The Row and the Boulevard

a novel by

Daniel Killman

GutenHaus Publishing
Nashville, Tennessee

This is a work of fiction. None of the characters are real. None of the events ever happened.

ISBN 978-0-615-18949-9

Printed in the United States of America.

First Edition, January 2008

Cover design by J. William Myers

Original typography by Hugh Daniel

GutenHaus Publishing - Nashville

For the three ladies in my life,

with all my love

PART ONE

FALL

Wherefore let him that thinketh he standeth
take heed lest he fall.

- I Corinthians 10:12, *KJV*

1

CHAD HARMON often found himself pondering things like paparazzi, gushing fans, and signing autographs. Such things were becoming commonplace in his life now. Perhaps it was true that the higher intellects never basked in a celebrity status. But on the other hand, maybe it was the ordinary, ineffectual people who had made that determination.

He reached out of the shower stall for a towel and began drying himself. His limited rehearsal time onstage at the Nashville Arena was slated for 11:15 a.m., so it was time to get moving. Tommy, his manager, was on his way over to drive him to the rehearsal, and Tommy was never late.

Chad had fantasized about a career such as this for most of his twenty-nine years, and here it was. Damned if they weren't calling him a *star*! But it was like another plane of existence. And he was almost sure that if someone were here to pinch his presently bare ass, he'd awaken and discover that none of this ever happened.

Tonight the "dream" would reach its pinnacle. Tonight would be the night of the annual Country Music Association awards, the Nashville music industry's grandest moment, televised on CBS.

"I wanna win," he declared as he switched on the blow dryer and began applying it to his carefully cropped blond hair. Yes, it seemed the perfect moment to say it out loud, with neither his fans nor the press around to hear him. So much for the claims of what an honor it is merely to be nominated. Let the meek inherit the earth, but give *him* a win.

"Bring it on," he muttered to his reflection in the bathroom mirror. "I'm due."

Tommy Matheson, his manager and closest friend, had spoken often about attitude and about the fair-weather friend that this business could be. Tommy always maintained that an artist must constantly take great care over all that he said and did, and it had never yet hurt anyone to keep his humility in place. Chad thought this to be reasonable enough advice.

"Aw, *man*!" he exclaimed as he looked at his wristwatch on the vanity. It was 10:29. He quickly switched off the blow dryer. "Get booking, Harmon!"

He dashed into the adjoining walk-in closet, grabbed a set of boxers from a drawer, and donned them. As soon as he'd thrown on a shirt, a pair of jeans, and boots, the doorbell sounded.

"Let's *do* it!" he shouted as he darted into the bedroom, picked up his guitar case resting at the side of his bed, and scampered out the door and down the stairs.

Chad was confident, eager, and set on a course for a fantasy coming true. But the wise counsel that Tommy had always offered would be needed in days to come, more than the young recording artist now realized. Being suddenly on top of the world, he could scarcely have conceived of that same world crumbling beneath him just as suddenly.

He still didn't really understand how it had happened so quickly. Nashville had seen the advent of more than a few country music legends over the years since the Opry's first broadcast back in 1925, and some were now saying *he* was to be the next.

Just two years and three months ago he had made his first "Writer's Night" appearance at the Bluebird Cafe, the small but legendary cocktail bar in the Green Hills area of Nashville. The Bluebird was a venue whose purpose had for many years been to springboard new Nashville talents.

"My name's Chad Harmon," he'd said as he took the stage that night. "I come from the proud state of Texas. And, like everybody else that comes here to the Bluebird, I'd like to share a few tunes I've written."

He had felt a good chemistry with the audience that night. He was careful wherever he performed to show an air of confidence, yet plenty of warmth and humanness. One of his natural gifts was that of "working an audience."

Tommy Matheson had by pure happenstance been invited to join a friend for drinks at the Bluebird that night. He'd invited Chad over to his table following Chad's performance. Though a big and warm heart beat within his big and burly frame, Tommy was seldom so assertive in meeting new artists. However, he knew that night that a very large talent had just appeared on the very small Bluebird stage.

"I'm Tommy Matheson, Vision Artists Unlimited."

"I'm Chad Harmon, singer, guitarist, songwriter." Chad had beamed that soon-to-be-famous smile. "Actually, I think I've heard of Vision Artists."

"I got my own start as a songwriter back in the late sixties," Tommy explained after they'd talked a while. "That led to havin' my own publishing house."

"I see," Chad said, silently hoping that this guy was to be his "angel." He could sure use a publishing deal to get a foot in, even if he didn't immediately land a recording contract.

"But I also manage artists," Tommy continued.

"Vision Artists Unlimited," Chad said, a light now dawning. "Of course."

"And even if it's me sayin' it, we're one of the best management companies in town."

Chad wondered whether this was that magic moment that he'd dreamed of. He not only wanted to write, perform, and record; he wanted it all. He craved stardom.

The next morning, with no hesitation, Tommy had his attorney set in motion the negotiations for Chad to go under the management of Vision Artists. He just as quickly made an appointment to see Broderick Richmond, known to most as "Rick," who served as CEO of Pioneer Records, headquartered across the street from

Vision Artists on Music Square East. Tommy took along a CD of four of Chad's tunes, a demo produced by Chad himself at a small studio on the Row.

Rick Richmond was anything but the warm and cordial type, yet Tommy seemed to have a way with him. Though preferring not to let it show, Rick actually had a tremendous respect for Tommy's assessment of talent.

From then on each day that passed seemed like an eternity to Chad as he continued his on-again-off-again labors with a temp agency in Nashville, though also playing a few club gigs here and there. By mid-January he had finally been signed with Pioneer for a one-album deal with a four-album option. With Chad now under the management of Vision Artists, Tommy's publishing house would publish the songs, three of which had been single-handedly written by Chad and several co-written with other writers. Rick Richmond was to produce the album.

"Geez, I don't think it's really hit home yet!" Chad exclaimed when Tommy took him to lunch at Bosco's in Hillsboro Village to celebrate the signing of the contracts. "It kind of takes your breath away. You think it will never happen, and then there it is! But I don't really understand *how* it all happened, to be honest."

"I'll tell ya somethin'. Most new artists don't have a clue as to how the business side of the music industry works," Tommy said. "But that's what I'm around for."

"I just want to keep singing. That's what *I'm* around for," Chad declared before ordering another beer.

He got his wish. A backup band of some of the finest available musicians was soon recruited. Tommy saw to it that his newest client played a few regional bookings here and there while waiting for the album to be recorded and released. In addition, Chad was the opening act for a few established artists in their concerts. He actually seemed to make as big a hit with the audiences as the headliner at such concerts. By the time of the album's release, Tommy would see to it that Chad was signed with a good booking agency.

Chad began working in the studio recording the album, which was carefully crafted with Rick's usual "power attitude," as some called it. Chad relished every minute of the recording experience, whether guitar playing, laying of vocal tracks, playbacks, retakes, or the mix. By late April the album had been completed.

"Fantastic!" Rick exclaimed when Chad's final vocal track had been laid. This had taken aback everyone in the studio. Most people thought of Rick as the impassive type, a man who seldom let his emotions go unharnessed.

At Rick's suggestion, the anxiously anticipated album was to be titled after Chad's own composed ballad "In the Rain," also to be released as a single.

The video of "In the Rain" was shot on location downtown near the Cumberland River, the Hard Rock Café serving as background. The rain to which the song referred had been forecast and had indeed fallen on that September night. A local actress, pretty, svelte, and appearing quite shapely when wet, was Chad's nonsinging costar. For the closing, the scene had dissolved to a bedroom, actually a set on a soundstage at NorthStar Studios, with both Chad and the actress slowly shedding their wet clothes and in each other's arms by the fadeout. That idea had been a concept of the video producer/director.

"Nothing like showing your butt to the world to become a star," Chad joked to Tommy on the set that day.

"Yeah, sure does make me know why they keep me on the administrative end of this business," Tommy laughed.

The album was released in early November. Chad, who reveled in playing his own CD over and over again at home and in his car, couldn't help feeling a bit anxious when sales made a merely respectable start the first few weeks, but Tommy assured him that he should be patient. Soon, thanks to a splashy marketing campaign on the part of the label, CDs started selling at full tilt. In December "In the Rain" soared to number one on the Billboard country charts where it was to remain for an incredible twelve weeks. Before dropping, it crossed over to the pop charts where it went to number one as well. The "Rain" video played constantly on the CMT and GAC channels and went to number one on the both networks' count-downs.

"Oh God! It's happening!" The words echoed in Chad's mind.

He traveled to New York and made appearances on *Live With Regis and Kelly* and *Late Show With David Letterman*, in addition to the numerous road gigs. *People Magazine* soon did a feature on the "rising country superstar" Chad Harmon, as did several other notable publications. In all his interviews Chad always appeared professional, relaxed, sure of himself. He needed no coaching from Tommy for this.

By spring he was making a nationwide sensation and was the talk of Music Row. The explosive success seemed phenomenal, even to the longtime professional Tommy Matheson.

A summer tour was booked to thirty-three cities, this time with Chad pleased to be the headliner rather than warm-up. Everywhere he played the audiences were ecstatic. Tommy marveled at how Chad seemed to hold those audiences in the palm of his hand like a seasoned pro.

A second single from the album, an up-tempo number called "She Wrote the Book," had climbed to number three on the charts during the early spring. Now a third, "Wicked Woman," was the number one country hit of the late summer. A video of the latter had been quickly turned out in the spring, this time shot in a live performance venue. That opportunity had come when Chad had been slated at the last minute to appear at a benefit concert for a local charity in the historic Ryman Auditorium.

As if all this weren't enough, the rising young star was at last invited to make his first appearance at the Grand Ole Opry, for which he would have to fly back to Nashville in between bookings in Denver and Salt Lake City.

"The Opry?!" he shouted when Tommy reached him by phone at his Chicago hotel room a week prior. "For real?"

"Yep," Tommy said.

An appearance on the Saturday night Opry was something every young wannabe country music star dreamed of, and Chad was no exception. The audience that night adored him.

No one, including Chad himself, had been quite prepared for the sudden stardom he'd achieved. When the CMA Award nominations were announced, to his delight but not shock, Chad was nominated for the Male Vocalist of the Year award, which was virtually unheard of for a new talent. The album received a nomination for Album of the Year. "In the Rain" was nominated for Single of the Year, an award going to the artist, and Song of the

Year, which went to the writer, in this case both being Chad. This was almost too much to process in his mind, he kept saying.

"A nomination for Entertainer of the Year, the granddaddy of 'em all, is just around the corner," Tommy said. "Just hang on for one or two years, bud."

"You have my word!" Chad exclaimed proudly.

Tommy vowed to always be there in every way possible for his client, and he assured Chad that he could always call on him for whatever he needed or had questions about. "This business can be pretty cold-hearted," Tommy said to him the day they'd gone to lunch to celebrate the signing of the contracts. "You can be the hottest stuff in town one day and ever'body's your friend, and next day you're yesterday's news."

On the day of the CMAs Chad had awakened feeling euphoric. Tommy had picked him up that morning, and they were now en route to the awards rehearsal. As Tommy took the Broadway exit off I-40, they heard a radio jock's speculation that Chad Harmon would probably take Male Vocalist of the Year that night. They both had to admit that this, though merely one man's prediction, was nonetheless exciting to hear.

"But whatever happens, I'll be okay," Chad said as Tommy lowered the volume on the car radio. "Losing any nominations the first time around is nothing to cry over."

"Glad ya got your head on straight about it," said Tommy as he steered his Jaguar into the parking facility adjoining the arena. "Not winnin' the first time out is nothin' to cry over, man. Gives ya someplace to go, and that's *up*."

"That's just the way I feel about it," Chad replied.

But in truth he knew that talk was cheap. As he'd said aloud in his bathroom not half an hour ago, he brazenly coveted those accolades because they meant having the validation of others in the industry.

The awaited night arrived. It was a tradition for nominated artists to arrive at the CMA Awards in chauffer-driven limousines provided by their respective labels. Upon arriving at the arena in his own limo, Chad was briefly interviewed and photographed by the local media people, which was another tradition.

Soon he was indoors and seated in his center aisle seat near the stage. After several handshakes and greetings from others in the business as they passed, Chad looked around and took stock of the scene around him. Television cameramen were completing camera checks. An announcement came over the public address system: "Five minutes till airtime. Please stand by."

He stole a glance at his date for the evening, seated to his right. She was an artist newly contracted with Pioneer. He had met her only a couple of hours before, their little rendezvous having been arranged by the label for publicity purposes. He'd heard of such things being done by movie studios in the old glamour days of Hollywood but had no idea it existed in Nashville until now. Oh well, she *was* cute, and she didn't seem like a total airhead. The problem was he now couldn't remember her name in order to introduce her to anyone else around him.

Neither the girl nor her name remained Chad's focus for long. For as he sat here at the CMA Awards, an artist nominated four-fold and quickly moving to the top, his thoughts went to someone who could neither be here nor watch by television.

Chad's mother Lydia had died of pancreatic cancer just over three years ago. He'd forever wonder why his mom had to be taken before her chance to see what great fortune had come his way.

Lydia had had a tremendous influence not just upon Chad's life but on the lives of many others as well. A very devout churchgoer back in Houston, where Chad was raised, she had been one of those rare individuals to whom people were drawn.

She had always admonished Chad to "be considerate, and just be plain nice to people." That would be true success, according to Mom, no matter whatever else happened. She'd never been over-bearing about it. Tough, yes, and a spiritual giant, but neither pious nor preachy. Somehow it was simply a pragmatic thing to her to practice the Golden Rule.

Seated here on CMA Awards night, he drifted back to the Houston hospital where he'd held Lydia in his arms just moments before she drew the last breath...

"Chad honey?"

"Yes, Mom, I'm here," he'd said, managing a smile for Lydia's sake.

"You got that something extra, Chad. I'm talking 'bout your music."

"Uh-huh," he was barely able to mutter.

"People are going to know it too, hon."

"You'll always be my first fan, Mom."

"But..." Her breath was waning.

"But don't forget to be good to people," he continued in her behalf. "Be kind to everybody, no matter who they are. Is that it, Mom?"

Growing still weaker, she was finally able to say, "Taught you well, haven't I?"

Chad couldn't offer another word, so he had simply bent over and embraced her. Holding her frail body close to his kept her from seeing his tears, which could no longer be contained. He was aware that at this very moment Lydia was going. He would swear forever that he'd felt her spirit rise up from her body, victorious. She'd lost the battle but won the war.

His father was home drunk at the time of the death. Chad had no brothers or sisters.

A modest insurance policy that Lydia had struggled to keep paid up over the years covered the costs of the funeral and burial. Fellow church members rallied to assist in any way possible with the arrangements. After all, they had lost a treasure.

The service was held at Lydia's non-denominational church, the humble place of worship where, starting at age thirteen, Chad had made his mother so proud, strumming his guitar and singing "Amazing Grace" or his own contemporary Christian tunes.

But now it was CMA Awards night, and, feeling that Lydia would prefer it so, Chad forced all regret from his mind. She was gone but never forgotten. That meant that she *was* here.

It was approximately two hours into the awards show when, after a commercial break, country super-star Lance Gayle, this year's host of the CMA Awards, was welcomed back onto the stage.

"Ya know, ever' once in a while a country artist comes along here in Nashville that's exceptional, kinda takes the whole world by storm," Gayle announced with a smile, actually reading from a teleprompter. "And that's what this next guy has done, without a doubt. Some people in the business keep tellin' me that if I feel like callin' it quits, I might not be missed as bad as I woulda been at one time...Come to think of it, that's the same news that my ex's attorney was tryin' to break to me just a little while back, but..."

The audience roared with laughter.

"...But what they were talkin' about was this next fella, and I gotta say he's a class act, and I'm proud to call 'im my buddy..."

Chad was eagerly waiting, guitar in hand, his band behind him. Within seconds the lighting would come up and the cameras focus on him. He would then perform not only in the presence of every important person in the business, but also for the first time to an audience numbering in the millions. Just minutes before, during a commercial break, he had been summoned from his seat for his performance on the show, his seat meanwhile being occupied by one of the "fillers" employed to assure that no seat appeared empty as cameras passed over. Before he could realize it, the moment was upon him.

"So here he is," shouted Gayle. "Won't you give a big warm welcome to the one and only Chad Harmon!"

Amidst the applause, Chad gave the downbeat, and the back-up band took the cue for "In the Rain." He passionately sang the tune already familiar to everyone. His entire soul seemed invested into what he sang, Tommy had always noted, and tonight was surely no exception.

As the song slowed to its finish, the televised tableau dissolved from a close-up of Chad to a long shot of the stage. The last chord was held while the audience exploded with an ovation that might have tested the limits of the Richter scale. Chad accepted it all with a nod and a smile.

The Male Vocalist of the Year award had been scheduled to immediately follow Chad's one-song performance on the program. Introduced next were Brent White and wife Leeza Hoffman, to present the award. After a bit of scripted repartee read by the spouses from teleprompters, Hoffman said, "The nominations for Male Vocalist of the Year are…"

The nominees' names were read in succession with a camera focusing on each one at his seat and a brief snippet of his most recent hit played after his name was read. A backstage cameraman caught Chad's close-up from the wings, a shot intended to look spontaneous but actually preplanned by the director of the awards show. Still awed by the experience of performing at the CMAs, Chad only heard the last name read in the succession of nominees, spoken by Miss Hoffman: "...and Chad Harmon."

"The envelope please...?" said White.

2

AN ARTICLE recently appeared in an issue of *Southern Life* magazine, which read as follows:

Bel Terre Boulevard:
A Step Back Into the Past,
Yet Beautifully Vital

Bel Terre, located in the southwest end of Nashville, Tennessee, is a place steeped in tradition and elegance. It takes its name from an antebellum plantation that still stands nearby as a tourist attraction. With a self-contained city government, Bel Terre has long been regarded as the epicenter of Nashville society. Indeed a bit of the Old South still thrives here to this day, complete with grand white-columned homes and refined southern accents that repeat the latest gossip over afternoon tea.

Stretching about two and a half miles through the heart of this mecca is Bel Terre Boulevard. Along the divided four-lane thoroughfare can be found many fine old homes as well as a few newer ones. It should be noted that the City of Bel Terre keeps a zoning commission that approves any building of new homes as well as renovations to existing ones. A journey down the Boulevard lends credence to the tenet that Bel Terre is "old money."

On Thanksgiving morning the "Boulevard Dash" takes place here. The Dash is an annual charity marathon run that boasts participants numbering over ten thousand.

At one end of the Boulevard is the beautiful Botanical Garden and Museum of Art, where the cream of society gathers once a year for the very elegant Nightingale Ball, a tradition that goes back for many generations. Well-bred ladies of Bel Terre have been known to commission their gowns for the event from the finest Parisian designers.

Near the same end of the Boulevard stands the grand Bel Terre Country Club with its surrounding golf course. Here the truly elite meet. One must have "connections" to procure membership at the club, though obviously another helpful asset for acceptance is a healthy bank account.

When visiting Music City USA, be sure to take a drive or perhaps a stroll down this elegant olden path. Bel Terre Boulevard has an enchantment all its own, a place that forever seems to speak of stately manners and grace.

Anna Lynn Jacobs
Staff Writer

The article had appeared with color photos of the country club, a few elegant homes, the main house of the garden estate, a semi-close-up of a beautiful blooming dogwood tree, and an action shot of scores of runners at the previous year's Boulevard Dash.

Robert Jackson Pritchard, age thirty-two and known to friends as "Jock," was among the very youngest homeowners on the "elegant olden path." Though often feeling a bit misplaced, he occupied his own home on the Boulevard.

Jock partnered as a tax estate attorney with Burch, Baxter, and Schultz, commonly known as BB&S, a prestigious law firm that occupied several floors of the Nashville Bank and Trust Building downtown. Family connections had helped secure Jock's affiliation with the firm immediately following law school.

"Thank you very much, ladies and gentlemen!" he bellowed while sprawled on his couch, viewing the CMA Awards. "You've been a wonderful audience!! *Goodnight, Nashville!!!*" With no one around, Jock could indulge a few fantasies while watching the telecast. He'd just finished crooning along with Chad Harmon on the hit song "In the Rain."

Jock was the son of George and Snooks Pritchard. Snooks had been a part of the original Bel Terre nobility all her life, George had "married in," and Jock had of course been a member of the society fold from the cradle. The entrenched social class of Bel Terre, of which they were a part, went back for many generations. Snooks had debuted years ago at the Bel Terre Country Club, where nowadays George regularly sharpened his golf swing.

George Pritchard had been a 1956 graduate of the Vanderbilt School of Law in Nashville. During his enrollment there, he'd met and courted Alicia Mae Ackerman, known as "Snooks," and had won her hand. The Pritchards had for many years remained childless, when suddenly Jock had come along quite unexpectedly in the autumn years of their marriage.

"We're endowed with the finest of dwellin' places Gawd evuh put on this uth, Robert J. Pritchard," Snooks had said to Jock often during his upbringing. The accent was a bit too thick and perhaps a bit bogus, some thought. But Snooks took tremendous pride in her Bel Terre heritage, never mind the fact that she spent half her time elsewhere, including the family's Palm Beach home throughout most of the winter.

During his childhood Jock had attended kindergarten through eighth grade at the Edgeworth School, a private institution near Bel Terre. Next had come high school at Bel Monte Academy, a long established and prominent school for young men on West End Avenue, just blocks from Edgeworth. Upon graduating from BMA, he'd accepted a scholarship to Yale, and Columbia School of Law had followed.

"There's no place like New York," Jock had exclaimed upon arriving home for Thanksgiving vacation during his first year of law school. "It's the center of civilization, you know. I think it's ...well, it's sort of become home to me."

This subtle declaration had raised an eyebrow or two at the dinner table. But Jock hadn't gone on to say that he was pondering a possible connection through a law school friend to go to work in production for a pop record label in the Big Apple, which would have meant abandoning everything he'd been educated for. He somehow hadn't found the courage to make that announcement.

Nor had he found the courage to forge ahead with such plans. After college and law school, Jock had dutifully returned to Nashville to occupy his place in society, enjoy the amenities of the Bel Terre Country Club, and assume a position at the great and prestigious Burch, Baxter, and Shultz.

For the past four years he'd lived here within blocks of his parents. And he was almost boringly certain that when the proper debutante, one of good breeding, came his way, he'd once again do what was expected of him: marry, have a couple of kids who'd go to Edgeworth, and so on.

"Damned if Harmon's not going to walk away with everything," Jock mumbled, focused on the awards show. "And rightly so."

He knew he was among the few Bel Terre residents watching the CMAs. Hell, the average resident here was surely more given to *opera* attendance, as opposed to Opry, he conjectured. But the music business had always fascinated Jock. A part of him would forever wonder what it would have been like to have his own place there. He had played guitar from childhood and had listened to the recordings of Waylon Jennings, Merle Haggard, and his favorite, Willie Nelson. Piano lessons had also been provided from age seven. He loved country music and always had.

As Jock watched the CMAs, his fantasies of being a star, crooning along as the various artists performed, were all in fun. However, those of writing, producing, and publishing were serious. Whatever his musings, he always had moments of indignation when pondering the music industry.

"Yeah, what's called talent in this ignorant town sometimes gets dressed up with plenty of slick producing to pass it off as something great," he grumbled to himself. "Shit, half of the fools down on the Row don't know one goddamned note on the scale from another. Why don't they stay on their tractors out in some cotton fields where they belong?"

He stopped.

"Give it a rest, Jock."

If people were to have heard his ravings at such moments, they'd have sized him up as the most pathetically jealous crybaby in Music City and would have been reasonably accurate in such an assessment. But how the hell *did* white trash freaks get to places of importance in the business? After all, there is true talent in the world.

He stopped himself again.

"Get over yourself, Jocko. Life is just a series of choices, man. You've made yours. So screw Music Row, screw everything!"

There. He'd vented. He'd be okay now. And besides, the Male Vocalist of the Year award was about to be presented, so it was time to lend his attention.

Leeza Hoffman opened the envelope, a smile coming across her face as she read, "The winner is..." and after the usual pregnant pause she said, "Chad Harmon!" The applause broke like cannon fire. A smiling Harmon was seen walking toward the podium to receive the award as the refrain of "In the Rain" was heard yet again.

Now speaking of talent, here it was, Jock thought. He'd listened to Harmon on the radio, on the CMT channel, and on the CD he'd purchased. From this guy came fresh music, skillfully crafted lyrics, and a voice and presence that were non-gimmicky.

All right, so the ignorant dickheads down on the Row can *show a little taste now and then.*

As Jock laughed at his own mental ramblings, which were a frequent occurrence, the phone rang. He muted the television audio with the remote and picked up the phone beside him.

"Hello."

"Jock, hi. It's Abe."

"Hi, Abe."

"Hadn't seen you all week. Just checking in."

"I thought it was supposed to be *me* who checks in with *you*," Jock said, with a chuckle.

"I wouldn't say that there's any law about it," replied Abe.

Nine months earlier Jock had undergone treatment for his drug addiction. He had since remained active in Twelve Step recovery, and Abe was his sponsor. During Christmas season of the previous year Jock's disease had come to a bottoming point when a skirmish had developed into a fistfight at the Wild Horse Saloon downtown, followed by an arrest. George and Snooks had intervened. In January they'd sent Jock to the Betty Ford Center in Los Angeles, the Pritchards themselves underwriting the cost.

"Ah don't mean to sound haughty," Snooks had haughtily declared, "but Ah would think you just nevuh can tell what dregs of humanity might be comin' in and out of these local treatment facilities. Why, ovuh thayuh at that Cumberland Heights, Ah hear you can see just about anything. They say it's just *pitiful*."

George went along with his son on the flight to L.A. for the admitting process at Betty Ford. Jock speculated that an out-of-town treatment would help preclude any disgrace to the family. As he'd cynically commented to his counselor at the center, "Yeah, maybe on the Coast it's in vogue to go to a high-class treatment center and maybe even a status symbol to have your own shrink. But on the home front, there's sure as hell no need to risk besmirching the family name, is there?"

During the latter part of Jock's four-week stay at Betty Ford, Family Week, as it was called, rolled around, a time when relatives were encouraged to visit the center and experience a series of meetings and personal counseling of their own. It was intended as a time of healing for families and encouragement as to their needed support in the patient's ongoing recovery process. With Jock being unmarried, the staff of Betty Ford had sought to include his parents, but due to a hectic social calendar the Pritchards hadn't been able to attend Family Week at all.

"But you can be shuwuh that we'll always be thayuh for our son," Snooks asserted when the counselor called to discuss Jock's recovery program. "And Ah've no doubt he's goin' to be just fine. He mainly was just needin' this time thayuh as a restoration, the way Ah see it."

After a thorough treatment program, Jock returned home to Nashville, where thankfully, BB&S had excused his absence with disability leave. For almost nine months now he had managed to remain "clean and sober."

Abe Feinstein was the retired chairman of the math department at Vanderbilt. Though quite the intellectual, Abe was in his own way a simple and practical man. He seemed as proficient at helping solve life's little problems as he probably had been at making the quadratic equation comprehensible to underclassmen.

"Been a week to die for at the office," Jock said to Abe.

"Beg your pardon?" asked Abe, although knowing that some lame joke had been intended by the remark.

"Wills, living wills, et cetera. And in my case, the tax analysis thereof."

"I see. Well, at any rate, it sounds like you're doing fine despite your workload. I'll let you get back to your restful evening."

"I was just watching the CMAs."

"Ah, yes. Country music. I actually attended the Grand Old Opry once at the Ryman back in the early sixties."

"You're kidding. Dr. Abraham Feinstein at the Opry. Well, for you, Abe, I'm sure that it was a lifelong dream come true," Jock quipped.

"No comment. You know that I'm not one to take a superior attitude."

"Oh, a humble drunk?" Jock said with mock sarcasm. "That would be almost a contradiction in terms, wouldn't it?"

"Now I think I've been insulted. I'm hanging up," Abe said, going along with the joke. He had taken a liking to this brash young fellow from their first meeting. "Will I see you soon?"

"I'll be at the meeting tomorrow," Jock said.

"Until then."

"Thanks for calling, Abe. Goodnight."

Jock clicked the phone off, laid it down and then un-muted the television. Though he'd missed Harmon's acceptance speech and commercials were now in progress, he toasted Chad with his bottle of Perrier. About damn time somebody truly deserving received recognition in the Music Row circus, he thought.

"Turn your mind off, Jock," he whispered, closing his eyes a moment. "Just turn your goddamned mind off."

Yes, he needed to get to a meeting. *Tomorrow.*

After Abe Feinstein hung up the phone, he tried dialing another number, one he'd dialed numerous times the last couple of days.

"Please pick up, Beth," he muttered pensively under his breath.

For a week now Abe had not heard from his daughter Beth, which was unusual. She and her husband lived in Brentwood, a suburb on the south end of town. As neither Abe nor his wife Liz had gotten a call from Beth in over a week, they'd begun to worry. They'd tried calling her the preceding day.

As had been the case since the previous day, only the answer machine picked up after four rings.

"Beth, *where are you*?"

Mystified, he hung up the phone, this time leaving no message.

Beth, age twenty-five, was the wife of Gary Segal, an attorney who at one time had been with Burch, Baxter, and Schultz, the same firm where Jock was employed. He had abruptly left two years ago and had temporarily pursued a private practice. Solid reasons were never offered, at least not to Abe, for Gary's leaving the firm.

"BB&S wasn't the place he felt at home," Beth had said. "It just didn't fit him."

An unsubstantiated report had gotten back to Abe, however, that Gary had parted company with BB&S after being disciplined by the firm for some sort of misconduct while on the job. In other words, he'd been dismissed, though Abe hadn't learned for what infraction. Gary had later ceased practicing law altogether and had moved on to work in his family's business, a successful boot and sportswear manufacturing company.

Abe decided that for at least another day he'd make light of the situation. He felt that as long as he didn't seem to worry too greatly, neither would his wife.

He somehow didn't feel right about calling Gary at work. He and his son-in-law had never gotten on that well. Beth was more than likely just busy with her work as an interior designer. Then too there was her social life.

Still and all, it was unlike Beth not to call for so long a time.

3

"HOW 'BOUT A SHOT of you holding the award up beside you, huh, Chad!" shouted a cameraman from *Country Weekly*, and Chad proudly obliged.

The cameraman was referring to the Male Vocalist of the Year award, though, in addition, the recording of "In the Rain" had by this time garnered Song of the Year and Single of the Year. The Album of the Year award had also gone to Chad Harmon. It had been a night to cherish!

Reporters and camera crews crowded the Green Room backstage at the arena. The news conference that followed the awards presentation was in progress. Though the show was still moving toward its finish onstage, representatives from all facets of the media could now interview winners and take advantage of some photo-ops.

"Can you tell us, Chad, when you'll be cutting a new album?" asked a reporter.

Smiling coyly, Chad, who now was guaranteed a second album very soon, replied, "I'll just wait and hope that it'll be real soon."

"You're being lauded by some as the most artistically and commercially promising young artist to come along since Elvis." Bertram Venneman, who'd spoken up, was the subtly patronizing reporter for ABC's *Good Morning, America.* "Do you think you're capable of living up to that claim, Mr. Harmon?"

There was a momentary silence in the room.

"There was only one 'King'," replied Chad. "All I want is to keep doing what I love, and I hope people will keep appreciating it."

"*Good boy,*" said Rick Richmond, a calculated sort of warmth to his tone as he walked up alongside Tommy, who was watching the press conference from the sidelines. "Handled old Venneman pretty well, I'd say. Self-denial, yet self-confidence. Public ought to eat that up, huh?"

"I've taught him well," said Tommy, shaking Rick's hand with equally programmed cordiality.

Tommy, like most on the Row, didn't find Richmond the most desirable guy to work with, but resisted becoming confrontational, even with Richmond insinuating that Tommy's client and friend was less than sincere.

"By the way," Tommy said, "Pioneer did well all the way around tonight, Rick. You oughta be proud."

"Absolutely. Well, Estelle's waiting for me. We want to get to the Plaza before everybody starts arriving. I'll let you be the one to tell Chad that we'll start talking about the new album next week. We'll let him get through the New Orleans booking. That concert is this weekend, right?"

"Yeah, it is."

"We'll be talking. Will I see you at the party?"

"Thanks, but Sandy and I are callin' it a night. She worked a full day."

"Goodnight then."

"'Night, Rick."

Rick moved on, leaving Tommy to project all of those new publishing opportunities ahead with another, brand new recording, Chad's second album. Yes, time to serve up new pieces of the Chad Harmon pie, plenty to go around.

"But I was told this pass would allow me to go backstage," Charlie insisted.

"Sorry, ma'am. The yellow passes allow you into the initial backstage area, but not to the Green Room."

"Well, a lot of good that does me," Charlie said in a huff.

"I really am sorry, ma'am. Those are the rules," said the guard. "Security gets really tight for CMA Awards."

Known to friends as Charlie, Charlene Cohen was secretary to Rick Richmond. She had hoped to get backstage and speak to a few of her friends. Her hopes were crushed now.

"It's okay, Charlie," said her friend Peggy Rose. "Why don't we just call it a night?"

"Guess that's all we can do," Charlie replied displaying one last frosty glare toward the security guard. She knew she'd later regret her rudeness toward this young man, who was, after all, guilty of nothing more than adhering to policy. Her looks and her charm, which were often useful tools on men, weren't going to faze this go-by-the-book guard.

"I don't understand why he has to be so pig-headed about it," Charlie mumbled. "I mean, do *we* look like terrorists?"

"Give it up, Charlie," said Peggy. "I guess things have to be that way for the CMAs."

The ladies turned and walked back toward the double doors they'd entered moments ago. At the last minute Charlie had been given a couple of tickets to the CMAs, though in the "nosebleed section," as she referred to it. Therefore, she had invited her friend Peggy, with whom she'd co-written a few tunes, to come along.

As the ladies arrived outside, Charlie spotted Rick Richmond and his wife Estelle getting into the Mercedes that had been delivered at the door. It struck her that Rick had the clout to arrange her triumphal entry into the great Green Room, and screw the security guard! She was about to shout out Rick's name to get his attention, but something made her stop.

"What?" asked Peggy in response to Charlie's fascination with something in the parking lot.

After a moment, Charlie said, "Nothing…Let's go."

"Charlie, what do you say we head over to Dalts, back in our part of town. I'd love a piece of malt cake. We'll both have to run a couple of extra miles to compensate in the morning, but what the hell."

"Sure. Why not?" answered Charlie, but with little enthusiasm.

They headed toward Charlie's car in the labyrinth of vehicles in the nearby lot.

"A night to tell your grandkids about," said Tommy. He and Chad shared an embrace, the press conference now having concluded.

Chad, about to depart along with his date for the Pioneer party, beamed. "God, what a rush! A few million people watching and listening to you! It's…beyond anything."

"You looked right at home up there, sweetie," said Sandy, Tommy's wife, giving Chad a kiss on the cheek.

"You got to see it?" Chad asked.

"I always have a monitor close by when I'm working backstage," she said. "Can't miss any of the fun."

Sandy, a makeup and hair designer, one of the most respected in the business, was adored by anyone who knew her. Many liked to rib Tommy that he had done better than he ever deserved by winning Sandy's heart years ago. Sandy had traveled with many stars and done makeovers on the likes of Reba and Dolly. She had beautified celebrities on the east and west coasts. Tonight she'd performed her artistry on Chad for the awards. She and Tommy had gotten unusually close to Tommy's newest young client.

"Can't you guys come to the party for at least a while?" Chad asked.

"It's been a long day. Besides, I think we just want to have our own private celebration in your honor," Sandy said as she took her husband's arm.

"Take a coupla days to rest up and recoup for New Orleans," said Tommy. "Then we gotta get ya back in the studio. I know I don't have to tell ya the new album is imminent. And Richmond doesn't wanna waste any time, I'm glad to report."

"Things don't let up on you once you're on a roll, honey," Sandy said almost pityingly to Chad.

"I hope they don't," Chad said. "The time has come. I intend to keep rockin' and rollin'."

They said their goodbyes, and Sandy hugged Chad once more before she and Tommy moved on. Chad and his date would soon be on their way to the party at Loew's Vanderbilt Plaza, where Chad would be as much the center of attention as he'd been at the awards presentation.

As the Mathesons moved down the hallway, Sandy couldn't help commenting, "It seems to me he could do with a bit of rest before the New Orleans booking."

"When you're ridin' the wave of success," said Tommy, "ya don't take a dive. Ya keep ridin'."

"Of course," she said. Sandy had been in her own business and married to Tommy long enough to know how demanding the entertainment industry could be. When success knocked, you answered.

However, as she looked back over her shoulder toward Chad, she felt something unexplainable. She couldn't understand why she had this nagging, disturbing feeling about Chad and New Orleans.

Bertram Venneman waited as his accompanying photographer Bud packed his equipment preparing to depart from the Green Room, their report having already been filed with the network. Smartly dressed and groomed, Venneman made quite a stark contrast to the young camera freak, a young man who seldom wore anything more than jeans, a tee shirt, and sneakers.

"Interesting specimen this Harmon guy," remarked Venneman with a smile. "Everyone seems to be touting him as the greatest to come along in decades. They're also saying that he's one of the most unblemished, unspoiled gentlemen they've ever known in this business."

"You know, I heard some pretty decent music tonight," said Bud, pretty much oblivious to the reporter's words. "Never went in for that country stuff much before."

Venneman, now in his early fifties, had been a senior editor with *Rolling Stone Magazine* for many years, and in the last four he'd also been contracted as the entertainment reporter for *Good Morning, America* on ABC. Rumor had it that Venneman was himself a frustrated musician in the classical genre and that he'd landed in journalism by default. Though his coverage of performers and reviews of their recordings had often been harsh and acerbic, this had only served to bolster his popularity. But some did wonder if Venneman truly hated music and those who made their living at it.

"The Achilles' Heel will rear its head somewhere along the way." He smiled. "I wonder if I'll be around to witness it when it does."

Venneman then began his walk back over to the nearby Hilton Hotel.

"Awwwwww, screw it!" Jock finally vented as he reached up and turned the bedside lamp back on, knowing that sleep was not to be soon forthcoming. The awards telecast had concluded a half hour ago.

Watching things like the CMA Awards brought his frustrations back again. He could criticize the talent of certain artists, blame those in positions of power for mediocrity in the business, maybe even suspect the moral compromises some had probably made to further themselves. But at least those people had followed their hearts.

Had Jock followed *his* heart? No, he had followed instructions. He had taken the easy way out and now was uneasy. He had chosen the way of comfort but was uncomfortable. But what could he do at this juncture? Piss everything away he'd worked toward?

What Jock did not have was an "in" to get directly involved in the business, not even in an administrative capacity. There'd probably be little to show for taking the plunge other than the misery of failing.

"So there's your answer, Jocko."

He'd programmed the data and accessed the solution. There was more in his life than he could ever be grateful for. He just had to find a way to be happy with his life, even if he had to be a little miserable, as if that made any sense.

Yes, it was time to see things as they were. Time to get on with life. Time to stop trying to live in a dream world, though he'd resolved to do so a thousand times before.

"And now time to get some sleep," he said as he turned out the light and rolled over.

And definitely time to get to a meeting, he thought. Tomorrow. Without fail.

"So..." she said, "tell me what it's like."

"What it's...like?" Chad was still clutching his awards. "Oh, you mean winning! It's great, Tracey. It's...just great."

He had finally relearned during the press conference chat that her name was Tracey Steel.

The limousine was traveling down Broadway, en route to the Pioneer label party at the Vanderbilt Plaza. Chad couldn't wait to get to the celebration and revel in the praise and adulation.

"You *should* feel honored," she said, as her hand came to rest on his leg.

So what? he thought. No harm in being friendly. Besides, she *was* cute.

"And it *has* been quite a night," she said with eyes pointed directly ahead. "And it's not over yet, you know."

"Uh-huh," said Chad.

Tracey's hand was still on his thigh. Chad merely fondled his awards.

Charlie and Peggy were having coffee at Dalts Grill in Lion's Head Village, a shopping center just a few blocks out of Bel Terre. Each had already knocked off a slice of the very rich malt cake that the establishment was known for. As they now sipped their refilled decaf, Charlie found herself unable to conceal her distraction from Peggy.

"C'mon, Charlie, is it worth all this?" asked Peggy, seeking to lighten the moment. "So you got backstage but not into the Green Room. You didn't get to see a few friends. They'll still be around for you to congratulate for a long time to come."

Charlie smiled. "Sorry, Peg. I hate to be such lousy company."

"What gets me is that you had the chance to go to the big Pioneer Records bash over at the Plaza, and you refused. People would kill for a chance to go to that party and rub shoulders with the people there." She smiled and said, "Including Chad Harmon, the hunk! You turn the party down but get bent out of shape about the Green Room issue. You're not making sense."

"I sort of got the impression that the invitation to the party – and in my case it was dropped by word of mouth, not engraved – it didn't...well, it didn't include extra guests."

"I *told* you before we went that we could go in separate cars, and you could head straight to the party after the awards. That would have been fine with me."

"It's not really just about the Green Room. It's just that..." Charlie stopped herself. "Let's save it for another time, okay?" She had almost come right out with it but had caught herself in time.

"Why am I feeling like I'm to blame for this? Tell you what, why don't you drop me by home? That way you can go on to the party and end your evening on a high point. My place is three minutes from the Plaza."

"I don't want to. Really, I'm ready to forget it now." Charlie managed a smile and raised her coffee cup. "So here's to our first CMA Awards. It was fun, wasn't it?"

"Yeah," said Peggy raising her cup to the toast, though still mystified by her friend's attitude.

Charlie knew that she most certainly was not making sense, as Peggy had said. Problem was she was not able to make sense, even to herself, out of what was going on in her life. But it was not something she felt comfortable discussing with Peggy. Not just now.

Chad had made the necessary rounds at the Pioneer gala, accepting handshakes, hugs, and congratulations. He hadn't found time to sample any of the culinary delights at the buffet, but waiters had seen to it that his wine glass never emptied. At just past 3 a.m. he decided it was time to go.

"Goodnight, Mrs. Richmond," he said to Rick's wife, taking her hand.

"It's Estelle," she said with a smile. She then shook hands with Tracey. "Nice to meet you, Tracey. And I wish you the best with your new recording deal."

"Thank you, Estelle," Tracey responded.

Chad felt a little woozy from the wine. He thus was glad for the limousine. He assumed the plan was for Tracey to be dropped at her place and that there were no expectations of her spending the night with him, despite the aggressive plays she'd made for him earlier. Chad just wanted to go home and revel in his glory alone, maybe jump up and down and shout a little.

"Shall we?" he said to Tracey.

"Yes. Goodnight, Estelle," said Tracey. "We've had a wonderful evening."

"Goodnight," said Estelle. "I hope to be seeing more of both of you in the future."

"Uh-huh," Chad murmured as he and Tracey made their exit. He wanted to roll his eyes at the "we" to which Tracey had referred, as if making sure everyone thought of the two of them as an item.

They hadn't offered their goodbyes to Rick, who was engaged in conversation with a Pioneer producer. It was just as well with Chad. He'd always found Rick a bit distant, keeping everyone at arm's length. Their relationship being a business one, it might just as well remain so.

Chad was still uncomfortable with the date charade, but hardly enough to let it ruin the evening. On a triumphant night like this there were few things that could dampen his spirits.

The driver opened the door of the limo for Chad and Tracey. After returning to the driver's seat, he pulled out onto West End and then took a right onto Twenty-first Avenue South. The limo's destination was Green Hills where both Chad and his date lived.

"I guess you'll need to tell the driver your address and maybe give directions," Chad said. "It'll be easiest to drop you first since your place is on the way to mine."

Never looking Chad's direction again, Tracey proceeded to do as he'd suggested. There would be no more wondering as to her possibly sleeping over with him. And no further conversation. Nor did Tracey put her hand on his leg as before.

Chad did, in chivalrous fashion, see her to her door where they exchanged a simple "Goodnight."

Chad was currently renting a condominium owned by Tommy and Sandy in the Burton Hills development. He'd judged the beautiful condo, offered to him by the Mathesons at a ridiculously low monthly rent, to be large enough to accommodate a family of five, and he lived alone.

It was a little before 4:00 a.m. when the limo pulled up to the condo. He said goodnight and thanks to the driver, hoping he was correct in assuming that tipping wasn't expected.

He unlocked the front door, entered the foyer, closed the door, and proceeded up the stairs. He quickly shed the tux, ran a warm shower in the stall of his bathroom, and stepped into it. It was then that he realized the makeup still remained on his face, though it would not for long.

After the shower he dried himself, opened a drawer, and took out a pair of silk pajama bottoms. After putting them on, he took a bathrobe from the hook of the dressing room door.

He had sobered slightly and decided to go back downstairs. He walked to the kitchen at the rear of the first floor. There on the center counter, to his amazement, was a beautiful flower arrangement and a chilled bottle of champagne. He opened the note that accompanied the flowers. It read:

> *No one in the business has ever deserved it more than you.*
>
> *We love you,*
> *Sandy and Tommy*

"What great friends," he thought. Perhaps you couldn't be quite sure about everybody on the Row, but the Mathesons were true-blue.

"Well…why not?" He uncorked the champagne bottle and found a glass in a cabinet above. He took the bottle with him as he walked into the semi-dark living room where he reclined on the couch.

He needed to take some more time to get relaxed before he could actually sleep. There was something other-worldly about what had happened to him over the last several hours. But Chad Harmon's time had come at last! And he would rise to greater and greater heights from here on. What else should he do but enjoy the ride?

"To the future," he said, as he raised his glass, drank, and then poured himself another.

4

"TELL HER THAT I'M SORRY but I got held up. I ought to be there in ten minutes or less," said Father Kris, speaking on his cell phone as he drove along West End Avenue on a beautiful autumn morning.

"I'll hold you to that," said Nancy Parker. Then she added, "Old Agnes Warfield is not one to be kept waiting, you know. She can't appreciate your having anything else to do besides meet with her. What's the old crow here for any way?"

"We're to plan a Christmas caroling trip to the retirement home that the young people are going to be doing," Kris replied, and he could just see Nancy rolling her eyes on the other end.

"*Christmas caroling?* That's bound to be at least two months away!" Nancy said.

"Yeah well, Agnes likes getting an early start." He found it sort of odd, his coming to Agnes Warfield's defense.

"Oh brother," was all he heard in response.

"Agnes is somebody you have to take as she is," said Kris good-naturedly. "I know she's a little pushy at times, but with all the good work she does, it's kind of hard to get upset with her."

"*Not* that hard, darling," she said curtly. "You sure you don't want me to tell her you got unavoidably tied up?"

"That won't be necessary," he said.

Kris Hartley served as an associate priest and assistant to the rector at St. John's Episcopal Church. The church, home of a large and prominent parish, stood at the intersection of Bel Terre Boulevard and Harding Road, the "main entrance," so to speak, into Bel Terre.

He was known to most as Father Kris. Now thirty-three years old, he had been born and reared in Asheville, North Carolina. Father Benjamin Allen, the current rector of St. John's Church, had served as rector of Kris's home parish when Kris was growing up. Kris's father, who'd been a custodian at the church, had died of a heart attack when Kris was only fourteen.

"By the way," said Nancy, "no one was on the front desk early this morning, so I was answering the phone. You had one call. A Mr. Abe Feinstein. He said to just call him when it's convenient. Are you moonlighting over at the Temple these days, darling?"

He was always amused by Nancy's sense of humor and her lack of pretense. She was the rector's secretary and thus a very pivotal member of the St. John's staff, but she stood on ceremony with no one.

"Moonlighting?" he played along. "Oh, didn't I tell you? I'm looking into converting. Talk on the street is that a rabbi gets better benefits; you know, retirement, insurance, et cetera."

"Benefits? How about the benefit of someone like me, who takes all those messages for you – Hel*lo*! – and even humors old Aggie, when it's *you* who've stood her up?"

"We could keep talking all morning, Nancy, but I'm going to be there in a couple of minutes anyway. Assure Agnes of that, if you will please."

"See you in a bit, hon. Meanwhile, I'll fix the old girl a second cup of tea."

"Thanks. You *are* quite a benefit, come to think of it," said Kris.

"Haven't I always told you that?" she said and hung up.

Kris closed the cell phone with a chuckle and continued up West End. After passing Saint Thomas Hospital, he pulled over to the curb as an ambulance raced from the opposite direction toward the hospital. Waiting at curbside gave him the opportunity to say a few morning prayers.

After committing his life to the priesthood, Kristoph William Hartley, as he'd been baptized, attended undergraduate school and seminary at Duke University, initially on a football scholarship. After ordination back at his home parish in Asheville and two years of deacon's service there, he'd received a phone call one day from Ben Allen regarding a position at St. John's, where Father Allen had served as rector for two years.

"We could do with a handsome young priest here at St. John's Church," Agnes Warfield said upon Kris's first day to visit the church, merely as a guest of Father Allen. It had been a weekday, and Agnes had been doing volunteer duty on the front desk of the church. "I'll even be bold enough to say that we could use a few youthful ideas too. In moderation, of course."

"Moderation is a good thing," Kris agreed, smiling at Agnes, to whom he took an immediate liking, no matter what anyone else thought.

His visit hadn't been talked about to anyone of the church as anything more than a friendly call from the son of an acquaintance of the rector, a young man who'd gone into the priesthood. But nobody pulled the wool over Agnes's eyes; she knew this fellow was here for an important reason.

"Just give it your prayerful consideration," Ben said as he and Kris said their good-byes. "You know I'll be behind whatever you decide."

Kris tried to sort his mixed feelings in the following two days. He'd envisioned himself eventually serving some small parish of his own when leaving his home church. Yet to be a part of a great and prosperous church such as St. John's, with all its diverse programs, would certainly be thrilling and seemed the divine plan. So in a couple of days he'd found himself picking up the phone, calling Ben, and saying, "The answer is yes, that is, if the offer still stands."

"It does," replied Ben happily.

It was a bit of a milestone for the conservative southern parish to call into its service a young African-American as one of its priests. But Kris was to find a very warm reception. He settled in at St. John's and found an apartment in the Richland Historic District off West End Avenue. Ladies of the church continuously baked for him and delivered their favorite dishes.

"That's a southern tradition in churches," Nancy had explained.

"I know," Kris said, "and I *like* the custom."

"Hey, I'm not knocking it," she said. "But I've wondered why church secretaries don't get treated with the same respect."

It was understood that Kris's main area of ministry would be with the youth of the church. He proved at EYC recreation time that he could throw a football better than any of the young men of the St. John's youth. However, he refrained from bragging that he had quarterbacked and led to a State Championship win his high school football team in Asheville several years back.

As for the teenage girls of the parish, few were willing to admit that they saw Father Kris as a "hottie," but many had seen fit to recommit themselves to church attendance and involvement in the youth program since he'd arrived.

Best of all, some said, Father Kris related well to all the young people. They opened up to him, and he touched their lives. They trusted and respected him. He seemed to many parents almost too good to be true.

Kris had meant more than small talk when he'd concurred with Agnes Warfield that moderation was a worthy virtue. He hadn't always experienced moderation in his life. A drinking problem had evidenced itself while he had been in seminary. He was later to learn that the disease was not terribly uncommon among the clergy of all faiths. He became involved in Twelve Step recovery as a first year seminary student and had now been sober for almost eleven years.

After the ambulance passed he drove the remaining few blocks to St. John's and pulled up to his designated parking place. Agnes evidently knew that Father Schmidt was on vacation, and she had taken the liberty of occupying his parking slot.

"And why not?" he said. "The church belongs to its people, and Agnes is a very special one."

Now, if he could just get inside and find a good strong cup of coffee before having to deal with the old girl.

"There are some very fine voices among those young people," said Agnes. "And, even if there weren't, it will mean a great deal to those folks to have them come."

The plans for the young people's caroling trip to the home for the aged were now in place. Kris would be responsible for getting the young people committed.

"It's very thoughtful of you to have spearheaded the project, Agnes," said Kris as he accompanied her to her car.

"I say it's you who's to be thanked, Father Kris," Agnes declared. "I don't think anybody else could have gotten those young folks involved in something like this. They *listen* to you, young man."

"I hope so," he replied. "And I try to make myself available to them."

"Whatever you do, you keep doing it," Agnes instructed almost sternly. "See you in church, Father Kris."

Kris opened the door of the aging Mercury for her.

"Good-bye, Agnes. Have a good day," he said.

As she slowly drove away, he returned indoors and proceeded to the church's main office where he checked his mail slot and found no new messages. He decided to have a look and see if Ben was in.

"Has Her Highness taken leave of us?" asked Nancy in a droll tone as he approached her desk.

"Yes, Agnes is gone," he replied with a smile. He indicated the rector's office door with a nod. "Is he in?"

"He is," she said.

The door was slightly ajar to Father Allen's office. As Kris peered through, he saw the rector hanging up the phone.

"Top of the morning," said Kris nudging the door open.

"Kris," said Ben. "Please come in. Have a seat."

"I just wanted to check in. I haven't seen you all week."

Kris noticed that Ben was getting up to close the door.

"Kris," Ben began. "I need to talk with you," said Ben with seriousness to his tone.

"Sure," he replied.

"Kris, you do such great work here. I couldn't have asked for a more outstanding young associate priest here in my work at St.

John's. Everyone adores you. I'd even be bold enough to say you are a *model* priest." He paused yet again while moving to occupy a chair next to Kris rather than at his desk. Kris waited a second for him to come to his point. "You're doing a wonderful work here, but…sometimes things happen we have no control over."

"What?" Kris inquired, now with growing concern.

"It's about Hunter Jamison."

Hunter was a sixteen-year-old member of the parish whom Kris had taken under his wing. A disturbed young man, Hunter had begun exploring the world of drugs about a year earlier. Since then, due largely to Kris's sponsorship and the local Cumberland Heights Treatment Center, he had undergone rehabilitation.

Hunter then adjusted to a productive life, active with St. John's EYC and on the debate team at BMA. There had been a few emotional setbacks to be worked through, but Kris continued to stay close to him and check up on him regularly. Though known as a quiet and withdrawn type, Hunter would often drop by Kris's office or call him up just to talk. And nothing had ever meant more to Kris than to see this dysfunctional kid getting his life together. Miracles did happen.

And the miracle was greater than most people knew, for Kris found that within this troubled young man was someone sensitive, caring, and wanting to do something special with his life. He even wondered whether Hunter might one day consider the priesthood, which would truly shock everyone.

But at the present moment Kris felt uneasy. Ben was leading up to something.

"What about Hunter?" Kris asked.

"The phone call I was just finishing when you came by was from Bill Jamison," Ben said. "It seems, Kris, that Hunter had been having a difficult week. At school, at home, just a bad week in general. Bill had plans to take him back to Cumberland Heights tomorrow if things didn't change. He wondered whether Hunter might need to go on some different medication."

"Did Hunter relapse, Ben? It happens, you know," said Kris, feeling anxious and realizing that he'd not been in touch with Hunter all week.

"Kris..." Ben's expression seemed even more ominous now. "Hunter overdosed this morning. His parents had kept him home from school, and he'd been alone in his room. They have no idea where he'd managed to get hold of the substance. He was rushed to St. Thomas about an hour ago."

Dear Lord...

"They," Ben continued, "well, they did all the usual stomach-pumping, CPR, et cetera."

Kris felt desperate. He wanted to plead with Ben, God, the doctors, or whomever.

"Kris…it's out of our hands now…I have to believe that means he's found peace."

Ben didn't have to explain any further. Devastated, sickened, Kris understood.

He sat alone at the desk in his office, his stomach in knots. He felt more grief-stricken than he'd ever been in his life. Even more than when his father had passed away.

No, it was anger he wanted to feel more than sadness. A wasted young life. Damn drugs! Damn anyone who ever had anything to do with dealing in them!

But then Kris suddenly thought about himself. He'd been too busy being the all-important man of the cloth this week to have even known that Hunter had been depressed. No need to blame fate, drugs, or drug dealers. *The fault, dear Brutus, is not in our stars, but in ourselves.*

The world contained many great egotists, like Father Kristoph Hartley, he now thought. But the poor unfortunates such as Hunter, who do well just to find a few fleeting moments of happiness in their miserable lives, get nothing but a marker over a grave, and the all too swift destiny of being a mere memory.

Unfortunately, Hunter, the world will recover from your passing very quickly and go about its business.

Though he was dreading it, he had to get over to the Jamisons' house. Since Kris had left Ben's office, Ben had gone on to the hospital where he was to perform the Ministration at the Time of Death, a church sacrament, at Bill Jamison's request. But soon Ben and the parents would be at the Jamison home, and it was as much Kris's responsibility to be there as it was Ben's.

He took his jacket from the back of his chair and headed for the door.

Bill Jamison was a self-made man, having years ago founded Jamison Distributing. He and Mary were not part of the inner circle of the elite Bel Terre Country Club set, though they owned a fine and beautiful home on the Boulevard. That home was of course to be a changed one after today. Kris, Ben, and the Jamisons were now in the living room.

As could be expected, Mary Jamison seemed in total shock, a blank expression on her face. She sat still and said almost nothing. She had served Ben and Kris fresh coffee despite their pleas that she not bother.

Bill looked as sad and broken as any man had ever looked but seemed to be coping somehow. Perhaps this was mostly out of necessity, Kris surmised. He had to be a support to Mary as well as their other son, Andrew, who'd soon be arriving home from the University of the South at Sewanee.

"I suppose God does things in His own way," said Bill, very despondently. "Hunter was just not able to deal with things in this world the way they are."

"And God understood that," said Ben. "That's how you've got to keep seeing it, Bill. When the tough times ahead close in on you, hold on to that thought." He paused a moment, then continued, "We're all a part of something bigger than ourselves. Hunter is forever loved by God."

Ben always had a way with turning a phrase yet making great sense. Kris's mind comprehended what Ben was saying, but his heart couldn't just now. There he could only feel bitterness.

"I'm not one to say the usual things said at such times, Bill," Ben continued, "but the church is here for you. As am I personally. If there's anything at all I can do, please call me."

"Thank you, Ben," said Bill.

They all stood and exchanged embraces. Mary now offered some of the few words she had spoken since Ben and Kris had arrived.

"Father Kris."

"Yes, Mrs. Jamison," Kris answered.

"Hunter would want you to do the service. Would you please?" Then she turned to Ben. "You understand, don't you, Ben?"

"Of course, Mary. I think that would be wonderful," said Ben warmly, but he waited on Kris's reply.

Kris managed to answer, "It would be an honor."

An honor, yes, but whether he'd be capable was another matter altogether. How would he get through it?

"We haven't gotten very far in the arrangements, but I suppose we will this afternoon," said Bill, still very sad and distant. "Someone will call you. We appreciate your open-mindedness about it, Ben."

"The idea sounds very fitting," Ben replied.

"I'll wait to hear from you," said Kris, shielding his reluctance as best he could.

Ben and Kris said their farewells to the Jamisons at the door and made their way toward their cars. Just steps away from Kris, Ben turned back to him and asked, "Are you okay, Kris?"

"Sure," he said, though he wasn't sure exactly what "okay" meant at times like these.

"It's tough, I know," said Ben as he walked over and put his hand on Kris's shoulder. "And the Jamisons are going to need a lot of support to get through this. I'm glad that you, perhaps more than I, will be there for them."

Kris managed a faint smile and nodded. After a moment, Ben continued on, got in his car, and drove away.

Standing here on the Boulevard, Kris looked up at the bright sun overhead and felt the cool, crisp air. The leaves were already on the verge of turning, autumn on the way. Hunter was never to look upon any of this beauty again. The fact that he, Kris Hartley, was still privileged to do so suddenly baffled him.

He started up his MR2 and headed up the Boulevard toward the church. After driving scarcely more than a block, he slowed to a stop and took the engine out of gear. Staring straight ahead for a moment, he knew that it was time to let it go.

He wept uncontrollably for several minutes.

5

CHARLIE AND PEGGY strolled down the sidewalk from "102" toward the parking lot. The noon meeting had just concluded. The house where the daily meeting took place, located on Bel Terre Boulevard and owned by St. John's Church, was commonly referred to by its street address, "102." It stood next to the church, having originally been intended as a rectory. The AA group met in a large room of the house, the space being provided as a service of the church. The group referred to itself as the Harding Road Group, though the house actually faced Bel Terre Boulevard.

"Are you up for lunch?" Peggy asked. "I ran my extra couple of miles this morning, like I said I would. Guess I'm entitled to a turkey sandwich over at Goldie's."

"I really don't have time, Peg," said Charlie. "I should head back to the office and get a few things done."

"Charlie, is everything all right?" inquired Peggy. "I don't know, you just seemed all through the meeting like you were kinda bummed about something. Anything you need to talk about?"

"You were plenty inquisitive about me last night," Charlie said rather abruptly. "Are we going to have to go there again?"

"All right, so you don't want to talk," Peggy recoiled. "I can live with that."

"No offense, Peg, but it's just that there are those days when a person is in a quiet mood," continued Charlie, still a bit terse. "It doesn't have to mean anything."

"Sure," said Peggy. "Guess I'd better go and do my own lunch thing. See ya."

Peggy walked on toward her car.

"Peggy." Charlie stopped her. There was a pause. "I'm sorry. I don't want to hurt your feelings. It doesn't have anything to do with you. It's just...it's just something I've got to work through on my own."

Peggy softened. "Look, Charlie, something's eating your gut alive. I can see it plain as day. And I just think you need to talk to *somebody*, even if it's not me. You need to deal with it, for your *own* sake, that's all."

Charlie looked at her beloved friend with her highlighted hair, body piercings, tattoos – everything about her was excessive. Yet Peggy was kind-hearted and a kick to co-write with.

"You're a true pal, Peg, and I don't want to do anything to offend you. So don't be angry with me. I'll get through this, but I surely don't need to lose a friend. I'm truly sorry."

Peggy looked at her, smiled, and then said, "Forget it. And you're not going to lose a friend, babe. Maybe lunch tomorrow, huh?"

"Count on it."

They shared a quick hug.

"Well, here I go," said Peggy. "After I grab a bite, I've got to go find a bikini."

Charlie laughed. "A bikini! Aren't you a little late? Or are you just catching end-of-the-year sales?"

"It's a costume in my new stand-up routine."

Peggy was a fledgling stand-up comic who had made a few appearances at Zanies, a local comedy club, though she waited tables several nights a week at J. Alexander's to earn her living.

"Your routine? I'll have to see that one," said Charlie.

"Bye now."

"Call me in the morning, Peg."

As Peggy drove away, Charlie unlocked her car, got in, and sat for a moment, thinking. Would she ever tell Peggy everything about the delicate situation she was facing? Was love supposed to bring as much pain as pleasure? She'd spent last evening feeling angst and frustration. Now she was on the verge of driving friends away.

Just as she started up the engine preparing to drive on to the office, there was a sudden tap on the window of the passenger side of her car.

Jock Pritchard and Abe Feinstein had been a few steps behind Charlie and Peggy as they had exited "102." It was the first chance of the week Jock had found to attend the Harding Road group meeting.

"I guess I'm feeling the old rut," Jock said. "The *winter of my discontent*."

"What's making you discontented?" asked Abe.

"Here I am, pulling down a hell of a salary," Jock continued, "got a beautiful home, a solid future, even a fine retirement plan."

"I understand," joked Abe. "You have my deepest sympathy."

Though knowing himself to be one of the biggest jokesters in town, Jock was in no mood for anyone else's jokes at the moment.

"But I've had dreams all my life, like anybody. The gotta-be-me thing, you know. Part of me ridicules that while part of me can't quit dreaming. So what the hell do I do?"

He'd said this almost derisively, as if daring the erudite professor to analyze and solve this one.

Abe thought for a little and then said, "Sometimes people do actually find a healthy compromise between different directions in which they're pulled. Sometimes there's a way to realize the illusive dream *after a fashion* without sacrificing practicality and common sense."

Jock was not impressed. "It seems to me either you go for a dream or you don't."

"If that's the way you see it, that's the way it is. I once heard it said that a man gets to a point he must simply 'accept or haul ass.' I think if you just keep searching you'll get to that point. It'll be one or the other."

"Such words of wisdom," Jock quipped. "Well, I'm sure glad we had this talk."

"You'll get my bill in the morning," Abe said.

Jock laughed. "Guess I'd better be getting on back to work. Thanks, Abe. I don't know exactly for what, but well, thanks just the same."

As they shook hands Abe said, "Have a good day, and stay in touch."

"Bye now."

As Abe walked on, Jock was thinking how it seemed, though Abe spoke in a lighthearted manner today, there was something weighing on him. He couldn't put his finger on it, but Abe was not quite himself.

But just then he caught sight of Charlie Cohen in the parking lot saying goodbye to her weird girlfriend, Peggy, and proceeding to her car. Charlie, with her shoulder-length brown hair, beautiful brown eyes, incredible tits, and great legs had caught his eye from the first day he'd come to Harding Road Group. Good thing, he thought, that she didn't know what went on in his mind. But then, hell, she *had* to know what most men thought when looking at her. She was no one's fool. That much he'd sensed.

Jock and Charlie had spoken only a few times, though Jock had certainly wanted to get to know this lady better. He found himself hurrying over to Charlie's car. Having spent a lot of his newfound recovery isolating himself, he decided it was time to open up. He might blow it and make an ass of himself, but what the hell! He had to find out.

He tapped on the window of the passenger side of her car.

Charlie lowered the window. The guy she'd always regarded as the budding young F. Lee Bailey was seeking her attention for something. He was an attractive guy. He never seemed to wear anything other than Armani suits, but what of it? She liked expensive things too. No need to scoff at those who could actually afford them.

"Hi," she said.

"Hi," Jock replied. "I haven't been here all week, and uh, I just thought I'd say hello." He tried to appear relaxed. "I, uh, I know this is your big week. I even looked to see if I spotted you in the audience last night on the awards telecast."

"Not much chance of that," she said. "Hard for the cameras to get a close-up shot of anything in the peanut gallery."

"Top balcony, huh?" he laughed. "That's the best they could do for you?"

She thought it cute, his slightly awkward attempts at making conversation. Even society dudes who partnered at big law firms could be shy. It was refreshing, and sort of sweet.

"Secretaries don't rate extremely high on awards night," she explained. "I was lucky to be there at all."

"Just the same, I'm envious."

She didn't look in a hurry to get away from him. Was he getting anywhere? he wondered.

"I..."

"Yes?" she smiled.

"Ah hell, here goes," he said, drawing a breath. "Is there any chance you'd care to...have dinner, or something?"

It dawned on Charlie that she had not been asked for a date in the conventional sense in over a year. She suddenly wondered how things could have ever come to that. For some reason she didn't quite know, she found herself smiling and saying, "Dinner would be nice."

Jock brightened. "Would it? I – I mean great!" They were both laughing now. "How about..."

"Yes?"

"...Saturday night?"

"I think that would work," she replied.

"Wonderful." He knew he was sweating. Was his face red?

"Why don't you give me a call, and I'll direct you to where I live. I'm listed in the book: Charlene Cohen."

"I'll call you."

"Now, I really have to go, Jock."

"Sure. I understand. I'll call you." *You said that, Jock.* "Uh, have a good afternoon."

Actually, he'd been glad to hear her say his name as he wasn't sure she even knew it.

He waved as he watched her drive away. Damn, she was hot! And the whole thing went pretty well. He walked on to his car. It was a great day after all.

As Charlie pulled out of the St. John's parking lot onto the Boulevard and then onto Harding, she wondered what had just happened. Moments ago she'd been wondering whether she was really in love with a man, feeling at once more joy and pain than ever in her life, and now she had just accepted a date with Perry Mason.

But then there was no reason not to do so…was there?

Charlie was suddenly aware that, though she'd just come out of a meeting, she was reflecting on how a drink, or just a few hits off a joint, used to help her calm down. She quickly breathed a prayer for serenity.

This situation had to be addressed. No doubt about it.

Father Kris noticed friends coming out of the meeting as he drove up the Boulevard. He continued all the way to Harding Road and would enter the front parking lot from there rather than cutting through the side lot. He was presently in no frame of mind to encounter the other group members and become engaged in conversation.

Entering the office of the church he noticed that there was still no one on the front desk. He hurried on up the stairs to his office, closed the door, picked up the phone, and asked Nancy to please hold all his calls.

Time passed as he tried to synthesize his thoughts. He prayed for guidance. Suddenly the phone on his desk rang. He picked it up.

"I really do need all calls held," he said abruptly.

"I know, hon," said Nancy, "but Bill Jamison has called, and so has Ben. The service is set for here on Saturday. One o'clock. Just thought you needed to know."

He paused. Less than forty-eight hours.

"Thanks, Nancy…Sorry I snapped."

"Need anything?"

"No. Oh, wait. Lord, yes. Please call Dalts and see if you can have Greg Smith paged, and try to explain things to him."

"Already taken care of. I caught him before he left his office."

"The chaplain at the penitentiary..."

"Talked to him too. And, by the way, he sent his condolences to us and to the family."

"There's the EYC Council."

"Don't worry. I'll still be here when they're arriving. I'll deal with it."

"I was to have dinner with Wallace and Martha Lynn Robbins tonight, but I'll take care of that on my own. I don't know if I'll go or not."

"I'll leave you alone now. Just give me a shout if you need anything."

"I will. Thanks, Nancy."

He hung up the phone still juggling the anger and the grief.

But enough self-pondering. He had to get past his emotions and prepare a sermon. No, it must be a *celebration eulogy* for Hunter. Yes, that was a start. Kris was resolved to get through this. He had no choice.

6

TOMMY HAD SPENT a good deal of the afternoon on the phone with Jake Hestor, his assistant at the publishing company, who was currently in Los Angeles.

"That's right. No rest for the wicked," Tommy joked, referring to the upcoming weekend gig in New Orleans, a trip he'd be making with Chad. A benefit concert for victims of Hurricane Katrina sponsored by the United Way had been booked at the New Orleans Fairgrounds.

"Man, this is the biggest 'winner-take-all' since Garth walked away with everything that one year," Jake said.

"Yep. And next year we're gonna hope for Entertainer of the Year," Tommy said proudly.

"I'd say odds have got to be pretty damn good after a start like this."

"I kept tellin' Chad not to get his hopes too high," Tommy continued, "and all the while mine were ridin' as high as they could be."

Tommy's successful publishing house, Associated Publishers, and Vision Artists Unlimited, his management firm, were housed together in an office facility on Music Row East. Jake's well-compensated position there had actually evolved into far more than just that of publishing assistant. Besides seeking out and signing new writers and publishing fresh new material, he served as an all-round right-hand man to Tommy. He was currently on the West Coast overseeing some bookings for some of Tommy's contracted artists.

Jake also went out of his way, perhaps to a fault, to keep the names of Tommy's artists before the important people in the entertainment industry as well as before the media. Rumor had it that Jake even leaked personal information that had anything to do with the artists to the tabloids. This would, after all, sell a few thousand more recordings, or so it was reasoned.

"I can't imagine that we don't have Jay Leno in the bag now. I'll stay on it," said Jake. "What about acting? Chad got any inclinations toward that?"

Tommy laughed. "Let's take a little more time before we try gettin' him in the movies, Jake. We don't know if he's gonna end up havin' a knack for that."

"Who cares? Elvis's acting was crap when he first started out, and nobody gave a shit," Jake reflected.

"Times've changed, Jake. The fans don't take to an artist failin' at somethin'. And certain parties in the media make it their business to find anything they can to take a man down."

"If it's all the same to you, I'm going to keep my eyes open."

"Well, I gotta go now," Tommy said with a snicker. "SESAC festivities are this afternoon, and I oughta make an appearance."

"Be sure to give my congrats to Chad."

They said their goodbyes. Tommy shook his head and laughed as he put the phone down. Jake, if perhaps a bit unprincipled at times, had consistently proven himself a gem both to Tommy's publishing house and the management firm.

As Tommy took his coat from the brass rack in his office and prepared to set out for SESAC the phone rang.

"Hello."

"Glad I caught you. It's Rick," said Rick Richmond. "I needed to share some news with you. The Pioneer board made a decision last week. To be honest, it was somewhat contingent on Chad's big win at the CMAs. But I thought it best not to go into it last night. I feel safe in saying that it'll be definite now, though the formality of the vote-taking is yet to happen."

"So what's up?" Tommy said.

"We're founding a major new subsidiary of the label, the name yet to be decided on. We want Chad to be the first artist on it. It's going to be promoted as focusing on 'country music for the masses.'"

"For the masses," Tommy repeated.

"It's going to be dedicated to developing Nashville music that has the broadest appeal, the biggest cross-over potential."

Tommy knew that the Pioneer people were prudent enough to realize that they had a goldmine in Chad Harmon. Chad's popularity with the pop and adult-contemporary audiences in addition to the lovers of traditional country had made both mechanical and airplay royalties escalate in a manner Pioneer hadn't experienced in a while. Now Chad's sweep of the CMAs signaled that it was time to milk a good thing for all it was worth.

"Sounds exciting," Tommy declared.

"The reason I'm calling is that we want to ask Chad to be at the press conference to announce the new subsidiary. It can be worked around his concert schedule."

"Sure. How soon?"

"A couple of weeks, give or take. Like I say, all the necessary business procedures have to take place first. Which is why I need to ask you to keep it all on the quiet for now."

"I understand. Uh, say, Rick?"

"Yeah?"

"We, of course, need to get around to talkin' about the album itself before long."

"Nobody knows that better than me. Believe me, I want that album out by spring, no later," Rick said. "Get Chad through the New Orleans booking this weekend, and we'll all try to talk next week."

"Will do," Tommy said. "Everything sounds great."

"Later," said Rick.

Tommy put down the phone. A new division of a renowned label, and evidently built around Chad. Yes, a towering thought, for sure.

But Tommy couldn't help feeling some trepidation regarding a new label subsidiary "geared toward the masses," perhaps signing acts that were more pop than country, hip-hop acts with a bit of country instrumentation thrown in. The issue had for years been a matter of controversy on the Row. Baby Boomers had now moved up to positions of power and leadership in the so-called country music business. Many had brought the sounds formerly heard in the pop genre along with them. But others in the business, Tommy for one, saw a great need to "get back to our roots."

One thing was sure: Chad was a country artist. Tommy knew that he should remain so, without a doubt. No transformation into anything trendy or gimmick-oriented, thank you. There'd been enough of the cutesy boy pop acts promoted in the country music market. Chad was pure country. Yet somehow he was not unlike others who had a flare for crossover potential. His accessible talent was the reason behind his becoming a deservedly huge success. And so far he'd done it without "selling out."

Tommy notified Trudy, his secretary, of where he'd be and headed out to SESAC. He'd share the label news with Chad later.

It was around 1:30 in the afternoon when Chad finally awoke. Thankfully, he had remembered to turn off the bedroom phone just before retiring so as to let the answering machine downstairs do its job.

His head throbbed a little, and as he looked in the bathroom mirror, his roadmap eyes were a sight. But that's what Tylenol and Visine were made for. Great celebrating had, after all, been in order last evening. He found what was needed quickly enough in the medicine chest.

"You'll be a gorgeous son of a gun once again in no time," he murmured as he put the drops in his eyes.

Then, after relieving himself, which was not a quick chore, considering all he'd drunk the previous night, he put on his slippers and robe and proceeded down the stairs. In the kitchen he prepared the coffee maker. Returning to the foyer, he was surprised to find that there were no messages on the answering machine, but then few people had access to the unpublished number. There was nothing to do but get the morning paper and relax.

He opened the front door and was glad to see *The Tennessean* right at the threshold. He picked up the paper, closed the door, and settled in on the living room couch.

Turning straight to the Living section, there it was bigger than life! A huge color photo of himself, occupying about one fourth of the front page of Section D, as he had performed "In the Rain" at the CMAs! It all came back. What a night it had been!

"Man, it really did happen!" he said. "It's right there in print. I have to be the luckiest man on the face of the earth!"

The article focused from the outset on the one biggest sensation of the CMA Awards night. And that sensation, the writer of the article attested, had been Chad Harmon, now the hottest act in town and fast becoming one of the hottest in the nation.

Several minutes later he sat at the center counter of the kitchen sipping coffee and continuing to peruse the newspaper article. But it came to him that there was something he couldn't avoid dealing with forever. He had promised Lydia to remain unspoiled, even in the face of his huge success. So here's where making good on that commitment began. He knew that he had to try contacting his dad in Houston at some point.

Buck Harmon had been a country artist on the rise in Nashville in the early 1960s. However, alcohol had destroyed his career. It had been a curious thing to Chad that there had been almost no one on the Row or in the media to pick up on the connection between the rising star Chad Harmon and the country artist of yesteryear, Buck Harmon. Too many days gone by it seemed, and Buck was forgotten.

Buck had just been asked to make his first appearance on the Opry when he went on one of his worst benders, and he was never invited back again. A prospective recording deal fell through as well. He eventually returned to his hometown of Houston and worked several local gigs in bars, that is, until he was instructed by the proprietors of all of them not to return.

Next he went from one blue-collar job to another, usually never keeping one for long. But he'd met Lydia, and they'd married. She had often been more of a breadwinner for the household than he, cleaning houses for a living. It was as if Buck was destined to go through life a failure.

For all his faults, Buck had always seemed like a congenial sort to most who met him, that is, if he'd been sober at the time. Chad had often considered it the height of improbability that his ne'er-do-well dad had somehow won Lydia's heart long ago. However, Lydia had a way of seeing the good in even the very lowest of all humanity.

"Yeah, just go on up to Nashville," Buck had said to Chad with a smirk upon Chad's announcement of his plans to move there. "You'll find out what's it's all about right quick. It's a tough old world, the music business. And full of assholes. And folks that want you to kiss theirs."

Because Buck had blown his chances decades ago, he could only belittle his son's dreams. Chad wondered, with a sneer, what dear old Dad must now be thinking.

But the fact stood that Chad was obligated to call Buck, not because of anything familial, but rather by his word to his mother. Besides, how would it look if he wrote his old man off as past history while he, Chad, climbed the ladder to success? Perhaps the burning need to call did stem from the desire to condescend to his has-been father, but he knew what had to be done, whatever the motivation.

"Guess there's no time like the present," he said with a sigh. He took the phone from the kitchen wall, dialed the number, and waited. He heard the phone ringing on the other end, and then came a shock.

"Hello," answered the voice of a woman.

He thought at first that he might have dialed the wrong number. But that number hadn't changed in over three decades. It had been his own through much of his childhood and youth.

After hesitating a few seconds, he said, "Uh, is this…is this Mr. Harmon's residence?"

"Yes, it is. This is Cora Eubanks." She seemed a woman of at least middle age or older. After a brief pause, she said with enthusiasm, "Oh, this must be Chad!"

"That's right," he said, still confused.

"I'm a friend of Buck's. I'm afraid he's out right now. I'm over here preparing some things for a dinner tonight. There are four of us who are getting together."

That Buck had friends with whom he actually socialized these days, or rather with whom he *drank*, was amusing to Chad.

The woman continued, "I feel very honored to be talking to you. We watched the awards last night. It was terribly exciting. Oh, forgive me, I haven't even offered my congratulations. It's all very wonderful for you. And, oh, your father was *so* proud."

"Uh...well, thanks. Please tell him I called."

"He'll be so sorry he missed you."

"Uh-huh," he fumbled.

"But certainly I will tell him you called," she added.

Strangely enough, she seemed a very refined, gracious lady.

"Would you mind if I got a phone number where you can be reached?" she continued. "I happen to know he's had a difficult time trying to get in touch."

Chad balked for a moment and then said, "Well, I'm afraid I'm leaving town. So it's kind of hard to say. Why don't I try later?"

"Please do, Chad. Buck is out doing some shopping. He decided he needed some fall clothes, though, heaven knows it doesn't get that cold down here. I think he'll be back by 4:00 at the very latest."

Buck shopping for a fall wardrobe? A lady friend in the house? Entertaining friends for dinner? Perhaps he had dialed the wrong number after all.

"Well, thanks, uh...?"

"Cora. Cora Eubanks."

"Uh-huh. Well, good-bye now." He clicked the phone off. "I'll be damned! A girlfriend!"

He'd envisioned Buck as having all the time in the world now to isolate and drink himself to death. And maybe he had found a female partner with some morbid need to play nursemaid to a sot.

Did he care about someone taking the place of his mother? No. That was something that happened when both parents of someone were equally loved by the son or daughter. He didn't love Buck. That love had been killed long ago. The whole thing was none of his concern. Let them do as they please.

He went back to the newspaper article, this time just to make sure he knew what artists and writers had won all the other awards. But it was impossible to keep from occasionally glancing back at the front page of the section where he himself was the featured attraction.

Cora Eubanks hung up the phone feeling encouraged that Buck's son had called. She knew that Buck had a sincere desire to contact Chad and earnest intentions of setting things right between himself and the son he'd wronged over the years.

"What a shame Buck wasn't here," she thought.

Buck would have to live for the rest of his days with the reality that he'd hurt his late wife incessantly, the wife who'd loved him, had always been there for him, and whom he'd failed miserably.

"I'll never have Lydia back, and I'll never have the chance to say I'm sorry," Buck had said. "That fact haunts me every day."

All that was left to Buck was Chad. Perhaps there was hope he could make amends to his son. Cora knew that this was of great importance to Buck.

Charlie was in the midst of some correspondence at her desk when Rick returned from a quick appearance at the SESAC event.

"Any calls?" he asked.

"Just Eric," Charlie replied, referring to Rick's nineteen-year-old son who attended the University of Tennessee in Knoxville. Then with a smile she added, "I think he needs money."

"I suppose he thinks that, with Pioneer sweeping the CMA Awards, his old man can now afford to put him up in a nice big apartment while he goes to school."

"Well, can't you?" Charlie joked.

"'Can I' or 'Will I'?"

"Never mind," was her simple closure to the subject.

"I'll call him later, maybe tonight from home," said Rick, seemingly bored with the subject. Then somewhat off-handedly he said, "How's my 5:30 looking?"

Charlie knew what was being inquired.

"It's still on," was the simple reply, Charlie being versed to a cryptic means of communication with Rick.

"Good," Rick responded as he walked into his office and closed the door.

She went about her work at the word processor, but only after checking her watch for the time. Two hours until 5:30. It seemed an eternity to have to wait.

7

"BMI," answered the receptionist.

"Mark Weinstock," Rick said.

It would be getting on toward 5:00 Eastern Time, Rick suddenly thought. He needed to call Mark now before Mark had left the office in New York.

Mark Weinstock worked in Special Projects at the New York City headquarters of Broadcast Music Incorporated. He'd worked in the same division of the Nashville office of the performance rights organization before moving on to BMI's national headquarters.

Mark's position with BMI was a full-time job. However, he was also secretly employed by Rick Richmond, who had founded a new publishing enterprise in New York under the name of New Works Unlimited. A post office box served as its mailing address. Weinstock's job was to actively solicit quality material from new songwriters. Serving as the owner of the publishing house, Rick would have sole propriety over songs released through this publishing venture.

The term "publishing," in its recording industry connotation, had little to do with the practice of printing sheet music for distribution and sales. Being the publisher for a song released on a recording basically meant owning the song going down on the recording. As Tommy had once explained it to Chad, it simply constituted one more way to divvy up the money. The artist, writer, publisher, and producer all took their respective cuts of royalties made from a song. The more titles a person had in the development of a single tune on a recording, whether producer, publisher, or writer, the more money that person would receive from sales of recordings and, more importantly, radio airplay.

"Mark, how's it looking?" he asked when Weinstock answered.

"Rick, hi. Looking great," said Mark. "Got a couple more tunes for you to hear which I think you'll like. One, believe it or not, is actually by a former Nashville writer who relocated in New York for some reason. There are demos of both. I sent it all by FedEx today. Seems to me like these would be really hot for Harmon, but you see what you think."

"Thanks. I will."

With a New York base of operations, it was a bit easier for Rick to be more discreet about his ownership of a publishing venture. That would certainly work best for everyone, he had decided. His intention was to act as publisher of most, if not all, the songs on the next Chad Harmon album.

It was almost 6:30 p.m. before Jock got away from the Burch, Baxter, and Schultz office. As he pulled out of the underground parking facility, he dialed Charlie's number on the cell phone, and eventually the voice mail picked up.

"Hi. It's Charlie. I'm not in. You know what to do." *Beep!*

"Hi, Charlie. It's Jock. Guess we'll touch base later about the directions to your place. But I wanted to let you know that I had an idea about Saturday night. I'd love to take you to the Bel Terre Country Club. Discounting all of those things you've read in the *Nashville Scene*, the claims about exclusiveness, none of which do I deny, the food is superb. I'll be talking to you before then about directions to your place, which is mainly why I was calling. Well, have a good rest of the week. Bye." And he heard the answering machine beep cut him off at just the right moment. He'd barely gotten it all in.

He turned right off of Fourth Avenue North onto Broadway. He popped in the Chad Harmon CD. Time for a little music.

Damn, it was a great day!

The moment that Jock was heading toward Green Hills Mall, his upcoming date for Saturday night lay in her bed, the covers pulled snug around her, feeling content, secure, cared for. At such times, all those moments in which Charlie had obsessed over the situation went right out of her mind.

At the foot of the bed, Rick was dressing himself. As he put on his trousers, she realized she remained attracted to him after the lovemaking, in the fleeting moments when he must now return to his *conventional* life.

"Any big plans for the upcoming weekend?" he asked her.

"No," she replied. "You?"

"No."

"Don't forget to call Eric," she said.

"Right," he answered.

Broderick Richmond, tall, handsome even at fifty, quite virile, powerful, respected, and wealthy, valued Charlie's company, and that was all she needed to know. She seemed to fill an empty space in his life just as he did in hers. And at these precious moments there simply was no purpose served by addressing the fact that he was married. There were many unhappy marriages in the world, and his was just another of them. No, it wasn't just a sex thing, she assured herself. Of course Rick treated her as if she were a goddess even in bed, thinking of her rather than just himself. But he was very open with her about himself and his life. Many would never have suspected Rick Richmond to be a man who could make himself even a little vulnerable, that he could be sweet and tender. But, Charlie now knew, at these special times they had together, few though they might be, he was just that with her.

Yes, to answer her own question of earlier today, she did love him. She found the arrangement, limited as it was for now, to be what she'd always needed. It worked for her. Their relationship brought her tremendous happiness at these times, and that was more than some people got in an entire lifetime.

Charlie rose and put on her robe. Rick looked at her and then pulled her toward him and into his arms.

"It's been wonderful, as always," he said looking at her.

"As always," Charlie agreed. "Rick?"

"Yes?"

"Would there ever be a weekend we could go away together? Just a chance to have some quality time. Maybe one of your New York trips?"

"I'd love it too, Charlie. But you might be disappointed to find how little free time I actually have on those trips," he said, though what was foremost in his mind was the fact that discretion would be damned near impossible with such a trip. But no need to say this to her.

"I wouldn't care. Just anything for a change." She paused, resolved not to sound whiny. "It's hard at times..."

"To settle for just a one- or two-hour rendezvous?" he asked.

She smiled again. He even seemed understanding of this.

"I can't keep any promises or commitments, baby." He looked at her and then said very pointedly, "That's why I never have made them." She nodded. He truly hadn't. "But…we'll see," he finally said, though concluding in his own mind it was out of the question.

She'd hang on to her hopes. Just one night spent together, one morning to awaken next to him.

"I really have to go now," he said.

"I know."

But both of them felt something as they embraced to say good-bye, the tension rising again, the body heat radiating through his clothing and her robe. He reached inside the front opening of her gown, drew her tightly against himself, and put his lips to hers.

However, they'd have to be quick this time. He really did have to leave soon.

There was only so much peace and quiet a man should experience following all the glory, or at least that's how Sandy Matheson had put it when she'd called Chad.

"You know I'm not going to take no for an answer, sweetie," she'd joked. "We haven't had a chance to celebrate with you."

"You don't have to twist my arm," Chad replied with a laugh.

The drive out to the Mathesons' took about forty-five minutes. They resided on a tract of land near Leiper's Fork, to the south of Nashville. Several stars' large, sprawling homes were found there of late. The Mathesons' home was a bit more understated, unpretentious, yet tasteful and spacious. Sandy herself had done all the decorating.

In the large barn were housed four Tennessee walking horses, favorite collectibles of the Mathesons. Stored in the barn as well was a sleigh, though Middle Tennessee seldom got blanketed with a heavy enough snow for sleigh rides. Nonetheless, if once in a lifetime it did occur, the sleigh was available, and the farm had ninety-two acres.

Sandy's late-planned dinner was tonight a mere threesome. Tommy, Sandy, and Chad all had felt a need to be low-key tonight. With a couple of pine logs crackling away in the stone fireplace of the den, they dined in the nearby breakfast room.

"As always, Sandy, everything was fantastic," said Chad as he laid his fork down. "The rack of lamb was superb."

"Thanks, sweetie. Glad you enjoyed it," Sandy replied. She then raised her glass of wine to Chad. "Here's to you. We're so proud of you."

Tommy joined her. "Amen!"

"I appreciate it, guys," said Chad. "You're the best. Both of you." He then smiled at Tommy and nodded his head in Sandy's direction. "How do you get one of these, Tommy?"

"You're askin' me?" said Tommy. "*I* don't even know how I got so lucky."

Tommy was a man who, after more than twenty years with his mate, still worshipped the ground she walked upon.

"I've had no complaints myself," said Sandy, lovingly taking Tommy's hand.

Chad wondered what it was like to share your life with someone you loved this much and from whom you received the same in return. He'd heard that it could surpass everything else in life, even performing, recording, and appearing in videos. He'd even written and sung about it himself, though never having yet found it.

Chad had brought along as a gift a Chardonnay that had been uncorked and finished before dinner. But the fine Zinfandel Sandy had served up with the lamb was wonderful, and he helped himself to yet another glass.

This time it was Chad who proposed the toast. "And now it's my turn. To the two of you, my best friends. And to all the success of Vision Artists at the CMAs."

Tommy and Sandy beamed. They'd never allowed themselves to get so close to one of Vision's contracted artists. Their business and their personal lives were generally two separate things. Yet Chad was special. He was like their adopted son.

"I've got an idea, sweetie," said Sandy. "It's getting late. Why don't you stay the night? There's a four-poster feather bed in one of the guest rooms. And, here in the country, we can guarantee you'll be waking up to the sound of a rooster crowing."

Truth to tell, Chad really had not relished going back to the empty condo and being alone, though he hadn't anticipated such an invitation.

"You don't think three's a crowd?" he said. "Tonight you two can finally be alone, now that the week's winding down."

"Actually we will be," said Sandy with a coy grin. "The guest bedroom is as far as you can get from ours."

"So's the rooster," Tommy added. "We like to sleep in, but there's no guaranteein' you will tomorrow."

Everyone laughed.

"Well, if you insist," Chad conceded.

"We do," said Sandy. "Care for coffee with dessert, sweetie?"

"Sure," murmured Chad. "I mean, no thanks. Maybe later." He continued on the wine.

Sandy had thought it a little impertinent to also express concern for Chad's drive back into town now that he had finished his fifth glass of wine and that his speech was becoming just a bit slurred. And besides, he was staying. So, enough said.

Father Kris was glad now that he'd kept the dinner date with Wallace and Martha Lynn Robbins. Two of the dearest people in the world to him since his coming to St. John's, the Robbinses, both in their seventies, were favorites of all in the community who knew them. Now occupying Martha Lynn's grand family home of generations past, located on the Boulevard, the two were among the most active in civic and social affairs as well as church activities. Yet they were actually simple people.

Martha Lynn had been raised a child of the Bel Terre Country Club set but had also been a close buddy of the late Sarah Cannon, a.k.a. Minnie Pearl. She'd hosted at her home everything from the Nightingale Ball Patron's Party to parish functions for St. John's Church. Though adept at being the proper hostess, she was equally content to merely sit and talk with the kitchen help. To Martha Lynn, there didn't seem to be any such thing as class distinctions.

As they walked him to the front door, Kris was aware that his spirits had lifted slightly this evening.

"I never have gotten close to Mary," said Martha Lynn, "but I have served on the vestry with Bill. He's always been a pleasant sort, it seemed to me. I just hate it for them."

"It's been a blow to us all," said Kris, "but I can't even imagine what the Jamisons are feeling."

"We've heard that young Hunter thought the world and all of you," Wallace said.

This struck a pang when it should have brought gratification. If Hunter had "thought the world and all" of him, it was a mystery to Kris that Hunter had not bothered calling him when he was at his darkest hour.

"Kris, I wanted to ask your opinion about something," said Martha Lynn.

"Yes?" he said.

"You know what a big supporter of our wonderful music program Bill Jamison has always been," she continued. "He underwrote the instrumentalists for one Christmas Eve service and also the Symphony for one of our major choir concerts. Well, you know, at times like these, people tend to feel the worst, with it being someone so young." She took a breath. "I think people need all the exalting of their hearts that they can get, particularly the Jamisons themselves."

"I would agree," said Kris.

"What about our having the choir sing at the service? Knowing what all the Jamisons have done for St. John's and how Bill and Mary love the music of the church, I think it's one of the best gifts we can give them. But I surely wanted to run it by you first, Father Kris."

"Well, it's a wonderful idea," Kris agreed. "But I guess it will depend on the choir being asked, and quickly."

"Of course."

Wallace now spoke. "You see, Kris, we want to give a special gift to the choir in Hunter's memory. That can sort of be done in exchange for the service, you see."

Kris was ready to cry again. God had put people like this on the earth to do great works that affect others right when they needed it. With parishioners like these, one could make a case for the lack of need for priests.

"We'll work everything out with Father Allen," said Martha Lynn. "We want to do the memorial gift anonymously."

"Well, this is so wonderful of you," Kris said. "It seems like everything is coming together. Thanks to folks like you, I believe we'll get through this tough time somehow."

Kris offered his farewell and thanks for the dinner and then went on to his car. He needed to get to bed and rest, not for his own sake, but for the fact that over the next two days he had an obligation to be a support to the Jamisons and the greatly saddened parish.

Charlie tossed back and forth in the bed.

As long as Rick had been with her, everything always seemed wonderful. And, after all, she'd consigned herself to their relationship being something with limitations, at least for now. After he left, however, the glory always quickly faded.

"I don't know how to deal with this," she finally said to herself.

She got up, walked to the living room, turned the television on but paid only passing attention to one after another music video playing on CMT.

That night Rick Richmond, well on his way to being one of the most successful record company executives in the history of Music Row, and his lovely wife Estelle had a late dinner, just the two of them, in the huge sun room off the back of their Brentwood home. The room where they dined overlooked the beautiful gardens and waterfall out back. A most delectable meal had been prepared and served by their cook, Mirella. It was to be a celebration dinner, they had decided, in honor of Pioneer's many wins at this year's CMA Awards.

After espressos, the couple retired to the master suite upstairs where they made passionate love together.

Yes, Rick and Estelle were the happiest of couples.

8

SOME NASHVILLIANS had long been bent on seeing the term "Music City USA" broadened in its meaning. Their desire was to see Nashville take its place alongside New York and Los Angeles as a major entertainment center of the nation. It was argued that the city must remain active in the expansion of all arts and entertainment forms.

Champion of such sentiments was Sarah Greeling, Chairman and CEO of Greeling International Industries, a company based in Nashville. Often said to be Nashville's "Patron Saint of the Arts," Mrs. Greeling had not only served on the boards of the local symphony, the ballet, the opera, and the Nashville Theatre Group, but she had also been the top monetary contributor to each through the charitable contributions of the company she headed.

Sarah's husband, Bradley J. Greeling, who'd been a descendant of several successful entrepreneurs and founder of Greeling International, had died from a brain tumor some years back, leaving his wife custodian over the multibillion-dollar, family-owned empire which comprised computer software services, investments, shipbuilding, and book, music and video distribution. All four of the Greeling's sons now served as heads over various companies in the Greeling International empire and occupied seats on the executive board.

While Bradley J. had remained at the helm of Greeling for over three decades, building the aggregate of companies, Sarah had served throughout most of those years as Director of Corporate and Community Affairs. It had been her privilege for many years to allocate three percent of Greeling's annual gross revenues toward various non-profit causes, but with particular consideration going toward the arts in Middle Tennessee.

"I want to see all of the arts thrive and flourish in Nashville, so that we, our children, and our grandchildren won't be deprived of the things of beauty in this world," Sarah had declared again and again.

The Greelings had been a devoted couple and loving parents to their children. Bradley J. had always involved his wife in important decisions. And now, in accordance with her late husband's wishes, Sarah had become CEO over Greeling. Some had truly doubted the proficiency of the family matriarch for the task at hand.

But Sarah Greeling, the businesswoman, executed her responsibilities with dedication, fairness, and intelligence. Perhaps most to her credit was her willingness to heed the advice of those in place around her. And Greeling International maintained its tradition of generosity and care over its thousands of employees worldwide, be they executives or clerks. Benefits and perks were such that the company experienced a very low turnover in its personnel.

Just before noon on Friday, Governor Tim Bennington took the elevator to the top floor of the fifteen-story Greeling International headquarters on West End Avenue. Mrs. Greeling had placed a call several days earlier inviting Tim to join her for lunch in one of the private dining rooms of the Greeling facility. With Sarah having been the chief supporter of his gubernatorial campaign, Tim was inclined to honor her invitations.

On the fifteenth floor was the large main dining hall for general employees, a separate one for executives, and two private ones for whatever purpose Mrs. Greeling or the other execs in the company might require. All food was prepared under the supervision of the company's master chef.

Stepping off the elevator, Tim was greeted by the manager of the dining room.

"Hello, Governor. Nice to have you with us again," she said.

"Hi. Good to see you too..." He fumbled a moment, although remembering her face.

"Ellen. Ellen Bane," she said.

"Of course, Ellen," he said with his usual bright smile while shaking her hand. "Always good to be back with you people here at Greeling."

"Mrs. Greeling will be along in a moment. Her secretary called up just now to say that she had received a call from Aaron, her son, who's heading the company in Brussels. But I'll show you on to the dining room."

"Thank you, Ellen."

Tim followed Ellen on to the room where a beautiful oak table was set for two. Garden salads were already in place. On the sideboard were a silver pitcher of water and a covered basket of bread.

After pouring the water, Ellen suggested she go ahead and take his lunch order since Mrs. Greeling's order for today had already been sent up by her secretary. Tim, as was his custom whenever he lunched at Greeling International, chose the chef's grilled chicken breast, house salad, and unsweetened iced tea.

Ellen went back out and quickly returned with the governor's tea plus a pitcher for refills, which she placed on the sideboard.

"Thank you," Tim said.

"You're welcome, Governor."

She went out again, and Tim took in the panoramic view of the city from the large picture window. But within a couple of minutes the door opened, and there was Sarah.

"Good afternoon, Tim," she said. Years of working with him on the Nashville Symphony board, the Vanderbilt University board of regents, and countless committees, added to the numerous social engagements they'd attended together over the years, made it hard for Sarah to address the governor by anything other than his first name.

"Hello, Sarah," he took her hand firmly in his. Cheek kissing was mostly reserved for social events in the evening and not daytime business meetings, he was careful to remember.

"I'm very grateful for your coming," she said, moving to her place at the table where the governor helped her with her chair. "Thank you."

"It was my pleasure to come," said Tim. "I always enjoy a visit with you and the chance to sample your chef's wares."

"Well, I see no reason not to come right to it. As you know, I was asked to chair the Symphony Hall Dedication Committee." She rolled her eyes a bit. "Just what I needed, another committee, if not a board, to serve on, and this one I'm chairing. I'm going to stop saying that I won't take on anything new, because as soon as I've gotten the words out I'm up to my ears in a new project."

She picked up her fork to begin, and the governor followed suit.

The Nashville Symphony had perhaps become Sarah's "baby" more than any of the other causes she supported, particularly in recent years as the orchestra had begun the building campaign for a new symphony hall. For some time now Sarah, among others, had strongly taken up the case for the orchestra needing its own home, like all the great symphonies of the world. Putting her money where her mouth was, Sarah had been forthcoming with a very generous pledge toward the new capital campaign, this over and above her annual gift to the symphony. A most ambitious fund drive had followed, in which Sarah had been actively involved. Next, an architect had been contracted, plans had been finalized and voted on by the steering committee, and groundbreaking had taken place.

"I have to say, Sarah, that nothing has ever impressed me more than the energy that I've seen you put behind this Symphony Hall," said the governor. "You can be proud. And the hall is going to be spectacular."

"I've never been more excited over anything," she said. "I feel like a child waiting for Christmas morning."

"I think all of Nashville shares the fervor with you," Tim replied.

"Though I complain about the time commitment involved in this dedication committee, which was actually a by-product of the steering committee, it's really terribly special to me. The concert should be treated as something of paramount importance."

The dedicatory concert had been set for late April the coming year. The hall was guaranteed its completion by spring.

"Let me share a few things with you," she continued. "No tours of any kind will be conducted prior to the opening. In fact, only those associated with the symphony, construction personnel, or other technical contractors will be allowed in the hall at any time leading up to the dedication." She paused, delighting in this. "I guess we're creating a bit of drama in preserving the mystery of it all. Even the news media will be barred prior to the dedication. They'll only be furnished with artists' renderings of the designed interior of the hall. But what I need to talk to you about, Tim, is the ball we're having for dedication night."

"Oh yes, the ball," he said smiling.

"And don't say it," she said with a pretended scowl. "Yes, we got the ball idea off the ground a bit late, but the committee is working diligently, and I'm putting some staff in our Community Affairs division at their disposal too."

"Excellent," said Tim, finding this more and more interesting.

"The concert will begin at 7:00 p.m., with guests for the gala ball being served cocktails and hors d'oeuvres at 6:00 in the hospitality room of the Symphony Hall.

"Oh, and, by the way, three different corporations are hosting menu samplings and wine samplings of the ball's bill of fare in the months leading up to the dedication, with chamber ensembles from the symphony performing at each. All three events will be treated as something special, and I think that they'll help lend an air of expectancy about the hall's opening. I hope you'll find it possible to attend one."

"I'll do my best," the governor said.

"But anyway, back to dedication night. The concert must end by 8:30, at which time the ball begins. The ballroom is actually going to be transformed for our event into a mini-replica of the Symphony Hall's interior. A New York scenic designer is taking this on for us. The set pieces will be built at a specially leased shop."

"Very impressive," Tim said.

"We're setting the cost of the dedication ball at one thousand per plate. The Patrons Party at my home the night before will be two thousand per person in addition to the ball charge."

"Two thousand. Well, great. Why not go for the gold?" Tim laughed. But he quickly decided his rhetoric needed working on.

"There's to be a forty-piece orchestra, contracted from local session players, to play for the ball."

"Can't ask for double duty the same evening from the symphony musicians themselves, I suppose," Tim said.

"Exactly, and do those union rules ever get sticky these days," said Sarah. "So the gala is where you come in, Tim."

"I'm listening," he said.

"We think it would be most fitting for you and Angela to be honorary co-chairs of the ball."

"You can count on it, Sarah. In fact, I'm flattered." And he was. This would look good. *Damn* good.

"Other co-chairs will be the mayor and his wife, and we've got a commitment from Al and Tipper Gore to be included as well."

"I'm very impressed, Sarah," he said. "No one will ever get ahead of you, will they?"

"So now my honorary chairmen are taken care of. I suppose the only other thing I'd ask is that, as governor, you please talk it up and help our city and state to feel and know the importance of this event, almost as if like a state holiday."

"I'll do whatever I can, Sarah," Tim said. "Count on it."

"Thank you, Tim," she said. "Oh, have you tried the vinaigrette dressing our chef is known for? It's truly outstanding and surprisingly low in fat."

Sarah's day was no busier than most, though she had a number of papers to sign relating to Greeling International business for one of the company attorneys. At 2:00 p.m. there was another meeting concerning the symphony hall dedication. This one was to be with Jason Goldwyn, executive director of the symphony.

Several years ago Goldwyn had assumed the position managing the orchestra when legal strategies were barely in progress to pull the symphony out of a bankrupt state. Chapter Eleven proceedings had begun in the wake of a severe cash-flow crisis. He had stepped in during reorganization and had played a major role in transforming the deficit-plagued orchestra to one that operated in the black exclusively, and all in a matter of a couple of years.

Goldwyn now was finding his position fraught with much more responsibility, but also greater excitement. The orchestra he loved working for was on the verge of owning and operating its own performance hall. It was to be a magnificent palace of music where classical and pop concerts alike would take place, all in a venue where plush elegance and impeccable acoustics had been planned according to the examples set by the greatest concert halls of the world.

Sarah shook Jason's hand as he entered her office on the fourteenth floor of the Greeling headquarters.

"Hello, Jason."

"Hi, Sarah," he said. "Anything new that the executive director of the Symphony should be made aware of?"

She laughed. "Actually there are a few things."

The two had become enormously close friends over the years. Goldwyn, who came from a management background on Music Row and who had thus brought his business skills along to the symphony position, had earned Sarah's respect as well as that of the rest of the symphony board.

She gestured that they should occupy the sitting area of her office where a few gas logs flickered in the fireplace on this chilly afternoon.

"Things have to happen quickly for the dedication," Sarah said. "We're on such a relatively short time frame all of a sudden. I can't believe how fast the days and months are passing."

"I know what you mean," he said. "I watched the flatbeds pull up to the dock just this morning with those incredible light fixtures to be hung in the hall."

Sarah nodded. "I had to stop going down every time I heard about a new development. I couldn't get any work done, and the hardhat they make me put on doesn't do a thing for my hair in the middle of a work day."

Jason laughed along with her.

"Well, anyway, on to business," she said. "I don't need to bring you up to speed on the ball since that's not your department, but I will say that everything is coming together beautifully for it. And the greatest news is that we have an underwriter for the expenses of the ball. Thus, I think we'll raise our targeted figure."

"An underwriter?" Jason asked.

"Ellen Mayhew. It seems she wanted to do this as a memorial to her late husband. She's very excited about it. And it now means that virtually everything raised will be clear profit."

"Wonderful," Jason said.

"Now about the concert itself..." she was about to go on.

"If you don't mind my interrupting, Sarah, let me tell you that Itzak Perleman's contract is not quite worked out." A slight smile crossed his face. "He's not in the habit of playing just one or two pieces on a concert, but I think we've helped his management understand the entire nature of this event."

"I see. What about the popular artists?"

"Dolly Parton, Garth Brooks, and Faith Hill are all a go."

"And the other classical artists?" she asked.

"We're working on a Metropolitan Opera vocalist, preferably a soprano. And we think Van Cliburn will return for this. He seems to want to be a part of the opening of this hall."

"It sounds as though you've been doing your job," said Sarah, "...as have I."

"Oh?" said Jason.

"One of our former employees in the video company, a graduate of the Columbia School of Broadcasting, managed to land an executive production job a few years ago with the A&E Network. We were happy for him because he had too much talent for us to keep him around. We hated to see him go because he was so liked by everyone, but, in all honesty, Bradley helped get him the job. A college and long-time golfing buddy of Brad's was at that time a vice-president with A&E."

"Interesting," said Jason.

"Since then, Larry has always seen himself as owing us a big favor, though we've assured him he doesn't." A bright grin was appearing on her face. "However, with his feeling so indebted to Greeling, I thought, why not just ask?"

"Ask?" Jason said.

"Jason, it seems that we have the chance to get the dedicatory concert televised nationally over A&E, and right during prime-time," Sarah said beaming.

The thrill of having a Nashville Symphony concert take its place on the national media scene was tempered by certain concerns Goldwyn couldn't dismiss. After a moment's pause in which he was careful to look quite pleased at the news, he said, "That all sounds very exciting, Sarah. It would be a wonderful thing to have happen, and I appreciate you're pursuit of this..."

"But...?" she said, detecting the trepidation on his part.

"Well, A&E is of course a for-profit as opposed to a not-for-profit organization, like PBS. It throws a whole different light on the negotiating of everybody's contract, not the least among which are the musicians in the orchestra."

"Do you really think that they'd create a major fuss when the orchestra has the chance to become nationally recognized?" Sarah queried.

"Not one musician I can think of in the orchestra would be less than thrilled at the prospect of seeing this happen. But the union they're a part of, well, that's another matter. And that's where it gets messy. Then, frankly, there are the technical concerns; cameras, lighting equipment, microphones being brought in to an untried space for its very first concert, and all this going out on national television. There would have to be special rehearsals, detailed sound checks, and who knows what all. And we've got the *local* media shut out until dedication night. Then there's the dilemma of the television crews having to work around our crew, who obviously will be doing their first concert in the hall. In all honesty, it makes things doubly complicated all the way around."

Sarah looked pleasant, not argumentative, as she said, "Jason, you seem to have begun a list of all the reasons this can't work. Can we now start looking at ways we can possibly *make* it work?"

After a moment Jason relaxed himself, never able to out-debate the likes of Sarah Greeling. "Yes…why don't we do that?"

"Thank you, Jason," she said with warm gratitude. "I really do want all your concerns allayed. In fact, I share them with you. First thing, we have to keep the concert in a ninety-minute time frame.

But that will be fine in that we'll all have a ball to get to, which I believe will draw a great amount of attention as well..."

9

"I DON'T KNOW what's going on, Izzy," Charlie said, sitting in a chair opposite the desk of Isobel Perez. "Up until a short while ago I hadn't had a drink craving in a long while. Now it seems to be in my every waking thought. It's...well, unsettling."

Charlie had decided to pay an afternoon visit to Isobel, who'd served as her counselor while she had been in the Cumberland Heights treatment program, admitted for detoxification.

"Of course it's unsettling. Drink cravings are supposed to be," said Isobel. Then, as if some intuitive senses were going to work she said, "Charlie, is there anything else that's maybe causing you some stress these days? Anything disturbing you?"

"No, not really."

It was only a half lie, Charlie told herself. To say that her relationship with Rick was stressing her out wasn't quite the way she would put it. Despite its limits, she loved him, and he made her happy.

As always, Isobel didn't seem to be lecturing Charlie, but was rather very warm and nurturing as she continued. "Sometimes we hold things in and don't even want to recognize them. We want to assure ourselves we're fine, that we can handle it. It seems better than to admit that we can't because nobody wants to be weak. But to *not* admit it means we're in denial, much the same as when we were telling ourselves that we could handle alcohol."

"Well, you know, everybody has hassles, little things that drive them crazy, and I'm no exception." Charlie was just a tad uneasy now, so she decided to make conversation. "In all honesty, I could sure use a little more money in my bank account, my monthly periods could be a little less severe, and, while we're at it, I guess I could sure use a steady boyfriend in my life."

Isobel laughed. "I just encourage you to remain honest with yourself, about what's troubling you, or about anything. I'm not saying you're a *dis*honest person, Charlie. But sometimes we just don't directly address our problems. It's a little easier, we think, to just look the other way rather than deal with them straight on. Is this making any sense?"

"I suppose," said Charlie.

"Honesty's the cornerstone. We can't get anywhere until we've gotten honest first. With *ourselves*. The first step of the program talks about being powerless. If we live in denial about that, we get resentful toward others, we become self-pitying, or we're fearful of things. In other words, we're just a mess!"

Charlie smiled, trying to take all of this in. Truth to tell, she now felt herself wanting to wrap this up. She wasn't comfortable disclosing the affair with Rick to Isobel. After all, it didn't really seem right to talk about it to another person. It involved a man who deserved his privacy, just like anyone else. "I'll keep taking the old inventory. Just like you told me a long time ago," she said.

"Good. We all have to keep taking responsibility over our own lives," Isobel continued. "No one else is responsible for our happiness. Only we, trusting in our Higher Power, can put our own lives together."

Charlie assured herself that she had no problem with such a concept. For certain she was taking charge over her own life and looking to no one but herself for her survival. And yeah, the "God" thing was part of it too, no doubt.

"And always remember this," Isobel concluded. "Talking to someone else is important. I can't say it enough."

Yes, Peggy had said the same thing earlier. But such rules were more easily talked about than carried out sometimes. "I guess I'd better let you get back to work," Charlie said, gathering her things. "I've kept you too long already."

"No, it's Friday, and the work week is winding down."

"Thanks for talking to me, Izzy."

"Glad for the chance to be of help, that is, if I have," Isobel said getting up.

"Your *friendship* is a big help," said Charlie, giving Isobel a big hug.

"Don't hesitate to call me at home if you need to," Isobel instructed.

"Don't be surprised if I do that," Charlie said.

"Stay sober, Charlie. But also stay happy."

Charlie saw herself out of the office in the treatment center complex and then to her car.

Isobel, experienced counselor that she was, didn't buy into all that her young friend had said. She knew there that was something going on that Charlie couldn't quite open up about just yet.

"With all due respect, gentleman, I introduced Harmon to this label." Rick Richmond was trying hard to contain his anger while addressing the board of directors of Pioneer Records in a special Friday afternoon meeting. Losing his temper would only work against him, though he quietly wanted to swear and spit in the faces of those six bastards seated around the table of the Pioneer conference room.

"We're aware, Rick, that you signed Harmon to the original contract," said Hugh Latimer, board chairman. "And we know you pursued Harmon as an artist for Pioneer. And, as you'll recall, we never made an issue of it the first time around, although certain ones of us thought we should. But you seemed so insistent and so dedicated to the project, we just somehow made the concession, whether against our better judgment or not."

"I was *very* insistent and *very* dedicated," said Rick with the most pleasant air he could muster. "I saw from the beginning what a rare artist Harmon was. Now the *nation* is starting to see it. It just seems to me, Hugh…uh, gentlemen…that it's in everyone's best interest that I remain in the position I was in with this artist from the first album. I feel I've proven myself with the quality of the product. And, if I may be so bold, gentlemen, it seems only *fair*."

"Rick," said Rupert Hodgins, vice chairman, "you know of the conflict of interests it's always been thought to be, a salaried executive taking the title and the monetary cut of 'producer' on a project. Not to mention the fact that the president of a label should be equally dedicated to every project coming forth from the label."

"I feel that I've always been exactly that," Rick said.

"And the first Chad Harmon album," continued Hodgins with affability, "is always going to be yours. Nothing can change that. And few men in your position can boast of such a thing."

Well, let me just jump up and down and shout "hooray," you goddamned patronizing prick! Rick wondered if his true feelings were showing to these fucking ignorant assholes.

"Rick," said Latimer, "your contract negotiations are coming around next year. Believe me, the board will be seeing you in a very positive light because of all you've done for the label. You'll actually be in a very good position."

There was almost a hint of discomfort evidenced on the faces of the other board members with Latimer now speaking so boldly in Richmond's behalf regarding contract renegotiations in front of everyone.

Rick, trying yet to contain himself, responded, "I have to say that I feel it would be only right for me to retain production over the second album, and, yes, any in the future. I've helped make this artist what he is. Gentlemen, are any of you aware that many of those musical nuances I developed on that first album are now used in Harmon's concerts? Everyone on the Row knows that any recording I've ever produced has always been nothing less than first rate.

"But this one with this very special, enormously talented artist was my crowning achievement, or so everyone tells me. I have a big part of my life invested in Chad Harmon. I do empathize with your position, gentlemen, and it is a point well taken."

Yes, time for a little humility, Rick thought.

"And I understand it has always been your feeling that a salaried executive taking a share in the profits of an artist's recording could be seen as a bit conflictive. But the circumstances here are very unique. A producer is what I've always been first and foremost, and I think it has been the main strength I've brought to my position as CEO of this label. And, if you'll pardon my saying so, I have signed to your label what could well be the talent of the millennium. I simply implore you all to allow me to remain at the helm of this project, one which I have been responsible for from the beginning."

Humility? Shit, this was *groveling*, a pose he'd never assumed. He wondered if the board members knew that. He also wondered if they had been affected enough by his oration.

But Rick was to soon learn that the board members had come into the meeting prepared to be unbending on this matter.

Jock was working late, doing some catch-up. Darkness was settling in over downtown. Most of the many BB&S employees were on their way home by now.

As he filed away the last of some papers, the latest rewrite on the estate of a wealthy old bitch that had staged a near-death drama at least twice to keep her relatives alert and in line, the phone in his office rang. With his secretary gone for the day, he hurried back in from the file room to answer.

"Jock Pritchard," he answered.

"Hi, Jock," the voice on the other end spoke.

"Charlie?"

"Yes," said Charlie.

"Good to hear from you," said Jock delightedly. "I'm looking forward to tomorrow night."

"Jock, have you heard any local news reports this evening?" asked Charlie.

"The news?"

"I got home a short time ago and turned on the six o'clock news on Channel 4." She paused a moment.

"Yeah?"

"I think, from what I've gathered, that you and Abe Feinstein are close," said Charlie.

"Sure," said Jock, becoming concerned. "Why?"

"Jock, it seems his daughter has been reported missing."

"Jesus! You're kidding!" Jock exclaimed. "And this is on the news?"

"Yeah. I hope it's all right to be calling you at work. I hate to be the herald of bad news. I just thought you'd want to know."

"Of course it's all right, and, yes, I do," said Jock, still shocked at the news. "Well, what exactly are they saying?"

"Actually the details are a little sketchy, at least in the news report. Something about her husband reporting her missing today. I guess maybe you know her name's Beth Segal. And then there was the mention of her father, Abraham Feinstein, a retired Vanderbilt professor."

Jock knew the story of Beth's husband, Gary Segal and his departure from his own law firm, BB&S, all too well. It had made quite a scandal, though he'd never spoken of it with Abe.

"There's a little more to it, Jock," she said.

"Go on."

"The news reports are focusing on a sort of bizarre twist to all this."

"What twist?" Jock was becoming more anxious.

"It seems, according to the reports, she's been missing for over a week," Charlie said. "But her husband only reported her missing today."

Father Kris turned the television off and looked up the number in his phone directory for Abraham Feinstein. The disturbing report on the evening news had caused him to suddenly remember Abe having left him a message the previous morning. He had been too preoccupied with the situation regarding Hunter to remember till now.

He located Abe's number and went to his kitchen phone. He wondered if he'd be able to get through to the Feinsteins at all. They could be speaking with the police, relatives, friends, and any number of others.

Yes, as he suspected, the line was busy. He hung up the phone.

"Dear Lord," he muttered under his breath.

Kris felt guilty now that he hadn't even returned Abe's call. He had always tried to be there for others. So why was he suddenly finding it so hard to reach out and help people now?

All he knew to do was to pray. But when your mind is reeling, the world is going into the ash can, and you can only feel pain and confusion, it could be the challenge of a lifetime to mutter petitions to God, he thought.

However, given the circumstances, it was all he knew to do or at least try to do.

Tommy and Chad took their first-class seats aboard Delta Airlines Flight 404. Some people in the airport terminal had noticed Chad and pointed him out. Two young girls had come up and asked for his autograph.

Something Chad knew he'd easily get used to was flying first class. The extra space around him was a welcome luxury. And who could argue with free cocktails?

Tommy was proud to have gotten word that afternoon that a *Saturday Night Live* gig for Chad was confirmed for December. And an appearance on NBC's *Today Show,* as part of their Friday concert series, was in the talking stages for next year. These had come through the connections of the Pioneer label, rather than through the William Morris Agency, which handled most of the concert bookings.

An attractive young flight attendant approached their row, as Chad and Tommy buckled in.

"Can I get you gentlemen anything?" she asked.

"Light beer please," replied Chad smiling.

"Guess I'll have the same," added Tommy.

"Of course," she said and went to fetch them.

Chad wondered whether Tommy had noticed that the flight attendant appeared quite concerned for their needs as soon as she'd recognized one of them to be Chad Harmon.

The attendant returned with the beers. "Are you gentlemen destined for New Orleans or going on elsewhere?" she asked.

"New Orleans," Tommy said. "Big concert hap'nin' there."

"Really?" she said. "Who are you going to see?"

Tommy smiled. “Well, I’m gonna get to see this guy right here,” he said, indicating Chad. “And, if he’s lucky, he’s gonna see a really big audience.”

“Oh, so you’re in the music business,” she said warmly. “You know, I just was transferred here to Nashville after being based in Cincinnati. But I seem to be spending more time in the air than here in town these days. I keep forgetting that the music business is really a big thing here.”

“You betcha,” said Tommy, unable to resist a subtle nudge of the elbow to his young client.

“Well, good luck. I hope it goes well,” she said to them both. Then to Chad she said, “Who knows, you might just be the next Randy Travis. Maybe we’ll even be seeing you on television one of these days.”

“You just never can tell,” chimed Tommy, loving every minute of this.

“Are you sure there’s nothing else I can do for you?” asked the pleasant attendant.

“Not a thing,” said Chad, with his face toward the window and quite ready for the flight attendant to move on now.

Abe hung up the phone after taking the call from Kris Hartley. He decided that he should now take the receiver off the hook and did so. He and Liz had said everything that needed to be said to the police regarding the investigation of Beth’s disappearance. They needed peace and quiet now, despite the best intentions of friends to call and express their concern.

Abe had tried to reach Kris yesterday just to talk, not having seen him for a couple of days. He’d so needed to talk about this with someone, and he’d always deeply respected the young priest who never failed to help anyone in need. His return call just now had been no exception.

“Abe,” said a very sad and frightened Liz as Abe walked back into the living room, “have you thought...have you been able to think...what it would be like to never have our Bethy again…for her to be gone for good?”

“Don’t let’s do this, Liz,” he said. “Please.”

"What if we just never know? What if she's just never seen or heard from again, and...never found."

This last had been said with a bit of a sob, though Liz was trying to stifle her emotions. Abe came to Liz, sat beside her on the couch, and took both her hands.

"All we can do right now is try to keep faith, Liz. It's all we've got."

After a moment, she nodded. There was a pause, then...

"Abe," she managed to say. "What about Gary?"

He didn't respond.

"How does he figure in? Abe, he knows something," she said. "Why else would he have waited all that time?"

"I don't know," said Abe, surely wondering all the same things his wife was voicing, yet not daring to mention them.

At that moment Gary Segal was at the police station downtown answering question after question. He'd been there most of the day since early afternoon when he had first reported his wife missing.

10

THE CHOIR OF ST. JOHN'S CHURCH sang the quiet hymn "Jerusalem, My Happy Home" as an introit to the service. Six young men, all Bel Monte Academy peers of Hunter Jamison, were serving as pallbearers, Father Kris and Ben processing behind the casket. The family took their place in the two front pews. Bill and Mary Jamison looked devastated, yet they were holding together somehow. The sanctuary was filled with supportive parishioners as well as young students and teachers from BMA.

Kris noticed that Agnes Warfield, who'd taught Hunter in elementary school, was seated near the front of the church, as were Wallace and Martha Lynn. The Pritchards, George and Snooks, whose son Jock attended Harding Road group, sat a few rows back. Kris remembered that George, in addition to being a fellow parishioner, was the Jamison's attorney. Even Sarah Greeling, the wealthy widow and now head of Greeling International, was here. Sarah, always so generous, had once chaired a capital campaign for the expansion of the church, and Bill Jamison had been an active part of the same campaign.

After the hymn finished, Father Kris came forward, prayer book in hand. Standing alongside the casket he read:

"I am the resurrection and the life, saith the Lord; he that believeth in me, though he were dead, yet shall he live; and whosoever liveth and believeth in me shall never die..."

Following the scripture readings Kris ascended the pulpit. Bowing his head, he repeated aloud the scriptural pre-sermon prayer:

"Let the words of my mouth and the meditations of our hearts be always acceptable in Thy sight, O Lord, our strength and our redeemer."

"Amen," said the people, who then were seated.

The church became still. After a moment Kris spoke.

"Speaking straight from the heart, I believe, makes more sense than preplanned words, especially when we're angry, hurting, confused. And I think that a lot of us have been all those things the last couple of days, at least to some degree. What we've all felt has been that Hunter shouldn't be gone from us. He should still be with us. He should still be attending school at BMA and church here at St. John's. He should still be going about all his activities. This just isn't right. It doesn't make sense. And we are, all of us perhaps, angry."

No doubt, he now had the attention of the congregation.

"But our feelings are no more than that. Just feelings. And we have to reflect on a scripture that says that 'we see through a glass, darkly' and that we only understand things 'in part.' Sometimes we tend to get a little arrogant and think our own wisdom is the most comprehensive that there could be. When it truly never is. It is only 'in part,' as the Apostle Paul put it.

"A little over a year ago I came to know Hunter Jamison. He became my friend. Hunter had faced some really rough times and had had issues, but he wanted to work through all of them." There was a brief need to stop and maintain control, in order to restrain his emotions. This was not the time for melodramatics. "We've all received a lot of God's grace, whoever we are, and there's a scripture that instructs, 'Freely ye have received; freely give.' It's pretty easy to forget that. But when we are giving, we are automatically *receiving*. Every time. When we're giving of ourselves in the most costly way, it's then that we're usually the happiest. It seems we all have to keep relearning that. But Hunter, I think, knew it far better than most of us. I know some things about Hunter that very few other people know. I feel it's fitting that I should share them.

"Hunter rode along with me a couple of times in my visits to the state correctional facility, a maximum-security prison, where I go once a month. He'd asked to do so. Hunter had a problem with all the luxury with which he had been blessed. He was actually a little uncomfortable with what he called his 'cushy lifestyle.' He didn't understand why *he* had always had it so good while others were born into environments where a life of crime was simply all they knew. Yes, Hunter loved being analytical. He was into 'cause and effect.' He actually said to me that there was just no basic difference between himself and some of those who were incarcerated. And he said he liked to go along to keep himself reminded. I have to tell you that blew me away."

Kris went on to share a couple of stories such as that of Hunter being the only male youth in the church to work with children last summer in the church's vacation church school program.

Finally, in summing up he said, "When I was first asked to get to know Hunter and to maybe help him with all the confusion in his life, it appeared to me that Hunter was a troubled young man. I remember praying for God to show me how to deal with him, how to reach out to him." Kris took the longest pause yet, still making the effort to keep the emotions in check. "And what do you think happened? Hunter helped *me*. He unknowingly reached out to *me*. Hunter changed *me*, and you know what? I'll never be the same again.

"So what do those feelings mean that I spoke of earlier, the feelings that none of this makes sense, that it just isn't right, that Hunter should be here? Perhaps that's my egotism, which I've certainly exercised before, going to work yet again. I *want* Hunter to be here! He affected me, and I want to keep on being affected. It was a wonderful thing."

He paused once more.

"But Hunter, I really believe, is resting now. This young man who found it very hard just to keep his mind at peace for an entire day is now at *total* peace. This young man who it seems seldom sought to take but rather to give...I like to think of him as having earned his wings...So, Hunter…fly."

There were one or two muffled sobs in the congregation. Kris was almost sure he even saw a tear glistening in rigid old Agnes's eye.

"Ben, our rector said something the other day. Pardon me, Ben, if I don't quote you totally verbatim. 'We're all a part of something greater than ourselves.' We're equally loved by God. I believe that. With everything in me, I believe that. There are no limits I could ever put on His grace, even if I wished to do so…That's a thought to take with us as we go from here today."

He crossed himself as did the congregation. "In the name of the Father, and of the Son, and of the Holy Ghost."

"Amen," responded the people.

Ben then led the people in the Lord's Prayer.

Following the prayer the choir stood and rendered a short and lovely anthem. At times questions had arisen at St. John's Church regarding the great amount of money spent annually on the parish music program, what with so many paid professional singers. But musical moments such as these, which in reality were pretty much regular occurrences here, led most parishioners to contend, "God is deserving of the finest."

At this moment, it was Kris's sentiment that Hunter was as well.

"In sure and certain hope of the resurrection to eternal life through our Lord Jesus Christ, we commend to Almighty God our brother Hunter; and we commit his body to the ground."

Kris now officiated at the Committal, the interment ritual at the Bellevue cemetery. Bright sunshine and slightly warming temperatures were lending a helping hand to this sad occasion. He tossed a handful of soil onto the casket as he continued. "Earth to earth, ashes to ashes, dust to dust. The Lord bless him and keep him, the Lord make his face to shine upon him and be gracious unto him, the Lord lift up his countenance upon him and give him peace."

"Amen," said the people.

Kris then offered the dismissal: “Let us go forth into the world, rejoicing in the power of the Spirit!”

“Thanks be to God!” responded all the people, concluding the ritual.

Next it was time to check in on Mary and Bill Jamison, Kris decided. As he walked toward them, Kris noticed that Mary was wiping away tears. Her tears had seemed few throughout the three-day ordeal, her pain having taken on the state of quiet numbness.

“My love and my prayers are with you, Mary,” said Kris, extending his hand to her where she sat in the row of folding chairs assembled for the family.

After a moment Mary looked up at Kris blankly and took his hand. “I think it all went rather well,” was all she said.

“I’m here if you need me,” he said.

She didn’t say another word but managed a wan smile.

Kris shook hands with Bill and his son Andrew, offering small greetings and what words of assurance he could, as did Ben who’d stood by merely as another mourner until now. After bidding their farewells and assurances of support to the Jamisons and speaking to several others of the parish, Ben and Kris walked on across the green lawn of the cemetery together toward their cars.

“Kris, you know that I don’t offer compliments unless I mean them,” said Ben. “But your message in the service was a great one. I, for one, needed to hear what I heard today.”

“Thank you, Ben,” Kris said.

“I’m sure that this is still tough for you,” Ben continued. “And it is for me too, but you were obviously closer to Hunter than I was. I’ve been where you are more times than I care to remember, and unfortunately, this probably won’t be the last time you’ll be in a situation of this sort. It hurts and you feel like maybe you’ve failed.”

Exactly, Kris thought.

“Just hang in there, Kris,” was all Ben said. He then embraced Kris, and the two men walked on to their cars.

It occurred to Kris that he wasn’t sure where he was going next. The thought of remaining alone in his apartment the rest of the day and evening seemed unbearable. But just then he had an idea. However, he would have to go home, change, and put in a phone call.

11

JOCK SIPPED A SODA and Charlie a Virgin Mary while waiting for their appetizers to arrive. Enrique was their server this evening, at Jock's request, thus assuring impeccable service, and perfectly paced, in Jock's opinion.

There was no one that Jock knew intimately tonight in the main dining room of the Bel Terre Country Club. However, there were one or two club members with whom he was barely on a first name basis. He couldn't resist mentioning one or two of them to Charlie, though in a whisper.

"Seated to my left and back toward the corner – please do not look abruptly – would be Wesley and Shirley Kendall. Their maid tried to kill Shirley by running her down with the family Mercedes in the driveway of their place up in Monteagle a few years back. Nobody seems to know the motive, or at least they're not telling."

Charlie didn't dare try sneaking a glimpse, although she was tempted.

"In the opposite corner and to my right is Eva Buckley with her husband, Gill Buckley, who's nearing eighty. Gill is Eva's fourth husband. Each of Eva's three previous hubbies died leaving her a little less fixed than she'd envisioned – estate lawyers hear about these things – so she's had to keep repeating the process.

"A few tables away behind you – you can look when you go to powder your nose – sits Bernard Chatworth, a multi-millionaire who's done time for tax evasion, an incident that received national attention due to the enormity of the debt. After the time served, Bernard returned happily to managing his very thriving real estate development firm. He and Meredith, his wife of nearly forty years, despite rumors of Bernard's numerous extramarital interests, are regulars here."

Charlie had taken this all in with contained astonishment.

"So now at last you're dining with the cream of society, Miss Cohen," Jock said with spurious grace and charm. "How do you feel?"

"Quite ordinary, from all you've said," she answered. "Boring, actually."

She was anything but boring, Jock thought. Charlie, dressed in a low-cut black chiffon dress with matching shawl, looked more beautiful than ever. Her dark hair was being worn up tonight, thus revealing the perfectly contoured neck and shoulders. Pearl earrings adorned her dainty ear lobes. It was a side of her that Jock had never seen until tonight, though he was pretty damned certain Charlie would look hot in army fatigues.

It was a matter of time before their conversation turned to the music world.

"Well, I guess what impresses me most about the music business here in Nashville is that it somehow maintains a small town feel," said Charlie. "I've never lived in New York or L.A., but the things I've heard from those who've been in the business on either coast and then come here lead me to believe that there just is no comparison."

"How so?" Jock asked.

"New York and L.A. are, I think, all the things you've ever heard and worse. The competitiveness, the ruthlessness."

"You really see things as being that different in Nashville?" he asked, though not wanting to seem argumentative in the face of her positive attitude.

"Oh, definitely," she answered. "There's sort of a family spirit to Music Row. People help each other out. I don't know if you can attribute that to southern hospitality or what exactly. But a lot of people in the business really are nice, or so it's always seemed to me."

Privately dismissing her naiveté for now, Jock said, "You mentioned earlier that you were from Cincinnati," he said. "Was it music that brought you here?"

"Not really. I 'backed in' to the business, as they say, although music had always been a part of my life. It just sort of happened. And recently, believe it or not, I've been trying my hand at songwriting."

"Songwriting? That's great. But tell me now, how exactly did you 'back in' to all this?" he inquired.

"My father, who still *walks* to temple on the Sabbath, wears the prayer shawl, the whole nine yards, well, he had a good friend from childhood who moved to Nashville a good many years ago to be director over the Akiva School."

"I've known about Akiva. Dinah Shore went there, right?"

"Yes. Well anyway, I was considering going to law school in those days, and Jacob Rappeport, who's my dad's friend I was talking about, suggested Vanderbilt. My father encouraged me to move here and look into it. I guess he also felt that Jacob could keep an eye on me. However, dear old Jacob, though he was a sweetheart who would have done anything for my dad or me, passed away from a stroke the year after I came. I lost interest in law school because by then the music bug had bitten me, I landed the job at Pioneer, I started writing a little, and well, now my poor dad is still wondering what in the world is to become of me. So there you have it."

Jock smiled. Interesting, he thought, how Charlie had pursued a law career, then ended up in the music business...Well, sort of. *He* had gone into law for real, yet he longed to be a part of the music scene.

"So what about your mother?" he asked.

"She died when I was two. My Aunt Rose came to live with us and helped raise me."

"I see," Jock said.

He was opting to let Charlie do most of the talking. After all, chicks liked to know that someone listened to them. But just then Enrique arrived with their grilled Portabella mushrooms.

“Ah, here we are,” said Jock as the appetizers were set in place.

“This looks wonderful,” said Charlie.

“Enjoy,” said the waiter. “Is there anything else for now, Mr. Pritchard?”

“Thanks, Enrique,” said Jock. “I think we’re fine.”

Charlie smiled. She concluded that she couldn’t find any fault with this country club way of doing things. She could get used to it quite easily.

A couple of miles away, at Dalts Grill, Father Kris Hartley was dining with Isobel Perez, who’d been his “stand-by date” for a couple of years now. Isobel saw other people, and Kris was free to do the same, yet the two were close and had long felt comfortable about calling each other up on a moment's notice to do dinner and a movie or whatever.

Isobel was cute, vivacious, and smart. The common ground she and Kris shared and which had brought them together was the Twelve Step program, both having been in recovery for a number of years. Kris had always been in awe of the work she did as a counselor at Cumberland Heights. She was also a parishioner of St. John’s Church. It was there that she and Kris had become acquainted. The two frequently shared experiences that they had had counseling others, comparing notes, so to speak, though always being discreet enough to speak of individuals anonymously. But tonight there was certainly no mystery regarding the identity of the person they were discussing. Hunter Jamison was still all that Kris could talk or even think about.

“I’ve never seen anything get to you like this before,” said Isobel, looking sympathetically at Kris.

They had finished dinner and were having coffee.

“I felt responsible for him,” Kris said sadly. “He looked to me for guidance. Izzy, I loved that kid. I never had a little brother, and I don’t know if I’ll ever have a son. But I think it was something sort of akin to that.”

“So Hunter had been on medication?” she asked.

“Yeah. But I swear what seemed to do him the most good was just getting on with life. Being proactive, you know. It was as if he got more on an even keel as he got involved in the things any normal kids do."

"Chemical imbalances are strange things," she said, reflecting. "They can be unpredictable."

"I should have seen this coming, Izzy. I've had enough training in counseling and heard enough stories about these kinds of things. Hunter was a special case. Being his sponsor, I should have known to stay on top of it."

There was a pause in their conversation.

"Funny. I sort of expected this to happen," Isobel said.

"*Expected it to happen*?" Kris said.

"I'm talking about you now, Kris. The feelings you're having. Guilt." Isobel drew a breath. "I'm afraid of making you angry, Kris, but you do have a bit of a tendency to want to *fix* people, though sometimes it's clear that you just can't. Hunter's gone now. Here's the ultimate case of 'just can't.' So you decide it's time to blame yourself."

"How can I not?" Kris's tone was almost defensive. "Hunter's well-being was entrusted to me."

"He was entrusted to you to do whatever you were capable of doing to help him. Which you did. But you're not God, Kris." She smiled, putting a hand on his where it rested on the table. "Always wanting to take on the burdens of others around you, or maybe the problems of the whole world, is not necessarily a healthy way to live."

He just looked at her a moment, saying nothing. Priests were supposed to take on people's problems, share their burdens, feel their pain. "Izzy, people do need to be there for each other in this world."

"Yes, people do. A good person makes himself available, as you have done. But, Kris, there's a difference between *caring* and – I hope you'll forgive me for this – trying to *control.*"

Kris wasn't quite sure whether to feel indignant. "You see me as a control freak?" he asked.

She smiled. "I see you as a very kind and caring man. But one who just occasionally forgets that he does have his limitations and that his *best* is all that he can do. The program has something to say about being 'powerless.' Let's see, the first step is it?"

He sulked a bit.

She continued. "But then beyond even our very *best* efforts, thankfully, there is still he Higher Power, and there always was, though we might have lost sight of that fact. And that has to be where we keep looking, right?"

Kris could find no other words to offer back just now. All he could do was look away.

Jock and Charlie were now enjoying southern pecan pie.

"Jock," she said, "what about the son-in-law? I mean, does anyone have any thoughts on why he waited so long to report her missing?"

"I'd imagine a lot of people are having a *lot* of thoughts right now about the whole thing, including thoughts about Gary Segal."

"Did you ever know him?"

"No. He was in another department of the firm."

"He's at Burch, Baxter, and Schultz?" Charlie asked, slightly startled.

"*Was*," Jock replied. "Got canned some time back for repeated sexual harassment. The firm was going to get sued big-time, so it made a hell of a lot more sense to fire him."

"This thing gets creepier as it goes along," Charlie said.

"And who knows where it's going to end?" Jock said. "Everybody's imagining the worst right now. Here's this beautiful young woman married to a weirdo that doesn't even bother to report her missing until a week after the fact. He hasn't communicated with any friends or relatives about it in the meantime either."

"Are *you* imagining the worst, Jock?" Charlie asked.

"Looking at things objectively..." he began, "for all I know, Segal's just a creep and a chauvinistic son of a bitch. However, I certainly haven't been a witness to any sort of foul play on his part, much the same as I wasn't there to witness O.J. doing anything to Nicole Brown and Ron Goldman on that summer night back in '94."

"God, what a comparison," said Charlie, a bit spooked.

"Yeah," said Jock, somewhat awed himself as he realized what he'd just said.

As they pulled up to the front of Isobel's condo in Bellevue, both she and Kris were aware that they'd been silent through most of the drive to her place. It hadn't been intended. Perhaps it was just a vigil in Hunter's memory.

Kris was actually very grateful that Isobel had helped him sort through some things this evening. He was trying his best to let go of the burden. But now he was aware that he needed to be in someone's presence tonight, someone who cared about him. He needed to feel loved. He and Isobel had never slept together in their two years of occasional dating. It had just seemed too complicated, given the absence of a formal commitment.

Kris, though not a virgin and not bound by a vow of celibacy like Catholic priests, took his position with the church seriously. When not feeling totally certain of a relationship and its future, a lot was at risk in exploring the intimate side. There was always the danger of someone being hurt, and possibly a scandal ensuing. It was not a puritanical stand but rather one of decency and common sense.

However, Kris wondered about tonight. Perhaps tonight was a case of things just being different. He felt he needed to be held. He was made of flesh and blood the same as the next man. He couldn't deny what he felt. But what about Isobel? How she felt must factor into the equation too. Just as he was wondering this, and as they pulled into the parking space in front of her condo, she spoke.

"Kris, why don't you come in for a while?"

"I'd like that," he said.

They got out of the car and were soon inside. As Kris made himself comfortable on the living room couch, Isobel busied herself in the kitchen. Knowing Kris's fondness for it, she decided to make cappuccinos. Several minutes later she rejoined him in the living room with a cup for Kris and one for herself.

"I heard you in there," said Kris with a smile. "So you broke down and bought a cappuccino machine."

"Last week. You kept saying I should," she said, taking a seat beside him on the couch.

He gazed at her. She was lovely. There'd always been something wonderful about Isobel. He had taken it for granted. He had been so consumed with his ministry that he'd neglected the other areas of his life that made him a human being.

"Izzy," he said, looking into her eyes, "you're quite a girl. All too often I haven't paid enough attention to that fact." It wasn't quite time, he felt, to stroke her hair and touch her cheek. Let her offer a word or an act of encouragement first.

She returned his smile a moment, then set her cup down on the coffee table.

"Kris," she said, "there's something I'd like to share with you. You've been special to me, and I've never had any greater friend."

Yes, he thought to himself, all too often relationships had to do with the physical side exclusively, and lovers never really learned to be friends.

Isobel seemed to be seeking the right words when she finally said, "Kris, I'll always cherish our friendship. Always."

"As will I."

She waited a moment, then, as gently as she knew how, she said, "Kris, I've met someone."

"I don't know, I guess it's like I've always just played it safe," said Jock after turning out of the side parking lot of the country club onto Harden Place, and then onto the Boulevard.

He and Charlie were en route to his house, which Charlie had agreed she'd like to see.

"This is going to sound like a cop-out, or maybe just like a spoiled brat," he continued, "but when you have an advantaged life that others would give everything to have, it's pretty hard to just dispense with it and go in a direction where there aren't any open doors. Hell, I sometimes think that those who don't have a lot to lose find it easier to go for broke and pursue an over-sized dream."

"But if it's what you really want..." she said.

"It's not that simple. I can't explain it really. You think I'm a spoiled brat?"

"No," she said. "But I'm not sure I agree that it's that much easier for those of us who don't have as much to lose materially.

Everybody pays a price. All people have their share of fears – fears of failing. There are times I wonder if I'm going to wake up one day an old woman who has nothing but her memories of all the things she aspired to and didn't achieve."

Jock thought about this. Okay, maybe there was something to what she said.

"Tell me," Charlie continued, "what do you do, play, write?"

"I've played guitar and keyboard since childhood," said Jock. "And I write too. Some people have actually told me they thought some of the stuff I'd written had real promise, but, aw hell, who knows?"

"Ever thought of co-writing with someone else? That's really the thing in Nashville, and I think there's a lot to be said for it. What makes a tune or a lyric work sometimes can be better determined by a team effort."

Jock knew of the common practice, but he'd never considered writing with another person. His writing was what it was. If anybody didn't like it, fine. Screw 'em. But he didn't need anyone to tell him how to "fix" a song of his creation. However, he elected not to voice this feeling to Charlie just now.

He pulled into his driveway. The house, which was illuminated by specially designed landscape lighting, was somewhat modest by the standards of the many huge homes on the Boulevard, yet a fine home just the same.

"This is lovely, Jock," said Charlie.

"Thanks," he said.

He pulled into a front parking space rather than driving around to the garage at the rear. He got out of the car and walked around to open Charlie's door.

"I'll give you the tour," he said, escorting her to the front door.

"Please do," she replied.

"My mom and her interior designer did the inside. I told them I wanted an eclectic decor, tasteful yet with an attitude, and not too frilly. Damned if they didn't do exactly what I'd asked."

Once inside he gave her the quick tour of the living room that boasted a large fireplace, fine furniture, and a Persian rug. Next came the dining room with an antique table formerly owned by his grandmother and a breakfront ordered from somewhere or other and filled with china his mother had insisted on supplying. He then showed Charlie the kitchen, guest room, and another room intended as a bedroom but currently used as his home office and den.

Finally he presented his master suite, complete with king-size bed, bear rugs on the floor, and provocative artwork on the walls. Jock felt sure that anyone could feel at home sharing this boudoir. But he sure as hell wouldn't press that issue. He tried to keep the member between his legs from pressing it as well.

"Coffee?" he asked Charlie.

"That would be nice," she said.

They returned to the kitchen where he put on a pot of decaf. Fifteen minutes later they were seated on the living room couch sipping away. They made casual conversation, though Jock was not focused. He could not get out of his mind the prospect of, as the English say, "shagging" her, right then and there.

Charlie sensed the tension in Jock. Try as he may, he wasn't too good at hiding his feelings, at least not those sorts of feelings. It grew as they kept on talking. It gave rise to an equally uneasy feeling for her. Theirs was now becoming a conversation about one thing while their minds and emotions were going in totally adverse directions. What he wanted was not going to happen, she had determined. It couldn't, not tonight. And that was that. Finally, she decided to just go ahead and address the issue head on. Honesty is the cornerstone, Isobel had kept emphasizing to her.

"I feel it's only fair to clear the air of something, Jock," she said flatly.

"Clear the air?" he said.

"I...I just can't sleep with you tonight."

Jock was to later remember that his mouth had probably hung open for a brief time as he stared wide-eyed at her. Then, after a moment, he erupted with laughter. Charlie was onto him, and it suddenly cracked him up. Several seconds passed, and he then fell back on the love seat still cackling.

For a moment it was her turn to stare at him. Who did the jerk think he was to laugh at her at such a moment? Nevertheless, at last a smile crossed her face. Then she found herself snickering. She didn't really understand why, but his laughter was somehow infectious.

No doubt Charlie had now quelled any hopes Jock had held of getting lucky tonight, and the whole thing was simply funny as hell. He managed to utter a question: "So does this mean..." he had to get the words out between the fits of laughter "...not even a good blow job?"

For this impertinence Charlie backhanded him across the upper arm. But almost instantly she was laughing with him again.

This went on for several minutes.

Kris lay in the dark stroking Franklin's fur, the dog's head resting on the side of the bed. A lot to be said for the old adage about "man's best friend."

A chapter in Kris's life had been closed tonight. The relationship with Isobel, at least as he'd known it, had ended. She'd been temperate and considerate in breaking the news. But their dating days were over. There was no use in wondering if it was his fault for not exploring the relationship further, or whether he'd just been too consumed with his own life.

We're all a part of something greater than ourselves.

Father Kris had to cling to a belief that he had his own purpose in life. He'd continue to seek it out. He was feeling maybe a little lonely just now, but not unbearably so. He'd be fine. He was somehow able, even at this very difficult time, to feel grateful for everything in his life. And it dawned upon him that he hadn't felt that way at all in several days.

12

THE FAMILIAR OPENING STRAINS of "In the Rain" sent the sell-out crowd into exultation before any lyrics were even sung. The first hit recording from the rising star was the closing number of the concert, and these days it was like an old friend with fans. There was a sellout crowd at the New Orleans Fairgrounds tonight, the remaining tickets having quickly sold the day or so following the telecast of the CMA awards. Chad Harmon had per-formed to what was perhaps the most enthusiastic audience he and the band had yet experienced.

Tommy marveled at how Chad's stage persona and his ability to hold an audience seemed to grow into something more and more commanding. He thought about the small handful of true legends that had graced the entertainment world, such as Sinatra, Elvis, the Beatles, the Stones, Streisand. Tonight, as this concert drew to its close, Tommy felt certain that Chad Harmon would in time take his place among them.

Finally the song slowed to its finish as the audience once again commended Chad with a deafening ovation. Chad re-moved the guitar strap, threw up an arm to wave his farewell, and shouted, "Thank you!! Goodnight, Big Easy! *Let your heart keep singing*!!!"

The exit line had been coined on the first night of the national tour in Detroit and had now become his signature. It seemed very fitting indeed to a city still seeking to rebuild, to regain its dignity. As Chad ran off the stage the fans had already risen to their feet. Tommy greeted him backstage, unable to contain his own pride. Whether because of the recent CMA sweep, the prospect of a new album, or the excitement of yet another new hit single, there just was something special in the air tonight.

"The world's gonna be yours, man," Tommy said, taking Chad by the hand, then embracing him.

"And I owe everything to you," Chad replied.

The roar of the crowd continued, the applause now taking on a pulsating rhythm accompanied by the stamping of feet. Chad and Tommy looked at one another and both knew that at least one encore was imminent.

"Go!" was all Tommy said as he gave Chad a shove sending him off and running back onstage. The audience cheered all the more as he reappeared.

The planned encore was "Card-Carryin' Country," the fourth Chad Harmon single now climbing the charts, currently at Number Three. It had been saved for the anticipated encore. Chad, ready to oblige his fans, took up the guitar again. He felt as though he could have performed on into the wee hours of the morning.

The band members had traveled to New Orleans on the new Chad Harmon tour bus. They had come down along with the road crew who would load in the set, sound equipment, special lighting, and other effects. A sound check with the musicians always followed the set-up, and the roadies had finished just in time for Chad to appear and run a couple of numbers that afternoon.

Chad and Tommy were now riding back to the InterContinental Hotel with the band members on the new coach, the concert having finally ended. Chad and the fellows had only journeyed to a handful of bookings in the bus, though many more would surely follow.

Tommy tried not to take a prudish attitude as Toby Stout, the bass guitarist of the group, took a flask of Schnapps from the bus's refrigerator and began passing it among the band members, Chad included. When Tommy went along on a concert gig, he was strict over the guys regarding their behavior only before and during a concert. What happened on their own time was none of his business. What *was* his business was whether the fellows got their jobs done as musicians, and they always did.

"Great show, Harmon!" said Stout as he handed the bottle to Chad for a second sip.

"Couldn't do it without you fellows," Chad answered.

"Awwwwww," the guys droned in unison

"Hell, we all know you're the star, Harmon," said drummer Billy Riddle as Chad took several gulps from the bottle, "but leave a little for the peons, will you!"

This was raucously echoed by the others.

"Hey, relax," said Chad, smiling, "there's a package store at the hotel. The next round's on me." This brought cheers from the guys.

As the bus rolled on toward the hotel, Tommy silently hoped that Chad wasn't to make a habit of this sort of partying with the musicians following every concert. Of course, New Orleans had always been one of the biggest party towns in the world. Tonight had been the first concert since the huge CMA win, and maybe they deserved a celebration.

However, Tommy's self-assurance waned just a bit when Billy said, "Hey, I got something better than liquid refreshment back at the room, we're talkin' some *good shit*, man. Don't anybody sweat it."

Amidst cheers from the others, Chad smiled and said, "You can always be depended on, Billy-Boy."

The rowdy laughter continued. Tommy was torn between being the custodial father figure and just looking the other way. For the moment, and with the stress of the concert now off, he chose the latter.

Chad's head was feeling light from the alcohol and a few hits off the joint that had been passed around back at the band's hotel suite.

It was a little after midnight. Tommy had retired for the night, hoping that the guys would follow soon after.

Chad and Billy were now on their way down the hotel elevator. They'd agreed to share a cab ride to the French Quarter. Chad felt he hadn't seen enough of the Crescent City with all its history and charm. And New Orleans, which was rebuilding itself these days with great pride, didn't roll up its sidewalks just because midnight had passed.

"We'll just go to Pat O'Brien's and maybe have one drink," Chad said. "I really need at least a little sleep before flying back to Nashville with Tommy in the morning."

"Yeah, sure," answered Billy.

Chad had always embraced a fine comradeship with his band members. Being the star didn't make him their superior. They were among the finest musicians in the business, and good fellows all. And they constituted his main circle of friends these days.

"I've been to New Orleans a few times in my day," said Billy to Chad. "I've even been once since Katrina. It's still a great town for good booze, good jazz..." and with a mischievous grin he added, "and there's a little something else that's not exactly in short supply around here, as I recall."

"Uh-huh," Chad said. He knew what Billy was alluding to. Billy loved female companionship perhaps even more than good liquor and good grass.

The thriving nightlife of the Quarter could almost convince a person that the city had never experienced such devastation in recent times. Four young Harmon fans that had attended the concert that evening shared a table at Pat O'Brien's with Chad and Billy. With the establishment packed at the time the guys arrived, the teenagers were only too glad to have the star be their guest. The two young girls were particularly enamored of the handsome Chad Harmon, who was nothing less than gracious and friendly toward them all.

Chad downed a Hurricane, the tall drink that the New Orleans French Quarter had always been famous for and which now seemed all too appropriate a name ever since the natural disaster that had forever changed this city.

After bidding the young fans farewell, Chad and Billy took a left turn out the front door and walked past Preservation Hall where a Dixieland combo droned away with "Just a Closer Walk With Thee." They proceeded on up the street, Chad's objective being to hail a cab and get back to the hotel.

"What a night, huh?" Billy said boisterously.

"Yeah," Chad answered, amused at his friend.

"The blond babe was really hot for you, the one seated to your left. You know, you could have given that chickie a memory to cherish forever, the night she got a little from a big-time star, Chad Harmon! That is, if her boyfriend hadn't been in the picture."

"Let me tell you something about the 'blond babe,' Billy-boy," Chad said. "She's in high school. They call that 'jail bait' where I come from."

"But old enough to have those awakening needs, right? And, if I'm not mistaken, you're old enough too."

"Sure, Billy," Chad said dismissingly.

But there was something to what crazy Billy had said. For the better part of two years he'd been damned near celibate. His entire life had been lived for one thing, and that was his music career. He had been willing to let everything else take a backseat in favor of the dreams that drove him on. But now that he had all he'd ever dreamed of, why shouldn't he start to think of other things?

"We take a turn here," said Billy pointing right up a street.

"We do?" asked Chad.

"Trust me on this one, man."

"Sure." Chad said with a little uncertainty as they walked on.

He let Billy lead the way, having no doubt that his friend knew the city better than he. After walking several blocks they arrived at a grand looking house, three stories tall, with wrought iron on all the windows. Billy rang the bell.

"Somebody you know live here?" Chad asked.

"You might say that," Billy said with a wry smile.

Before Chad could ask any further questions the door opened, and an attractive woman, perhaps in her early fifties and dressed very smartly, stood looking pleasantly at first Billy, then Chad.

"Yes, may I help you?" she said.

"I was here on my last trip to New Orleans," Billy charmingly said to the woman. "I remember you."

"I'm sorry that I can't say the same," she said, smiling. "But do come in please."

Billy entered, Chad following a bit behind him as the woman closed the door and secured the computer-activated lock. It was beginning to dawn on Chad where they had arrived. Somehow he didn't protest, though he was suddenly struck with a major case of nerves.

"I'm Marlene," said the woman.

"Of course, Marlene," Billy quickly replied.

It was amazing to Chad how charming and polished Billy could seem even when he'd consumed as much liquor as Chad himself had.

"Why don't you make yourselves at home in the sitting room," Marlene said. "Someone will be with you very shortly." She had indicated the very lavish room to the right off the entry hall. They walked into the room, one that seemed to Chad to be as fine and stately as any front parlor across town in the Garden District must be. "The bar is there," she said, pointing toward what appeared to be an antique armoire which, with its doors opened, revealed that it had been converted into a bar and liquor cabinet. "We're on the honor system as far as drinks go. You'll find a note pad there for recording your tab."

"Very nice," replied Billy.

"Let's see," continued Marlene, "I believe Shannon and Clarice are available right now. Let me check and be sure. At any rate, there's no hurry about deciding. Make yourselves at home."

She walked out and down the hall.

"You get it, no?" Billy asked quietly with a grin.

"I get it," whispered Chad nervously. "Look, Billy, I don't know about this."

"Aw, relax, dude. New Orleans is a place where this is thought of as a business just like any other."

"Come on, Billy..."

"Like she said, there's no hurry about anything anyway. You can take your time."

"Yeah, but..."

"You're a man of means now. And you're still single, free as the wind. It's an accepted thing here, man. And if you don't have enough cash, would you believe they take Visa?" Billy laughed. "Whadaya say, huh?"

Chad, still a little tense, replied, "Okay, I got my Visa. But what I don't have with me right this minute is...you know."

"Neither do I, man. But do you think they're crazy enough to not keep such things on hand here? A first-class place like this knows how to be safe."

"Point taken. But..."

From the entry hall two young ladies, probably in their mid- to late twenties, appeared.

"Hi. I'm Shannon." A redhead.

"I'm Clarice." Blond.

They were refined and sophisticated, Chad noted. Though meeting two of these types of girls for the first time, or at least for the first time with his being a prospective client, he somehow felt more at ease than he thought he would have at such a moment. They appeared so normal, so very nice.

Especially Clarice.

"I'm originally from Dallas," she said. "I moved here a little less than a year ago. After finishing at SMU, I was offered a job with a marketing firm here in town. New Orleans was just getting back on its feet after the Katrina thing. But a little earlier this year there came some lay-offs. And, well, you know how that goes. It's the most recently employed who leave first."

"I understand," said Chad. "I'm from Texas too. Houston."

"Really?" she said.

"I moved to Nashville three years ago."

They had just moments ago retired to a private bedroom on the third floor, a room with beautiful, though not flashy, decor. There was no mirror over the bed, evidently no big-screen television for viewing porn, no whips, chains, or vibrators – at least not in plain sight.

She sat on the chaise near the bed. Chad sat at the foot of the great bed. He couldn't quite figure how he should handle himself physically, whether to cross his legs, fold his arms, or whatever. He was certain he must look like a virginal teenager on a first date.

Her loveliness still captivated him. And *baffled* him. She had such charm and yes, true class. This was not the type of girl you met in a brothel, or so he'd have thought.

"It's something I never do, but I want to tell you my real name. It's not Clarice. It's Melinda. Melinda Holstrom," she said. "I somehow feel like being who I really am, and I think I can do that with you."

"Of course, Melinda." said Chad. "Uh, well, my name really is Chad."

"Yes, I know." She paused. "I have a confession. Admittedly, I'm not a connoisseur of country music, and I wasn't at the concert tonight, but I happened to have seen the awards Wednesday night. I had been channel-surfing, and I somehow ended up on the awards show."

"I see."

"You're Chad Harmon."

He smiled. "Guilty."

"I really can't believe it. Just a few nights ago I was looking at you on national television, and I've also been seeing the ads for the concert. And I think I read this morning that it had sold out."

"Right."

"And here you are." She stopped and smiled. "I suppose I'm acting like I'm, what do they call it, star-struck? Now I feel self-conscious, and I wanted so to appear above that. More intelligent, you know."

"Oh, please," he said. "I'm feeling self-conscious like you wouldn't believe. You can't imagine the case of jitters I've got."

She was somehow touched by this. "Jitters?"

"Yeah."

"You've never...I mean..." She chose her words with care. "...well, you never have been in a place of business such as this before?"

"I'm afraid I haven't," he said, a bit relieved, the air having been cleared by getting things out in the open.

"Well, you see," said Melinda, "up until a few months ago, *I'd* never been in a place like this either. That's the truth."

"I don't find that unbelievable."

"But it pays far better than anything else I could be doing. And you wouldn't believe how un-intimidating the clientele is here, very upscale actually. They're not admitted otherwise. And then there's Marlene. She's wonderful. One of the sweetest people I've ever met. Like a mother to me. The mother I never had."

"Is your mother deceased?" asked Chad.

"No. But we're not close." She didn't seem bitter, but rather as if stating a simple fact. "I was an only child, and not a planned one at all. My mother had her career goals. I'm sure I got in the way. I absolutely adored my father. He was wonderful. He was both a father and mother to me. He had no choice. But he died when I was thirteen."

"I'm sorry," said Chad.

"I got into SMU on a scholarship, graduated with a degree in business administration, and..." She smiled. "Well, now just look at where a good education can lead a girl."

Chad was forced to laugh along with her.

"I went a couple of years to Rice, basic liberal arts, you know," Chad said, "but music seemed to be what my life was about. My mother even supported me on that one."

"I don't communicate with my mother that much," continued Melinda, "but that's fine. With her *and* with me. And, as I said, I love Marlene. She's actually a parent figure in a lot of people's lives."

After a moment Chad said, "I know what it's like to come from an unhappy home. But I've got to say, I wasn't entirely shafted in that area. My mother was the wonderful one of *my* two parents." He paused a moment. "And you know, somehow I feel pretty sure, without your even describing him, that your father was a heck of a guy."

"Indeed he was," she said. "Whether I'm prejudiced or not, I feel he was as great a man as ever lived."

"And my mother," Chad said, "was the salt of the earth, the most perfect human being I think I ever knew." He stopped a moment. "She died shortly before I moved to Nashville."

Melinda was touched. "We do have some things in common, don't we?"

They had made love, slowly and tenderly. Chad had been careful to treat her as if she were royalty, not his hireling for the night. He mused to himself that there was no reason why he shouldn't take advantage of such things as this, especially now that he had, as Billy had put it, the *means*.

Melinda currently lay in the crook of his arm, her eyes looking toward the ceiling.

"What's on your mind?" he asked.

"Nothing in particular," she replied. "Well, actually, I was thinking how...how it's never been quite like this."

"What do you mean?" he asked.

"You're different."

"Different?"

"But I don't let myself focus on it too much. I can't."

"I think I'm missing something here," said Chad.

"You are who you are." She'd said this almost sadly. "And you have your place in life. And I have *my* place in life."

"Melinda, please don't start talking about *stations* people have in society. I don't see myself as better than someone else, you or anybody."

"No, of course you don't. That's not what I meant. It's just ...well, it's just that you have a path you're meant to keep going down in this world. And you have to stay with it. It's who you are."

"Yeah...?" Chad said, still not understanding her point.

"Why does life have to be so unfair?" she asked. "And why is loving someone and finding a life you can truly share with a person so difficult? Perhaps impossible."

"Well, it might happen for you one day."

She sat up, wrapped her arms around her legs, almost seeming frustrated and continued, "That's what I want: just old-fashioned romance. And with a good and decent man."

"Like I say, maybe in time you'll find just that."

She looked at him and then turned away. "You seem optimistic in my behalf."

"Melinda, you're lovely. And you can be anything you want to be in life. You have everything in the world going for you."

"You think so?" she murmured.

"For sure," said Chad, "if that's what you make up your mind to. I should know. I've made a few dreams come true for myself."

"I feel like I'm going to always long for what I can't have, what I truly know down deep can't suit me."

"Can't suit you?"

"You don't get it, Harmon. What I want is never going to be mine, because, and I know this..." She looked directly at him. "The guy truly worth having is going to be out of my reach. And the things that put him out of my reach are what make him special. A no-win situation."

He was keenly aware that her gaze was fixed firmly on himself, and he hoped she didn't mean what he thought. An old torch song came to mind as he wondered if Melinda "had it bad and that ain't good." And for *him*, Chad Harmon. After this one brief encounter did this chick think that she was in love with him? Maybe she *was* star-struck in the worst possible way. Now a little uneasy with all this, he tried to lighten the moment.

"Melinda, you've just got to hang on. I think life holds a lot for you. And maybe great things are just around the corner."

"Perhaps so." She'd said this nonchalantly, perhaps no longer seeing the point of debating the matter.

A part of him wanted to disappear, what with the conversation turning so serious. Strangely, another part wanted this moment to last a lifetime. She was, after all, unlike any girl he had ever been with.

Eventually, he motioned for her to lie back in the crook of his arm. She did so. They pulled the covers up snug and just savored a time of closeness in silence. No doubt, he had found great pleasure in Melinda's company. There was something peaceful and beautiful about this moment that they were sharing together.

It seemed that maybe an hour or so more had passed when he said, "I guess I'd better get dressed."

But just then he thought he heard a certain commotion somewhere in the house, maybe from the floor below. There were loud voices.

"What's the racket all about?" he asked.

Melinda didn't answer. Like him she just paused and listened. Then she got up, donned a dressing gown and went to the door. She opened it slightly, listening to the uproar as it seemed to grow in volume. Doors were being banged open and someone, a man, was shouting something.

A look of fear and shock appeared on Melinda's face. She still said nothing.

"Melinda, what is it? What's going on?" Feeling alarmed, he jumped up and pulled on his trousers.

After a second or two she said, "Oh God, no. It can't be. Not now."

"What?!" Chad demanded.

But Melinda said nothing else. Chad walked over to the partly opened door and listened to the sounds from downstairs. It took a moment to sink in, but he now related to Melinda's bewilderment. The sound he now heard was the voice of a man reading someone his rights.

13

"THE PROJECT'S BEEN MINE from the beginning!" said Rick with as much hostility and rage as his wife had ever seen in him. "I created Chad Harmon. I *am* Chad Harmon, goddammit!"

A pall had been cast over the Richmond household throughout the weekend. Estelle had sensed something weighing on Rick from the moment she had met him for dinner Friday evening. She hadn't even needed to look directly into his face or engage him in conversation to know it. It was in the air about him.

During a late Saturday morning brunch at the Richmond home, he'd finally exploded and divulged to Estelle what was up, the Pioneer board's ruling that neither he nor any label executive would act as a producer over any part of an artist's recording from here on out. Rick's livid account to his wife of the board meeting came only after he'd first gone out to his personal driving range on the back stretch of the Richmond property and smacked away at the golf balls, each swing serving as a blow at the imagined face of one after another director of the Pioneer board.

"Take my word for it," Rick snarled, "Latimer, Hodgins, and the other sons of bitches have got their jealousies beneath those fine, gentlemanly façades. Somebody accountable to *them* making big money, maybe one day more than any record producer ever did, is more than they can stand, so it's time to put our CEO in his fucking place!" Rick didn't go on to say that the clandestine New York publishing venture was now a futile effort, since Estelle, like most, had no knowledge of the company he'd been forming.

"I'm so sorry, darling," she said as they went for an afternoon drive. "But, though it might not seem much comfort now, the first album is going to sell even greater than before, especially now with the awards having happened and thus giving new impetus. Everyone will know that you started it all."

"Harmon is going to sell more recordings than any artist in years," Rick responded acidly. "The artist to whom I gave his start, that I brought to the label, and that I've helped make what he is today! They *know* that. Someone else is going to produce him from here on out, and that is shit! It smells of self-importance on the part of the idiots who have about as much place on the board of a label as a goddamned dog!"

Feeling helpless, Estelle didn't know anything else to say.

Early on Sunday Rick called and instructed his attorney Phillip Smothers to meet him at the Pioneer office at 7:30 that very morning. He didn't offer to explain why, and Phil always remained flexible when Broderick Richmond beckoned, even to the point of changing family weekend plans.

Rick led Phil into his office and came right to the point. He relayed the entire story of the board meeting, at least from his own perspective. Phil already knew the scenario of Harmon's career rise, and how, according to Richmond, Rick himself had discovered Chad Harmon when no one else knew he existed, and how he alone had then made Harmon everything he was. But the story was to be presented again this morning in copious detail.

Rick had scheduled the meeting to inquire whether there was anything at all on which a lawsuit could possibly be built, a lawsuit against the board ruling. He knew that it would make for strained relations with the board, should he pursue such a thing. But that was something he could live with better than the directors if it ever came to that.

"Rick, I'm sorry," said Smothers after perusing some of the file copies of artist contracts, Rick's own contract as CEO, and the one for Chad Harmon. "I just can't see anything that a solid case could stand on. Pioneer has clearly spelled things out. They're under no obligation to you for anything."

"I gave you these contracts to review purely as a formality, Phil," said Rick testily. "I want to know if there's anything *outside* we can pursue, not something in the goddamned Pioneer contracts. I know the contracts are standard. But what about *other* things we could possibly build a case around?"

"First of all, Rick, there's no precedent here," Smothers said. "Frankly, I've never known of a label executive suing his board, and…"

"There's a first for everything, isn't there?" Rick snapped.

Smothers ignored the interruption and continued, "Secondly, I can't think of a thing, except maybe malicious intent on the part of the board, for which you'd have the burden of proof. I think we'd have to have solid evidence that there was a deliberate conspiracy on the part of some of the directors to sabotage your career. Then and only then *might* there be some sympathy toward your having propriety over Harmon's work with the label. However, I feel I have to say that the whole thing would still be questionable. If such a case actually went to trial, which would be a mess, and for *you* I mean, well, the outcome would depend on the sentiments of the jurors. It would be shaky at best."

Rick looked away, quietly seething. It seemed he wasn't going to get anywhere in the legal realm, according to Phil Smothers. Nonetheless, he'd keep his options open, at least in his own mind. Yes, there were other more aggressive and ruthless attorneys who might be more skilled at playing hardball, the sort of attorneys who had names, names he could now afford to retain, given his success of late.

And he was determined that the same success would continue.

It was pretty much thought of as customary for a gentleman to call a lady after a date if that date had seemed to go well. It had, Jock thought to himself, notwithstanding Charlie's having quenched the flame by her delicate disclosure that she wasn't quite ready for exploring the physical side of a relationship.

Snooks had meanwhile called early to ask if he was going to be in church. She and his dad were going to the late service and then on to Sunday brunch at the country club. Jock had said thanks but had declined his mother's invitation to church. Working at his law practice all during the week, tedious as it was to him, meant that his weekends were saved for relaxation and recreation.

He dialed Charlie's number. The phone rang four times before the answer machine picked up. Yes, he'd waited late enough to call. *Too* late. Unless it was just a case of her not wanting to take any calls. Of course, if she had Caller I.D., maybe she just did not want to talk to *him*. He chose not to leave a message but instead put the receiver back down. Perhaps leaving a recorded message might look a little too forward, too pathetically eager. But then wouldn't reaching her directly have seemed the same?

You've got to get a life, Jocko. What the hell is there about this chick that's making you act like an adolescent?

He walked across the bedroom to where his old guitar stood against the wall. He hadn't touched it in quite a while. He now picked it up, sat on the bed, and strummed a few licks. He thought about Charlie, who, like others, forged ahead with her dreams even in the face of frustration and possible failure. She had courage and brains.

Well, I'll be damned.

Something was dawning on Jock just now. He'd had thoughts moments ago about getting a life. He was now becoming more and more aware that perhaps there *was* a certain life he wanted. A life with Charlie.

Charlie was driving to the Pioneer office to retrieve a couple of song lyrics that were saved on the hard drive of her office computer. She and Peggy had talked about possibly getting together on Sunday for a co-writing session.

As she pulled up to the back entrance of the Pioneer office, she was surprised to see Rick's Mercedes parked near the door. She couldn't imagine what he could be doing at the office on a Sunday morning. There was a Lincoln Town Car parked next to it. She had never been to the office on Sunday, but for all she knew, it was a frequent thing for Rick to do. She stepped out of her car and, using her office key, opened the back door. Upon doing so, she almost ran headlong into Rick and his attorney, Phillip Smothers.

"Oh," she exclaimed, then smiled. "Pardon me."

"Sorry if we startled you," said Smothers.

"What are you doing here on a Sunday, Charlie?" asked Rick abruptly, and immediately she surmised the chill was on.

"I just wanted to pull up and print something on my computer, some song lyrics I've been working on," Charlie answered. "I forgot to do it on Friday."

"I'll be going now. If you'll excuse me," said Smothers as he moved past Charlie and on to his car.

Rick turned and walked back toward his office without offering another word to her. Something was up with him, for sure. With trepidation she slowly walked toward his office door that had been left slightly ajar as he entered.

After a moment's hesitation she said, "I didn't know I'd find anyone else here on a Sunday."

"Normally you wouldn't," Rick answered without looking up at her. He was putting some files back together that had been on his desk.

After a few seconds in which he still seemed to hardly acknowledge her presence, she continued, "Rick, is there anything...?"

"I'm going to have to get home soon," he said, getting up from his desk and going toward the file cabinet. "Estelle made lunch plans with some of our friends." He then lowered his voice almost to a whisper, though, as far she could tell, no one else was in the office building. He didn't look at her as he spoke. "Although it's a coincidence our both being here, it's not a great idea our remaining so. Not alone."

He picked up his cashmere blazer from the chair and walked past her out the door, not saying another word.

"Of course," she said quietly, though feeling hurt.

There was something to what he'd said. They had to be discreet at every turn. As she watched him go out the back entrance she wanted to ask him what was wrong, and to also ask if there was a chance she'd see him again soon. But she let it go.

Rick started up his Mercedes, still frustrated by the lack of encouragement he'd received from Smothers. Then he sat for a moment thinking about Charlie.

Was there a possibility that...? But how? He'd always gone out of his way to be very careful, almost beyond reason, to protect the privacy over the thing with Charlie. He'd never once closed the door of his office when she was there with him. He'd never called her from his home phone or even the office phone, never taken her to lunch, and, like a moment ago, had refused to speak with her about anything but business while in the office, even when there didn't seem to be anyone around to hear.

He thought of the born-again Christian freaks on the board. He guessed that there was always the slight possibility that gossip had started to spread about the affair. The board members getting wind of his arrangement with Charlie would surely have caused those fine, upstanding gentlemen to see him as guilty of "conduct unbecoming." And now they could be out to slowly undo him based on pious moral grounds. Hollywood this simply was not. Nashville was still the "Buckle of the Bible Belt," as the term went. Old-fashioned values were embraced here, and they especially were by certain board fellows, he thought.

Rick was certain that he'd taken every possible precaution, but ...but what about Charlie? As he drove out of the parking lot and up Music Square East toward the traffic circle he was forced to wonder if the little bitch had simply been unable to keep her mouth shut. Could she have disclosed it to even *one* person, perhaps a bosom friend, her affair with Broderick Richmond, the powerful head of Pioneer Records? Women loved to wag their tongues. Sometimes they just couldn't hold even the deepest secret of their hearts inside and tell no one. And just let another female learn of the choice little tidbit, then look out!

Charlie Cohen had been an excellent secretary and always a great fuck. But had the whole thing come at a huge price?

Rick had always felt that it was he who ran the label *and* the board. But now it seemed as though they were out to take him down a notch. Call him paranoid, but somehow he couldn't dismiss the thought. The board members wanted and needed his administrative expertise, yet they seemed to have an ever-growing personal dislike of him, and there had to be reasons.

He turned onto Demonbreun Street and then entered the on-ramp to the interstate heading south to Brentwood. He was already calculating what he'd do next about the situation.

"Oh, Charlie, I forgot. God, I completely forgot about our getting together!" moaned Peggy as she opened the door to her apartment.

"Well, we didn't really confirm it. And I didn't call ahead. Is there something wrong?" Charlie asked, though she noticed that Peggy looked dreadful.

"I'm afraid I'm coming down with the flu," Peggy answered. "Charlie, I'm so sorry I didn't call you. But you really don't want to be around me right now."

Charlie could tell by Peggy's pale coloring, red eyes, and raspy voice that she was surely feeling miserable.

"The flu," said Charlie. "Oh no."

"I started feeling a chill last night. But, oh God, this has come on *fast*."

"Say no more. I understand."

Charlie actually wasn't in the state of mind for creativity after her unsettling encounter with Rick, though some friendly company would have been welcome.

"I'll call you tomorrow, babe," said Peggy. "Charlie, I really hate this happening."

"Forget it, Peg," said Charlie. "I should have called you at some point during the weekend to confirm. Just get some rest and get well."

"I'll try. I swear I don't understand this. And it's so early in the season to get sick, you know. But, really, I'm feeling horrible."

"Take care of yourself, and just let it run its course."

"Right," Peggy said weakly.

"Bye now," Charlie said.

"Bye, Charlie. Once again, sorry."

"Don't give it another thought. Just get well."

As Charlie walked back to her car, she felt her depression deepening a bit. She'd looked forward to some time with Peggy, if for no other reason than to take her mind off Rick.

After arriving back at her apartment and finding no message from Jock, which was another thing she'd sort of hoped for, she thought, why not go to the mall? Exactly what she'd be shopping for, she didn't know. But the trip was something with which to busy herself, and so off she went.

At that same moment, Jock, giving up on reaching Charlie, finally accepted the nagging invitation from Snooks to come along to a benefit that evening for St. John's Kindergarten. It was a cause with which she'd involved herself off and on over the years since Jock's early childhood. The event was being held at the home of Snooks's very dear friend Ellen Mayhew.

Not exactly the Sunday he'd envisioned, but there it was.

14

"YOU'RE WHERE?!"

Tommy had been awakened by Chad's call at a little before 7:00 a.m. Chad quickly relayed only the necessary details, and Tommy in a matter of minutes was dressed, in a cab, and on his way to the police headquarters. After going through the procedures of signing papers, posting bond for both Chad and Billy, retrieving their personal effects, and so forth, the time was near 8:00 a.m. Tommy had foreseen that they couldn't possibly make it to the airport in time for the flight home, so he'd called the airline on his cell phone while en route to the police station and had thankfully been able to book a later flight.

From the moment Chad called, it had been Tommy's fear that the news media would somehow get word of the incident. His fears were confirmed. A few members of the press, including several photographers, were waiting outside the station as Chad Harmon, the rising country star and recent multiple CMA winner, came out along with Tommy and Billy.

"Mr. Harmon, could you please give us a statement!" shouted one almost smirking reporter.

"Were you with an employee of the establishment at the time of the raid, Mr. Harmon?!" shouted another.

"Why don't you all go to hell?! Get a goddamned life!" Chad said in a heated voice while barely looking back at the reporters, which caused Tommy to hustle him even more quickly into the waiting cab. Billy had already entered the cab from the opposite side. Tommy had tipped the driver to wait outside the station.

"Take us back to the InterContinental Hotel," Tommy quickly instructed the driver. Then he quietly said to Chad, "Ya gotta keep it cool, man. Don't react to 'em. Ya just play right into their hands when ya do."

As they drove away, Chad looked back at what seemed like his enemy now, the press. Worse still, Tommy was certain that within hours, maybe minutes, a press release with accompanying photos would be going nationwide.

"Tommy," said Chad contritely as they rode back to the hotel, "thanks, and...I'm sorry."

Tommy didn't respond at first but finally said, "All we can do now's wait it out. Just get past it. And we will, with time."

Back at the hotel, while packing, Chad gave a quick account of the whole thing, the late night trip to the Quarter, Billy's detour to the cathouse, and so on.

"What gets me," Chad said, "is that everybody says the whole situation is overlooked here. It's an *accepted* thing. The places stay in business all the time. But all of a sudden, the vice decides to stage a raid. I don't get it." Tommy said nothing. After a moment Chad reluctantly continued. "There's something else, Tommy."

"What?" Tommy said. "Let me have it!"

"They evidently tipped off the press that they were going to do this. News people were waiting outside the place, just like back there at the police station."

Tommy could tell by Chad's face there was more. "And…?"

"One of the cops was pushing me along, being a real asshole, you know, just loving every minute of it…and I…I let go of a few choice words at him. Yeah, I did it there too."

Tommy saw that Billy and the other band members made it onto the bus for their trip home. The fellows were making light of the arrest, in fact ribbing Billy about it.

"I'll tell you one thing, man," Billy said, almost proudly, "the price of getting laid is getting pretty steep, huh?" The guys all laughed. "Shit," continued Billy, "I really think I should've at least gotten a refund from the place."

The fellows howled even more, but the look on Tommy's face unmistakably said that he had no appreciation for the humor, and they soon decided to knock it off.

Things were silent in the cab as Chad and Tommy rode to the airport. There was nothing left to be said. For Chad it was sinking in now. Being led to a squad car by police, photographed, fingerprinted and detained had all been humiliating and frightening. But now the true shame of it was setting in. He felt almost glad for the first time that Lydia wasn't alive to learn of this. To what extent the *world* learned of it remained to be seen. How much attention would this be given by the media? He shuddered to think of all those reporters who had been waiting outside the house of prostitution as well as at the police station. He was a star merely on the rise as of yet, Chad tried to assure himself. Just maybe the whole thing would be downplayed or even passed over by most of the media. He found himself hoping for an earth-shaking news day tomorrow, anything short of a thermonuclear war, something that would force other items of interest into relative obscurity.

As they rode to the airport, it occurred to Tommy that he hadn't called Sandy. Close to Chad as they were, she would be devastated to hear it first from some news source, should the story spread that quickly. He'd maybe try to get alone somewhere at the airport to phone her on his cell. He didn't want to have the conversation in front of Chad.

The cab pulled up to the curbside check-in stand. Tommy and Chad got out, and the cabbie removed their bags from the trunk. Tommy paid the cabbie. They stepped up to the stand, and Tommy presented the tickets.

Just then an older model Buick pulled up to the spot at the curb that the cab had vacated. An overweight woman in a polyester pantsuit and sporting a beehive hairdo stepped out of the car, her husband obviously delivering her to the airport.

"My Lord, Chester!" she was heard to exclaim to her husband softly as if trying to be discreet, though not speaking quite softly enough. "That's *him*. That's that country singer. The one that they was showin' on the news this mornin'…least I think that's him."

The man, unlike his wife, made no attempt at speaking quietly. "He don't look like somebody in that big a trouble to me. Course, if you know the right people you probably don't even have to pay any fine or nothin'."

Tommy and Chad didn't turn around. They finished up their business at the check-in stand and quickly moved on into the terminal.

"*Welcome aboard Flight 1709 for Nashville…*"

Chad and Tommy made their way down the aisle of first the forward and then the rear cabin of the aircraft. They were forced by the change in plans to fly coach, their seats E and F, Row 20. As they moved down the aisle, Chad was almost certain he could hear the passengers' thoughts: "There's the country redneck that hangs out in whorehouses. Thinks he's hot shit, I'll bet."

He took the window seat and Tommy the middle. He knew that Tommy, who always flew first class, must be quite uncomfortable, large man that he was. An elderly woman occupied the aisle seat. It pained Chad to know that Tommy's plans had been altered because of his own doings. They should have just ridden back to Nashville on the bus with the fellows, he thought. But on the other hand, this way they would at least be arriving home in a couple of hours. Chad wanted to be nowhere but home right now.

"*Flight attendants prepare for departure.*"

After take-off, Chad was hoping that he'd be able to soon fall asleep. Exhaustion would probably be setting in from all the sleep deprivation. However, his mind for the first time went back to Melinda, Clarice, or whoever she was. They hadn't had any further communication following the raid.

"Damn it, isn't there any fire escape," he'd shouted, "or any back stairs?!"

"I'm sorry, there's not," Melissa answered.

"But, you don't understand, I've got to get out of here!"

As he recalled, no further words had passed between them. He wondered how she and the other employees lived under those conditions, never knowing when there might be a bust. Jesus, what a way to live!

"Can I get you something to drink?" asked the flight attendant, suddenly bringing him back to the present.

"Nothing," murmured Chad as he turned his head toward the window for the duration of the flight. No complimentary cocktails in coach anyway.

Tommy read a newspaper that he'd found in the magazine rack at the front of the aircraft while boarding. The unfortunate incident had taken place in the wee hours of the morning, and so it couldn't have made it into the morning papers.

Chad had finally begun to drift off when Tommy nudged him with his elbow.

"We're landin'," Tommy said.

Sandy was to meet the flight. Tommy had reached her while in the air, calling from the airline phone, regarding the flight change. Being seated on the almost full aircraft, he hadn't been able to break the awful news. He knew that each minute could possibly mean the further and further spreading of the story, and he longed to get Chad home.

As they came out of the baggage claim area to the temporary parking, Sandy was waiting, a bright smile on her face. Tommy quickly surmised that she knew nothing of the incident.

"Hi, fellas," she said happily.

She and Tommy kissed. She also gave Chad a warm hug.

"Hey, darlin'," said Tommy, quietly and hurriedly.

"Hi," said Chad.

Sandy instantly sensed that something was up. She noticed the leftover smell of alcohol on Chad's breath, the foul, stale odor of liquor still being processed by the bodily organs.

"You and Chad go on and get in the car, and I'll grab the rest of the luggage," Tommy said rather abruptly. He wanted Chad out of sight.

"Okay, sure," said Sandy, still bemused.

Just then some shouts were heard across the parking lot: "Mr. Harmon!" "Hey, Chad!"

Instantly Tommy and Chad both turned, shocked, expecting the worst. But there stood two teenage girls, one of them holding pen and pad in hand.

"May I please have an autograph?" inquired one girl adoringly.

"We really love you, Mr. Harmon," said the other girl.

Sandy and Tommy delivered Chad to the Burton Hills condo, they said their good-byes, and Chad retreated inside. The conversation between everyone had been restrained as they'd traveled from the airport.

Chad went directly to the refrigerator, took out a cold beer, and turned it up. He needed to unwind. He was now safe in his own environment. Everything now seemed a bad dream, as if it really hadn't taken place. After finishing the beer he quickly took out another cold one, opened it, and drank. The vague memory of it all now was partly due to the fatigue coming over him. He hadn't had quality sleep in God knows how long now. As soon as the second brew was downed, he deemed it fitting to have just one more. He needed to quickly loosen up and get some sleep. He opened yet another.

Suddenly it occurred to him that he'd left his carry-on bag in Sandy's Mercedes when they had dropped him off a moment ago. Damn! It contained his shaving kit. In the kit was a bagged portion of the grass Billy had shared with the guys back at the hotel suite. A few hits off a joint right now would undoubtedly help him to unwind. Getting a little high had always been one of the best sleep inducers he'd ever known.

The phone rang. With any luck, it would be Tommy and Sandy saying that they had noticed the bag and were returning with it. He picked up the receiver of the hall phone and answered.

"Mr. Chad Harmon," said a male voice on the other end.

"Speaking," Chad replied.

"Mr. Harmon, my name is Robert Hendley. I'm with UPI, and I was hoping to get a statement regarding..."

Chad abruptly pressed the receiver button. Then, looking down at the digital display on the answering machine, he noticed that there were three messages displayed on the digital screen. Dropping the receiver, he nervously unplugged the phone cable and the power cord of the device. Next he took even the batteries out of the compartment on the underside, hoping that this would permanently delete any and all stored messages.

"Oh God!" he shouted aloud. How had they managed to get the unpublished number? And what sort of hell would he be in for in the coming days?

Tommy wanted to concentrate on other things about his premier client, such as the up and coming *Saturday Night Live* appearance, several other important gigs, the next album, and the material it would contain. But it was a given that he and Sandy would have to discuss Chad's regrettable New Orleans experience for a while, and today certainly would not be the last time Tommy would be required to address it.

"Don't be too quick to judge him, Tommy," said Sandy as they arrived back at the farmhouse.

"I'm not judgin' 'im," said Tommy. "The guy's human. I know that. But he should use just a little better judgment. He's a man of notoriety now, and he was a visitor in a major city makin' a major public appearance – and for a benefit. And where does he end up celebratin'? A whorehouse. I'd just like to think maybe he'd set a better example for the band members."

They had noticed the piece of luggage when they were almost home, and Tommy had called Chad on his own cell to ask about getting it back to him, but there was a constant busy signal, despite the fact that Chad had Call Waiting. Chad also failed to answer his cell phone. Probably he had disconnected the house phone in order to get some sleep, Tommy decided.

Tommy and Sandy were finishing lunch in the breakfast room looking out on the farmyard. Sandy debated something in her mind for a moment. She knew how Tommy loved Chad. Chad was the "kid brother" that Tommy had never had. She didn't want to be offensive in what she said.

"Tommy, since you brought up his sense of judgment," she began, seeking to tread lightly, and she paused again.

"Come on, out with it, babe," he said. "What're you gettin' at?"

"Tommy, had he been drinking? Sometimes the judgment can be marred by alcohol, you know."

"Yeah, well, Chad and the guys do a little partyin'." Tommy shrugged. "Well, okay, they party a hell of a lot. After the concerts, when the stress is off, they can relax. They passed around a bottle on the bus. I just didn't think of it as bein' all that terrible."

"Having a drink or two isn't necessarily a terrible thing for anyone," she said. "But do you really have any idea how much he drank?"

Tommy was still making light of it. "No doubt they *all* had a fair amount. Did you ever see any band members that didn't love boozin' it up when they thought the time was right?"

"Of course not," she answered. "But do you have any idea how often Chad does?"

Tommy wasn't sure he liked where this was going. "What're you sayin', Sandy?"

"Just that maybe..." She stopped again. She knew her husband like a book and could almost read his every thought, especially when he glared the way he now was doing. "Tommy, it isn't a bad thing to suggest that a person might have a problem and need some help. The only wrong thing is seeing it, and then sitting by and doing nothing."

He got up and put his napkin on the table. "Sandy, I think just maybe you been readin' a few too many books or watchin' too much Oprah. I'm gonna go feed the horses. Might take a ride too."

Sandy, feeling frustrated, watched him go out the door and then to the barn. Tommy always let the cowboy in him come out when he was troubled, angry, confused, or just didn't want to talk. Or *all* those things.

Something told her not to press the issue about Chad just now.

Chad stretched out onto the bed. His mind was a mesh of many things; the concert last night, the trip to the brothel, Melissa, the arrest.

But at least now he was to the point of being able to forget. That is, after the sixth beer. It was all becoming a sort of faded limbo. And having unhooked the phone, he knew it wasn't to be a bother anymore.

Everything was pretty much fine now. He was relaxed. Yes, very relaxed. Eyelids were heavy. Time to rest now, thank God. Time to let it all go.

15

THE "ST. JOHN'S BASH" was an annual event benefiting St. John's Kindergarten, which technically was a pre-school. Jock, like many other Bel Terre children, had attended the school in his childhood. This year the event was to be held at the sumptuous home of Ellen Mayhew, which was located just off of Bel Terre Boulevard. Ellen, widow of the insurance company magnate Jim Mayhew, was a native of Jasper, Alabama, though not everyone knew this. She had once attended school at Belmont College, now Belmont University. During her enrollment there she had met her entrepreneur husband. It was noted by some that the title "St. John's Bash" didn't seem quite "high tone" enough for this year's event, what with its being at the lavish Mayhew residence.

Snooks and Ellen, who were best of friends, spent much of their time together, whether in Palm Beach or in Nashville. Jock, who'd met up with his parents at the benefit party, assumed that his mother probably had about as much heartfelt interest now in the flourishing of the kindergarten as she did in a Braves baseball game. But it was a tradition with her, not to mention that it was this year being held at her friend's home.

"Ah'm just delighted you brought this handsome son of yours along, Snooks," said Ellen as she accepted the obligatory kiss on the cheek from Jock. "Robert, Ah think it's been a good ten yeuhs or so now since Ah've seen you."

"Well, those years have been kind to you, Ellen," said Jock cordially. "You look as lovely as ever." *Not that a little cosmetic surgery had anything to do with it in your case, hell no!*

As he moved on to the hors d'oeuvres table in the dining room, he suddenly began to wonder what he was doing at this soirée. Nothing bored him more than pretentious affairs of this sort. And these days he couldn't even have a few good stiff drinks to get him through it. But what the hell, he had to have dinner some way or other. So he'd eat, sip on a soda, say a few "howdy-do's," and then be on his way.

Moving around the table and helping himself to the caterer's wares, he was approached by a middle-aged man also filling his plate.

"Hello, Jock," said the man.

Jock immediately recognized the bearded face as that of Albert Scruggins, a Vanderbilt law professor who'd been a friend of his father for many years. Scruggins had become a father late in life, and his child now attended the pre-school.

"Hello, Mr. Scruggins," he said, shaking the man's hand while balancing his plate in the other.

"How's your work with BB&S these days?"

"Just great," Jock lied.

"I always knew you were bound for great things, Jock," said Scruggins in a slight New England accent. "I could always understand Columbia snatching you away from us, but I can't say that I was thrilled about it."

As if you could have gotten *me in a Nashville college once I was out of high school.* "Well, Columbia was an experience," Jock said. "But at least I came home for law practice. And I've never regretted that." But a truism dawned on him, one about lawyers being lying assholes.

"After you've served yourself, Jock, would you care to join me out in the gardens?" asked Scruggins. "There's a quiet little nook back in the far corner where we can have a chat."

It sounded as if Scruggins wanted to talk privately about something, maybe something of marginal importance, Jock supposed.

"Sure," he replied. *There's no one else to bullshit with at this rip-roaring wingding anyway.*

"I have to say, I find the whole thing pretty intriguing," said Father Kris. "I guess it's always going to be controversial. But then I can't criticize what I don't completely understand."

Kris, in attendance along with the other St. John's priests at the Bash, was engaged in conversation with Nelda Fairbank, a native Nashvillian and longtime parishioner of St. John's, who'd caused more than a little stir over the years with her "ghost-busting" as she sometimes referred to it. Nelda, a lady who managed to hold on to her southern belle attractiveness quite well to now be past seventy, was also quite the character, in Kris's opinion. In addition to being a bit of a socialite in her own right, and one who had grandchildren at St. John's Kindergarten, Nelda had for many years been in the business of relieving homes plus their disgruntled and sometimes frightened residents of "restless spirits."

"Well, now honey, listen," she said, "I can't impress upon you enough the fact that it's just not like what you see in the movies, *Poltergeist*, *Amityville Horror*, and the like. It's never, I repeat, *never* that way."

The discussion Kris and Nelda were having on this subject had followed the previous topic of death and the afterlife. Kris couldn't at this point remember whether it was he or Nelda who had segued their conversation in this direction. But Nelda, in her "ministry" as she saw it to be, and Kris in his, both had had their experiences in dealing with death.

They were seated in the library of the house. No one else was currently present.

"People tend to think of horrible, ghoulish creatures screaming out," Nelda continued, "or maybe the walls and floor turning to rubber. My Lord, that's only in Hollywood. I'll say it once again, it's not like that at all."

Kris smiled, his mind actually quite open to all this, and his curiosity as well. "What *is* it like then, Mrs. Fairbank? I'd really like to know." He was aware that one retired priest, one who'd occupied an emeritus position on St. John's staff, had years ago denounced Fairbank's spiritual exercises as pagan and not at all embraced by the church. Not that that was to deter Nelda one whit.

"Call me Nelda, honey," she said in a gentle drawl, "First of all, it's not black magic. It has no origin whatsoever in the rites of witch doctors, sorcerers, and such as that. Would you care to know where it has its basis, Father Kris?"

"I would," he said.

"In the Bible. The inspired Word of God."

"The Bible. Well, that's something I've certainly staked a lot on in my work," he said with a smile.

"Most of what you read at one of my services, as I like to call them, is straight out of the scriptures."

"Really?"

"Honey, listen. I've had people call me over the years who are just desperate, I repeat, *desperate. Absolutely at their wits end!* I'm often told that my reputation precedes me and that my name has really gotten around. But after all, I've been on local radio talking about it, had articles written up about me in magazines, so I guess it was to be expected. But that means that while some scoff, others need my help because they simply don't know where else to turn."

Nelda went on to describe a few of her experiences over the years. What surprised Kris was how he himself was starting to buy into what she was saying, whatever skepticism he might have had now melting away.

"What's most important to understand," she said, "is that you are not, I repeat, *not*, when involved in my ministry, 'casting out demons.' You are simply helping *restless* spirits find the peace to move on rather than tarry."

"Does that mean," asked Kris, "helping them move on…to heaven?"

"That's the way I like to put it, Father. But to each his own." Then a smile came over her face, and she went to a whisper. "It's interesting I should be sharing a story with you about this while we're here – in Ellen's home, I mean. And I hope I finish it before anyone else enters the room..." She definitely had his attention now.

"It was a couple of months after Jim Mayhew died," Nelda continued. "I got a call from Ellen's personal secretary. Ellen was off in Bermuda or some such place. It seems that one of the maids had sworn up and down that Mr. Jim's ghost was roaming the halls of this very house, Father Kris. She wanted to know, the secretary did, if I would come over here and do an exorcism, I repeat, an *exorcism*! Can you imagine? Well, bless her heart, I had to tell her that I don't do exorcisms, but that I'd come and do whatever was possible for me to do." Nelda started to laugh. "I got over here, honey, and she had the servants of the house *all lined up in the front foyer*. My God, there must have been six or seven. Well, I pronounced what blessing I could on the place. So, Father Kris, you must be seated on hallowed ground as we speak."

Kris laughed along with her.

"But honey, this is what I mean about people's preconceived ideas concerning this," she continued. "An *exorcism*! First of all, you cannot, I repeat, *cannot* order a man out of his own house. Second, going through this ritual might help you stop feeling afraid or whatever it is you *are* feeling, but what about the poor man himself? Just suppose, though deceased, a man really is unsettled about things and still needing to be ministered to?"

Kris now knew that Nelda was sincere in what she did. She had never accepted any pay for her work. But then he gathered that she'd pretty much always been financially comfortable. So why would someone like Nelda pursue something that was quackery when it seemed, at least in some circles, a social stigma?

But was there truly a social stigma attached to Nelda Fairbank? This woman counted among her personal friends former British Prime Minister Margaret Thatcher, two foreign ambassadors, and the elite of a few southern cities.

Kris purposed in his heart to get to know Nelda Fairbank a little better than he had in the past.

"It's going to be the hottest topic of conversation at Nashville cocktail parties that people have had for some time. But I'm sure you know that," said Scruggins.

"And the most sensational story the local news people have had to exploit in a while too," Jock added.

Scruggins and Jock were in a remote part of the gardens behind the house. A few other guests were also braving the mildly cool night eating and socializing in the back garden area of the Mayhew residence. However, they were just far enough away that Jock and Scruggins could talk privately.

Scruggins continued. "Segal is going to have a very uncomfortable time even living in Nashville, let alone trying to work."

"The whole thing is pretty bizarre," Jock said, reflecting sadly on his personal connection. "God, what the parents of young Liz are going though. I spoke to Abe Feinstein the other day."

"Oh, you mean that you know Dr. Feinstein personally?" asked Scruggins.

"Yes. I assumed you did too."

"I'm afraid I never have gotten closely acquainted with anyone over in the mathematics department. Big university, you know. We of the law school tend to remain kind of self-contained." Scruggins hesitated a moment. "I had no idea you had a personal connection with the Feinsteins." Jock noted that the comment had been made almost with a look of concern. There was something on Scruggins' mind Jock couldn't yet figure. Scruggins continued. "Segal is in deep trouble. Whatever ends up happening, whatever does or does not come to light regarding the disappearance of the wife, he's got problems. Potentially of a criminal nature."

"No shit," said Jock with a smirk.

"Gary Segal came over to the department yesterday. Guess he took a chance that he would find the most dedicated law professors working on a Saturday. I was there for a meeting and was briefly back in my office when he knocked on my door."

"He was at the law school?" Jock asked.

"He's a graduate, you know. And he doesn't feel comfortable approaching any of the law offices in town, with all the attention being given this thing."

"I'll bet he doesn't," Jock sneered. "And I wouldn't suspect that he's about to be nominated for Man of the Year anytime soon either."

Scruggins looked at him a moment. “Jock, you and I hopefully are committed to a fundamental belief that a man is innocent until proven guilty. Also that everyone is entitled to legal representation. Am I right?”

Jock curtailed his sarcasm. “Sure.”

“Would you share my passion when I say, God help us when we begin to excuse the denying of anyone, whoever that person is, those constitutional rights?”

“Of course. But what’s your point, Al?”

Scruggins took a breath. “Jock, I have some long-time friends on staff at Columbia. I went to law school with a couple of them. I’ve gotten reports from some colleagues there about your work while you were enrolled. I know you not only trained for litigation, but you were said to have shown the most promise in that area of anyone that had come through Columbia in years.”

“I did pretty well,” Jock said blandly.

“In early days you were Outstanding Oralist, then in your last year went on the school’s team to the national finals of the Moot Court competition, and took first place.”

“That’s right.”

“It’s none of my business, of course...” *That’s right, it’s not.* “...but I’ve always been unable to figure your coming home to work in estate taxes, albeit with a very great firm.”

“It’s what was open to me here on the home front. And it’s pretty stress-free,” Jock said.

“Jock, Gary Segal is looking very hard for a legal ‘non-insider’ to represent him. I can understand his being apprehensive about approaching certain attorneys on the local scene. Some of them probably aren’t going to touch him with a ten-foot pole anyway.”

“So what are you getting at, Al?” asked Jock, though the picture was becoming clear.

“This thing is going to be sensationalized, as you pointed out, especially if a trial of some sort eventually takes place. Of course, there can be no charge filed against him till some proof – a body for starters – is produced. But it’s the chance for a young, smart attorney to start building a major career.”

“Someone like myself,” said Jock rather curtly.

“Yes,” was all Scruggins replied.

"Segal's quick move to retain legal council is quite intriguing," Jock said. "And I'm sure it will be perceived that way by others too. He isn't even being charged with anything at this point."

"Gary's never gotten a lawyer of his own because he never could foresee particularly needing one. But things could change rapidly for him. People are talking, and opinions are being formed. He's already being put on trial by the press and by the 'court of public opinion'."

"Yeah, I suppose." Segal certainly *was* already being convicted around town, as Scruggin's said. Jock remembered even now the few conversations he'd already had with others, including Charlie, about the situation.

"There is a bit of a conflict on your part. I understand that, Jock," said Scruggins. "As I said, I didn't know you had a personal connection to the family. Therefore, it's for you to decide."

Suddenly he was seized with thoughts about the Segal family, the money, the power, and his desire to make it on his own, not just relying on his own family's wealth and connections. But he soon dismissed it.

"I don't have to decide, Al. I know. There's no way I can take Segal on as a client. Apart from everything personal, I've made my career choice already." Jock wondered why he didn't say this with a deeper conviction. But he knew why. He hated estate tax analysis. He was bored shitless with it.

"People do make career moves, Jock," said Scruggins. But then almost with what seemed to Jock like a condescending smile, he added, "However, I understand."

"I appreciate your thinking of me, Al," said Jock, "and I also appreciate the complimentary words."

"You're welcome," said Scruggins with a handshake.

Jock could almost swear he sensed Scruggins silently saying to give him a call should he change his mind.

"I've enjoyed talking with you, Nelda," said Kris warmly, taking Nelda Fairbank's hand.

"The pleasure was mine, Father Kris," Nelda said.

Both had said their farewells and their thanks to the hostess and were now waiting in front of the house along with a few others for the valets to return with their respective automobiles. Nelda's quiet and soft-spoken husband watched for their vehicle.

"I have to confess," said Kris coyly, "that I would like to know more about the…ghost-busting, I believe you called it."

"I'll be more than happy to share with you anything I can," she said cordially. "Honey, I'll even gladly, I repeat, *gladly* welcome your coming along, should I get a call from someone."

Kris's first thought was, what would people think if word got around that he'd accompanied Nelda on one of her purgings? He had a certain reputation he had to protect at St. John's Church.

"That would be very kind of you," he said.

"Here's the car, darlin'," said her husband as the car appeared.

They bade their goodbyes and Kris waved as the car drove away. As Kris's car came through the front gates, he was feeling a greater inclination toward learning more about Nelda's "ministry."

"But Robert dahlin', you're not leavin' already," said Snooks.

"Yeah, I guess so, Mom," he said. "Time to get home, got a big day tomorrow."

"Well now, a Patron's gift bag is waitin' in thayuh for you. The bags are all lined up neatly goin' up the back stayuhs. Isn't it sweet the way they did them?"

"Patron's bag?" he asked.

"On the reply card that went along with the invitation, Daddy and Ah replied for you on the Patron level along with ourselves. We thought the extra money was worth it to support somethin' we truly cherish like our kindergarten."

"Of course," Jock replied, but wanting to get the hell out of here.

"Ah'll go get the bag. They're really the cutest things, brown papuh sacks rolled up to look like little children's school lunches."

As she headed toward the back of the house Jock stood in the entry hall looking into the main parlor. He noticed again Albert Scruggins, now engaged in conversation with the headmistress of the preschool.

The whole thing nagged at him. He wanted to make it in the world on his own, make a name for himself, even if he looked a bit like an opportunist. Shit, everyone who made a name in the legal profession had made some compromises, he told himself. Should he be any different?

There was, of course, his friendship with Abe, which meant a great deal to him. He couldn't help wondering what his friend, and everyone else for that matter, would think if he should involve himself in this.

But just last evening he had presented the facts, those that he knew of the case, to Charlie over dinner, stressing the importance of objectivity rather than bias when looking at things. He believed in those principles. Yes, Gary was entitled to legal representation. And Scruggins had said that he, Robert Jackson Pritchard, had the stuff great attorneys were made of, the kind needed at desperate moments.

Snooks returned with the goody bag.

"Thayuh," she said, handing the bag to him. "Glad ya came, dahling."

"Thanks, Mom," he said and gave her a quick kiss on the cheek. He headed up the hall to the front of the house with her, ready to escape at last.

16

"A POLICE CRACK-DOWN on a New Orleans brothel over the weekend sent both prostitutes and their clientele to jail. The raid was made noteworthy in that one of the new top names in entertainment was included in the arrest...

"Chad Harmon, country music heartthrob and multiple winner at Nashville's CMA Awards just last week, was placed under arrest along with nine others a little after 4:00 a.m. Sunday.

"According to sources, Harmon, who has sold over two million recordings and is perhaps best known for the crossover hit 'In the Rain,' offered no comment upon leaving police headquarters, other than a few choice words that we cannot quote here.

"The recording star had performed the preceding evening for a sell-out crowd at the New Orleans Fairgrounds, a benefit concert for victims of Hurricane Katrina. Following the concert, Harmon reportedly had enjoyed a night of celebrating in the New Orleans French Quarter concluding with a visit to the house of prostitution.

"A spokesperson in the office of the Nashville management firm that oversees Harmon's career told CNN that 'Mr. Harmon deeply regrets the unfortunate incident' and said that Harmon simply wishes to 'put this in the past and move on with his musical career.'"

Jennifer Eldridge, the CNN News anchorperson, paused briefly then said:

"Today in Baghdad..."

"So now what do you make of the infamous Chad Harmon bust Saturday night?" asked Wolfie O'Dell, popular radio personality of Nashville's WCAN.

"Well, no matter what they say, he's the cutest thing to come along in a long time," answered Lisa Hodges, his on-air sidekick.

"Mr. Harmon shakes your bushes, huh, girl?"

At this Lisa let go with one of her characteristic cackles. Many listeners agreed that Miss Hodges was on the morning broadcast to assure the radio listeners of knowing when the "star" O'Dell was being funny.

"Well, I gotta say this..." Wolfie continued.

"What?" said Lisa, still giggling.

"Ol' Mr. Chad was sure shakin' the wrong bushes last Saturday night."

And another round of the hyena laughter resounded from Lisa, who then said, "Now that's kinda mean."

O'Dell said, "Yeah, well, I do believe it's time now to go the traffic report…"

"*Please* do," Lisa giggled.

Exceeding speed limits as much as he dared traveling up Hillsboro Road toward Burton Hills, Tommy turned the radio off in disgust. The obnoxious disc jockey's on-air humor was something he didn't need. He knew Wolverine O'Dell personally and had never considered the guy his cup of tea, either as a radio figure or as a human being, the term used loosely. But at the present moment he felt like going to the station and shoving the radio microphone down the jerk's offensive throat. Decency and propriety, it seemed, had long since gone out of the entertainment industry, and most everywhere else in the world for that matter.

Tommy had continually gotten a busy signal when trying Chad's number. Of course, it was early in the day for musicians, and the receiver was probably still off the hook. But with things unfolding in the media over the last twenty-four hours, and Trudy already taking call after call at the office from concerned friends and press people alike, he thought it time to check on Chad.

Perhaps even worse than just a report of the event, a few local stations had actually run the footage of Chad being led out of the establishment spewing all his foul language, the words themselves bleeped out. Why couldn't the damned press just leave bad enough alone? Tommy wondered.

He pulled into the front driveway of the condo, got out, and went to the door. After he'd rung the doorbell and waited a minute or so, he rang again. With no success, he took out his own key to the condo and opened the door.

"Chad?"

There was silence.

"Chad!" he said again, a little louder, but still with no response.

Walking quickly back through the hallway to the kitchen and adjoining den he saw no one. What he did see was an almost empty gin bottle, a half pint, on the kitchen counter. Checking the trash can under the sink, he noted that there were several beer cans.

"Alright, Harmon. Time to start layin' off," said Tommy under his breath.

He went back up the hall and noticed that not only was the answering system disconnected from the phone jack, but the power cord was also unhooked, and batteries from the machine had been taken out.

"Poor guy," he muttered. "Guess they've already been givin' 'im the business."

He thought he'd better call for him one more time rather than risk scaring him to death by barging into his bedroom.

"Chad! Where ya hidin', man?"

He turned and proceeded up the stairs. Arriving at the master bedroom he slowly crept in. There Chad lay sprawled on the bed snoring, his naked body only half covered by the sheet. Tommy felt relieved to see that he was pretty much fine. But he suddenly caught the faintest whiff of some foul stench in the air. He made his way into the master bath and it grew more pungent. Lying in the commode was un-flushed puke.

"God," said Tommy under his breath and quickly flushed the commode. But there were also splatterings on the front of the tank and the back of the toilet seat.

He looked under the vanity for a bathroom cleanser. Finding none, he opened the closet. None there either. For lack of anything better, he ran water in the sink and created a lather from the hand soap dispenser. Taking a washcloth from the rack he did a quick cleanup, then tossed the cloth into the closet hamper.

"How many of my artists you think I'd do this for, Harmon?" Tommy mumbled.

Before exiting the bathroom, he spotted in the adjacent closet a can of air freshener, of which he made generous use.

As Tommy walked back into the bedroom, Chad snoozed on. It seemed that his young friend had not only learned an important lesson about discreet behavior but also about the effects of over-indulgence.

"Yeah, keep on gettin' ya beauty rest," muttered Tommy with a snicker as he walked out of the room. "We'll talk later."

At his Houston home Buck Harmon's eyes and ears had become suddenly attuned when Chad's name was mentioned as he sipped his morning coffee. He had become accustomed to seeing his son in the limelight, and however negative their relationship might have been of late, he had always taken great pride in Chad. But the news report now coming over nationally televised morning news was something different.

"...house of prostitution...arrest..." The words sounded ugly and yet spoken with such ease by the reporter.

Just how many women, including hookers, Buck had slept with during the years of his marriage to Lydia he didn't remember. Now that his wife was gone he wanted no one but her back in his life. What makes men go after glitter when they have gold within their grasp? It makes no sense, he thought.

But time to think about his son now. A lousy and embarrassing thing had befallen him. And just as his career was burgeoning, just as things were going his way.

"Chad," he said sadly. "Aw, Chad..." Though Buck had of late been pretty much rejected by his son, he felt great sadness and a concern for him. "I wish I could see you, son," said Buck aloud.

"What the fuck do you want now, prick?" was Rick's thought, answering Hugh Latimer's call while still at home on Monday morning.

But things became interesting as he learned Latimer's reason for calling, which was to break the news of Chad Harmon's arrest. Rick hadn't turned on a radio or television, nor had he taken the time to look at the morning paper.

"Jesus!" Rick almost shouted aloud in response.

Latimer was quite distraught that the label's newest and most successful artist, one that they were to build a new label division around, had been involved in a scandal like this. Should they postpone the announcement of the subsidiary, the press conference in which Harmon was to be present?

The conversation continued, which was mainly Latimer's while Rick listened, his mind calculating. The board chairman kept anguishing over the offense that certain fans might take at this. Rick pondered how Latimer was railing on about morality but that there was evidently no morality bone to pick with him personally. This must all mean that the board guys hadn't found out about the arrangement with Charlie after all. Yes, Rick concluded, the secret was still safe. But the banner waving over appropriate conduct gave him all the more reason to be even more careful now, perhaps even break it off completely with Charlie for a while.

What none of this did, however, was rectify the situation of all the sons of bitches on the board having taken from him his production rights on Harmon's future recordings.

"I'll give you a call later, Hugh," said Rick who needed time to think everything through.

"I'll wait to hear from you, Rick," said Latimer. "I'm afraid we're faced with some damage control."

After they hung up, Rick drove on to work. At about 10:30 he sat at his desk thinking, plotting. He once again went and pulled the Chad Harmon contract from the files for perusing. He read it and then sat pondering things further. At last he was resolved.

"Fuck all of them!" Rick suddenly said aloud to himself as he picked up the phone and dialed Latimer's work number.

"Mr. Latimer's office," answered the overly polite secretary at Latimer's insurance company.

"Put me through to Latimer," he said imperiously. "Broderick Richmond calling."

Latimer came on the phone, "Hello, Rick."

"Hugh, I've been thinking since we spoke this morning, and there's something I wanted to take up with you before talking to the other directors."

It sickened Rick to offer any flattery at all to this asshole.

"Yes?" said Latimer.

"It's about our standard company contract for artists."

"Go on."

"There is a morals clause in every contract."

A pause.

"I hadn't thought about it." Latimer sounded as though he had a sinking feeling.

You hadn't thought. What a surprise, you ignorant dickhead. "I think it's something we're going to have to take a good hard look at," Rick said, feigning deep sadness.

This was the first of the conversations he was to have with all the board members. If every director didn't agree as to what action must now be taken, he'd pit them one against another, and in the end he'd control this. If nothing else, he'd shame the pious thinkers into what was right according to their fine Christian principles.

It would be a small victory, not a full retribution, but there was nothing else left.

Chad awoke with head throbbing. He looked at his bedside clock. It was 11:15. He got up, went to the bathroom, and peed. He then started down the stairs, all those horrors of the previous day's experience coming back to him. As long as he stayed tucked in bed it was as if he was away from the world, nothing really able to get to him.

Stopping at the front door, he debated whether to get the morning paper. He figured he had to face it all at some point, so he opened the door and picked up *The Tennessean.* He opened the paper, and on the right-hand side of the front page was the story, the headline reading, "Music Row's Most Celebrated New Talent Arrested."

"Aw, God!" he shouted, throwing the paper across the hallway. Just days ago the news media had been in a love affair with him. Now things had turned, and the honeymoon had ended.

He walked on up the hall and into the kitchen. About to go through the motions of making the morning coffee, he stopped, not really wanting coffee after all. He had no clue just what he was going to do with himself now. There was no concert booked for a few weeks and no scheduled rehearsals with the band either. And, though off days usually meant time to write, he was in no place emotionally to let the creative juices flow.

Maybe he needed to get out in the country somewhere, away from civilization. Tommy and Sandy's farm came to mind, but Tommy was probably still too upset with him. Better to steer clear of him for a day or two.

Just then he looked down at the counter. There was a handwritten note:

> *Hey, sleeping beauty!*
> *Welcome back to life. I just wanted to check on you. I'll be at the office. Call me later.*
> *Tommy*

Chad's eyes turned misty thinking of his tried and true friend always looking out for him. But he assured himself he was going to be fine. After all, Tommy had said they'd work through it, get past it.

Chad knew that he had to.

The board meeting was set for 5:00 p.m. By early afternoon Charlie had finished placing calls to all the board members, though having no idea what the specially called meeting was to be about, the regular monthly meeting having taken place only days ago.

She'd also been unable to discern why Rick seemed so remote, almost as if he were angry with her. He'd always kept his distance in the work place for discretion's sake, but this was different.

Finally Rick called her into his office, as usual not asking her to close the door behind her.

"I've managed to reach or at least leave messages with all the board," she said. "Everything is set. And the conference room is booked."

"Good." He maintained an officious nature, hardly looking at her. "Now about the West End meetings usually set for 5:30…"

She brightened a bit, attentive to the code that only she and Rick were privy to. Her apartment wasn't on West End Avenue but rather in Bellevue. However, this was meant to refer to her place, where she and Rick always had their "meetings" together. "Shall I schedule later in the week?" she asked.

"No," he said flatly. "In fact, maybe not at all in the near future."

She wasn't sure she'd heard correctly. Her mind couldn't take it in, though she was accustomed to the esoteric means of communication. It almost sounded as if he was breaking off the relationship. But no, that couldn't be the case.

"Not at all?" she asked, a little shaken though trying not to show it.

"Not for the time being," he answered, still without emotion and still not looking at her.

She stood there several seconds with no response.

"One more thing," he said. "For today's meeting, I need you to pull copies of three or four random artist contracts on file. I have the Harmon contract already."

She hardly heard him but finally answered, "Of course."

"That'll be all," he said and then turned away, walking over to his private wet bar for a fresh cup of coffee.

After a moment she walked out.

"This time I'm afraid *I'm* the bearer of bad news," said Jock after Charlie answered the phone back at her desk.

Jock had wanted to talk only about his upcoming meeting at Vanderbilt this afternoon, but he'd been interrupted by the information he had just received, which he knew he needed to pass on to Charlie.

"Oh, hi, Jock," Charlie said. Still hurt and confused by Rick's words, she'd hardly heard what Jock had said.

"Esther Bullard – I think you know her, she comes to Harding Road group – well, her daughter's a paralegal here at BB&S. And Esther is Peggy Rose's sponsor in the program."

"Right," said Charlie, though still distracted.

"Esther stopped in at Peggy's place to check on her on the way to work this morning. She'd tried calling her and didn't get an answer. She also remembered Peggy calling her yesterday and that she mentioned being sick."

"That's right. I went by Peggy's place yesterday. We'd talked about a writing session. She was coming down with the flu, so I didn't stay. What's going on?"

There was a pause, and Jock said, "I knew you two were good friends. But...well, it seems it's not exactly the flu, Charlie."

"What do you mean?"

"Esther called for an ambulance after finding Peggy delirious when she got there. Peggy had this incredibly high fever."

"Dear God," gasped Charlie. "An ambulance! Where did they take her?"

"Centennial," he said. "The emergency room first, but then they admitted her."

"I'll get over there now," Charlie said quickly, preparing to leave. "I really ought to be with her."

"Charlie," Jock interrupted. "Charlie, you can go there if you want, but I'm sure you're not going to be able to see her."

"Why not?"

"They have her on a ventilator. She's getting constant attention from the doctors. Charlie, I'm afraid it looks bad."

Somehow at that moment all that flashed in Charlie's mind were two things; the fact that she had ruined Peggy's night at the CMAs with her own depressed mood, and having snapped rudely at Peggy the very next day when her friend had expressed concern for her. She was suddenly filled with shame.

After a few miserable seconds she said, "I'm going there now." Without another word she hung up the phone, grabbed her purse, and headed for the door.

"Please tell Rick there's an emergency I've got to see about," she shouted over her shoulder to an office clerk. "I've got to go to Centennial Hospital. I'll be back later."

Rick was fielding calls a good deal of the afternoon from people in the business regarding the breaking news story of Chad Harmon's infamous New Orleans adventure and subsequent trip to the police station. Most wanted to just share the dirt and crack a joke or two.

It seemed the story was the talk of the Row and of the airwaves as well. There had even been a disdainful comment wheedled by a press person from the pastor of the Church of Tomorrow, a huge local charismatic congregation. The church counted among its fold several born again country stars and others in the business.

A certain irony was occurring to Rick. Chad Harmon was in a position to possibly sell more recordings than ever before as a result of all the negative publicity. People craved sensational news. He had already taken a few calls from people wanting to absorb the scandalous details. After all, didn't the most gruesome accident on the highway always attract the greatest number of onlookers? Such was the case with human beings. Chad Harmon might now have the chance to become a bigger star that ever – and as a direct result of a scandal!

"What a fucking shame to see the end of something legendary before it even gets going," he said with a sneer.

He decided to call the last board member to plant the necessary seeds for the "emergency" meeting. According to Charlie's note, she'd reached all but Rupert Hodgins before leaving. The little bitch had rushed out for the afternoon for some reason or other, so he'd have to place his own call.

"Mr. Hodgins's office," answered yet another perky secretary.

"Put me through to Rupert," he ordered. "It's Richmond."

Rick's resolve was quite firm. If he wasn't going to produce Chad Harmon, no one was.

Bertram Venneman sat at the computer in his Manhattan office. While covering the CMA awards for *Good Morning, America*, he had gathered material for a feature article on Chad Harmon to appear in the November issue of *Rolling Stone*.

As he was now downloading the breaking news story off the Internet, Venneman knew that his article already in progress must now take on an entirely different spirit. He chuckled to himself, knowing that this assignment would be far more interesting than originally thought.

17

"I'M STARTING TO WONDER if she's in a state of shock that she's never going to come out of."

Bill Jamison was meeting with Father Kris in Kris's office. Kris was trying to offer whatever counsel he could to the broken man.

"Mary has always been an open sort of person. Now it's like she's shut herself up inside of a cocoon. She's *without* emotion, almost...almost like she's not really there."

"I've heard you say that you were going to ask the doctor to prescribe some anti-depressants?" Kris asked. "I wonder, Bill, if a sort of numbness can come with those medications. It's assumed in such cases that that's the only way a person can deal with the pain at a time like this."

"No, you don't understand. Mary hasn't seen the doctor. And she refuses any medical help. She says she doesn't want to medicate her emotions. The way she puts it, it won't help for her to go into a vacuum. She says she *needs* to feel."

"And yet she seems to be in a vacuum anyway," said Kris.

"Exactly," Bill replied.

"I suppose, Bill, that I have to admire Mary, in a way. I think it takes bravery to just face the pain straight on. Still, I'm sure it's disturbing to see her the way she is if help is what she's really needing."

"She eats, but not much," Bill continued. "She has little to say. Spends a good deal of time just sitting with her hands folded. She may take a short walk outdoors but never leaves our yard." He paused a moment. "Sometimes she goes in Hunter's room, closes the door, and doesn't come out for a long while. I have no idea what she does there. I hear no crying from her while she's there. I don't understand it, and I don't know what to do about it."

Kris was touched that Bill should now be so drawn to him for whatever pastoral help might be needed, due to Kris's connection with Hunter. Yet he also was learning what it was like to help shoulder the most unpleasant burdens of parishioners, and it was not enjoyable.

"Bill, I wish I could offer more profound advice, but all I can say is just keep on being there for Mary any way you can. She'll be in my prayers, I assure you. But be sure to take care of *yourself*, Bill. I don't think it's a bad idea to look into a support group. For grief, you know. Maybe you should look into some counseling for yourself. Whatever it takes. You've got to look after your personal needs in order to be able to be there for Mary. And for Andrew."

Bill sat quietly and took in all that Kris was saying. "Well…I appreciate your listening, Father Kris," he finally said as he stood up. "I'll be going now."

"Please call on me anytime you or Mary feel the need," said Kris as he got up, shook Bill's hand, and began to see him out.

Bill stopped at the door.

"Married couples are supposed to share everything, Father," he said looking down. Then looking at Kris one last time he added, "And that includes grief. Wouldn't you agree?"

Kris merely nodded, unable to offer anything further. Bill then went out the door, Kris closing it behind him.

Not yet being a parent, he could only imagine what it was like to lose a child, and so tragically. Simply to get up out of bed and face another day must be an almost unbearable task.

Only seconds after Jamison disappeared Kris's phone rang. He picked it up.

"Kris Hartley," he answered.

"Hello, Father Kris. This is Esther Bullard. From the Harding Road group, you know."

"Of course, Esther. How are you?"

"Haven't seen you much lately, Father," she said.

"No, I haven't made it to the meeting the last week or so. I've been swamped."

Esther was one tough old broad, Kris had surmised. She was a plainspoken recovering alcoholic who was a regular at the Harding Road Group. She'd been in the program for nearly thirty years. Though sometimes using language that could give a sailor pause, she was respected by everyone, including Kris.

"Always seems to be that way for you preachers," she said.

"You're so right," Kris chuckled.

"Well, Father, I hate to do it, but I'm about to make things even a little messier for you."

"How so?" he said.

"Don't know why we always feel like we've got to inform you specifically of the bad things going on with the group members. But then, like I say, no one would ever consider letting up on a preacher."

"What is it, Esther?"

"I think you know Peggy Rose."

"Of course I know Peggy. Quite an interesting girl, I've always thought."

"Well, things are a bit more *interesting* than we'd like them to be today," she said.

"Oh?" Kris asked.

"Poor little thing got really sick over the weekend. She called me yesterday. Then, well, something told me to go by and see her this morning on my way in to work. She's got no family in town." Kris could have sworn that he could sense Esther, of all people, becoming a bit emotional. "She's a very, *very* sick little girl, Father Kris."

She went on to relay all the facts, those she understood, of the rare form of meningitis that the doctors had tentatively diagnosed, and that she was now on life support.

"Life support?" Kris almost gasped.

"They really want to help her hang on until her parents get here from Chicago."

Hang on? Kris had that feeling yet again that the world around him was going to hell and that he was unable to do anything about it. He quickly determined from Esther which hospital and was off in a flash.

Jock wasn't able to immediately join the others at the hospital. He hadn't been close to Peggy, but Charlie was supposedly her best friend. However, his going there would have to wait. He had put in the call from his home to Scruggins' home early that morning and had taken off work from BB&S at noon. He'd agreed to meet Scruggins and Gary Segal at 2:00 p.m. at Scruggins' office on the Vanderbilt campus.

Heading toward the Vanderbilt law school, Jock reaffirmed to himself that he wasn't all that serious about taking Segal on as a client.

"I'm just agreeing to meet and talk," he'd said to Scruggins when calling him. "I need for that to be understood."

His representing Segal might necessitate his leaving BB&S. But then it could possibly open up a door to his going into private practice. No more of that tedious shit he faced on a day-to-day basis. It was simply time to keep the avenues open, Jock thought as he pulled into the law school parking lot. After all, as Al Scruggins had said, Segal *was* a citizen and thus entitled to representation.

"I'm sure they're doing everything possible, honey," said Esther Bullard seeking to comfort Charlie, who was terribly frightened. Only problem was, Esther thought, there was nobody to reassure *herself.*

The two were in the hallway adjacent to the waiting room of the Critical Care Unit and were praying that some news would come soon. Peggy's parents were due in just after 3:00 p.m., and Esther had agreed to go and meet their flight.

"When I saw her yesterday," Charlie said, "she looked terrible, but then the flu always does that to anyone. I had no idea this was something so...so awful." She wasn't able to say the word *deadly*, though it had been tucked away somewhere in a corner of her mind. Charlie thought about how she cherished her friendship with Peggy. This was a nightmare.

"None of us had any way of knowing," assured Esther. "Hell, if I'd known, I'd have been right there yesterday, never left her side. And I can't figure what made me go by and check up on her today, except maybe the Lord."

Kris got off the nearby elevator and spotted Charlie and Esther. Both women were slightly comforted to see Father Kris Hartley, a living treasure to the Harding Road Group.

"Do you know anything more?" he asked them.

Esther replied, "No more than what I told you when we talked, Father."

Just then, Doctor Scranton, who'd met with Esther earlier when Peggy had been transferred to the CCU, appeared from around the corner. Kris, Charlie, and Esther stood as he approached.

"Have Miss Rose's parents arrived yet?" he asked.

"No, Doctor. Their plane's due in a little after 3:00, and I'm meeting it," Esther quickly said. "So please consider me her family in the meantime. Can you tell me anything at all, Doctor?"

Scranton balked for a moment as if not quite sure whether to proceed. Then, with a bit of reluctance and after looking away a moment, he said, "Miz...?"

"Bullard," she said.

"Miz Bullard," he continued, "I'm terribly sorry to have to tell you this..."

Jock hadn't taken a particular dislike to Gary Segal. The average-looking and seemingly mild-mannered man had said little thus far. Al Scruggins had done most of the talking as the three met in Scruggins' office behind a closed door.

Only a few brief times had Jock allowed his mind to host a passing thought about the young daughter of his close friend Abe, a young lady now missing for a week, and who, for all he knew, was chopped up and bagged somewhere.

"Gary feels, and I agree, considering the sensational nature of what's happened with his wife and the high profile the case of her disappearance is already taking on, all meetings between his legal counsel and himself need to be as covert as possible. No lunches in restaurants, et cetera."

Jock said as politely as possible, "I'm all business in my work. I seldom do lunch."

Segal smiled and said, "That's good. I'm the same way."

"I should make something else clear," Jock continued. "Before I could consider this, you need to know that I would need some sort of a retainer. This would be an entirely new direction for me to go professionally."

Both gentlemen gave a nod of respect to this. Jock continued, "But having said that, I suppose I have to also say that I'm not exactly sure what that direction would be. In other words, I don't know what sort of legal representation you're seeking at this point, Mr. Segal, or what it is exactly that you're needing my services for."

"Please call me Gary," said Segal, though Jock wasn't sure how comfortable he was about being on a first-name basis with the man. "Everyone needs to know that they 'have a lawyer,' pardon the expression. You see, I never have retained one, and, however terrible the current circumstances are, now seems the time for me to do so."

"Also, Jock," Scruggins said, "the recent unfortunate events happen to coincide with the eminent retirement of Marcus Jacobs, who has been general counsel for Segal Industries for a number of years." Jock knew well of Marcus Jacobs, as did most people in the legal circles of Nashville. Now in his seventies, the retirement of the legendary Jacobs to be effective the first of next year had been the talk around town already.

Scruggins continued. "As I mentioned last evening, Jock, it's been known, perhaps more than you realize, what a great litigation attorney you could be, with your standings in the moot court of your day, plus your reputation at Columbia. But you've also had experience now in the area of probate."

"Your reputation has even been known to me," said Segal.

Jock couldn't help being awed by the fact, if it was indeed a fact, that he had been the talk of many a lawyer, Segal himself being one.

"I'm flattered, gentleman," Jock said.

"Jock, Gary would like you to consider coming on now as his personal counsel for which a seventy-five thousand dollar retainer is offered." Jock was further struck by this more than respectable amount. "You can also expect no less than two hundred and fifty an hour for your work representing him personally in whatever capacity becomes necessary."

Segal now took over. "I of course hope that that *isn't* going to become necessary, but if it does, I'd feel comfortable knowing that I had someone like yourself to count on. But I have something much more immediate to present to you…May I call you Jock?"

"Yes," Jock said.

"The entire Segal family has gotten involved in the discussions regarding you. Maybe you're aware of the success my family has seen over the years with Segal Industries." Jock nodded that he did. "A general counsel for the corporation is about to be needed, with a starting salary of four hundred and fifty thousand per year."

The reason Jock had been summoned here today was becoming quite clear. He wondered if the astonishment that he'd felt at the mention of the fee had been obvious to the two gentlemen.

Charlie drove out of the Centennial Hospital parking facility in a daze. Perhaps it hadn't really registered with her mind as of yet. Maybe she just wasn't able to let it sink in, a means of protecting herself.

Yet the truth remained that Peggy was gone. Charlie would have no more lunches or evenings out with her sweet, wacky, wonderful friend. There would be no more co-writing songs with Peggy. No more seeing Peggy at the Harding Road meetings. No fun times, like the countless ones they'd shared. How could it be? Her dearest friend dead?

"Oh God!" she cried aloud.

The very deadly and almost unheard of strain of meningitis had taken Peggy's young life in less than two days. Charlie, in a state of limbo, thought she could remember the doctor saying that the disease, at least as they had now diagnosed it, affects only one in half a million people. But Peggy had been on the unlucky end of those odds.

Charlie, Esther, and Father Kris had parted company just a few moments ago. Esther was on her way toward the horrible duty of meeting the Roses' flight and breaking the news to them. She'd respectfully declined Kris's offer to go along, feeling that it was better not to have too many people around at such times. Esther was a far braver human being than herself, Charlie thought.

And now she was just driving, though where she didn't know. She proceeded south on Twenty-fifth to West End Avenue but was hardly cognizant of her surroundings. She simply was moving on somewhere, anywhere.

By early afternoon with his head still aching, Chad considered a run to the store for Tylenol and beer. But he hated the prospect of possibly being recognized, with all the publicity now surrounding him.

Then he thought of something. Reclining on the living room sofa, he picked up his cell and put in the number for Ted Halsey, the road manager for the group.

"Hello."

"Ted, it's Chad."

"How ya holdin' up, man?"

"Fair. But I got a problem, Ted. I really don't want to go to the store. You know, people notice me these days."

"What 're ya needin', man?"

"Well, the old beer stock is running a little low."

"Say no more. I was goin' by Kroger anyway today. Can ya wait a coupla hours?"

"Oh yeah, sure."

"Consider it done, my man."

"You're a good guy, Teddy."

They both closed up their phones. Still sprawled on the sofa, Chad realized that he hadn't mentioned to Ted his needing the Tylenol.

Oh well, the old head would probably be getting better soon anyway.

"One very noted clergyman has already put in a call to the label." Rick had carefully scripted all the lies, at least in his mind, in order to effectively address the Pioneer board. "He even has mentioned drafting a letter to our label, copied to Vision Artist Unlimited and the Country Music Association, which he plans to have signed by some other prominent clergymen in town. And of course, the press hasn't missed the chance to play up Chad's moment of swearing at the media as he left the police station. That's upset some people all the more." He wondered if any of the board members might ask the identity of the non-existent minister, to which he'd only be able to reply that the man had wished to remain anonymous for now. But luckily Hugh Lattimer jumped in.

"It seems that a lot of people were holding Mr. Harmon up as a shining example to the young," said Lattimer. "His wholesome image and his songs have been something they've held in high esteem. Unfortunately, that causes people to take even greater offense now. The worst thing is the clip of him leaving the…the business establishment." Hugh Lattimer, fine, decent, upstanding gentleman that he was, was proving to be an even greater ally in his crafted plan than Rick had anticipated. Lattimer was genuinely crushed by all these goings-on with Chad Harmon.

"The public can be shamelessly fickle," said Rick, putting on his best disdainful expression. As for the "wholesomeness" spoken of and the "example to the young," he wondered if any of these fucking idiots had ever bothered turning on CMT and seeing the suggestive video of "In the Rain" with its brief nudity. Apparently not.

"We've talked about opening a Christian music division of the label next year," spoke up Gregory Chase, a thirty-something businessman, new to the board this year, and who usually remained rather quiet at the board meetings. "What sort of reflection is this going to have on that prospect? I think we have to look at that too."

It was time for another fabrication, Rick thought. "A reporter at *The Tennessean* called while I was at lunch and left a voice mail message," he said. "It seems the morals clause we have in our standard contract, as do most of the other labels in town, is known to someone down at the paper. He wanted a comment related to the morals clause and Harmon. I declined. For now."

This brought a dead silence to the room.

Rick knew that the others were more than likely assuming him to be jumping on this more aggressively due to his indignation at being forbidden to produce any further Harmon recordings. Yet, just as he'd plotted, they seemed to be feeling a certain gravity to the situation.

"This is all simply terrible," said Rupert Hodgins. The others didn't have to echo his sentiments; it showed in their faces. It was as if they all somehow knew even now what the outcome of this meeting was going to be.

Rick knew that victory, albeit bittersweet, was his.

By the time Jock arrived at the hospital, his friends had gone their various ways. He learned the sad news about Peggy from the CCU nurse. He pitied Peggy's family, but he also was concerned as to how Charlie was handling everything.

As he drove away from Centennial, he immediately tried reaching her at the work, at home, and at her cell, but it was to no avail.

Greg Chase, the Pioneer board member, was also a close friend of Tommy and Sandy Matheson. They all attended the same rural church a few miles outside Franklin. Excusing himself from the board meeting for a moment, he dialed the number for Vision Artists on his cell. Trudy, the receptionist, answered, and he asked to be put through to Tommy.

"Gregory Chase calling," he said.

"I'm afraid Tommy's gone for the day," she replied.

"Could you please give me his home or cell number?"

Greg was a close enough friend to the Mathesons that he wanted to break the bad news to Tommy himself, although he dreaded it.

Charlie pulled into the parking lot of her apartment complex a little before 5:00. After leaving the hospital, she'd driven around town and wasn't sure just where she had been. She was still hardly aware of the world around her, though the truth had registered more deeply and she'd let go and cried for a very long time.

As she parked in a space near her building, she tried to pull herself together. She looked into the rear view mirror. Why she should care how she looked she didn't know. After all, her life wasn't a thing of great value. It was a life going nowhere. Her closest friend that she loved so much was gone. And she had no one who cared for her in a deep and personal way. In fact, the one man she loved belonged with someone else. Despite all that, she hadn't slept her way into any great writing or publishing deal. She had nothing to show for her efforts.

As she was looking in the mirror she caught sight of Kenny, the young grounds keeper. He was sitting on a short brick wall connecting to one of the buildings, in a secluded spot. Though not a particularly bright young man, he had always seemed pleasant. Currently Kenny was puffing discreetly on a joint with little regard for who might be watching. And Charlie surely knew a joint when she saw one.

He was about to get into his own car and drive away. Without deliberation, she got out of her car, walked toward the young man, and immediately saw him tuck the joint under his hand, though not disposing of it.

"Hi," she said.

"Hi," he replied as she continued strolling toward him. "Something I could help you with, ma'am?"

She flatly said, "Guess I could use a friend." She stretched out her hand the direction of his, the hand concealing the joint.

Kenny smiled. Nothing to worry about, he decided. *This chick is cool.*

It was as if Jock had somehow already known that he would take this step. Ever since Scruggins had approached him it had been there in his mind, though he'd never allowed himself to admit it. Yet, as it had turned out, Segal's proposal was beyond his dreams. He was about to become a new man, powerful and financially comfortable in his own right, not so dependent upon his family's resources.

He wasn't sure just how he'd go about telling everyone, his parents, the firm, and especially Abe. Abe Feinstein had been such a special friend. And now this new turn of events! He hoped Abe was the intelligent and clear-thinking man he'd always seemed to be. Surely he would find it in his heart to understand.

Jock decided that he couldn't agonize over that at the present moment. Damn it, he was entitled to his opportunity to revel in this moment.

But he wanted to do so with Charlie. He picked up the phone to try her number once more.

Charlie let the phone ring as she headed out the door, not waiting to hear the message Jock left. She didn't want to talk to anyone. She was just high enough to be mellowed, not stoned out of her mind. Her driving should be okay. She'd make it to the liquor store just fine.

She'd get back, and that would be that.

As he arrived back at his apartment, Kris, feeling about as low as he ever had, decided that it would be a good thing to get in touch with his original sponsor in the Twelve Step program, Buddy McMasters.

Buddy had been a member of the AA group Kris had attended while enrolled at Duke. A retired officer of the Marines now in his late sixties, he'd been spoken of as the "kick-ass" type among the many young men he sponsored in recovery. Kris had determined early on that this was what he'd needed, though the tough, hard-nosed ex-Marine was as far from Kris in lifestyle and disposition as could be. But for all the things he wasn't, Buddy was the best specimen of someone living and working the program of anyone

Kris knew. Buddy was the one man he could talk to about the toughest issues.

Isobel had been right. Kris occasionally forgot that he couldn't solve the entire world's problems. But when certain moments of helplessness came along, he felt weak and worthless. Where did such feelings come from? Most recently, when the terrible news of Peggy had been revealed, there'd been no words of assurance he knew to offer Charlie and Esther.

"Well, I'll be damned!" Buddy shouted warmly upon getting the call from Kris. "Good to hear from you, my friend."

"Good to hear your voice too, Buddy," Kris said.

"And how's life treating the young padre?"

"I'll be honest. Not the greatest, Buddy."

"Is that so? Well, Kris, my boy, let me hear about it."

There were tears rolling down Kris's cheeks. But he prepared to let it all out with his old friend.

Tommy was as angry as he had ever been after Greg Chase had called him with the news. He'd immediately tried calling Rick but couldn't reach him. He didn't know how, but he'd have to fight this thing. He couldn't let this happen and destroy Chad's career. Probably no other label in town would touch Chad Harmon if Pioneer dropped him in the wake of the scandal. That such a thing could happen in these permissive, crazy times seemed ludicrous. Tommy couldn't get his mind around it. This was the Bible Belt, yes, but were Pioneer's board people living in the Victorian Age? Something about this simply didn't add up.

It was now late evening. He headed to Chad's place, though he wasn't sure why. He didn't really want to talk about it to Chad until he had it confirmed from Rick. Yet something made him want to check in on his young pal.

Like yesterday, getting no answer at the door, he went in on his own key. There on the living room couch was Chad, passed out. A few beer cans as well as a near empty vodka bottle were nearby. This all irritated Tommy.

"Ya gotta get your damned act together, Harmon!" he said to the sleeping Chad.

But then suddenly and for some unknown reason he stopped. He stood and looked at Chad a long while, pondering what Sandy had said. But Tommy said aloud, "Gotta get a grip on things. That's all there is to it."

Yet no matter what he said, something was now weighing on Tommy. He didn't want to face it, but it was facing *him.* In fact, the day was full of lousy things that had to be faced and dealt with. It had always been his assumption that when a person needs to make a change, they just need to *make a change*. It had hardly occurred to him that there were those who simply were not capable of doing so. Sandy had said something.

The only wrong thing is seeing a person who needs help, then sitting by and doing nothing.

Rick took I-40 to the Old Hickory exit in Bellevue feeling a bit vindicated after the meeting in which he'd arranged things so that Chad Harmon as a recording artist, Pioneer's goose that laid the golden egg, was history. It was now past 9:00 p.m. The meeting had run on for more than two hours. He'd stayed behind to chat with some of the board people for a few minutes.

Earlier that day he'd tabled things with Charlie, feeling it best to do so since the Pioneer board could maybe be onto him and punishing him. But now he'd had a change of heart, and Charlie was always one to forgive. Estelle was indisposed for the evening, a meeting of one of her charities or something. After the stress, the anger, the battle, and everything else today, he was horny. He had tried calling her on his cell but couldn't reach her.

He pulled into the parking lot at Charlie's building. Putting on his cap and dark glasses, as was his custom, he got out of his car and proceeded straight for Charlie's door. He didn't even knock before unlocking and opening the door.

"Charlie?"

There was no answer. Looking around he finally found her in the bedroom asleep on the bed though several lights were still on in the place. He quickly determined that she was shit-faced. He had heard stories about her having gotten sober and maybe being in AA. Evidently that had been a crock.

"Well, what the hell," he said looking at her. Women were often a lot of fun at times like these.

He turned out the lights in the room, undressed, and came to her. Most of her clothes remained on, so he started removing them.

"Bedtime, baby," he said.

Charlie was to later remember this vaguely, a terrible, foggy recollection. She would remember wanting it to happen, yet not really wanting it. She would remember still being filled with grief and guilt, alcohol not really medicating her feelings. She would remember that this time Rick seemed very different, almost angry, brutal, fiercely driven. She would remember him smothering her mouth with his, almost cutting off her breath. She would remember being too physically weak to offer any resistance as he violently thrust himself in and out of her.

But then she might just as well accept that this was who she was and what she was. In the final analysis she was nothing more than Rick Richmond's whore.

PART II

WINTER

Yet time serves wherein you may redeem
Your banished honors and restore yourselves
Into the good thoughts of the world again.

- Shakespeare, *Henry IV, Part I*

18

"AND THAT SIX YARDS will be good for a Titans first down!"

Tommy and Chad cheered along with the rest of the fans. Chad's spirits seemed to have lifted just a bit for the first time in weeks, or so it seemed to Tommy as he observed him from the corner of his eye. The two were attending a playoff game at the Coliseum, the Tennessee Titans versus the Tampa Bay Buccaneers. A frigid wind was chilling the crowd on this Sunday in January. The game had remained a dead heat throughout, and now in the third quarter, the score was 27-24, Tampa Bay.

"I'm going to get some coffee," Chad announced as he got up.

"Aw man, we're gonna score in a minute," said Tommy.

"I'll catch it on the monitors inside," Chad said.

"Might as well bring me some too," Tommy said, hardly taking his eyes off the field.

"Sure," Chad said as he turned and walked up the steps toward the concession area.

Tommy's Club Section seats on the forty-five yard line were a luxury, even on a blustery winter day like this one. Chad was glad that he'd finally agreed to come along. The past three months had been the most trying of his life, but he was surviving. Tommy had finally intervened regarding the problem with alcohol. With his life pretty much in the toilet, Chad had offered little resistance.

Having finally agreed to go to treatment for his addiction, he'd flown with Tommy to Sierra Tucson, a treatment facility located in the Santa Catalina Mountains of Arizona. The month spent there had seemed to be helpful. In fact, Chad realized that as time grew near to leave, he was a little apprehensive about returning to the outside world.

But by mid-November he had come home to Nashville. There had only been a couple of concerts to cancel, the fall and winter generally being more of a down time for country artists, a time to rest from road weariness and a time to write and record new material.

After returning home, Chad had played a few road gigs and a couple of local benefits. He even made another whirlwind trip to New York City with Tommy in December and made the scheduled appearance on *Saturday Night Live*. His performance went well, with only a few news media sources making mention of it being Harmon's first major television appearance since his arrest.

Thus far he had remained clean and sober. However, as friends and associates noticed, he didn't seem the happy, gregarious Chad Harmon they'd known before. But that was to be expected for a while, Tommy surmised.

On the bright side, one new song, released at about the time of the September debacle, had climbed up the charts and made it to number seven. Ironically, the song, recorded during the previous summer, was titled "Great Days," which now seemed hauntingly reminiscent of the artist's former world, the one that had come crashing down.

As for the scandal itself and the subsequent cancellation of Chad's contract, the press had gone on a typical joyride. There'd been the expected cries of indignation from the Harmon supporters and a few public condemnations of his actions from the "holy and righteous."

"Some people just have to get behind a cause. But, ya know, sometime or other people gotta get on with their lives," Tommy claimed. "Just gotta wait it out."

It remained to be seen what would happen as far as a recording contract. For the time being Chad was financially secure, but he knew that living was more than *making* a living. He was born to write and to sing. Many well-known Nashville recording artists at times found themselves suddenly without a record label. That was nothing new. Would *he* find a new recording home? Time would tell.

Chad wore his sunglasses and a Titans cap today. He'd also begun sporting a new set of whiskers. This didn't necessarily keep him from being noticed, but that was something he'd have to get used to. Before, people would recognize him and think of the great new rising country music legend. Now he was certain that their first thought was that this was that guy who got busted screwing around in a whorehouse.

"Two coffees, black," he said to the counter attendant at the concession area.

A huge roar rose from the crowd both seated and standing in the enclosed area of the Club Section watching the game on the television monitors. Running back Chris Brown was making a wide-open run toward the goal line. "*Touchdown, Titans!*"

Chad noticed that the spectators around him, some of them as intoxicated as he'd surely been in times past, were directing their attention to something besides him. Great. He wanted no notoriety today.

"Thanks," he said, paying for the two coffees.

"Anytime, Mister Harmon," replied the counter attendant with a smirk and a wink.

Oh well…

Father Kris had been invited to Sunday brunch with Nelda and Reuben Fairbank at the grand Bel Terre Country Club following the Sunday morning services at St. John's. The Fairbanks had wanted for some time now to have Kris as their guest for dinner or lunch, as well-bred southerners did to demonstrate their hospitality. What if his was the only face "of color" in attendance today? Times had changed, even here in Nashville. Even at the exclusive country club. The Fairbanks and Kris were currently at the dessert buffet sampling the chef's creations.

"What hurts more than anything, Father Kris, is the criticism of people against something they simply don't understand. Why, I've been called everything from a heretic to a psychopath. And from fellow parishioners, I repeat, *fellow parishioners*, members of the household of faith, calling me Satanic or a nutcase or whatever."

"I suppose sometimes people's lack of understanding leads to fear," Kris said.

"And the truth of it is," Nelda continued, "that it's all about helping people, both the living and the deceased, offering them a ministry unlike any other, but an extremely important one."

"Nelda, if I may ask, what would you say has been the…well, the most *memorable* call you've made in your…" Kris fumbled for words.

"My ghost-busting?" she said with a smile.

He laughed. "I forgot you like to refer to it that way. And I hope I'm not sounding like I'm interrogating you."

"Not at all," she said. "Well, let's see…Perhaps it was when I received a call from the father of a little girl who had died of, I think it was…leukemia, yes, that's what it was. They lived over in south Nashville, the Nolensville Road area. Oh, I guess this was about twenty or so years ago. They had, oh, a couple of other children, I think, and *they* were both healthy, thank the Lord. But the mother – I swear their names all escape me – I'm getting just a little older, don't you know – well anyway, she had been grieving something terrible. But the main reason she was grieving was that she was certain the *little girl* couldn't let go of *her*, the mother. They swore they had heard footsteps in the little girl's room and in the hall. And both the mother and the father just knew that the child was terrified, I repeat, *terrified* of death. Well, after the call, of course here I came. We began the usual way, the scripture reading, you know. After a while I asked the parents to speak to their daughter, just say whatever they felt they needed to say to her. They told her how much they loved her and always would, things such as that. It was sort of their time to say everything that was left unsaid to their child at that point. That's something that's very important, Father Kris."

"Yes." Kris was touched by the story.

"Then a little later – and by this time I was truly feeling the mother's desperation about the child's anxiety – I said, 'honey, there is nothing for you to be afraid of at all. And you know your mommy and daddy love you. And God does too.'" Nelda paused. "'Walk toward the light now, honey. Walk toward the light. It's all right. There's nothing for you to be afraid of. Just move on toward the light, sweetheart.' That's a common thing in such moments, you know. You've heard about people seeing the bright lights when they've experienced temporary death, like on an operating table or something like that."

"I have," Kris said.

"So that's what I told the child to do."

Kris asked, "Did she? I mean, did you feel that she 'walked toward the light'?"

"After a moment, yes. There was a little weeping and mourning to be done. Because the poor people had actually let go of their little girl, you see. They could have held on, but they let her go. And, you know, Father Kris, there are times when you might even wonder – I certainly have – whether the visit, the call I made, was more about that, those left behind needing to find the peace to let go, more than being about the departed needing to move on."

"At any rate, I suppose you feel that you've offered a special service to such people," Kris said.

"That's the point, Father Kris," Nelda replied smiling. "Well, have we all got what we're needing?"

The three had finally made their way down the massive table, Nelda having halted the progression now and then to stop and dramatically emphasize a point. She had stocked her plate with samplings of several delights. Kris and Mr. Fairbank had decided on a helping of the bread pudding and hard sauce.

"I think we're all in good shape, darlin'," said Mr. Fairbank, one of the few things he'd said of late, usually content to let Nelda do most of the talking.

"It looks wonderful," Kris agreed, and the three headed back to their table.

"The desserts here are delectable, I repeat, *delectable*," she continued, as they arrived back at the table.

The Titans had managed an exciting win over Tampa Bay, 37-34. Tommy and Chad were now making their way to the parking lot directly adjacent to the stadium, another one of the amenities provided for Club Section members.

"What a game, huh?" Tommy said.

"Yeah, it was," Chad replied.

The two men were bundled in their parkas, caps, gloves, and whatever else might help keep them warm since the wintry weather was far from letting up. In fact, there'd been talk of some possible snow in the forecast.

As they got inside Tommy's Jaguar, Chad said with a snide grin, "On a night like tonight, I'll bet one of Sandy's hot buttered rums would hit the spot. Yes sir!"

"Very funny," Tommy smiled. He started up the engine and headed toward the on-ramp to the interstate. "Would you settle for a hot chocolate?"

"Thanks, but to tell you the truth, I'd like to get home."

The rum joke had actually caused Tommy to think about something that had been on his mind. It seemed as good a time as any to broach the subject again.

"Given any more thought to meetings?" he asked.

Chad balked a moment then said, "Yeah, a little." A pause. "No, not really very much."

"Been a coupla months now."

"So?" Chad knew Tommy's concerns and didn't exactly know why he was prompting him to articulate them again.

"I can't help feelin' like things could get better if you did, man. I hear from a lot of people that their meetings are somethin' they really look forward to...once they get goin' to 'em. And they say that they're necessary. I'm pretty sure that that's what you heard at Sierra Tucson too."

"I keep in touch with the counselor back at Sierra."

"Ya mean *he* keeps in touch with *you*...on occasions."

"I've got you and Sandy to talk to and to look out for me. What more could a guy need?"

Not to be taken in by Chad's humorous affection, Tommy said, "What ya *need* is a sponsor, man. Somebody that's been right where you are."

"Nobody's been *right* where I am," Chad retorted.

"Oooo, soundin' a little bit like a big ol' pity party. Ya think nobody else's ever had his dirty laundry aired in public before? Ever'body's got issues, man. Ever' man or woman alive has got some crap tucked away in a secret closet somewhere. Okay, so yours got exposed for a lotta folks to see, and now people know you're just as human as they are."

Chad was listening. After all, he was a captive audience at the moment riding in Tommy's car.

After a minute or so Tommy said, "Look, life's gotta go on, bud. And yeah, I know you're not drinkin'. But ya need to get …well, ya need to get *better*. You're meant to be somethin' in this world. And there's more for ya in life than you're findin' right now. I really think I know what I'm talkin' 'bout. And I think the professionals at Sierra Tucson do too."

Kris was on his way up the Boulevard following his brunch with the Fairbanks when his cell phone rang.

"Kris, it's Ben."

"Yes, Ben."

"I'm afraid I've got some bad news. Agnes Warfield was taken to Saint Thomas a couple of hours ago. It's her heart again. I got word as soon as I got home from the service."

"Is it serious?"

"It is. Her niece took her to the ER, but she's in the CCU now. I'm here. She's been conscious at times. I knew you and she had a close friendship. I thought I'd better call you."

"Of course. And I'm on my way." He took the turn from the Boulevard onto Harding Road. Saint Thomas Hospital was located only a few blocks away.

Agnes had experienced heart disease earlier in life in addition to surviving breast cancer. She'd had a pacemaker installed several years earlier, Kris recalled. Progressing well into eighty-something years now, she was bound to have become more fragile. The imperious, sometimes overbearing Agnes, who was frequently the butt of jokes around the parish, was a very special person to Kris. Her self-sacrifice for people in ways seldom known to her fellow parishioners had been inspiring to him. He had even found it interesting that, despite her years, she found no age barrier between herself and Kris, nor had she a racial barrier, for that matter.

Soon he stepped off the elevator near the Critical Care Unit. Ben was there, a few relatives, and one or two parishioners. Even Nancy, the parish secretary who supposedly disliked Agnes intensely, was there and misty-eyed.

"She's been asking to see you, Kris," Ben said rather hurriedly.

"She has?" Kris said. The haste with which Ben had said this made Kris think that time must be of the essence.

"She's pretty weak now." Then Ben added quietly to Kris, "But she's as lucid as can be."

Without another word said, Kris proceeded on through the door to the CCU. Hospital personnel, he'd learned, were somehow less apt to question those in clerical collars. So he didn't bother asking if it was all right to go in to Agnes.

Kris had hopefully learned his tough lessons about control. He couldn't "fix" the world around him. Agnes had lived a long and productive life and wouldn't want him to pray for a repair of any situation such as hers just now. *Owe no man anything, save to love one another.*

Hooked up to the various intravenous tubes, she lay still and with her eyes presently closed. A nurse was checking vital signs. When she saw Kris, she smiled and moved on. He approached the bedside and stood quietly. Soon Agnes's eyes opened.

"Father Kris." Her languid tone couldn't belie her weak state.

"Hello, Agnes," he said with a smile as he took her hand.

"There's something I want to tell you, Father."

"Yes?"

Almost like a child who just can't wait to divulge a big secret, she said, "I haven't told Father Allen. I wanted you to be the first to know. I'm leaving a bequest to the youth ministry of the church and another to the Kindergarten. It's something I planned a good while back. It's all been worked out."

He wanted at once to laugh and to cry. "That's wonderful," he said. His guess was that retired schoolteachers could hardly have amassed great fortunes like several of the wealthy parishioners at St. John's Church, but then wasn't the "widow's mite" the most blessed and beautiful?

"My life has been so good. I want to give back. I've also done a little something for the retirement home. I never had to go live there myself like so many of my friends. I suppose I was fortunate. But I wanted to do something for them."

"That's just great, Agnes."

Her voice was weakening all the more with each word, and her fragile hand in his was cold. "You're going to have a wonderful ministry, Father Kris. All your life you're going to. I just know it." The no-nonsense, staid personality he'd known was dropping its guard. Warmth and tenderness had never been the style of the stern and rigid schoolteacher. Nelda had just that afternoon mentioned something about death bringing out those things that hadn't been said but that needed to be.

"Thank you, Agnes. I hope so."

There was a full minute or so in which she said nothing, and then she spoke again. "It's strange, Father Kris," she said, "…but I've been sort of drifting off every now and then…sort of dozing …And, like in a dream, don't you know, I've been sure that I've seen lights, very bright lights off in the distance. I've heard… about that kind of thing before."

"Yes," he said, fighting a lump in his throat.

"But I waited on you, Father."

After a moment he said, "It's all right, Agnes." A pause. "You can walk on toward the light."

Nothing more was said. He held her hand a while longer. She soon closed her eyes, never to open them again.

19

"STILL NO FURTHER EVIDENCE has surfaced in the case of the disappearance of Brentwood interior designer Beth Segal a little over three months ago," reported Carolyn Rucker on the WAB-TV Evening News.

The haunting mystery of Beth Segal and her husband's belated reporting of the fact that she was missing had been the source of gossip, speculation, police investigation, and news stories in all facets of the local media. It had become the premier conversation topic at both the family dinner tables and all the Nashville social functions.

Jock Pritchard had resigned from Burch, Baxter, and Schultz in December and then assumed the position of legal counsel for Segal Industries beginning January 1. However, he had actually learned very little about the Segal family. He'd had the chance to meet the widowed patriarch, Joshua Segal, now pushing eighty, only one time. Mr. Segal was in failing health and of late had preferred to keep a low profile in the community, with all the current publicity surrounding his son.

Jock also had learned little regarding the business of which he was to be a part. It was a precarious time within Segal Industries as employees, along with everyone else, wondered about the fate of its acting president, Mr. Gary Segal. The boot and sportswear company, which had grown over the last couple of decades into a multi-million-dollar business, now seemed clouded in fear and apprehension. Thus, business had fallen off, a few employees had actually left the company during the scare, and no one was certain of who was in charge.

"Here I am on the payroll, and I'm not doing *shit*," Jock said to a friend after the first couple of weeks at the company. "I can't get much information from anyone because there's no one to ask."

He wondered constantly how and through whom one could get acquainted with all the inner workings of this damned company, whose legal matters he was to oversee. Nonetheless, he had his own secretary and an office at the headquarters of Segal Industries in the Burton Hills office complex in Green Hills.

The reaction of Jock's parents to the news of his career change, once he had summoned the nerve to actually tell them, had been about what he'd expected.

"Why would anyone want to leave a firm like BB&S when you have the future you're assured of there?" George exclaimed. "And why would you want to involve yourself in the uncertain situation surrounding that young Segal fellow?"

"But Jock, what on uth will people say?" was Snooks's only concern.

Jock had received the seventy-five thousand dollar retainer for representing Gary up front in addition to his healthy salary as general counsel for Segal Industries. Not only was this practically unheard of, but it was also pretty damned bizarre, Jock thought. No need for his services in legal representation had actually come out of the case involving Beth's disappearance. No charges could be filed against Gary Segal at this juncture, due to the lack of evidence. Jock had offered the retainer back to Gary, who, to Jock's dismay, had flatly refused it.

"We made a deal," Gary had said. "I can't accept it. It's been worth it to have you come aboard with us at Segal."

Keeping the retainer made Jock feel a bit uneasy. He thought it almost unethical to take it. He also wasn't sure he wanted this kind of indebtedness to Gary Segal.

He hadn't once faced Abe with the news about becoming the attorney for Abe's son-in-law and the Segal family throughout these last three months. Abe would surely learn of it in time. Jock had seen Abe only once when Beth had been reported missing, and he'd then wished Abe and his wife the best, telling him that they and their daughter were in his thoughts. He had ceased attending the Harding Road Group.

As for Charlie, Jock had seen her three or four times since her relapse. After being released from Cumberland Heights following her treatment, she'd twice declined Jock's invitation to have lunch with him. He assumed she was heeding the common treatment center advice to avoid new serious relationships in the earlier time of recovery. The people at Betty Ford Center had given him that same shit when he had been a patient there. Charlie was, in effect, starting over with her journey to recovery. He'd been saddened to learn of her relapse but hadn't probed the subject. The sudden death of her friend and co-writer Peggy had probably been the precipitating factor. Damn, life was hard sometimes!

On this snowy Monday morning he sat at his desk sipping his coffee and reading the morning paper as the phone rang.

"Jock Pritchard."

"Hello, Jock. How are you?"

Jock gulped down a scalding sip of coffee before speaking. "Hello…Abe?"

"Yes."

Jock wasn't sure what he should say next. He felt his stomach dropping elevator style.

"I guess the greater question would be, how are you, Abe?"

"Just right," said Abe.

The reply was Abe's standard way of acknowledging that he was in God's hands, in God's will. Ergo, things were just as they should be with him.

"How's Liz?" Jock asked.

"She's bearing up. Actually, better than I thought she would."

"That's good to hear. Abe, I…I'm not sure I know what to say." He might as well clear the air at this point. "I feel…well, embarrassed, Abe."

"Yes, I understand. And I guess that's the reason I wanted to call."

Jock was awestruck.

"Thank you, Abe. Abe, is there a possibility, that we, well, can we have lunch sometime?"

"Of course."

Abe's quick acceptance made Jock feel both gratification and dread.

"I don't suppose there's any chance you're free today?" asked Jock.

"Well, believe it or not, I'm going to brave the weather and go to the meeting at the usual time. But if you want to maybe meet afterward."

"Sure. What about our old favorite, Café Nonna? That way you won't have far to drive home in the snow."

"That'll be fine. Say 1:30?"

"Sounds good."

"See you then," Abe said.

"Abe," Jock said. "Thanks for calling."

"You're welcome, Jock."

They hung up.

Holy shit! How many times had Jock pondered just how he'd handle the situation when finally contacting his former sponsor and friend? And Abe had had the graciousness to contact *him.*

Jock wondered what the group members over at Harding Road thought of him at this point. Did they see him as a traitor who'd sold out, or who had gone over the Dark Side of the Force? People just loved to trash someone in whose shoes they had never walked. Aw well, screw 'em.

For now it was back to the morning paper.

"Abe, I think about you every day. I really do," said Jock.

As planned, the two were lunching at Café Nonna on Murphy Road, just blocks from Abe's home. They had almost finished their pasta now. A light snow was still coming down.

"Thank you, Jock," Abe said.

Jock noticed his manner seemed serious yet not extremely sad or depressed. That much was encouraging.

"I would assume that the not knowing must be the most difficult part," Jock said.

There was a pause.

"It is."

"If I can be so inquisitive, Abe," Jock proceeded warily, "How do you cope? How do you deal with the unresolved, the lack of closure?"

"Doesn't our program teach us that we take one day at a time?"

Jock nodded. Abe continued.

"That's really all that any one of us has, no matter what we're facing. Just today…It's one more lesson, albeit the hardest I've ever faced, in learning to just live and keep doing the next right thing."

"Abe, I need for you to know this." It was hard to press ahead to this, but Jock knew he had to. "I took the position with the Segal family purely as a career move, a step up, you know. I saw it as a means of bettering myself, to find more independence."

"There's no need for an explanation, Jock. We do what we do, all of us. I made up my mind not to take it personally."

Jock felt a twinge of guilt. Abe and Liz were suffering through the horrible situation involving their daughter, and it occurred to him that he had made this lunch date for the purpose of quieting his own guilt more than to comfort his friend.

"That means a lot, Abe, to hear you say that."

After a moment Abe, looking down, said, "There isn't going to be a charge against Gary."

Had this been intended as a question or a statement? Jock had felt all along that avoiding this was better for both parties, but here it was. "It's difficult for there to be a charge without substantial evidence and without…" and he drew his breath. It seemed crass and insensitive to refer to the vanished daughter of his friend that way.

But Abe finished the sentence for him: "...without a body."

Not another word was said for a while. Jock hoped that nothing regarding the case or Gary Segal would be said again today.

After another few seconds, Abe said, "If I could be honest with you, my friend…"

"Please do."

"I meant what I said about not taking personally what you've done with your professional life…But I suppose what has hurt is you're feeling that you had to pull away from me, Jock, to ignore and avoid me. It's not you're taking a job with the family of my son-in-law that I'm thinking about, but your doing away with our friendship. I've been your sponsor, Jock, and if that's never to be again, surely you know that I'm accepting of that. But I'd like to think that our friendship could remain."

Though it was tough seeing himself as the first-rate asshole he was, Jock was forced to realize that he'd deserted a great and wonderful friend at a time when that friend had most needed the support of those who cared about him. Apologizing was something Jock had virtually never done in his life, but…

"I hope it will always. I'm sorry, Abe. Please forgive me."

After a moment, Abe said, "I do, Jock. And thanks."

Their waiter arrived with the check.

"And thanks for lunch," Abe said. "I *hope* I'm safe in assuming that lunch is on you, now that you're in the big league of lawyers."

Jock chuckled at this. What a great thing it was to have his friendship with Abe back again.

"Absolutely," he answered.

Ron Wilkins had been Jock's friend since their elementary school days at Edgeworth. They had also graduated from BMA together. Sharing an interest in music, the two had played in a rock band briefly during their high school years. Ron had earned a music business degree at Belmont University and gone on to work in Artists and Repertoire at Sony Records. Like his friend Jock, Ron was a wannabe songwriter.

After lunch with Abe, Jock had happened to run into Ron at the Produce Place, a small neighborhood market just down the road from Café Nonna. The two hadn't seen each other in several years. Jock had stopped to purchase some fresh fruit after deciding not to return to the humdrum of the office for the afternoon.

"So how are things going at Sony these days?" asked Jock.

"Pretty well. Aw, I'm not setting the world on fire, financially speaking, but I look forward to every day coming."

"How many years now at Sony?"

"Eight," Ron answered. "Some people didn't make it in today because of the weather, so the rest of us decided to take an afternoon vacation."

"I just made the same decision," Jock said.

"I read about you and the new position with Segal. Saw it in the paper."

"Yeah. That's been quite a change," Jock said. Then with some disdain he added, "And when you consider my connection with the Segal family these days, I sure as hell can't stay out of the public eye."

"I guess not," Ron said. "I don't suppose you find any time for writing these days."

"Songwriting? Are you kidding?" Jock smirked. "Breaking into a new career is enough to have on my plate."

"Yeah, I guess so," said Ron.

However, Jock suddenly realized the irony in what he'd just said. He was actually still trying to find enough work to stay busy.

"What about you?" he asked Ron.

"Oh yeah, I keep at it. I don't have a publishing deal or anything like that. But I've had a couple of tunes on hold for artists, one of them for Montgomery Gentry."

"Well, that sounds encouraging."

"Yeah, well, as they tell you, it sort of gets you excited, but a song on hold doesn't necessarily lead to anything."

Despite this admission, Ron seemed a happy man.

"Ah well, stick with it," Jock encouraged, though feeling that most people who decided to go the route of writing and pitching their tunes were banging their heads against the wall. "At least you're working within the business, and you have some ongoing connections."

"To a certain degree. It can sometimes help."

There was just something different about his friend from days gone by. Perhaps it mostly had to do with the fact that they'd both matured, but Ron seemed more content than Jock had ever remembered him.

"Say, Jock," Ron continued, "since you're taking off the rest of the day, why don't you come on by my place? I'll show you my recording studio in the back of the house. It's just a few blocks over, on Meadowbrook."

"Sure," he answered, though not really knowing why in hell he did. He'd come to feel so far removed from the world Ron still lived in that it would seem to hold little interest to him now.

"You can just follow me over," Ron said as the two stepped up to the checkout stand.

From the Produce Place there were only two turns to get to Ron's house. Jock followed him as they both drove slowly up the quiet and currently snow-covered street.

The Richland-West End Historic District, between West End Avenue and Murphy Road near the heart of the city, had warmth, charm, and was like a step back into yesteryear. Old homes ranged from grand and elegant on Richland Avenue to relatively quaint on other streets. Throughout the neighborhood were sidewalks, large shade trees, and front porch swings.

The Wilkins home on Meadowbrook Avenue was modest but charming and well maintained. It was a two-story house. Inside, it was tasteful and very livable. It certainly had the lived-in look, but then two children resided here.

Off the back of the house was an extension added on by Ron himself a few years earlier where the small recording studio was to be found. It was a sixteen-track studio. There was a booth for the control board, another for a drummer, and yet another for vocals, plus pretty much all the needed accoutrements. There were two guitars, one acoustic and one electric, both on stands in the center of the studio. There were also two stacked synthesizers.

"There is a girl who works as a clerk at Sony and who writes. She came in just before Christmas. She's into the Gospel thing. She put down three really good tunes. She had her own musicians, people she knew personally, and she was quite a talented gal. I especially enjoyed that," Ron said.

"So you're able to make a little money on the side doing it?" asked Jock.

"Aw, not a fortune. That's not what I'm into it for. I'm mainly just having a good time."

"Well, it all looks great, Ron. I'm happy for you."

Before long each had picked up a guitar, Jock the acoustic, Ron the electric. They played around with a few tunes from their former high school days. After that, Ron, a keyboard player as well as guitarist, went to the synthesizer and shared two tunes he'd most recently co-written with other writers.

They reminisced over the old times at BMA. It was the most relaxing afternoon Jock had spent in a good while.

Soon Shirley, Ron's wife, and their two boys were back from an outing in the snow, and the five of them enjoyed hot chocolate, which Shirley had made. Ron's boys, Luke, eight, and Jacob, five, were spunky kids. They were typical boys, high-spirited, but a lot of fun to be around. They immediately took a liking to Jock, and he enjoyed horsing around with them. He found himself pondering how good it would be to have a family of his own one day.

"Well, if ever you decide you want to do a little more jamming or even maybe put something down on tape that you write, just let me know," said Ron when it was time for Jock to say goodbye.

"Thanks for the offer, Ron," Jock replied. "But I guess my new career is going to be about all I can handle for a while." And what a fucking lie, he thought to himself.

"I understand. Well, I'd say that it's a hell of an opportunity for you, Jock, this Segal Industries thing."

"Believe me, it is," Jock said. "Well, it's nice to have seen you again, Shirley. And thanks for the hot chocolate."

"You're welcome, Jock," she said smiling and taking his hand. "And I hope you'll come back again."

"We'll have to see to it that he does," Ron agreed.

Strange, Jock thought. He was from a well-to-do family and was now in one of the most lucrative legal positions in town. But he was reluctant to leave the humble, happy abode of the Wilkins clan and return to his own home. He was feeling almost envious.

"See ya, guys," he said smiling at Ron's boys playing in the living room. "Enjoy your day out of school."

The boys in turn bade their goodbyes. Ron saw him out to his car, and soon Jock was driving away.

What was it like? he wondered. Not to be guaranteed the sort of financial comfort he had been born into, to have a fairly simple job like Ron's, and yet to have everything that completed your life. No doubt his high school buddy Ron Wilkins had a damned good thing going.

"But then so do I," Jock quickly assured himself.

20

CHARLIE HAD NEVER RETURNED to her job at Pioneer after that last night with Rick at her apartment. But she had returned to Cumberland Heights. Her relapse into addiction had been a devastating one. The Cumberland Heights philosophy was that a person in such a state of despair needed to leave his or her own world for a time and go to another one, there to be cared for, nurtured, and hopefully prepared for a return to conventional life.

Charlie hadn't lost *all* will to go on, or so it seemed. It was two days after becoming intoxicated that she had finally called Esther Bullard and asked for help. Charlie knew that poor Esther, having been Peggy's sponsor, had her hands full already dealing with Peggy's death and assisting her heartbroken parents in every way possible. She knew that another burden was the last thing the poor woman needed. Nevertheless, Esther had come on the fly. She took Charlie under her wing just as if she were her own sick child and helped get her "cleaned up," as she'd put it, in time for Peggy's funeral the next day, though Charlie had said she didn't wish to go to the funeral.

"Yes, you're going," Esther declared in the spirit of a WAC sergeant. So off to the funeral Charlie had gone and there mourned along with Peggy's parents, Esther, and many others.

Esther had also called Charlie's father, who had come to town immediately. She went along with Charlie and her father for the admitting process at Cumberland Heights.

After a treatment program lasting three weeks, she was released. Her father, who had remained in town for her entire stay, went home three days later. Charlie resumed her attendance at the Harding Road meetings. It was terribly painful going back to her home group, with Peggy never to be there again.

A couple of weeks following her departure from treatment, Charlie landed a job through the help of a fellow group member at Dillard's Department Store at Green Hills Mall. Selling cosmetics for Clinique seemed perfect for her, at least to her Clinique employers, beautiful and chic as she was. And Charlie was comfortable enough at the job, not particularly liking or disliking it.

She couldn't bear to return to her songwriting, as Peggy had been her co-writer. She had no idea where life was headed. All she knew to do was to keep plodding along "one day at a time." In fact, for her it was taking *one moment* at a time within a given day. To keep on breathing, eating, sleeping, not drinking or drugging, was pretty much her full-time occupation now, as she waited for life to get better. If it ever did.

Charlie tried to put the tawdry affair with Rick out of her mind, especially the night she'd been too drunk to offer any resistance to him. After finally divulging to Esther her past history with Rick, she asked Esther to call Pioneer for her and to tell them she would not be able to return to work, at least for the time being. After a few days had passed, Esther spoke with the other secretary at the Pioneer office regarding Charlie's need to return to Cumberland Heights, since she'd never had any of her calls to Rick returned. Esther had advised, and Charlie had agreed, that she should never return to Pioneer at all.

Having Esther Bullard as a sponsor was certainly an experience Charlie had never contemplated before. Plainspoken, direct, and plenty tough was how Charlie had always pictured the old broad from the stories she'd heard Peggy tell. And Esther was all that. But Charlie respected her nonetheless.

Soon after her release from Cumberland Heights, she called a locksmith and had the locks changed on her apartment door.

On this Monday evening, Charlie clocked out and left the mall, ending what today had been an early shift at the Clinique counter. The day had been a slow one for business due to the weather.

After traveling a few miles south on Hillsboro Road, her cell phone rang.

"Hello."

"Charlie?"

"Jock?"

"Yeah. I figured you might be on dinner break or leaving for the day."

"I went in at nine this morning, so I'm heading home."

After an awkward moment Jock continued.

"How are you?"

"Fine. You?"

"Doing well. I've been thinking about you and wondering how you were."

"By the way," she said, "Happy New Year. I guess we haven't run into each other yet this year."

"No, we haven't. And Happy New Year to you. Some snow we got yesterday and this morning, huh?"

"Yes. I'm being careful driving home, but actually the roads seem fine."

"I've had no trouble whenever I was out today." After another awkward pause he continued, "I've been sitting around this afternoon piddling with my guitar. That's something I haven't done in quite a while."

Charlie didn't respond.

"Charlie, have you got any plans for the evening?"

She hesitated. "Just a quiet evening at home, maybe reading this book that Esther gave me on spiritual living."

"Great." This was not going according to plan, but he forged ahead. "Well, I…I had this notion about getting together, you and I. I wanted to share with you a couple of songs I've written. It's like, I don't know, all of a sudden somehow I'm sort of cranked up about the writing thing again. And it's the first time that's happened in a long time."

"You're kidding." Trying to sidestep the prospect of seeing him, she jokingly said, "You mean lawyers like you have time for such frivolous things?"

"Oh, plenty of time," he answered, "especially when you're doing next to nothing at work."

She thought a moment. She truly wanted nothing that reminded her of the music industry right now. It brought Peggy to mind, but also Rick Richmond.

"Well, Jock, I..."

"You know, I had an unusual afternoon. I ran into an old buddy from high school. I used to play in a band with him. He took me to see his studio on the back of his house, and we jammed a little, just like the old days. Somehow the old bug bit me, and, well, I'm just having some fun with it this time, not taking it all too seriously, you know."

"So what made you think of me?" she asked.

"Why wouldn't I?" he said. "I just feel like sharing this with someone, and who else would there be? I thought if there's anybody who'd understand and take some interest, it would be you."

He evidently still thought of her as a songwriter. That was the last thing she wanted to be categorized as these days.

"Well..." she groped.

"Aw, come on. How about I pick up some Chinese for us, huh? There's a good place out there near you, I think. And I promise I won't stay late."

She hated to say no, in a way. He was being so persistent, and he had been patient with her for not seeing him socially. "Well, okay," she finally said with a bit of reluctance. She hadn't considered herself particularly good company of late.

"Ah, great. I'll phone in the order and be right out," he said.

"Jock," she said abruptly.

"Yeah?"

"Give me a little time to get home, get clothes changed, you know."

"Oh, sure," he said. "Say, half an hour?"

"Well, it's six twenty-five. I just left the store. Can we make it seven thirty?"

"Whatever you say. See ya."

After hanging up, Charlie wondered for a moment if it had been the right thing to say yes. Perhaps she was giving encouragement to him when she knew full well that she was not up to dating anyone. Almost automatically she dialed Esther's number on the cell. It was considered the proper procedure to call one's sponsor when in doubt or troubled about something.

"Well, I don't see anything to get worried about," Esther said when presented with the situation. "It seems to me like he's just being friendly. And I'd imagine you're doing a pretty good job of keeping it that way. Just friends, I mean."

"Right," Charlie agreed.

"'Course I know Jock from the meeting, though I don't think he's been there much lately. I sometimes think he kinda needs to get his head on a little straighter, but basically he's a pretty decent fellow."

"So you think I'm doing the right thing?" Charlie asked.

"Didn't I make it clear enough?" Esther said. "Sure, honey, I think that's just fine. Might do you good to have a little company."

They ended the conversation just as Charlie was nearing her apartment complex.

"I didn't say there was anything 'sub-standard,' as you put it, about the song," Charlie said emphatically. "I just was suggesting that maybe it needed a little less fluff. Let the words speak for themselves, without feeling you have to dress them up. The magic of country music has always been its simplicity, the down-to-earth, heartfelt human emotions."

Jock, having proudly completed the first tune he'd wanted her to hear and still holding the guitar, had seemed a bit offended at Charlie's comments about the song, even though he'd solicited them.

"It seems to me a song just *is* what it is," Jock said, and to Charlie his tone seemed defensive and dogmatic, much like the confrontational lawyer in litigation. "If it's a bit too high-tone for, shall we say, less educated tastes, well, isn't that the listener's problem, not the songwriter's?"

"Jock, I thought you said you weren't taking things all that seriously this time," Charlie said.

"I'm not. But if I disagree, I think it's my right to say so."

There was a pause.

"Granted. But all I meant was, although your song might say something that's real and from your heart, and though it may be something that means a great deal to you personally, why not see to it that it communicates to others just what they need to feel with you?"

"Some people like apples, some people oranges," he argued. "If someone doesn't turn on to a songwriter's way of expressing himself, that's that person's prerogative. But every creative person has to be true to himself."

"You're missing the point, Jock," Charlie said.

"Well, what *is* the point?" he asked rather curtly.

"I'll tell you, if you'll maybe come down off your high horse for just a moment!" Charlie fired back.

He drew a breath. No, he hadn't intended on an argument with Charlie. In fact, that wasn't what he wanted at all. "Fine," he said calmly. "I've dismounted, madam. Go ahead and rip old Jock a new asshole."

She sighed at his sarcasm but then continued. "When you have a creative talent, I think you should want it to be something that touches as many people as possible. And your talent is obvious to me, Jock. You know what you're doing. You can write, no doubt. But the kind of writing Nashville prides itself in has a straight-forward, no-nonsense approach. And that is what fans everywhere have come to expect of it and to love about it. The turns of phrases are just plain gut-level, honest, extremely human. Any person could relate to them."

He was more subdued now. Deep inside he had to question whether Charlie was right in what she was saying. After all, she was no fool. But if she was right, where in hell did all this leave *him*? "Okay. Okay, so let's say you're right," he began. "The fact remains that I'm a writer who is what he is. I don't know how to be anything else. So, considering what you've just said, what do I do?"

Though knowing she'd broached this topic with Jock before, she said, "Perhaps you really should consider co-writing."

"I know that's the big thing around Nashville, co-writing. But," he said tentatively, "I don't know. I'm not sure it's what I should do."

"Why not?"

"Well, apart from everything else, I'm not too damned sure I could get along with anybody," he said with a sardonic smile.

Without smiling back, she said, "That I could imagine."

He laughed. "Touché."

She now let the faint hint of a smile show through. "Well, are you going to let me hear another one?"

"Like a sheep led to the slaughter?" He was now putting the guitar aside.

"Aw, come on, Jock. You're a big boy. You're not afraid of a girl beating up on you, are you?"

"I'm not into pain, thank you."

"Please. It's what you came over for. I really do want to hear what you're doing, and, contrary to what you may think, I *like* what you're doing. I think it has enormous potential. I really do."

He was a bit humbled now, though apprehensive. After all, she had decided to become a damned critic. "Potential, huh?"

"Yes," she said. "And, believe it or not, I mean that in the most positive way."

"Tell you what. You know the other thing I came over for: to eat. I think our cashew chicken and egg rolls are getting cold."

"Oh, that's right. I forgot," she laughed, rising from the couch and heading toward the kitchen. "I'll put them in the oven."

"And then, *after* we've eaten, I'll let you hear yet another of my finest work, and you can continue tearing me to pieces."

"My pleasure," she shouted from the kitchen.

She was somehow enjoying matching wits with this somewhat arrogant jerk.

Charlie had put on her overcoat to walk Jock out to his car. She loved that feeling of a snowy night and wanted to take it in. But maybe it had more to do with being afraid of him trying to kiss her goodnight if she told him goodbye at the door, although it had been understood that this was not a date.

"Thanks for letting me come by," Jock said, toting the guitar in its case. "And, I'm sorry if I overreacted a little, about the songs, you know."

"Jock, I want to tell you something," she said.

"I'm listening."

"I told you before, and I meant it, I think that your writing is very good. I have to say that there was something truly wonderful that I heard in that last song, what was it…?"

"'Love Me a Little Less'," he said.

"Yes. Jock, it's beautiful. Really."

"But…?" he said.

"What do you mean?" she asked

"Your criticism still holds regarding my writing. Uh, let's see, too 'fluffy' or something along those lines. Needs to be kept more simple, more direct."

"Now that you bring it up, yes. But your basic creativity is there." She continued, "And that's why I still think you ought to consider co-writing with someone."

"Well, though it may not seem like it, Charlie, considering the way I behave," he said, "I also really meant what *I* said about just having some fun with it. Hell, I made my choices a long time ago. I'm an attorney. I guess it's no big deal either way."

"Maybe it *is*," she said. "I think something really good that has the chance to be something great ought to be made great."

"Great?" he said. "You sound like I'm the man to write the next big smash hit. Look, Charlie, you know good and well there are thousands of writers in this town, many of them desperate for work, and all of whom fancy themselves to be the creator of the next number one hit. So maybe at least one of them ought to have his chance, instead of me."

"It's a long shot, getting a song released to a major artist. But I'm not sure that that's all that this is about," she said.

"What are you saying?"

"Are you happy, Jock?"

"Happy?" he laughed. "That's a pretty relative term, you know. There's happy and there's happy. I've got a lot going for me with a new career, in case you haven't heard."

"Yes, I've heard," she replied. "But, interestingly enough, not from you. I haven't heard you say one thing about the new job all evening long. All I've heard about is your enthusiasm over getting back into your music."

"Come on, Charlie, what do you think I'm going to do? Ditch a career and become a songwriter. Boy, just what this town needs, another one of those."

"No, I don't think you're going to ditch a career. But I don't see why you should ditch your music either."

"I'm not. Like you said, I'm getting back into it."

"So why not be the best you can be at whatever you do?" she inquired. Then, without hesitation, she added, "You ought to be co-writing with someone."

Standing there in the snow-covered parking lot, he set the guitar case down on the hood of his car and opened it. "You know, it so happens I have a lyric sheet for 'Love Me A Little Less' right in here. You think so much of it *and* you think it needs a co-writer, well, have at it. By God, it's yours." He took the sheet out and handed it to her.

In total surprise she said, "Oh, no. That's not what I meant."

"Maybe not, but how about it?"

"I'm just not the person, Jock. And besides, I'm not doing any writing these days."

"And why is that?" he said.

After a brief moment she said, "I'm concentrating on my recovery program, and that's all I need to focus on right now." She didn't go on to say that songwriting now made her think of Peggy and that it was too painful. That was her business.

"Seems to me you've been out of Cumberland Heights a good while now. Maybe you need to start thinking about getting on with life."

She wanted to lash back at his impertinence but rather chose to ignore it. "Jock, the answer is no. What about your friend Ron? He might be just the person. You said you go way back as friends."

"He's got too much going on right now. Besides, Ron doesn't have the passion for this song you have. I believe you said you heard something 'truly wonderful' in it."

"Jock," she said trying to pass the lyric sheet back to him, "I'm not taking this. That's final."

With a smile he said, "Neither am I" as he got into his car and closed the car door.

"Jock!" she protested as he started up his motor. "Jock, damn it!"

It was to no avail. He backed the car out and soon was driving away, as Charlie stood still holding the lyric sheet in her hand.

"Well, to hell with you," she said and headed back into her apartment.

As he drove away, Jock considered what had just happened. Had he gone too far? Inasmuch as Charlie was the one person in the world whose affection he most wanted to win, perhaps he was going about it the wrong way.

Winning the affection of Charlie Cohen. Somehow, he hadn't given that a sustained thought for several weeks. His pursuit of a new career had been the main driving force in his life. But he had enjoyed dinner with her, singing to her, and yes, even sparring with her. Oh, for sure he wanted to do more than that with her. Hell, he wanted to jump her bones. But it went deeper.

"I'm in love," he said.

Lush romantic words, especially clichés, just were not his style, either as a songwriter or as a man. Yet, by God, he, Jock Pritchard was a man in love. Time to admit it. He loved and wanted Charlie Cohen.

A half hour or so after Jock had driven away, Charlie had brushed her teeth and was in bed with the book Esther had given her. But she wasn't able to concentrate. She looked across the room, and there it lay, the lyric sheet that Jock had brazenly left in her hands while proudly driving away, the asshole.

"No," she said aloud to herself. "I'm not ready to write again."

And she certainly *did not* wish to give any satisfaction to that idiot, as if he had won, as if he were able to manipulate her.

"So that's that."

She opened the book once again and made what was to be a vain attempt to focus her attention on it.

21

CHAD HAD COME to the meeting more to mollify Tommy than anything else, due to his friend's dogged insistence about the need for meetings. After all, he owed much to Tommy. As it turned out, however, he wasn't entirely sorry he'd come. It was heartening to hear from those who dealt with some of the same issues he faced, as had been the case at Sierra Tucson.

The group called itself the Harding Road Group and met in a house adjacent to a church in Bel Terre. In Chad's behalf, Tommy had researched online the local group meetings around Nashville, and this one had surfaced. It met each weekday at noon.

There seemed to be people here much like Chad had gotten to know at Sierra Tucson, with certain exceptions. At Sierra, sophisticated and educated individuals had been the norm, as one might expect at such an expensive facility. The difference here was that the intellectual and handsomely dressed coexisted alongside blue-collar workers and scantily clad college students. Freaky musicians who had probably been cocaine addicts rubbed shoulders with the bank execs and doctors whose social drinking or other substance abuses had gotten out of hand. No doubt, the disease of addiction was no respecter of persons and was no stranger to those either on Music Row or on Bel Terre Boulevard.

Within this one meeting more than one story had been shared of sexual abuse. There'd been at least three failed marriages talked about and a wrecked career too. Chad momentarily wondered if he'd merely hit the group meeting on a particularly active day. He also asked himself why people should need soap operas and daytime talk shows for high drama when meetings like this existed.

Seated in an inconspicuous corner of the room, Chad had not shared aloud in the group today, nor had he introduced himself to the group when newcomers were given an opportunity to do so at the start of the meeting. It wasn't time for that, he decided. And besides, his notoriety as Chad Harmon was still the big issue. He wanted his anonymity along with the rest of them.

General conversation ensued among the members after the meeting ended. Those in business attire promptly headed back to their jobs, having attended on their lunch breaks. Others chatted and shook hands or hugged one another.

A fellow who seemed to be popular among the crowd, Chad noticed, was a young black man in a clerical collar. It had certainly been demonstrated at Sierra Tucson that the disease of addiction was no respecter of persons or position. And this man of the cloth, who looked to be about Chad's own age, was unashamed to let it be known that he dealt with the same affliction as all the others around him. Interesting.

Without speaking to anyone, Chad moved on toward the door. The meeting had been a good experience, but he wanted to get home now.

It was Friday. Just as the previous Sunday night and Monday had brought snow and frigid temperatures, now a high-pressure system was promoting a thaw and milder weather. Most of the snow was gone from the ground. Arriving outside, Chad put on his suede jacket and headed toward his car.

As he neared his vehicle he heard someone, almost in a shout, say, "You're new around Harding Road, aren't you?"

He turned and was surprised to see that it was the young clergyman he'd taken note of inside now addressing him.

"Yeah," he answered as the guy approached him. "That's right."

"I'm Kris. Kris Hartley," said the guy, extending his hand.

He had an instinctive feeling that the clergyman didn't know Chad Harmon from Adam and was obviously not a country music fan, which actually put Chad at ease. "I'm Chad," he said, shaking his hand.

"I hope you'll come back," Kris said.

"I'm sure I will." Chad wasn't actually sure whether he would or not. "Good meeting."

"Yes, it was. We have all kinds of people here," Kris said.

"So I noticed," Chad replied.

"I guess you know we meet every weekday."

"Uh, yeah. I was told about the website that lists all the local meeting, locations, times, stuff like that."

"Great. Live close by?"

"Sort of. Burton Hills. I have a condo there."

"Ah, that's a nice area."

"Of course, I have a steal of a deal, renting from a good friend right now. I look forward to buying someday soon."

"So what do you do, Chad, if I may ask?" Kris inquired

"I'm in the music business," he replied.

"Really? You know, I thought I might have heard your name."

"So where are you employed?" Chad asked. Then indicating the clerical collar, he added, "It's obvious what *line* of work you're in."

Gesturing toward the large and sprawling St. John's Church directly adjacent to where they stood, Kris replied, "Right there."

"Oh yeah? You're the pastor there?" Chad asked.

"Actually, the head clergy is called *rector*," Kris said, "but no, I'm one of four *associates* to the rector."

"Big church, huh?" Chad said.

Their casual dialogue continued on. Soon, realizing they were on the verge of spending the afternoon in a parking lot, Kris asked, "Would you care to go grab some lunch?"

Chad hesitated a moment but then replied, "I guess I would." Then thinking of the prospect of being seen publicly and being whispered about, he said, "Is there some place, well, sort of quiet in the neighborhood?"

"Well, there's Sonobana over in Lion's Head Village. Are you into Japanese?"

"Sure."

They got in their respective automobiles to head to Sonobana. Chad wasn't sure why he was interested in talking with the priest, but he was. And at least Kris didn't seem morbidly interested in Chad's private woes. Actually, the guy seemed genuine.

Over lunch Chad finally disclosed to Kris the full story of who he was, his profession, and the arrest last fall. Kris seemed interested and sympathetic, not shocked or judgmental.

After they'd finished eating, Kris invited Chad to come to his office back at St. John's Church to keep their conversation going. Though he had a co-writing session scheduled at 3:00 p.m. with Billy Riddle, Chad said yes.

Following Kris back to St. John's, Chad called Billy, who, as it turned out, was not really up to any writing today. They arrived back at the church, and Kris led Chad upstairs to his office after stopping to ask the receptionist to please hold his calls for the time being.

"Tell me something, Father," said Chad after they'd visited in Kris's office for a while. "You seem like you have a pretty good handle on this sobriety thing. You've gone for a lot of years now without a drink, right?"

"A little over ten," Kris replied.

"You haven't had a craving for alcohol at all, in a long time, I assume."

"That's right."

"Never relapsed?"

"No."

"I was just wondering, why do you continue on with the AA thing? Are the meetings still that important to you?"

"Excellent question," Kris said. "In my case, it has more to do now with quality of life than fighting to stay sober. The Twelve Step program is a guide for living, no matter where you are in your journey. The program sort of reiterates everything that anyone of wisdom ever said, or at least that's my opinion. I see the twelve steps as more or less restating all the principles Christ advocated. I think they help a person be a better Christian or Jew or Muslim, whatever. I suppose I need to be reminded of what works because I forget. And a bit of humility and doing the next right thing does work."

Chad had listened with interest. "So you see this as an ongoing thing for you no matter how long you've been sober?" he asked.

"I need the principles of the program more today than I did years ago," Kris replied. "And if it ain't broke, don't break it. Wouldn't you agree?"

Next Chad shared with Kris his experiences as a musician and songwriter, his background and upbringing in Houston, his quick rise to the top in the Nashville music industry, and once again the disaster that came his way last September. It was the first time he'd spoken about himself so candidly since his days at Sierra Tucson.

Before either of them could realize it, it was nearly 4:00 p.m.

"Guess I should be going now," he said. "I enjoyed talking, Father Kris."

"Just 'Kris'" will do," he said. "And I enjoyed it as well."

"Have a good weekend," Chad said as he shook Kris's hand. "Hope we meet up again."

"Oh, by the way, I happen to have an extra copy of the Big Book. Do you have one?"

Kris felt embarrassed at the mention of the textbook of the Twelve Step program, not having kept a copy when leaving the treatment center. He'd been advised to keep one handy of course, but actually he hadn't read it at all since leaving the facility. "Uh, no, I misplaced mine," he lied.

Kris reached to the bookshelf behind his desk and produced a copy of the book. He handed it to Chad. "Let me know what you think," he said with a smile.

Chad smiled and was certain that this guy was on to him. "Sure."

"Oh, by the way," Kris said as he reached inside his top desk drawer, "I keep a calling card with my numbers on it. Since I spent good money on these at Office Depot and hardly ever think to give any out, please take one. Give me a call sometime."

"I will," Chad said and took the card.

They said their goodbyes and Chad was on his way.

At home that evening Chad finished a quiet dinner of leftover chicken and then watched the evening news. Next he picked up his guitar and spent a half hour or so playing around with a new tune he'd been writing.

At about a quarter past seven he went upstairs and got ready for bed. It was early, but he planned to spend the evening finishing the new paperback novel he'd begun a couple of nights ago. After brushing his teeth and firing up the gas logs in the bedroom fireplace, he climbed into bed and picked up the novel. But before he could get started the Big Book that Kris had given him came to mind. It was all the way downstairs on the kitchen counter, he remembered. There was of course plenty of time to read it. He'd get around to it.

However, after a moment, he soon found himself getting up and heading down the stairs for the book. Soon he was back in bed reading chapter after chapter. This was not the Friday evening he had planned, but that was fine. He wasn't bored as he read.

"I beg your pardon?"

"You heard me correctly, Father Kris. She's taken to sleeping in Hunter's room," was the reply.

Kris, just having finished a late dinner at his apartment, was taking a call from Bill Jamison, who still confided in him regarding his wife's handling, or lack of handling, the grief over the loss of their son Hunter.

"You mean all night?" Kris asked.

"For the last two nights," Bill said.

"Bill, I wish I knew what to say to you. I'm so sorry this is all happening. I know it's tough on you. So, she still refuses any grief counseling?"

"Totally. I'm thinking now she doesn't want to acknowledge that Hunter is even gone. A few relatives were in for Christmas, including our son Andrew of course. She somehow managed to talk a little over Christmas dinner, but after everyone left she went back to being solemn and despondent. But…well, those words don't really describe her attitude. It's more like a nothingness, a *lack* of emotion."

"Bill, do you want me to talk to her?" Kris asked.

Bill seemed to hesitate on the other end then said, "Perhaps. I don't hold out a lot of hope that it will accomplish anything. But I don't know what else there is to do."

"Are you both going to be home tomorrow?" Kris asked.

"Yes, we are. I hate to spoil your Saturday."

"Not an issue, and you won't," Kris said. "Like you say, I don't know what I can do, if anything. But I'll try."

"Thank you, Father Kris."

After putting the phone down and serving up a big helping of Kibbles and Chunks to an impatient Franklin, Kris began to ponder the prospects of tomorrow. There wasn't much left to say to Mary that hadn't already been said, he thought.

Lord, give some guidance.

Before he could ponder the situation any further, the phone rang again. Kris noticed it was nearing 10:00 p.m. as he took up the receiver.

"Hello."

"Hello, Father Kris – I mean 'Kris'?"

"Yes."

"Chad Harmon."

"Chad. Hi."

"Hope I'm not calling too late."

"Not at all. I just finished dinner a moment ago."

"Wow. And I thought musicians were the only night people."

"I'm not just a night person, man. I'm a twenty-four/seven person. Occupational hazard for priests, you know."

Chad hesitated briefly then said, "Well, here goes. They tell you at Sierra Tucson that you need what's called a *sponsor*." No response from Kris, so Chad continued. "I know you've heard about such things."

"Most definitely," Kris said.

Chad hesitated again then said, "Well, I need one, I guess." Again no immediate response from Kris. "Could you maybe think about…" Chad said, and then he forged ahead, "…well, would you oblige?" This had been tough for Chad. Asking for help was not his strong suit.

"Glad to," was Kris's reply.

"Really?" Chad said.

"Yeah."

"Just like that, huh?"

"Of course."

"Well, I guess that settles that," was all Chad knew to say.

"I guess it does," Kris agreed.

Chad wasn't able to see him smiling. Kris knew that the AA program was for those who truly wanted it and were "willing to go to any length to get it," as the saying went.

"Call me anytime. Every day, if you wish."

"Oh yeah?" Chad said, then he joked, "Like, anytime of the day or night?"

"Well," Kris replied, "if it's, say, three o'clock in the morning, I'd appreciate your making it an emergency."

"If you insist," Chad laughed.

"Would you like to maybe meet again next week?" Kris asked.

"Sure."

"Tuesday, after the meeting?"

"That'll work."

"In the meantime, why don't you maybe read the book?"

"I'm way ahead of you," Chad said proudly.

"Great."

"Well, I guess that's it for now. Thanks, Kris."

"You're welcome, Chad," Kris said.

"See you Tuesday."

After they said their goodbyes and Kris put down the phone, something occurred to him. He probably should drop by a store somewhere tomorrow and see if he could find a Chad Harmon CD. It would actually be fun and interesting to get acquainted with his new friend's music.

Noticing that Franklin had just finished lapping up the belated dinner, Kris knew it was time for their evening walk. He went to the closet and got the leash, which always made Franklin cavort with joy.

Putting the receiver down, Chad reopened the book, still questioning if there really was something to this working of the steps. He'd give it some thought. Time would tell whether it would make any difference to him personally.

22

"WHY DID I EVER agree to do this?" Charlie silently asked herself. There definitely had to be a streak of masochism in her, she concluded.

It was Saturday afternoon. She had met with Jock to "discuss," as he'd put it, the song "Love Me a Little Less." Co-writing with this egocentric idiot had been the last thing she'd ever intended. He'd called the previous day and proposed getting together and talking about the song. Once he'd shown up at her doorstep, things had actually evolved into a co-writing session. Why hadn't she seen this coming?

They each had their guitars. Their deliberation was going much as it had on Monday night. In fact, it seemed almost a rehash of that same conversation.

"Jock, you asked for my input, and now I'm giving it," Charlie said, trying to keep her cool.

"I just can't see what a two-bar tag on the end of a verse does for it," Jock protested. "It's throwing off the overall structure of the song."

"It just gives emphasis to the final refrain as you go into it," she said. "But Jock, you're still trying to think of songwriting as something so technical, something that would make a good grade in a music theory class. That's a proper strategy if you're out to write a symphony, but not for a country song."

"Oh yeah?" he said proudly. "Do you think maybe you underestimate the demographics? It's been known for some time that people who listen to country aren't necessarily backward rednecks. A lot of educated people, people who care about things like form and structure, have an appreciation for it too."

"Form and structure are all well and good. But emotion, things of the soul and of the human spirit, are what it's most about," she said.

His tone seemed a bit testy as he said, "I don't say that you have to be stuffy about it, but I'm damned if I can see why *every* freaking rule ought to be broken, and why a writer has to go out of his way to show himself unschooled and ignorant." He then took on a gentler tone for a moment. "What's wrong with a little class, Charlie?"

She drew a deep breath. "We go around and around like this, Jock," she said.

"It seems we do," he agreed very matter-of-factly.

"Jock." She paused. "I don't think this is going to work."

"What isn't?"

"Our writing together."

"Who's co-writing? I just wanted to go over the song with you, and get your feedback."

"Oh, *please*! You left the song with me telling me to 'have at it.' And when two people get together to work out a new tune in progress, that's known as co-writing, and you damn well know it!"

"Oh yeah?" he said with a grin. "So we're writing together after all, huh?"

"No, we're not!" she shouted. "That's what I'm saying. It's not going to work."

"Come on, Charlie, so we have a few disagreements. I think that's normal."

"Disagreements?! Jesus, it's like there can be no such thing as anybody disagreeing with *you*, Jock. *You* have all the answers and *you're* not to be questioned. You don't want collaboration. You want someone who'll automatically validate everything you do. Well, by God, that is not how co-writing works!"

"Hey, hey, Charlie, chill. You don't have to get so upset. Sorry if I seem a little opinionated."

"*A little opinionated!* Jock, as far as you're concerned, you know everything, and nobody else knows a damned thing!"

"All right, I'm *sorry*," he protested.

His manner wasn't exactly contrite. That wasn't Jock's style. So why did she feel the tendency to let it go, to excuse his behavior when he acted like an asshole?

"Tell you what," he continued. "Why don't we lay it aside and go for a walk?"

"A walk?"

"Sure. The weather's cooperating. No more frigid temperatures until next week, the weatherman says."

"Well…" She truly had no legitimate excuse, though her mind raced to try and find one.

"Come on, it'll be good for us," he said. "We need to clear our minds. And I think we each need to, shall we say, settle ourselves down a little."

The way Charlie saw it, she might need to "settle down," but Jock needed to grow up. Go figure why she was letting him get away with so much. Surely it wasn't because he was, after all, cute, in a homespun sort of way.

"Well, maybe for just a few minutes," she said tentatively.

The few minutes walk had passed into over half an hour as Charlie and Jock strolled the grounds of Charlie's complex. The sun was shining, and it seemed almost like an early spring day. As planned, at least by Jock, they'd both begun to relax.

"So far I'm still just tending to some simple financial matters. Just bullshit stuff." He was discussing his new job, though "job" seemed a misnomer, he claimed. It was actually more like a new place merely to draw a healthy paycheck, at least at this point. "But I guess when they need me for something really meaty, they'll let me know."

"Jock," Charlie said, "if I'm…well, you know, treading on the client confidentiality thing, you can say so. But I was wondering, has Gary Segal shown any sadness at the disappearance of his wife?"

"You're only as inquisitive as the next person," Jock said. "I haven't actually seen him that much. When I have, he hasn't really acted like much of anything you could describe. He's sort of a dry personality."

"Jock, what do you think really happened?" Charlie asked and then paused. "Sorry. That's one too many questions, isn't it?"

"I'm afraid it is," he answered with a smile.

Charlie continued to feel that Jock was disenchanted with his new career. But she wasn't going to question or lecture him any further about it. They kept walking on.

After a while, Jock looked at Charlie silently for a moment as they kept walking. She looked back at him. "I was thinking …" he began.

"What?" she said.

"I was thinking how grateful I am that you don't seem to judge me or look at me like I'm shit. I mean, because of the career move I've made. After all, Abe and I have been close, as you know."

"Have you taken a lot of flack about it?" she asked.

He thought a moment. "Actually, no. Except maybe from my folks. But I knew that that was coming."

"Well," Charlie said, "I guess maybe you really haven't been around people that much, people who've known both you and Abe."

He almost glared at her. "You're talking about the Harding Road group," he said. "And my attendance – or lack thereof."

"You keep saying yourself how things at the office aren't exactly pressing. You've got lots of time on your hands."

No response. He just kept walking. "All right," he finally said. "So I'm a cowardly little shit. But you're right that I don't relish seeing people glower because I'm the goddamned Benedict Arnold of Nashville, or whatever they've labeled me by now."

"You seem to have drawn quite a conclusion for yourself about people, Jock." she declared. "If someone takes that attitude, that's just the way it is, and I promise I'll put you at the top of my 'feel sorry for' list. But, you know, you're already assuming that they *will* feel that way without giving anyone a chance."

She thought that she almost saw a hint of a smile in his brief silence.

He finally said, "You know, you have a way of pissing me off sometimes, Charlie."

"Ditto," she replied without missing a beat.

Both of them took a breath and then laughed.

"So, I'm no fun to write with, huh?" he grinned at her.

"Oh, I don't know. Maybe there's hope for you. Maybe you'll get better, get more used to taking suggestions," she replied.

"And, who knows, maybe you'll get more open-minded about a little bit of musical sophistication." She said nothing. It was only he who laughed this time. After a moment he said, "I'll work on my…uh, *character defects*, I think they're called. Promise."

She looked back at him and smiled. Maybe there was hope for this jerk. But just then she noticed something as she looked down. She was taken aback to find that they'd been holding hands for the last few minutes, and she'd hardly realized it until now.

"It seems to me like we've already had a conversation a lot like this," Esther said.

"Yeah, but, well, it wasn't a date before," Charlie added. "This more or less would be…I think."

Charlie, committed to contacting her sponsor with her personal concerns, had phoned Esther immediately upon Jock's departure from her apartment. Jock had just invited her to have dinner on Sunday night, and she'd told him she'd think about it.

"Well, are you wanting to go out with him?" Esther asked very plainly.

"I…" Charlie began, "…I don't know."

"Well, it sounds to me like maybe you do, honey."

"Yeah, sure, in a way, I do. I miss going out and having fun. It would be wonderful to just go have a nice dinner."

"Do you like the guy, Charlie?" Esther was never one to mince words.

Charlie found herself speechless. How should she answer that? She hadn't actually posed such a question to herself in a direct way. "Well," she began, "I guess I sort of do. I mean, you know, he's a nice guy. Despite the fact that he can be a real pill sometimes."

"What man can't?" Esther said. "And for that matter, what one of us gals can't be a bitch on the right day?"

Charlie laughed. She knew that *she* was anything but perfect. She could be headstrong, self-pitying, and temperamental. And no one who is perfect relapses in her disease of addiction.

"So you think I should go?" Charlie asked.

"I think you have to decide that according to how you feel," was the simple reply.

"I see."

"Just take things slow. What's meant to work out will work out."

After a moment Charlie said, "Right. Well, thanks, Esther."

"Anytime, hon."

After hanging up Charlie sat and considered the situation. She walked to the couch and picked up the guitar. Looking at the lyric sheet again of "Love Me a Little Less," she began to reread the very sensitive words that Jock had conceived. Yes, it still needed refining, but the essence of the lyric as well as the lush tune had touched her deeply.

Jock was a unique guy. Yes, she concluded, it was okay to like him.

Jock felt as if he had no right to call Abe Feinstein, at least not on the same basis as he had done in the past. He'd hurt his friend. Now approaching him for help was very difficult. Yet Abe had reconnected with him, of his own volition. So, right or wrong, he placed the call.

"Hello,"

"Abe, hi. It's Jock."

"Yes, Jock."

"I hope you're doing well."

"Just right. You?"

"Fine." Jock said as he took a deep breath, "Abe, can I come over and see you next week?"

"Of course."

"Can we make it as early as Monday morning?"

"Sure."

"I thought maybe around ten. That'd give us plenty of time to talk before the meeting."

"Ten will work fine."

"Great." After a second or two, Jock said, "Thank you, Abe."

"You're welcome, Jock. See you Monday."

A damned remarkable man, Jock thought, as he was about to hang up the phone. But just before he did so, the call waiting tone sounded in his ear. He clicked the button. It was Charlie calling with an answer about Sunday.

Come Sunday evening Jock and Charlie dined at F. Scott's in Green Hills. They discussed everything from music to current events. Later that evening when Jock drove Charlie home and saw her to the door, he kissed her goodnight. He didn't solicit an invitation to come inside, but rather just gave her a quick kiss, which she received without issue. She thanked him for a wonderful evening, smiled coyly, and told him goodnight.

Sneaking a peak out the window a moment later, she saw Jock walking toward his car. He leapt up in the air and clicked his heels together before getting in his car.

She smiled. Yes, he's a handful, she thought to herself.

23

ABE HAD GUESSED the intention behind Jock's request to meet, that of resuming the sponsorship. But he couldn't help wondering how they'd go about making things the same between them again. The knowledge of Jock's association with his son-in-law would always be there, a reminder of what had all but destroyed his life and that of his wife.

The thought of never again seeing their precious daughter was something Abe and his wife dealt with every day and would for the rest of their lives. Settling things between himself and Jock, as far as their friendship was concerned, had been one thing. However, the prospect of sponsoring Jock the same as he had done before now suddenly seemed conflictive, considering Jock's professional affiliation. Somehow Abe couldn't quite put it all into perspective.

It took him a day or so to settle the matter within himself. When contacting Jock just days ago, it had been out of his own need to find closure to at least some of his feelings. Now he was going to be asked to humbly give of himself and help a young man who had become a part the Segal family business. What was he to do?

Jock was seated on the living room couch of the Feinstein home facing Abe, as he'd done so many times in the past.

"Abe," Jock said, "I wanted to ask...and God knows I can't believe I'm doing this, because I feel that I basically have no right to do so. I'm a self-serving son of a bitch. But yet you made me feel almost as if I wasn't the other day. You know, I think that's a rare gift you have."

"What is?" Abe inquired.

"Making someone feel as if he's something special, not worthless, not a piece of garbage. And undeserving though I may be, I want to humbly ask you if you could be my sponsor again." There was a lump in his throat. "Will you please?"

For reasons Abe didn't quite understand, he felt tears welling up in his eyes as Jock spoke. It wasn't grief. It was something else.

"Yes," was his reply, and a giant stride was made toward at least some peace, peace as he hadn't known in a long while. Any selfish tendencies he had were being shed. He was doing what was good for someone else and not himself, no matter how hard, and the catharsis was indescribable.

"Thank you, Abe," Jock said, unable to hold his head up any longer. "Thank you."

It would soon be Jock's turn to get teary-eyed. He felt honored beyond measure to count Abe Feinstein as his friend.

Chad met with Father Kris after the Tuesday meeting.

He'd been surprised to learn that Kris had suggested they start from scratch, that is, at the beginning of the twelve steps, as if he were a new person in sobriety. He was a little indignant at this idea. He'd been paced through the steps at Sierra Tucson and therefore couldn't see the point. However, he chose not to voice any resistance. He'd let Kris call the shots. For now.

"I'm glad to hear you've read the entire book," Kris said, "And I'm impressed."

"Guess I didn't have anything else really pressing to do this weekend," Chad said.

"And have you made your list?"

"My list?"

"You know, Step Four."

"Oh, that. Well, I kind of did that at Sierra Tucson. They have you do all that sort of thing while you're there."

"You know," said Kris, "I find more and more as I go on how useful it is to reexamine myself in the same way I did when I began with this program. It helps me to see how I can keep making my life better."

"So, are you suggesting that I go through that process again?" Chad asked, trying hard not to sound belittling or argumentative.

"It can't hurt. Everything about this program ends up working in our behalf. As for my own life, I was brought up with spiritual values, and I embraced them – as best I knew how. But I never found anything like humility and self-denial, not really, not until I got into this program. I supposedly knew all about being a decent human being, law-abiding and such as that. But I never really grasped the part about 'love thy neighbor,' especially when I was the one who was right and the other person wrong, or at least as *I* saw it. I never got the part about caring for someone else more than myself, and I never knew what it meant to see someone who was a real jackass as a person who needed to be loved. There was no way I could do any of that before."

This was all well and good, Chad thought, and he was sure Kris meant it sincerely. However, it was hard to buy in to the concept of going though all this again. To commit to an exercise of making a list of all the reasons Santa Claus shouldn't come see him this year seemed juvenile, a waste of time.

"I see," was all Chad said with a forced smile and not really knowing if he'd proceed with what the priest was suggesting.

"I have to tell you, man," Kris said, "I'm blown away by your musical talents. I went to the record store on Saturday and got the *In the Rain* CD. I'm by no means an authority on country music, but I was impressed by the quality of it. I feel pretty honored to be sponsoring somebody so important."

"I don't know for sure how true *that* is anymore," Chad said.

"Well, things have a way of working out in life," Kris said.

That's easy for you to say, the admired man of God.

Kris continued. "All you really need to devote your attention toward right now is your spiritual side. I believe everything else will fall into place if you do that first. Could be that your career won't proceed exactly as you'd planned, but it will be what it's meant to be."

The sunny attitude Kris exuded was actually annoying to Chad. It was hard to embrace the prospects of life not going on in at least some fashion after what he'd planned. What did Kris mean to imply? Was he suggesting that he might have to give up his career? "Sure," Chad finally said. "I guess that's it, huh?"

"Well, if there's anything else you need to talk about, I'm here. Tell me, what are you doing these days, performing, writing?"

"I'm doing a little writing. The band rehearses every now and then for a few road gigs we've got coming up. And my manager and I are searching for a record label."

"I see. Any prospects?'

"No."

"I obviously don't know much about how your business works. But I would think there's got to be a dark hour for everything. And, at the risk of sounding trite, life has a way of moving forward. It all works out somehow."

"I guess we'll see," said Chad, not feeling positive at this point. "Well, I'll let you get to work. I know you have a lot going on, considering your job."

As they both stood up, Kris said, "Yeah well, this could be considered my job too. Please remember to call me anytime."

They shook hands, and Chad moved toward the door.

"I will," Chad said somewhat falsely.

He descended the stairs, went out the set of double doors, and got in his car. Driving away from the church, Chad was feeling more down than encouraged after meeting with Kris. The gray, cold weather was closing in on Nashville yet again, and it was as if Chad felt the cold wrapping up his heart as well. If he never was to return to the success he'd known in the business, then he didn't have a clue as to where he was headed.

He drove on toward his condo in Green Hills. A bit of an effort was needed to move that direction and not toward a liquor store. So often in the past he'd escaped from whatever was negative by medicating his emotions the usual way. It was the first time he'd felt an inclination toward a drink in a good while. And damned if it wasn't following, if not a direct result of, getting into this AA thing, as people had insisted he do.

Somehow he kept moving on toward home. To give in to liquor probably meant self-destruction. On the other hand, he wondered what the alternatives could be.

"I want you to just finish the song. I really mean it," Jock said.

He had made his daily call to Charlie, who was at home, off work for the day.

"What?" she said, surprised.

"I want you to finish it, just as I said the night I drove away and left it with you."

"I'm not sure I understand," she said.

"Charlie, I know I can act like an asshole. You're right about what you said. I need to open myself up to other people's ideas. Co-writing is just what I've needed all along, and I've been too damned self-assured to see that. That's why I'm asking you to take 'Love Me a Little Less' wherever it needs to go. You put on the finishing touch. Although I was being sort of cocky about it when I turned it over to you that night, I think that's because I really knew down deep that you were right in the things you were saying."

Was this really Jock? she wondered. A guy stubborn as hell and with an ego as big as all outdoors was becoming solicitous of *her* ideas. If she didn't know better, she'd swear Jock Pritchard was at last open to true collaboration.

"Jock, I want to make sure I'm clear on this. You're not going to protest at all, no matter what I do with it?"

"That's right."

She couldn't help wondering whether his change of heart had, at least in part, an ulterior motive, a ploy to finally get her in bed, trying to appear the modest, sensitive guy and not a macho creep. But suspicion wasn't a virtue, and for now she would give Jock the benefit of the doubt.

"Well, after all, the song was originally yours." She paused. "What do you want me to do, or I guess I should ask, what is the next step after I do what I do?"

"Let's schedule a time at Ron's studio and demo the song," he replied.

"Oh, I haven't done demo work in quite a while," she said.

"I'll be covering the cost," Jock continued. "Ron's rates are reasonable. I guess we need to also consider taking in one or two other tunes, as long as we're there."

"Yeah, that would be nice," she said. "Are you considering one of your other songs, one of the ones I heard the night you were over here?"

"Why not think about an idea of your own for another song? I know you've been a writer for a good while now. Surely you've got something worth developing and putting down."

She had done that in the past, but that had ended with Peggy. She wasn't sure she was up to revisiting that at the present time. "Oh, I don't know," she said. "I'll think about it."

"I hope you will. And *I'll* get the chance to take a whack at it and let you know what changes *I* think it needs."

"I knew you had a motive," she said, feeling a smile come across her face. "And I'm sure you can't wait."

"Remember now, baby, what collaboration is all about," he said in a playfully patronizing tone.

"Yes, well, we'll see," she said.

"I'm looking forward to hearing what comes of it all. I think we might just create some really hot stuff."

"Who knows?"

He continued, "Hey, tonight there's an in-the-round being done by three writers, one of them being Ron Wilkins, down at Twelfth and Porter's. Would you like to go?"

"That sounds like fun," she said. "I've been to only one of those." She stopped, once again thinking of Peggy, with whom she'd attended an in-the-round showcase. "It was a few months back."

"Can I pick you up at 7:00?"

She paused only a moment. "Sure."

They said their goodbyes.

The evening at Twelfth and Porter's was something she knew she'd enjoy, a small group of writers showcasing and jamming together on each other's tunes for an audience. Recreation of any kind was something she hadn't experienced in quite a while.

But for now there was one thing she wanted to do. She walked to the end table next to her living room couch and picked up the lyric sheet yet again to "Love Me a Little Less." She took her guitar from its case and began working the tune.

24

"*HOW* MUCH DID YOU SAY?!" Father Kris said in awe.

"Fifty thousand dollars," answered Ben Allen.

Ben had come to Kris's office early to inform him that the youth ministry of the church was to receive the bequest after all the proper paper work had gone through. Fifty thousand was a fairly respectable gift for a few of the wealthy parishioners at St. John's Church, Kris thought, but it seemed a veritable fortune for a retired teacher. So much for the "widow's mite" he had anticipated.

"I had no idea Agnes could have managed to save that sum of money," Kris exclaimed.

"My conversations with the BB&S people," Ben explained, "revealed that Agnes pretty much lived a simple life all of her eighty-four years. When she would receive her own inheritances from certain relatives who'd passed on before her, such as her six siblings, she put aside the majority of it into savings. She wasn't worthy to spend other's hard-earned money, she said. I knew you'd want to know about this, Kris."

Kris would spend the remainder of his morning marveling and thanking Agnes. However, more astonishing news was yet to come. He received a phone call from Cumberland Heights late that morning.

"A wonderful gift of fifty thousand dollars is on its way to Cumberland Heights," said the development director. "And it was left in your honor. We wish to say that we're very proud for you and for ourselves, Father Hartley."

Kris knew he could not have been more shocked or humbled. His disease and his recovery program were not things he'd worn on his sleeve. He'd never spoken about it openly from the pulpit or in general conversations with church folk, and certainly never with Agnes personally. Yet somehow she'd learned the truth and had had such respect for it, she'd done this in his name. This was almost more than he could stand.

When Agnes had followed destiny and "walked toward the light," it had meant that others were now to benefit from her life, perhaps far more so than when she'd lived. No doubt, parishioners who'd talked about, joked about, and avoided Agnes, what with her feisty personality and sometimes overbearing ways, would now be forced to rethink their opinions. *We see through a glass darkly.*

That afternoon Chad paid another visit to Father Kris. Chad had completed his most recent step work. The revelation of someone's most protected secrets was nothing new to Kris. No one could shock him with an admission of sordid details. Human beings always needed to talk to someone, and he pitied those in the world dealing with guilt or other issues while having no one with whom to do just that.

"So there you have it, Father," Chad said casually in closing.

Kris smiled. "Congratulations. You survived."

"Yeah, I guess." Then he joked, "Are you going to give me a penance now?"

"No, it doesn't work that way," said Kris. "On second thought, yes, I will give you a penance. Keep going through the steps."

"Just give you an inch, and you want a mile, huh?" Chad joked.

"You got it," Kris laughed. "And, by the way, I promise that your confidence is well placed. I always say that to anyone who divulges anything personal to me, and I always keep my word. Nothing will go beyond this room."

After a moment Chad said, "Guess we're going to get to that part about, uh, what do they call it, *amends*?"

"It'll happen," Kris said simply.

"Ah well, we'll see about it all in good time."

"I'm sure of it."

"Like I said, give you an inch," Chad ironically scoffed.

They talked a while longer. Chad was glad that this ordeal was over, and he frankly did not look forward to any further steps. Nevertheless, he realized that he was feeling better.

The good day that Chad had been enjoying was not to last after leaving Kris's office.

The light flurries were continuing to fall as he pulled into the Walgreen's parking lot on Hillsboro Road. He had remembered needing a few personal items and made the stop. In case the snow did get heavier, which the weather forecast was still iffy about, he didn't want to have to venture out again.

After entering the store he took a shopping cart and headed toward the aisle where toothpastes, floss and the like were found. While perusing the brands of mouthwash he heard a voice from behind him.

"You're the Harmon guy."

He turned to see a middle-aged man of average appearance.

"Chad Harmon," Chad replied smiling.

"Yeah, I thought so," said the man, not smiling. "My daughter had a CD of yours. She bought it last summer. You know how young teenage girls are. I'd seen to it she and my son both quit listening to the rock stuff a good while back, especially with the things I was seeing on MTV. Guess it would have been just as well to stick with rock music."

Chad felt a sinking in his stomach. He turned and started to move on, but the man blocked him and all but got in his face.

"Then I heard about the trash video on CMT after all that mess in New Orleans happened, and I pretty much understood. I wasn't surprised at all after that. Young people have enough garbage to fill their minds up with. But somebody like you comes along with a polished image, and all they need is for you to show them what life is supposed to be like. It's because of you and others like you that the world's going to hell, but I'm sure you don't even care."

"Sir, I'd like to move on now," Chad said seeking to negotiate his way around the man.

"I'll tell you something," the belligerent man said, not willing to let Chad pass until he'd had his say. "You're finished. Anybody with any sense knows it."

"Sir," Chad said, feeling his heart pounding and blood rushing to his head, "I'd like to move on and finish my shopping now. I wish you'd just let me do that."

As Chad was finally able to break away, the man got in one last jab that was loud enough to be heard throughout the store: "Why don't you move to California where all the nuts and faggots are? I'd say you belong there. Nashville doesn't need you!"

Chad simply kept moving, his heart pounding like it hadn't done since the day of the arrest. Somehow the horror of that night in New Orleans was now coming back. He chose not to finish his shopping. He abandoned the shopping cart in the next aisle, zipped his parka, and headed for the door. There had been a moment back there when he'd felt like striking the maniac. The fact that doing so could have landed him back in jail was possibly all that had restrained him. He couldn't verbally respond, partly because he was nearly speechless, partly because he knew there was no use trying to reason with that sort of person.

By the time he got to his car he was still shaking. "Damn!" he shouted after he was inside the vehicle. He had known that such people existed in the world. Maybe it had just been a matter of time until he directly encountered one.

But the last thing that the freak had uttered somehow stuck with him: *Nashville doesn't need you.* Chad Harmon was a past sensation. Damaged goods.

After a while he started up the car. He hadn't gotten the items he needed from the store, but that was the furthest thing from his mind just now. He drove home feeling miserable and angry.

After Chad had left his office, Father Kris considered his situation. It gave him a sense of satisfaction, the help he was able to give

Chad, someone in recovery from his disease. But he kept thinking about Hunter.

Kris regretted that he had been unsuccessful in making any sort of breakthrough with Mary Jamison, who yet remained distant and uncommunicative. He tended to feel he was letting Bill down. But even that very feeling was that codependency demon rearing its head yet again. Playing God was something he simply could not do any longer. Mary, much like her late son, was a case he could have no power over.

It was strange, Kris thought, how Chad Harmon had certain parallels with Hunter Jamison, whom he'd also sponsored. Hunter, though younger, had been quite talented in his own right, resistant toward the program at first, and just as spirited and full of personality as Chad. Hunter had faced demons few have had to face. Yet Chad, on the other hand, was dealing with the demons of scandal, the invasive news media, and now the coldness of the music industry.

But while he pondered Hunter's memory, something occurred to Kris all in a flash. It suddenly came to him how he'd known the name of Chad Harmon when first meeting him. Though not having been much of a country music enthusiast in the past, he now recalled that Hunter had been a very strong one. He was almost sure now that Hunter had owned the Harmon CD and had even talked about Chad Harmon's music to Kris. Yes, that was where he'd heard Chad's name! It had taken him all this time to make the connection, and it now seemed a bizarre coincidence. Strangely, it made him feel a new bond with Chad, and somehow more of a closeness with Hunter.

"You sure?" Tommy asked, talking to Chad over the phone.

"Yeah, the roads are probably going to be getting a little slick after dark," Chad said. "Maybe it would just be better to stay put."

Chad had accepted an invitation a couple of days before to join Tommy and Sandy for dinner along with a few other of the music business folk but now was reneging. Weather was his excuse.

"Maybe you're right," Tommy said.

"Tell Sandy I'll miss her cooking," Chad said.

"Hey, Chad, call me nosey, but is ever'thing okay?"

"Yeah, Tommy, everything's fine." Chad's tone was playful. "Don't worry, I'm being a good boy and going to the meetings, even doing the 'Steps' thing."

"Proud a' ya." Tommy said, though all of his concerns weren't totally assuaged.

"Well, have a good evening, and I'll see you guys soon," Chad said.

"Sure," Tommy replied. "If you change your mind, the door's always open."

Afternoon passed into evening. Chad flipped through a few magazines, turned the television on to channel surf, ate a brief bite of dinner, showered, and then switched on the gas logs in his fireplace.

But he couldn't forget the encounter with the raving lunatic at Walgreen's. He also couldn't put his musical future and all of its uncertainty out of his mind.

Sometimes when a person squirms long enough, bothered by something, it finally occurs to him to ask for help, Father Kris often said. He had told Chad to call anytime. That was what a sponsor was for, he'd insisted. Chad somehow wasn't inclined to immediately do so.

Biting the bullet, he finally made the call. There was nothing else left to do. After Kris answered, Chad relayed the whole story; the incident at Walgreen's, the volatile anger that he'd felt, and his fears regarding the future prospects for his musical career.

"I don't know if you tend to talk like an analyst," Chad said. "But before you have a chance to ask *how I feel* about all this, I'm going to tell you exactly *what* I felt at that moment. I felt like hitting that crazy, sick son of a bitch in the nose."

"So noted," was Kris's reply. "I understand, man. And I'm sorry you had such a rotten afternoon. But you know, I can assure you that a guy like the one you're describing has a lot more issues in his own life than even he knows."

"But what does a creep like that gain from saying something like that to somebody?"

"Relax, Chad. I know the type of person you're talking about. You just happened to be in his path. You provided him the outlet he needed for venting the anger and whatever else has been boiling over in his mind.

"But let's talk about you instead of him. We all have moments where someone else upsets us, though, believe me, I recognize that your moment seems like a doozey when compared to some others. However, the lesson is the same: Don't let another person determine how you're going to feel."

There was a momentary silence.

"Say that again?" Chad said.

"Other people are going to anger you, disappoint you, frighten you, make you sad, all kinds of things. And that includes people you love as well as people like this guy whom you don't even know. That's the story of most anybody's life. But, you know, the world is made up of people, flesh and blood, who are just trying to find their way, like you. And they're going to let you down now and then, maybe even piss you off, that is, if you tend to depend on them to always please you.

"But each person, and that means *you*, is responsible for his own happiness. Serenity happens inside of *you*. It doesn't come from the world around you, or from other people doing things the way you think they should." Kris paused and then asked, "Am I making any sense?" There was quiet on the other end for a moment. "Chad?"

"Yeah, I'm here," he replied. "I'm just thinking."

"Good."

"But don't I have a right to feel some outrage over something like this?" Chad asked.

"You'd hardly be human if you didn't have that tendency. But that's different from letting it take control of you. The asshole – I'm talking in your terms – probably is not bothered a bit right now by the encounter he had with you today at Walgreen's. But you are, despite the fact you feel *he* was the one who was out of line. What's wrong with this picture? And if you let him control how you feel, he's won and you've lost. He's the one you think was wrong, yet he goes on being the victor and you the victim. Doesn't make sense, does it? Don't be a victim, Chad. Don't let him win."

Chad felt there was wisdom in what he was hearing.

Kris continued. "Listen to me, Chad. I grew up a young black man in the South. I suffered some indignities that had to do with my race, though not nearly so many as previous generations in my family. Then I lost my father at a young age, and I didn't know how I'd afford to go to college. I wondered when my time would come, when my miracle of deliverance and justice would happen.

"But I learned that *I've* got to make my life what it's going to be. No waiting around for it. I'm responsible for finding my own peace of mind. If I wait for it to just somehow show up on my doorstep, or for the world to give it to me, I'll wait forever. And life won't get better. It'll get worse. What would be the point?"

Chad would hash this around a good while longer, after he and Kris ended their phone conversation. He at least felt some better because of the conversation. His anger and frustration were a bit subdued.

25

"DEAR SIRS:

I regret to inform you that I must offer up my notice…"

This was scary. Throughout his legal career he'd sought to demonstrate only the most professional behavior. A sense of responsibility, fairness, and decency was the hallmark of a great attorney. Or at least those had been the words of one very idealistic law school instructor in Jock's past.

It was Monday morning and Jock Pritchard, sitting at his office computer, was drafting a letter of resignation from his position at Segal Industries, which he planned to present as soon as possible.

"...I realize that my assuming this position only to resign within weeks must seem unprofessional at best. Yet for me to remain in a position to which I cannot wholeheartedly devote myself is all the worse for your company. Segal Industries needs and deserves a legal representative who can serve the company and effectively meet its needs. I'm sorry to say that I feel I cannot."

In addition, Jock made out a check returning the full seventy-five thousand dollar retainer to Gary. It seemed, at least at this juncture, that Segal wasn't going to need any representation in litigation.

How the hell could he have ever considered taking a job like this with a hope of being fulfilled in it? But he knew the answer.

This was all a result of his consuming desire to rise to a high level of importance and "respectability."

Due to the unsettled nature of the company these days, he was in a quandary over exactly how to tender this resignation. Should it be mailed to someone in the family? That seemed a coward's way out. No, he'd have to call Gary and ask to meet at the Burton Hills office. He recoiled at the thought. Perhaps the strongest reason he was not continuing was the intense desire not to have anything further to do with Gary Segal. But it seemed the only proper way to go about it.

As he sat in his office, idle as he'd been since his arrival, it was almost funny how his mind was already racing ahead to things like the scheduled recording session with Charlie over at Ron's and writing more songs. Furthest from his mind were new job prospects and how to go about searching for them. Had he gone crazy at last?

Summoning all the courage he could, he picked up the phone and dialed Gary's home number. After a couple of rings, Gary picked up. They scheduled a 4:00 p.m. meeting. Gary would be at the office by then, he said.

"No way!" Charlie said, almost incredulous at what Jock had just told her.

"It's true, babe," he said.

"If you don't mind my asking, how did Gary Segal react?"

"We don't meet till 4:00 p.m. today. I have the letter all ready."

"Well, what are you going to do now, now that you're through at Segal's?"

"I wish I knew."

"You're not even concerned about that, are you?"

"There's plenty of time to do that. I gotta get through this last meeting with Segal today first."

The two were sitting in his car outside Dillard's in the Green Hills Mall parking lot. He had met her there at 11:00 a.m. and she had left her car, so that the two might grab an early lunch at the nearby Green Hills Grille. Charlie was due at work at 12:30. He'd saved the news until after lunch, so they could simply eat and enjoy one another's company.

"Jock," she said, "I'm proud of you. I know you've done the right thing."

Hearing these words from Charlie meant more to him than anything else, he thought to himself. "Thank you, Charlie."

She then leaned over and kissed his cheek, which delighted him even more but made him thankful, for modesty's sake, that he was in a sitting position, so as not to embarrass himself. All kisses between them thus far had been initiated by Jock, and their relationship hadn't yet made it to the bedroom.

"Well, duty calls," she said, gathering her purse.

"Are we going to run the tunes tonight?"

"Well, I'll work until 10:00, and I have early shift tomorrow. Can it wait until tomorrow night?"

"Sure," he said, though disappointed.

"But I'll tell you what," she consoled. "I'll cook a special dinner tomorrow night, and we'll celebrate then."

"Gee, I never celebrated *quitting* a job before," he laughed. "But you got a deal."

"But I want to call you during dinner break and find out how it went with Segal. Will you be home?"

"If not, I'll be on my cell," he said.

"Right," she said, opening the car door.

Taking her arm, Jock drew her closer. It was he who gave a kiss to her this time and not on the cheek. She found herself wanting to melt in his arms right then and there.

When they finally pulled away from one other, she smiled a bit sheepishly. "Bye," she said and got out.

"Bye," he answered, never taking his eyes off of her as she walked away. In fact he sat watching until she disappeared from sight before even starting up the car.

"God, she is one wonderful woman!"

The meeting with Gary Segal went as Jock had expected. Segal's first reaction had been one of surprise. But he never became angry or antagonistic.

"There's no way we can persuade you to change your mind?"

"I'm sorry. I'm afraid not."

Finally they parted company with a handshake and Jock's deepest apologies for having, to at least some extent, wasted the company's time. He also handed to Segal a separate envelope with the check for the full amount of the retainer. Segal hadn't really protested, nor had he gone out of his way to persuade Jock to stay on. Jock now knew that he'd been hired mainly to be on hand as a litigating attorney for Gary, when and if his services were needed. It was becoming more and more evident that such services were probably never to be needed at all. There was no solid case against Gary.

It was over. Time to pack his things and go.

Jock received the call from Charlie at her dinner hour to learn how the meeting had gone. He decided to call her again late that night after she'd gotten home. He was a bit lonely and wanted to talk to her since he was not going to be seeing her that evening.

"What did you do all evening?" she asked.

"Fooled around with the guitar, of course," he answered, "and tried writing a little."

"Good for you," she said. "I look forward to Sunday."

She was referring to the recording session that had been set up with Ron Wilkins at his home studio.

"Yeah, I can't wait," Jock said.

"The musicians are booked?"

"Ron took care of that part. Just a bass and a drummer, that's all. I'll lay the keyboard tracks after doing guitar."

"Are you going to pick me up?"

"How about 10:00 sharp?" he said. "The other two musicians will be meeting us at 11:30. We'll just get there a little early and talk through a few things with Ron."

"Well, it sounds like you've thought of everything. Now Jock, though I'd love to go on talking, I really would, I do have early shift tomorrow, and I need to get some sleep. Which will, of course, allow me to be in good form tomorrow evening so I can fix the dinner I promised."

"I'll let you go," he conceded. "Have a great day tomorrow."

After they'd hung up, Charlie realized she was feeling better and better about things, about her writing, about her relationship with Jock, about life. Maybe she was moving toward normalcy in her life. She had to admit she was feeling closer to a guy who had just up and quit his job with no prospect of another, and she didn't care one bit. In fact, his leaving Segal was the best news she could have heard from him.

She began to undress. She then washed her face, brushed her teeth, and then climbed into the bed with a magazine.

It couldn't have been more than fifteen minutes since she and Jock had hung up that the phone rang again. Charlie smiled. He probably just had to say one last goodnight to her. She laughed to herself, but it would have to be a short conversation this time. She picked up the phone.

"Hello."

"Charlie?" said an all too familiar voice on the other end.

She felt her stomach knot up and her breath almost leave her body. Fear, dread, guilt, sickness in general seized her all at once. It was Rick.

"Yes," she finally said.

"I've been wondering how you were. To tell you the truth, I've been concerned about you."

There was another helpless pause, then, "Well, I…"

"I'd heard that you got back home a couple of months ago, and that you were now working."

"Yes. I am."

"I hope everything is well with you." He paused. "Charlie, there's something I just need to say. If you've decided Pioneer just isn't the place for you, I understand. That's fine. And I truly want to wish you the best."

"Thanks," she said, still feeling very uneasy and almost as if she wanted to run and hide somewhere safe.

"Well, I hope our paths cross somewhere along the way. And I hope they do so soon." He paused. "You're very special to me, Charlie, and I've always thought highly of you. I hope you know that. You deserve the best in life, you really do." She said nothing in response to this. She didn't know what to say. "I'll let you go. I know it's late," he said. "If there's ever anything I can do for you, anything that I can help you with, please don't hesitate to call."

"Yes," she said, knowing how awkward her voice must sound. "Goodbye."

"Goodbye, Charlie."

She heard the connection click off. After a few seconds she put down the phone. Catching her breath, she felt as if she had just run up a few flights of stairs.

Why had he called? What did he actually want? Or perhaps a more pertinent question would be, why was she reacting the way she was? It all frightened her, no doubt because of past history and things she was desperate to forget. She was also angry because she felt almost violated, though he hadn't physically set foot in her presence.

But was it something much, much darker? Was she still drawn to him? The strong, the powerful, and, as she'd once thought, the very caring Rick Richmond, CEO of Pioneer Records, one of the most successful labels on Music Row and in the world. To this day she remained under the spell he'd always been able to cast, and it seemed it would always be that way.

Things had been getting so much easier, so much better in her life. And now this. Why? Why did it happen now?

The good night's sleep that she'd told Jock she needed was not to be.

Throughout the dinner at Charlie's place the next evening nothing had gone awry that Jock could pinpoint. Her lasagna was delicious. She looked radiant as ever. Her conversation had been animated and warm.

But something was different. He saw nothing in her face, nor did he hear anything strange in her voice. There was no tangible evidence, yet something just wasn't quite right. He had gotten to know Charlie too well and become too close to her not to pick up on it.

They got through the early part of the weekend pretty much routinely. But at one point Jock casually asked her if everything was okay with her.

"Of course," she replied, "why wouldn't it be?"

But this didn't allay his concerns.

Sunday arrived, the day of the demo recording session. It was cold and windy. Jock dropped by, picked her up even earlier than originally planned, and they enjoyed a full breakfast at Le Peep in Bel Terre before going on to Ron's.

Laying the basic tracks for the two songs took barely over an hour. Charlie had chosen not to write any new material, as Jock had suggested she try to do. She had simply participated in the development of his.

The bass player and the drummer Ron had booked for the session were fine musicians, quick to pick up the tunes and nice fellows to work with. Jock played guitar. Ron always engineered the work done in his own studio, so he was at the soundboard. Charlie watched, listened, and commented when asked to do so. After the bass player and drummer left, Ron added a few effects here and there, a guitar solo track, a keyboard track, et cetera. A subtle synthesized string patch was added underneath the tune, this done by Jock. The time came for the vocals, which it was agreed, would be done by Jock also. The up-tempo song came first, then the ballad "Love Me a Little Less."

"Two, three, four…" came the count-off heard on the tape followed by the introduction to the song. Jock was poised, with headphones on, at the microphone in the recording booth. He sang the song word for word, note for note just as Charlie had revised it. Jock had proven himself a man of his word.

As the lush tune began to unfold, the efforts of their labors, the fruit of their collaboration, it became difficult for Charlie to listen. The beauty of the song, which was something created from and now sung from Jock's heart, actually affected her in ways that were unwelcome. It was breathtakingly lovely, but she hurt terribly inside.

All at once she stood, grabbed her coat, and walked out of the studio as the song continued. Her leaving was unnoticed by Jock and Ron. Arriving outside, she found that Jock's car was, of course, locked. She had wanted to get inside the car for privacy. For lack of any other option, she wrapped her coat tightly around her, raised the collar about her neck, and walked, taking a brisk stride down the sidewalk.

Tears came to her eyes. She put on her sunglasses that luckily were in her coat pocket and simply walked on. Eventually she wept outright. She cursed her own efforts at seeking happiness. That was something that came to other people, never to her.

Charlie had developed a great affection for Jock. No doubt he was crazy about her and would do anything for her. And to this day she still loved – and still hated – Rick Richmond. How was she to deal with such convoluted emotions?

Jock came outside looking for Charlie before proceeding on with the sound mix. After calling for her, he finally found her a block or so away still walking. Noticing that her face was tear-stained, he asked why, but she offered no answers, at least for now. Finally, disturbed by her state, he drove her home without doing the final mix with Ron. Though she had been crying, she now was silent. He kept asking whether he had done or said something wrong, but she answered no.

They drove into the parking lot of her complex. Jock sought one last time to make a breakthrough. "Charlie, you know how I feel," he said. "And I wish you could just talk to me about whatever it is. We'll deal with it, no matter what. Apparently you're not dealing with it very well *alone*."

After a moment, though unable to look at him, she said, "But, you see, I have to. I have to just work through this on my own, Jock. Believe me, it has nothing whatsoever to do with you."

"I'm sorry, but it does! Because I happen to love you, Charlie!" *Jesus Christ!* He'd said it. And for the first time. And he'd thought he'd never be able.

She closed her eyes a minute, as if unable to bear a certain pain. "I'm going in now, Jock. *Please* don't see me to the door."

She got out of the car and ran toward her apartment. Jock, though feeling almost like a pent up animal bursting to get out of confinement, somehow found it possible to respect her wishes and not follow her.

Charlie got inside quickly. She cried for a couple of hours more off and on before finally calling Esther.

26

"UGHHH!" CHAD SHOUTED in defeat as he missed yet another shot.

He and Father Kris had now played three sets of racquetball at Whitworth Racquet Club. It was Monday afternoon. Chad had preferred playing on a weekday when Kris had an afternoon off. Fewer people were there at such a time, and he remained wary of the public eye.

Kris had by now won three sets in a row.

"Told you I was out of shape," Chad said, struggling to catch his breath.

The next morning the two began a program of running in the early morning with a couple of St. John's parishioners. Kris and the two men had begun the program a year or so earlier. It took a tremendous commitment on Chad's part as they met at 5:30 each weekday morning for a five-mile run on the Boulevard, but he was determined he would do this. For Chad's first morning out the guys generously slowed their pace to accommodate their new recruit's level of fitness.

"We'll have to get you involved in the Boulevard Dash next Thanksgiving," said Kris to Chad.

After this first day's run on a mildly cool morning, Kris and Chad took a slow walk around the back parking lot of St. John's

Church sipping bottles of Dasani, which Kris had had the forethought to bring along.

As Chad worked on catching his breath a sudden and painful cramp developed in his right calf. “Aw *man*!” he exclaimed, favoring the affected limb. “Just what I need!”

“What?” asked Kris.

“A damn leg cramp!” Chad answered in pain.

The two men sat down on a low concrete wall surrounding the parking lot, and Kris instructed Chad to take the shoe and sock off so that he could help massage the cramp out of the muscle.

“Try taking some deep breaths,” Kris coached him.

“You have just all kinds of ministering gifts, huh, Father Kris?” Chad said, still in pain, as Kris kneaded the muscle.

These days Chad found himself more and more at ease with Kris when discussing his spiritual journey. He now thought of Kris as a pal, not someone to whom he was to be held accountable, like a military officer.

“So how’s the Step Nine thing?” Kris asked.

“Funny you should bring that up,” Chad replied. “I’ve been wanting to ask you something. I’m sure you don’t do this ‘amends’ thing in every little situation going back over your entire life, right?”

“If you mean like trying to look up every last person to whom I might have said or done something unseemly all the way back in my kindergarten days, of course not,” said Kris as he continued to work the tight muscle in Chad’s leg. “As for myself, I think the making of amends to someone is for my own benefit perhaps more than the other person’s.”

Chad wasn’t sure he understood.

“I guess we just have a way of knowing when we need to say we’re sorry.” Kris said. “It starts weighing on us.”

With a boorish sort of grin, Chad asked, “What’s your juiciest ‘amends’ story, Father Kris?”

“So you want some good dirt, huh?” Kris said smiling.

“Sure, why not?”

“Well, let’s see. I guess it was back in seminary at Duke when I first got sober. There had been this chick, an undergrad, a really beautiful girl, with whom I’d had a fling. I had very rudely dumped her when I met her roommate, who happened to be even more gorgeous."

"*Woo-hoo!*" exclaimed Chad, amused to think of Kris, revered man of the cloth, as a heartbreaker.

"So," Kris continued, "I felt this need to tell Sandra – that was her name – that I'd been a jerk and that I was deeply sorry. I just somehow knew I had to make those amends."

"Was Sandra impressed?"

"She looked me straight in the eye, agreed with me that I was a jerk, and told me to fuck off. She didn't care to hear anything else I had to say."

Chad abruptly spewed a mouthful of water down the front of his sweatshirt. "*Excuse me?*"

"Not all stories like these are going to have a heart-warming ending, Chad," Kris advised. "Like I said, I look at the making of amends as being for my own benefit, if it's something I have a personal need of doing. Sometimes it's pretty hard. Those that are the most costly to me end up being the most important, and they change *me*. I get better…And I think *you're* better now."

He had indicated Chad's tortured leg, now relieved after the massaging Kris had given it. As Chad began to put the sock and shoe back onto his foot, Kris looked at his friend and was suddenly taken aback. It wasn't a feeling totally foreign to him. *But, Dear God, what's going on?* He tried to quickly put it out of his mind, as he had many times throughout his life.

The two continued chatting a while, said their goodbyes, and headed to their respective homes. Kris had yet another workday at the church ahead of him. Right now there was no time to dwell on such questions as the unsettling ones he was having about himself.

Arriving back at the condo, Chad planned to sleep a little more, maybe do some writing. He'd then perhaps go to the Harding Road meeting.

Melinda, a.k.a. Clarice, back in New Orleans so many months ago, had been on his mind of late. Funny, but Kris's narrative had touched a nerve. Though never one to think of himself as superior to others, or so he'd always told himself, he had taken precisely that attitude in the excitement of the moment so many months ago, when the arrest had occurred. He had behaved as if she were merely the insignificant whore and he the upstanding person, and an important star to boot, one who just didn't deserve to be part of this arrest. And he hadn't said another word to her following the incident.

Strange how the memory kept coming back and haunting him. He had known Melinda for only part of an evening. Some might think he had some serious guilt trip issues, being so concerned about a hooker. But he wondered where Melinda was and how she was doing. She had been unlike anyone he'd ever expected to find in a brothel; pretty, sweet, sensitive, charming, intelligent. Yes, she'd merely been someone trying to find her way in this dark and oftentimes unwelcoming world. Not unlike himself.

Chad knew he'd have to give this more thought. Just what he'd do about it was uncertain.

He received the call from Cora Eubanks only after Cora had first contacted Pioneer Records, had been referred to the Vision Artists Unlimited office, and then had managed to finally speak directly to Tommy Matheson. Tommy had in turn given her Chad's unlisted home number, something he would virtually never do, except in the case of very extenuating circumstances.

"When did it happen?" Chad asked.

"Last night," Cora said. "For some reason he called me instead of dialing 911. I called for an ambulance immediately. Poor man, I suppose he was so frightened and in such pain he just did all he could manage to think of doing."

"And how is he now?"

"He's resting," she said, and Chad could tell she'd been crying. After a moment she continued. "But it was a massive heart attack, Chad. They've hooked him up to all that medical equipment. I don't exactly know for sure how much the doctor is going to be willing to tell me, since I'm not a blood relative. They've asked about his family, and I knew that that meant you, of course."

Chad had thought so many times about Buck, the father he'd grown to despise years ago. His thoughts about the man in recent months had changed to a surprising degree. Nevertheless, he'd procrastinated about contacting him, as before.

He knew that, in his own way, he'd been becoming all the things that he had hated in his father. Chad had let all the people down who cared about him or had been good to him, such as Tommy and Sandy, the band, all his friends, Melinda, and so on. Covering his own ass had trumped everything else all his life. In all the months since beginning his recovery program, he hadn't once tried to get in touch with Buck. Yes, add Buck to the list of people he had let down. The revelation of all this was hard to accept, yet accept it he must.

"I'll get there as soon as I can," Chad said without giving it another thought.

He quickly got the information regarding the hospital name, location, and so forth, and soon they hung up. Next he called Tommy, who immediately had Trudy book the next available flight to Houston for Chad.

"You think you're okay goin' by yourself?" Tommy asked.

"Yeah, sure," Chad replied.

"Somebody'll call you with the flight info."

"Thanks, Tommy," he said and they both hung up.

Next he called Kris at the church. He barely reached Kris before he left for the noon meeting. Kris couldn't help feeling the same concerns as Tommy.

"I guess you have to do this alone, but please get in touch with me as soon as you can, as soon as you know anything, huh?"

The call waiting tone sounded on Chad's phone, and he looked down at the Caller I.D.

"Sure, I'll call," said Chad. "I have to sign off now, Kris. The Vision Artists office folks are calling about my flight."

"Take care," Kris said.

"Bye," said Chad, and he clicked the button. "Yeah."

"Chad, it's Trudy at the office. The quickest I could get you out was at 2:35 p.m. on Southwest. Takes a little under two hours. Got a pen?"

"Yes."

She proceeded to give him flight, gate, and seat numbers, all of which he nervously jotted down. A cab seemed the fastest thing once he'd arrived, so she'd arranged no car rental. "You'll have to hurry, of course," Trudy said, "since they want you there an hour ahead. Oh, wait, Tommy wants to speak to you again."

In a few seconds Tommy was on the line. "Hey, buddy."

"Hi."

"I'll be by to get ya. I'm gonna drive ya."

"Thanks, Tommy," Chad said, on the brink of tears.

"Can you be ready in an hour?" Tommy said.

"Easily," Chad replied.

Chad had no concert bookings for the next few weeks. Only some rehearsals with the band would have to be cancelled. If such an unfortunate thing had to occur, at least the timing was suitable.

Father Kris vaguely knew the story about Buck Harmon, the promising country artist of the sixties, although Chad had seemed somewhat reluctant to talk about his father. He hoped and prayed that Chad had the chance to see Buck before it was too late.

After attending the noonday meeting he arrived back at the church just after 1:00 p.m. Before going upstairs to his office, he stopped at the mail slots to see if he had received any calls or mail, which he had not.

Coming out of the main office was Sarah Greeling, who had dropped by to present a check covering the cost of the up-coming Sunday's altar flowers, which were to be in memory of her late husband Bradley. As anyone connected with the church knew, the wealthy Greeling family had been the parish's most significant monetary contributors for years, both before and since Bradley's death.

"Hello, Father Kris," she said.

"Hello, Mrs. Greeling," he said. "How are you?"

"Very well, thank you. I've been here taking care of the flowers for Sunday."

"That's very good of you."

"Father Kris, it's been months now, and although my schedule remains chaotic, that's no excuse for not at least dropping you a card in the mail. I've wanted for such a long time to tell you how touched I was by your message at the funeral for Hunter Jamison in the fall."

"Thank you. That's nice to hear."

"Bill Jamison and I have served on boards together, and of course we've known one another through church. We were all devastated by the tragedy, and it was quite beautiful to hear such inspiring words. They truly were that to me, and I'm sure they were to the Jamisons."

"Thank you, Mrs. Greeling. Hunter was a special young man to me."

"You know, I'm sorry I don't get to see more of you, Father Kris," Mrs. Greeling said. "I hope that I can have you to dinner sometime. You'll note that I use the word 'hope' because of the way my hectic life keeps moving along."

"I'd consider it an honor, but I do understand," Kris said. "I'm aware that you're heading into a busy time. I've been reading in the paper about the dedication concert and the ball. It's becoming quite the talk of the town."

"Oh, yes," she said. "It's taking far more of my time than I'd planned. But then, I've said *that* before."

"People don't usually realize how much work goes into such an event, I suppose."

"You're quite right. One headache after another keeps arising with the ball plans. But then I keep hearing that the same thing keeps occurring with the concert itself. I heard just yesterday that yet another of the performers set to appear has had to withdraw, and orchestrations for the particular piece he had written had already been commissioned."

A thought came to Kris, and he almost didn't hear her next words.

"But," she continued, "I'll remain determined that my family and I have some of your time, Father Kris. Perhaps after the dedication of the hall."

"I'll look forward to that," he said.

After they said their goodbyes, he proceeded up the stairs to his office, all the while thinking what a shame it was that money, such as the Greeling empire had, couldn't buy another earthly chance for Hunter Jamison. He'd even settle for such a chance for Mary, who also seemed to have, in her own way, left the world behind.

By the time he got to his office and closed the door, his mind was going to work on something else. *Another of the performers has had to cancel.* He had no idea whether the idea was feasible, if he dared to pursue it. Something told him that it would seem almost presumptuous of him, while something else said, *ye have not because ye ask not*. It was certain to Kris that the good we do in another's behalf remains the most important of all our doings.

Nearly a half hour passed after the chance meeting with Mrs. Greeling. He looked in the phone directory, found the number, and dialed. A receptionist answered.

"Could I have Mrs. Greeling's office, please?" he said.

Greeling International was just blocks from St. John's Church. Kris assumed that Mrs. Greeling had been headed back there when leaving a short time ago.

A secretary answered, "Mrs. Greeling's office."

"Uh yes, this is Father Kristoph Hartley. I'm an acquaintance of Mrs. Greeling through St. John's Church."

"Yes, Father Hartley."

"I don't know if I need to speak with Mrs. Greeling directly. But I was hoping to get a brief meeting with her sometime in the very near future."

"Would you wait a moment, please, Father Hartley?"

"Yes."

There was the customary "on hold" music while Kris wondered how strange this would seem to Mrs. Greeling, as if he'd counted the minutes until she could have arrived back at the office before calling. And he'd pretty much done exactly that.

The receptionist's voice came back on. "Can you possibly meet at 4:30 this afternoon, Father?" she said to his surprise.

"Yes. Yes, I can."

"You know where we're located on West End."

"I do."

"Please come to the front desk, sign in, get a security badge, and they'll direct you to the fifteenth floor."

"Thank you. I'll be there at 4:30."

"Goodbye now," said the secretary.

Geez, that was almost too easy.

But then nothing was really accomplished just yet.

Mrs. Greeling's office was warm and inviting, much like the most genteel Bel Terre lady's sitting rooms might be, with fine wood paneled walls and bookshelves, a fireplace, and beautiful yet not pretentious furnishings.

Kris and Mrs. Greeling were in the sitting area. He'd begun with great thanks that she'd agreed to see him on such short notice at this busy time. However, she smiled and assured Kris that she was delighted to see him. Thus, he figured, it was time to simply come right out and say what he'd come to say.

"Mrs. Greeling. I've pursued a career of reaching out to people because I've thought, and still do, that that was my true vocation. There's been someone to whom I've been in a personal ministry. I'll admit he's become a close friend and someone that I think highly of. His name is Chad Harmon. He's a country artist. Does the name happen to be familiar to you?"

Sarah indicated that yes, it rang a bell but that she couldn't remember anything specific.

Kris then gave a very candid account of the sad story of Chad's rise and fall, though in a concise edition. He did not seek to gloss over the truth. He followed up with the report of how Chad was picking up the pieces of his life.

"You know, I seem to recall some very interesting things I was hearing, or maybe reading," Sarah said. "Actually, this was before the scandal broke, I think. It had to do with Mr. Harmon being 'possibly the greatest talent to come along in Nashville in years' or something along those lines. I'm quite sure now that I heard that."

"I've little doubt you did," Kris agreed.

He now felt moved to divulge something else, something that he seldom discussed with fellow parishioners. He opened up about his own disease with which he'd been in recovery for some years now, through the grace of God. Chad, he went on to explain, was someone he was sponsoring in recovery, just as he had done with Hunter Jamison.

Having now said all this, Kris got to the reason he had come here. No sense in turning back now. "I wondered, Mrs. Greeling, if you could be of any help in determining whether a performance by Mr. Harmon could be possible with the Symphony. Many pop and country artists have appeared with orchestras and have done so specifically with the Nashville Symphony. I've read that some will do so with the dedication concert."

"And would you have in mind that specific concert, Father Kris?" she asked with a smile.

He took a second or two before saying, "Yes ma'am, perhaps I would."

A moment passed as Mrs. Greeling merely gazed into the air.

Kris, suddenly wondering whether he'd maybe gone too far, said, "Mrs. Greeling, if I've…"

"I was just thinking about something. I was thinking how the church has always been there for me, actually for *us*, I should say. There was a dark time in our own lives, my late husband's and mine. It was a good many years back. I don't know whether you're aware of it, Father Kris, but Bradley faced criminal prosecution. Father Jacobs, James Jacobs was his name, our rector at the time, came and testified on Brad's behalf. A character witness."

Kris did remember hearing something of what she was talking about, now that it had been mentioned. It had been a case in which Bradley J. Greeling had been charged with insider trading. It was interesting to hear Mrs. Greeling speak candidly about the incident just as he had been so open with her.

"My husband was far from being a perfect man, Father Kris, though his heart was basically in the place of doing what was right. Always. And, as far as this particular charge went, he was indeed innocent. Finally, and thankfully, he was cleared of all charges. Father Jacobs, we always knew, helped make the difference. But I suppose that's just one of the many instances of the church being there for me." She looked at Kris and went on, "And as long as we have genuine men of God like you, Father Kris, I'm sure it will continue to be there for its people."

Kris felt at once gratified and a bit embarrassed.

"I suppose I can't promise anything. I usually feel it's not my place to involve myself in the artistic matters of the orchestra. But I will see what I can do."

Kris took a breath. "Thank you, Mrs. Greeling," he said.

The two continued visiting for several minutes. Afterward, Kris departed feeling hopeful and encouraged. But only time could tell what was to become of all this. Meanwhile, he would say nothing to Chad.

27

JOCK HAD SPOKEN to Charlie once since the recording session on Sunday. At her request, however, he hadn't tried to see her. He had seen her from across the room at Monday's Harding Road Group meeting, after which she'd quickly fled before he had a chance to approach her. For two days now he'd agonized over the situation, unable to devote heartfelt attention to writing, job seeking, or anything else. Had he lost her? Was she blowing him off? And if so, why?

Come Monday evening, he decided to call Esther Bullard. Surely she knew something, though what she knew and what she would divulge might be two different things.

"Has she opened up to you about the whole thing?" Jock asked with obvious exasperation. "I really need to know what's bothering her, Esther. I want to help her if I can!"

"I've talked to her three or four times about it," Esther said. "She's going to be okay, if you just give her enough time."

"I'd love to share your optimism, Esther. Hell, I'm desperate to. I care for Charlie very much."

"Well now, if you're thinking about cross examining me, I'm sure you know about confidentiality, you being a lawyer and all."

She'd said all this in a good spirit, but *what* she said pissed him off nonetheless.

"Well, it so happens it's all I can think about," he said. Finally thinking he might as well lay it on the line with her, he added, "I love Charlie, Esther."

"I'll buy that. But you know good and well that Charlie's going to have to be the one to talk to you about it herself. It's going to have to come on her own time."

"Yeah," he finally conceded. "Okay, you win."

"It's not a matter of winning anything, it's just doing the right thing, and I think you know that," she said. "Now you listen to me, young fellow. She's a wonderful gal. I believe that, same as you. And I believe it when you say you're crazy about her. But you're just going to have to have a little patience, and that's all there is to it." He didn't respond. "Tell you what I'll do. I'll talk to her and let her know that I think the time's coming when she's going have to talk to you. And that she owes you that much."

Jock's spirits lifted faintly. "Fine," he said.

"Keep your chin up," she said in closing. "What's meant to be is going to be."

He paused then finally said, "Thanks, Esther."

"Any time."

After the phone call, he decided to go for a walk and burn off some of the early dinner he'd eaten and perhaps burn off some restlessness as well.

With a delay in his flight and the cab driver fighting the evening traffic, it was nearly 6:30 before Chad reached the V.A. Medical Center in Houston. Till now he'd come to take for granted the almost small-town feel of Nashville when compared with Houston.

The woman at the information desk directed him to the CCU, and there he was asked at the nurse's station to please wait. Overhearing him speaking to the nurses, Cora Eubanks walked up. "Hello, Chad," she said.

He turned and beheld a somewhat dainty woman, very neatly dressed. The woman his father had kept company with was neither completely unattractive nor pretty. She appeared to be perhaps in her mid-sixties.

"Hi. Are you…?" he said.

"Yes, I'm Cora." And she took his hand.

"Thank you for calling me, Ms. Eubanks," he said as they strolled a few steps down the hall.

"Please call me Cora. I'm so glad you came." She motioned toward a waiting room. "The doctor is with him right now."

"Any change?" Chad asked as they made their way toward the waiting room.

"I really don't know. I can't seem to find out a whole lot." She stopped and gathered her courage. "But he is very weak, Chad. That much I can tell you."

He took this to be her way of saying that she felt it was time to prepare for the worst. They continued to chat. She informed him how Buck's lifestyle had pretty much been routine right up until the heart attack, which had happened early that morning. However, he had seemed to be a little more easily tired out in recent weeks.

After some time and more conversation about the events of the last twelve hours, Cora felt obliged to share something else with him. "Chad, I feel like there's something you should understand. Maybe it's not important to you, maybe it is. But I just think that I should say it."

"Yes?" he said.

"Your father and I, we…" She sought to find the right words. "We have been nothing more than very close friends. Really that's true."

"Well, Cora, I suppose that's none of my…"

"But I wanted you to know, Chad," she said. "You see, my husband passed away less than a year after your mother. My life was over, I thought. Oh, I still miss him terribly. And just like Buck, I have a grown-up son living out-of-state." Then after a pensive moment she said, "I'm sure I'll go to my grave one day having loved only one man in all my life, my husband. And there's something else you must know. Your father has always felt the same way toward Lydia. No matter what you may think, however things may have appeared all through the years, Buck loved your mother more than anything else in this world, Chad. He failed her in countless ways, yes. And he's lived with that regret ever since she died. He's wanted to take back all the past and hated that he couldn't."

Chad found himself hanging on every word she said.

"And people do change. Sometimes, when we get to our lowest point in life, a miracle just happens that changes even the most *unlovely* of us all. That's what happened with Buck. I've never seen a person hunger for a better way of living quite like your father. To say that he's been a completely happy man would of course be less than right, because he's lived with the memory of your mother, all the wrong he did, and how he can't make it up to her because of it being too late."

He focused on a word she'd said. Change. He was learning about change. He'd been undergoing a lot of it himself lately.

"Though he'll never have the chance to make it up to your mother," Cora continued, "he's tried to hold onto the hope that he'd have that chance with you."

Chad realized he was about to cry. "Thank you, Cora, for all your words. They've meant a lot…I needed to hear them."

"You're very welcome, Chad."

There was a pause.

"So…how did you happen to meet, if I may ask?" he finally said.

"We were in the same home group, and it just turned out we had similar situations in common."

"Excuse me?" Chad said. "Did you say 'home group'?"

"Yes, that's right," Cora replied. "And it was just a coincidence that we came into the AA program at about the same time."

"Well, it seems to me that we got two options here, girl."

As it happened, Charlie had dropped by Esther's apartment that evening almost immediately after Jock's call to Esther.

"What do you mean?" Charlie asked.

"You can either tell him that it's over and you never want to see him again, or you can just sit down and tell him the whole truth. At any rate, the poor guy needs to get on with his life. He's climbing walls. He's nuts about you, but I probably don't have to tell you that."

The thought of sending Jock away once and for all was devastating to Charlie. She told herself that that was because it would hurt him so. Yet the idea of telling him everything regarding Rick was almost unthinkable. She felt that she could never have the nerve to do it, however weak and cowardly that meant she was.

"I don't know, Esther," Charlie said, turning away and almost wanting to plead for one more option. "I'm just not sure if I can do either of those things. I hear what you're saying, and it makes sense. But, oh God, I don't know if I could ever tell Jock about the whole…the whole 'Rick' thing."

"What's it really all about with you, Charlie?" Esther asked. And her words seemed to insist that Charlie look her in the eye.

"What do you mean?" Charlie asked.

"What's this thing with Richmond really all about where you're concerned? I want to know."

"Well, I've told you," Charlie said. "There's a part of me that still is affected by him. My God, he's another woman's husband!"

"You know what?" said Esther. "Seems to me you're a girl with average human emotions. Okay, so you feel like the worthless bastard can still get you all worked up. Girl, that doesn't make you a tramp. Taking it and going with it, well now, that'd be different. But I got a pretty strong feeling that's not going to be happening again." Esther drew a breath and said, "What you're really feeling is guilt. Isn't that right, Charlie?"

"Well, of course I feel guilty," Charlie answered emphatically. "My God, look what I did, Esther, and for how long. *Adultery*."

"Do you think there's anybody alive that hasn't got something in their past that they regret, something they're ashamed of?" She stopped to give Charlie a moment to digest everything she was saying. "It's guilt you're feeling, but it's because you're thinking maybe you're not worthy of Jock. Is that it, Charlie?" Charlie didn't answer. "And you're scared to death of being honest with him, because that just might cost you the whole thing. He might not ever look at you the same way again. Might even lose him." Still no response from Charlie. "So what you're doing is keeping him dangling. I think, kiddo, you better consider what's right here and what's wrong." Esther gave one more pause as if to emphasize her point, then she added, "Do the next right thing, Charlie. It's time."

Chad was nervous but not at all hesitant to do what he had to do. No, it was what he *wanted* to do. It had been a long time coming, and he'd been granted this opportunity at the eleventh hour.

Walking into the Critical Care Unit he immediately saw the room to the left where Buck was lying. It was not a room in the conventional sense, more of an open cubicle facing the nurse's station at center, all the patients in the unit having the same type arrangement.

"May I go in?" he asked the nearby nurse.

"Yes," she said politely. "Try to keep it short."

He nodded and proceeded toward his father's bedside. Though already having expectations of a not-so-pretty sight, he wasn't completely prepared for what he saw. Buck's eyes were presently closed. He appeared older and thinner than Chad remembered him. There were several intravenous tubes of various kinds hooked up to his wrist and neck. A small facemask provided oxygen.

The man that he'd decided he hated long ago was lying there before him, and he knew that he'd never really had any hate for him at all. Funny how certain things end up not mattering when one comes down to the final analysis. He thought of the man lying here as the rising country star of yesteryear, now long forgotten. And now dying. A man who had shown great promise and who'd had big-time aspirations was on his deathbed unnoticed by the world.

Chad now realized that the bond with his father, no matter how dysfunctional, had made him call his dad that one time in the last four years. It had not been out of a humble sense of obligation, as he'd congratulated himself, but rather out of the bond he still felt with Buck, albeit hidden so far away that even he couldn't see it.

He slowly approached the bedside. Buck's breathing was very audible. When Chad stood directly beside him, Buck's eyes soon opened.

"Chad," he said, speaking through the oxygen mask.

"Hey, Buck," Chad said.

"I…I can't believe it," said Buck, his voice pathetically weak.

"It's me," Chad said with a jovial grin. "In the flesh."

Both men knew that he was making light of things because of the moment. It somehow helped. Buck smiled as best he could.

"It means more to me than anything else could have," Buck said.

It seemed there should be so much to say, millions of things. Neither one could find the words. Perhaps, Chad thought, it didn't matter so much. He looked at his father lying there, and the release from everything he'd held on to was so freeing that he thought he'd never experience anything like it again. Sobs came forth out of him that he tried to hold back but couldn't. He began to weep outright, and it actually was a bit embarrassing.

Buck slowly and listlessly reached out and took his hand. Chad held it tightly. He then drew closer and laid himself across his father's chest. He was reminded of that same type moment with Lydia. Tears came from sadness, yes. This was a sad time. But it seemed there was sometimes a fine line between sadness and joy. When two hearts are brought back together, which never were really apart in the first place, there is unspeakable peace. Yet Chad did manage to speak one thing.

"Buck…I…" He couldn't get the words out.

"I love you too, son," came the weak voice of his father.

Charlie had gone home and gotten herself ready for bed after visiting with Esther. She knew that bedtime reading wasn't going to be productive, the words appearing on the page yet not making contact with her mind.

It was now past 11:00. Thank God she had tomorrow off from work, because she felt pretty sure that sleep wasn't forthcoming. Sitting up in her bed, the lamp beside her still on, she pondered how simple things could be if there were such a thing as making the past magically go away. It would make so much more sense than the reality of people having to face and deal with crap in their lives.

At nearly 11:30 the phone rang beside her bed.

"Oh God," she muttered.

She wasn't ready to talk to Jock. Why couldn't he just leave her alone for now?

A second ring made her reach, then hesitate. She didn't know what to say to him. How exactly would she put him off this time?

The third ring came, and she knew that the answer machine in the kitchen would pick up after the fourth.

"Jock, give it up!" she shouted at the phone. "You've just got to give me my space. I need some time!" But feeling frustration with him and perhaps ready to tell him so, she suddenly picked up the receiver. "Yes?" she said almost harshly.

"Charlie?"

Her stomach did exactly what it had done the last time. This time, however, she thankfully didn't become breathless.

"Rick?"

"How are you?" She didn't have an answer. "I know it's late," he said. "I apologize. And I hope I didn't wake you."

Rick Richmond could be so warm and so pleasant. He had that engaging way with people. Or at least with her. She never used to understand those who characterized him as cold and aloof. Rick's charm was unsurpassed.

"You didn't," she said.

"I'm glad. I just wanted to say hello again. I keep wondering about you and how you're doing." Once again she said nothing. "Charlie," he said. "What can I say? I've missed seeing you."

It was bizarre to realize, yet part of her wanted to react with the receptiveness she knew he was fishing for. The torn emotions, the tug-of-war, were confusing, frightening.

"I really have missed our times together," he said after some silence. "I guess I'll have to go on missing you as a secretary. But I hate the thought of...well, of losing you."

She was determined that this time not only would she not lose her breath, but she wouldn't experience heart failure either. The so-called human emotions to which Esther referred were quite strong. But somehow, miraculously, something else won out over those feelings and took charge.

"Rick," she said abruptly, "I don't want you to call anymore." There was nothing said for several seconds. "Rick...It's over. It was over a long time ago, in fact. I don't want you to call me, and I don't want to see you ever again." She had really done it! She, Charlie Cohen, had been able to do the impossible. "My life is going in a new direction. I mean that I'm getting my life together for the first time. I don't have to live a life in shame anymore. The last time you called you said something about me deserving the best in life. I think so too. I *want* the best in life, not third rate."

While he waited a moment to respond to her, she caught her breath, though she was trembling like someone in shock.

"I guess there's nothing more to say," he said, and she almost felt sorry for him. *Almost.*

"No," she confirmed. Then she added, "Actually, there is one more thing to say, Rick."

"Yes?"

"Go fuck yourself," was her simple closure to the conversation.

She hung up the phone and trembled only for a few minutes more.

Buck Harmon died at 11:50 p.m. Central Standard Time. Chad was at his side. A few other friends Cora had contacted had gathered and were in the waiting room.

Chad was thankful that he'd been the one alone with his father, the one to first notice the horizontal line on the EKG machine. Buck had passed very peacefully. After kissing Buck, he went and gave the news to all the friends in the waiting room. Cora embraced him a moment, and a few others did as well.

"I need to make a couple of calls," he said to them, politely excusing himself.

Walking to the end of the hall where there was another sitting area, this one devoid of people, he took out his cell and phoned Tommy.

"He's gone," he said when Tommy answered.

"I'm sorry, buddy," Tommy said.

"I got here in time, and, well, I'll tell you all about it someday. There's a lot to tell."

"I'll look forward to hearin' it," Tommy assured.

"I'll stay on a couple of days to see to the arrangements."

"Any way I can help, lemme know," Tommy said.

"Thanks. But what he wanted was very simple, come to find out. Cremation, and no funeral service."

"Just let us know when you wanna come home."

"Right." Chad stopped, almost emotional now. "Tommy?"

"Yeah, bud."

"I've never known a friend like you."

Trying not to get choked up himself, Tommy replied, "Well, I'll always be here for ya, bud,"

"I know. Just like you always have been."

They soon hung up, and Chad proceeded to call Kris, just as he'd promised.

28

SEVERAL FRIENDS OF JOCK, young professionals with whom he'd gone through elementary school and high school, had recently invited him to join a group of guys in their early morning rigors of running on the Boulevard. Getting up at 5:15 a.m. for a time of "male bonding" seemed less than inviting to Jock at first, but he'd finally agreed.

That first morning he'd been surprised to learn that Father Kris Hartley from his church was one of the participants in the morning exercise. Jock, not an avid churchgoer, had known the young priest only from a distance, even though they had both the Harding Road Group and St. John's Church in common. He'd felt that he and a man of the cloth probably wouldn't have that much in common to talk about. That is, until today.

Later in the day the two sat next to each other at the Harding Road meeting. Jock initiated a conversation with Kris following the meeting. As most of the others drifted out of the room, Jock came to the point.

"I feel like you're probably well connected with individuals here in the community, Father Kris. I wouldn't doubt you're more closely acquainted with people in the parish than I am these days, despite my being a lifelong member. To tell you the truth, I've sort of drifted away from extremely active church attendance."

In truth, they both knew that Jock hadn't attended church at all in years.

"And I wanted to ask a favor of you," Jock continued.

"Sure," Kris said.

"If you could just keep your eyes and ears open about the various law practices we have represented at St. John's Church, which are many, I happen to know. And if you might know of someone who might be seeking a new junior partner in a firm, a young attorney who's sort of made a public ass of himself by having taken and then promptly quit a job, please let me know."

Kris smiled and nodded. He knew, like most around town, the story involving Jock and the Segal family. He found it interesting, nonetheless, that Jock would be sharing this with him.

"I've been thinking a lot about this," Jock said, "and yes, I'm even willing to go right back into estate tax work if that's what's meant to be. But at any rate, I really do need to go back to work at some point. I don't have to worry about whether I'll eat or not, but I need to move on in some way or other."

"I understand." Kris knew now that Jock Pritchard, of all people, was actually finding a trace of humility in his life. Jock's coming to Kris was perhaps a sign that he was truly seeking a spiritual way of living. Though not exactly sure what help he could ever be, he added, "You never really know what might happen. Sometimes opportunities are just around the corner."

Charlie was at once frustrated and relieved that she'd been unsuccessful in reaching Jock that morning, either at home or on his cell. She didn't relish the thought of telling him everything, though she knew the time had come to do so.

Jock had disconnected his bedroom phone to get some extra sleep following the morning run, and he hadn't remembered to reconnect it when reawaking. Eventually, he had gone on to the meeting, where he always kept his cell phone turned off.

It was a good thing that this was a workday, Charlie decided. It kept her preoccupied and gave her a reason to pace, working on her feet as she did. She finally made the decision that she'd wait until the end of the day before trying Jock again.

Tommy had had an errand to run near the Bel Terre area and had taken a chance on Father Kris Hartley being available. He wanted to meet the "sponsor" whom he'd heard Chad speak of so fondly and who was making such a difference in his young friend's life, plus Chad had asked that a message be delivered. Therefore, he'd dropped by Kris's office at the church, and he and Kris instantly became friends.

"He wanted to be routed through New Orleans for his flight home?" Kris asked.

"He asked for an *overnight* stay in New Orleans comin' back," Tommy answered. "Beats the heck outta me. You'd think that that would be the last place he'd wanna go. I can't figure it. But he'll be home by Friday. So I'm doin' what he asked. He wanted me to let ya know."

"I appreciate it, Tommy. It's good to have the chance to finally meet you." Kris then asked, "Concerning Chad, how did he seem to you?"

"He sounds as good as I've ever heard him sound. He just said there was somethin' there in New Orleans he had to do. Said it was important."

"Well, I guess it must be," Kris said. In truth, he had an idea what it might all be about.

"He was determined. But anyway," said Tommy, changing his tone a bit, "I wanted to say thanks, Father Kris, for helpin' Chad. You see, I sorta took 'im under my wing right from the start. My wife and I both think of Chad like family now."

"So I've heard, Tommy," Kris said. "He feels the same way toward you. He's spoken of you to me several times. Tommy, if I may ask, how's his career looking, from your perspective?"

"He's got a few fairly decent gigs lined up in the spring," Tommy answered. "We're still shoppin' 'im around to some other labels. Don't know where that's gonna lead. Time'll tell. I'm goin' at it every way I know to. And it's sorta hard 'cause it's a transition time in my company."

"Transition?" said Kris.

"I've signed a coupla new writers, lost some others, and I'm maybe about to sign one or two more. Besides all that, my legal rep left town, so I'm lookin' for a new lawyer for my company."

"A lawyer?" Kris asked.

"Yeah. Somebody that negotiates contracts, stuff like that. You see, all my artists, when they get signed to a label, also new staff writers with the publishing house, each song that gets released – ever'thing in the whole business requires a contract, which requires a lawyer to execute it."

"If I may just ask, Tommy," Kris said, "does someone in that position usually have to have some special training or experience, or, well, do they simply have to be an attorney?"

"Well, I guess it helps to be experienced in entertainment law. Most people in that field pretty much do that exclusively."

"I see. Could an attorney just make a decision to start doing that as a new career?"

"Hard for me to say," said Tommy. "There's not that much I know about law as a whole, which is why I need lawyers in the first place."

"I see," Kris said.

Father Kris's call had taken Jock by surprise, to say the very least. He and Kris had parted company barely three hours ago.

He was now at the desk of his home office, his mind feverishly running. Entertainment law. He'd never given a serious thought to such a thing. That probably was because he had been too self-important to consider dealing with the people down on the Row, those toward whom he had always taken a condescending attitude. After all, he'd always felt, that is, in times past, that he surely knew a better way of doing things than any of them.

But it suddenly was a fascinating concept. Hell, yeah! Why not? Entertainment law! Something that Abe had said months ago was now coming back to him. Something about people finding a suitable compromise between different paths that they might have taken in life. At the time he'd paid little attention.

He'd dealt with regrets for so long over not following his heart where music was concerned, yet at the same time he'd had a great appreciation for the law, thus feeling constantly ambivalent. He couldn't count the times he'd felt torn between his two great passions, never conceiving of the prospect of a marriage of the two. He wondered if even Abe himself had known how prophetic his words could be.

Kris had informed Jock that he could contact Vision Artists Unlimited and ask to speak with Tommy Matheson as soon as he wished. The Latin phrase *carpe diem* came to mind, and Jock picked up the phone.

Charlie, working at the Clinique counter, was impatiently waiting for the day to pass. Feeling anxiety, she had managed to rearrange every item displayed on every counter when she wasn't waiting on a customer. As the time dragged, she became more and more fretful. A great guy had loved her for a long time now, and she'd been too mixed up to appreciate it. It was as if this was her punishment.

At a little after 5:00 p.m., with just under an hour until she was to be off work, she looked across the aisle at the Elizabeth Arden counter and saw a very lovely woman, a customer who looked strangely familiar. In a split second Charlie realized the woman's identity, and her heart immediately palpitated.

Estelle Richmond.

No sooner had this realization come than the ringing of a cell phone in Mrs. Richmond's purse was heard. Estelle quickly took it out.

"Hello."

Charlie tried to busy herself once again and not even look in Estelle's direction, let alone eavesdrop. But she couldn't help overhearing her words.

"Yes…Oh, not again…Well, of course if you can't get out of it…How late?…Oh, I see." There was deep disappointment in her voice. "…No, I'll just let Mirella go home early, and I'll fix something for myself…Yes, Rick, I – I understand…Of course…Yes…Goodbye."

Charlie stole one more glance in Estelle's direction. She was returning the phone to her purse. Charlie turned away, trying to look preoccupied again, but in doing so she knocked a few bottles of exfoliant off the counter. She nervously bent down, picked them up, and reorganized them onto the counter, trying desperately to appear unshaken. As she sneaked one last peek, she could almost swear Estelle was wiping away a tear.

But in a split second her heart raced again as Estelle was giving up on Liz Arden and coming over to the Clinique counter! Before she could think of what to do, Estelle addressed her.

"Pardon me, miss," she said, with unhidden heartbreak in her face. "Could you show me whatever wonderful new products you might have in?"

Charlie took a breath. "New products?"

"I suppose that sounds a little vague." She smiled poignantly. "I just mean that I would like to see whatever new and promising things you might have…that might help a middle-aged woman become newly beautiful."

At that moment Charlie felt more compassion than she had perhaps ever felt for anyone in her life. Her fear and nervousness were replaced now by pity. Estelle was a broken woman trying desperately to win back the love of her husband. The husband who found his satisfaction elsewhere.

Charlie set out to help her in whatever way she might. "Well," she said, "we do have this new foundation just in…"

Tommy had put off meeting with Jock until 6:30 due to a late afternoon appointment already scheduled. They met and talked at length, until finally Tommy invited Jock to join him for dinner at Sunset Grill in nearby Hillsboro Village, so that they could continue their discussion. Jock became even more excited over the business and all it might now entail for him.

Charlie, after leaving work at 6:00, was to find even more frustration in trying to reach Jock, who'd turned his cell phone off yet again while heavily involved in conversation with Tommy.

Charlie could almost hear even now what Esther would say: Jock had waited a long time, now *she* could wait, and what's meant to be is going to be.

Tommy and Jock finished their dinner and kept talking for a while. At about 9:30 Tommy suggested they make a run back over to the Vision Artists office so that he could give Jock copies of a few of the company's past contracts on file there. They departed after Tommy sprang for the dinner, as he'd insisted. The two men then returned to the office for another forty-five minutes discussing some details.

Charlie went to bed in defeat by 10:30 p.m., exhausted from all her efforts and the frustration of not reaching Jock.

29

"CORA," SAID CHAD over the cell phone while riding in a cab now nearing the Houston Airport, "there's no way I could ever thank you for what you've done. You've made the difference for Buck and me."

"It meant a lot to *me* to help," said Cora. "You see, Chad, Buck had become my best friend."

"I'm almost at the airport. I'd better sign off."

"Goodbye, Chad."

"Thank you again, Cora."

He closed the cell phone, paid the cabbie, and got out to check his luggage at the curb. He had been booked by request on an early flight out of Houston, 7:35 a.m. on Southwest. The flight time was barely over an hour. He flew to New Orleans, claimed luggage, and went by cab to the InterContinental Hotel, where he'd stayed on that infamous trip to the Big Easy.

After checking in, shaving, showering, and having some breakfast just before the hotel buffet closed, he went back to his room and took the yellow pages out of the dresser drawer. He'd always known that most escort and massage services were listed, but he didn't know exactly how to identify by name the establishment he'd visited with Billy that night. The only thing he could recall was the name Marlene, the proprietress.

"Make Your Day AND NIGHT!...MA-ma MI-a...Men's Night Out"..." It seemed that Marlene's name would prove to be no help in his search, but then addresses weren't listed with the business names anyway. Interesting, Chad thought, that no matter how great the natural devastation a city experienced, such as a Hurricane Katrina, the oldest business in the world would always flourish.

He decided to rest up a bit, having gotten very little sleep the past night. Everything requiring his attention in Houston had been taken care of. Buck's personal affairs had been simple, and easily settled. Chad had given Cora full charge to dispose of Buck's few assets at her own discretion. All that had mattered to Chad was the healing of the relationship with his father, which had happened.

After awakening a little past noon, he got up and changed his clothes. Setting out on foot to find the place seemed his only remaining option. Fortunately, the weather was mild and sunny, which was not all that uncommon for New Orleans in February. And all he knew to do was to start from Point A, which meant Pat O'Brien's. That was where he and Billy had begun walking that night. That much he could remember, though having been half intoxicated at the time. Asking a street vendor for directions, he was led to nearby St. Peter Street where O'Brien's was located. He went on from there, seeking to retrace the steps he and Billy had taken that night.

He took a turn down what he thought might be the correct street and kept looking at all the buildings, trying his best to remember. He was about to give up and try another street when he spotted what he thought could be the house. It had been nighttime then, so it was hard to say. The wrought iron gates on the windows looked familiar. He approached the house. The solid oak door with a brass buzzer located alongside it said that this was possibly it.

He of course felt a lot of trepidation, the memories of that night now rolling over him in waves. But he drew his breath and pushed the button. After a moment, unlike that night, the door didn't open, but a female voice came over the small speaker next to the switch.

"May I help you?"

"Uh, yes," he answered nervously, "I was wondering whether there was someone here named Marlene."

"May I ask the nature of your business please?"

"Yes, I'm not wanting any – that is to say, I'm just wanting to hopefully speak with Marlene. I sort of need some help with a personal matter."

This time there was a pause, and the female voice said, "May I ask your name?"

Aw shit! But he had come this far, and so he finally answered, "Chad. Chad Harmon."

There was another brief pause.

"One moment please."

While he stood waiting he didn't dare look to see who might be watching. His sunglasses were in place, but turning around would give anybody a chance to see at least part of his face.

At last the door opened, and Marlene appeared. She was the attractive middle-aged lady he remembered, although now dressed in a chic blouse and black pants. Her manner was as pleasant and dignified as before.

"Is there something I can help you with?" she asked.

"Yes ma'am," he said. "As I said, I'm Chad Harmon. I…I was here several months ago as a…visitor."

"Yes," she said. "I remember."

"You do?" he said.

"One of the more unfortunate nights. And unfortunate for you, I'm afraid."

"You *do* remember."

"I'm blessed to have a very good memory," she said. "It has its advantages in my work."

"Yes, I…I'm sure," he said. "May I ask, Marlene, if there is still a young lady here…well, she went by the name of Clarice at that time. But I happen to know that her name is Melinda."

She looked at him a moment then said, "Mr. Harmon, wouldn't you care to come inside off the street? We can talk in the parlor."

He balked a moment then said, "Sure."

She led him into the plush sitting area where he'd first met Melinda months ago. They both took a seat on the couch. Chad was torn between desperation to be out of the place and wanting to know about Melinda.

"I'm afraid Melinda's no longer with us," Marlene said.

"She's not?" he responded with a sinking feeling.

"She got a job in restaurant management."

"Restaurant management?"

"Melinda was never really cut out for this line of work," she said. "You see, Mr. Harmon, she was, and still is, almost like a daughter to me. She's quite a special person."

This touched him. "That's interesting," he said. "I recall her talking about you. I think the feelings are mutual."

"We're very close," Marlene confirmed.

"You said a restaurant?"

"Jobert's, out on the Lakefront. It's a fine restaurant. It's managed to get back into business as usual quite well since Katrina. And Melinda's very good at her job."

"I've no doubt."

"It's Jobert's, with a J. They're open daily for both lunch and dinner. She should be there today, I think. And I would imagine the lunch rush slacks off in about another hour or so. I'll write down the phone number for you." Chad looked surprised as she got up and went across the room for a pad and pen. "Yes, of course, I *am* disclosing a lot of information to you," explained Marlene as she wrote. "I suppose because I feel it's safe to do so in your case, Mr. Harmon. I'm usually a pretty good judge of character. Another thing that has its advantages in my line of work."

They talked a bit more before Marlene saw him to the door. Chad had somehow found himself becoming more comfortable in the moment.

"Well," he said stopping just outside the door, "thank you, Marlene. Thank you very much."

"You're welcome, Chad," she said and then added, "and good luck."

He was about to turn and go. But he stopped, looked at her one last time, leaned toward her, kissed her cheek, and then departed.

This took Marlene by surprise. However, she soon smiled and chuckled to herself as she watched him disappear up the street.

Determined as ever, Charlie had placed a call at 7:00 a.m. to Jock. She was taking no chances on his getting away from the house early this time. It was her day off from work. If he was in town, which she was beginning to doubt, surely he was at home at this hour of the morning.

As she heard the ringing begin, a horrific thought suddenly crossed her mind. What if he was bedded down with someone, having given up on that neurotic, indecisive, ice-cold little bitch Charlie Cohen?

Just then Jock picked up.

"Charlie!" he answered, recognizing the number on his Caller ID.

"I, uh…Jock, hi," she said. "How…how are things?"

"Things are just great. And you?"

"Good," she awkwardly replied. "Jock, I really want to talk to you."

"I'd like that," he agreed. "I have some news I need to share with you too."

"You do?" she said. "I – I mean, good. That's good."

Her mind went back to that day last fall when he'd tapped on her car window in the parking lot after the Harding Road group meeting. It had been *he* who'd been awkward making conversation with *her* that day.

"Are you working today?" he asked

"No. My day off."

"How about lunch?"

"Of course."

"I was in town and I just wanted to say hello," Chad said, having made the phone call to Jobert's. "Actually, I'd like to see you, if I may."

"Oh?" Melinda said, mystified. "Well, I'm afraid I'll need to be here at the time the dinner rush begins, which is around 5:30, but then I'll take the evening off tonight. So maybe later, if you'd like."

Marlene had called ahead and notified her that he'd probably be contacting her, but she was still finding this hard to believe.

"Is there a chance I could see you this afternoon?" he asked.

"Well…"

"Please."

After a moment, she conceded, "I suppose you could come out to Jobert's. That is, if you'd like."

"I would."

"There's a quiet nook in a corner of the restaurant where we could sit and talk, I guess."

"I'm downtown. But I'll see you soon," he said and hung up.

Melinda couldn't have been more confounded if it had been the Prince of Wales calling. After all these months, Chad Harmon getting in touch with her now was the most curious thing on earth that could have happened. She was fascinated, doubtful, expectant, and a little scared. For three months she had been building a new life for herself through her work. Marlene had helped her get the job through a personal connection. What would send Chad Harmon back to find her after all this time? Marlene had felt comfortable about the whole thing, enough to tip him off as to how to find her. Nevertheless, she'd be full of anxiety until he arrived.

For over four months Melinda hadn't gone a single day without thinking of Chad, which had seemed ridiculous at the time. Now *he* was on his way to see *her*!

She forced herself to go back to the restaurant expenditures she had been dealing with for the time being. He'd be close to half an hour coming out from downtown.

Charlie had never seen Jock so exuberant. It was as if he'd found what he'd been searching for all his life, and nothing could make him happier.

He'd gotten held up with some people at the Visions Artists office and hadn't been able to pick her up until nearly 2:00 p.m.

"I'm going to start right in drawing up contracts for two new writers Tommy is signing. There's also to be a new recording artist signed soon. And in time, there'll be the record label contracts, and all that. Jesus! It's all coming together, Charlie!"

"Jock, I'm very happy for you," Charlie assured.

They were lunching at Provence, a bakery-café in Hillsboro Village. All through lunch, Jock had been so garrulous over the new career she'd had no chance to discuss the subject weighing on her mind.

"But you were right about something, Charlie."

"I was?"

"When you said that I didn't have to ditch my own music, because of a career. And, by God, I won't. Oh, I'll keep at it for my own fulfillment, and whatever comes of it or doesn't, I'll be fine. But, hell, I'll *have* a career!

"And you were right about something else, my need to co-write. I think it was Helen Keller who said that alone we can do little, but together we can do so much."

She had never imagined Jock could be like this. He was philosophical, a bit humble, and above all, centered, content. But all that actually made her even more nervous about coming forward with her own information.

"I've spent my life trying to be a decent, law-abiding, pretty much live-and-let-live kind of guy," Chad said. "I don't think I ever did anyone deliberate harm, at least not that I can recall…But you get to a point, as you pursue the program of living that I have lately, that you have to adopt a new perspective on things, especially on yourself. When I did that, I realized – I really did – that I've looked out for myself first. All my life. My own dreams, getting my own way, being right and making sure everybody understood that I was."

He paused. "I looked out *only* for myself that night. I had no concern about anything but saving my own precious hide, though that was to no avail of course. I didn't care what became of anyone else involved, including you. It was all about *me*, which is how I've lived most of my life. But, you know, the fact that I wasn't able to make a clean break that night ironically ended up being the best thing that could have happened for me, because it led to where I am now.

"I've got a close friend back home in Nashville. Actually, he's what's called my sponsor. He says that everything's a part of the 'perfect whole' in the ordered universe. Everything just fits together to form the greater plan. Even the very worst things and the things we just can't understand."

He dropped his eyes and became very contrite. "There is also within the structure of this program, Melinda, this thing about making amends to people you've wronged. I want to do that. I'm extremely sorry for how I acted that night. After my talk earlier that evening about not seeing myself as better than anyone else, people not really having stations in life, I took a position of superiority. I believed that I was deserving of getting out, of not being included with you others, because I was who I was. Anyone else besides me, to hell with them. I never spoke another word to you, nor did I try to look you up…That is until now. And I'd like to ask you to accept my apology, Melinda."

She hadn't been able to take her eyes off him once during this oration. Sitting here in this dark corner of the restaurant, sipping coffee with Chad Harmon, it was like the world was a different one than it had been before he had walked through the door that afternoon. This guy had surely changed. In fact, he'd affected her, such that she wasn't sure she'd ever be the same again either. Everything he had said had been nothing short of astounding.

"I do, Chad," she said, almost fighting back tears. "I do, and thank you."

After a moment he spoke once again. "Thank *you*, Melinda."

To Chad, Melinda was every bit as delicate and lovely as he'd remembered her from that one night.

"Jock, it's my turn to talk now!" Charlie finally said as if about to explode.

Startled, he looked at her as they walked out the back door of Provence. They had finished their lunch, during which Jock had covered everything from his upcoming duties with the artists and writers under Tommy's management to how great a guy Tommy was going to be to work with, and finally laughing speculation about what George and Snooks would say regarding this one. They were now on their way back to his car in the back parking lot. They stopped and stood beside his BMW.

"Sure, babe," he said, wide-eyed at her outburst. "I, uh – I'm sorry.…Go ahead. I'm listening."

"There's something I've needed for a long time to tell you, and I kept thinking I just couldn't."

"Do you want to get in the car?" he asked.

"No," she said, hardly hearing him, "I just want you to listen to me for a minute please."

He looked around, hopped up and perched himself on the fender of the car facing her. With a nod of the head and a gesture, not daring to offer another word, he cued her to proceed. Charlie paced a bit, seeking to pull her thoughts together.

"Jock, I have to first say that I think you're wonderful. I think so today even more than before. And I'm so proud of you. You can't imagine how happy I am that you've found your niche in life. You've searched a long time." *Oh God, can I really go through with this?* "I just needed to say that to you before we completely change the spirit of the conversation. I feel like…you might not want to see me again when I'm through telling you what I have to tell you."

With an almost ridiculing smile he said, "Charlie, come on…"

"Jock, please! We agreed it was my turn to speak! And I'm not going to get this out if I don't hurry it along!"

He hushed, folded his hands, and made himself as comfortable as he could atop the vehicle fender.

Sometimes looking up at him, sometimes looking away, often pacing, other times standing still, she let go with the entire story of her long-term affair with Rick Richmond right there in the parking lot. She held nothing back. She included the fact that she had still been involved with Rick at the time she'd begun dating Jock. At times she almost became tearful, but she forced herself not to, determined not to be the drama queen.

Finally she said, "Jock, I just couldn't keep it from you. And if it's a lot more information than you needed and bargained for, I apologize. But I couldn't go on without you knowing." She was silent a moment, as was Jock. So she continued. "If you need some time away from me, I'll understand, I really will. But I just have to say…I…" and she couldn't believe these words were about to come from her, maybe because she'd never wanted to admit them to herself, "…I love you, Jock."

He just sat looking at her. After a moment passed, he jumped down from the fender of the car and hoisted her up, setting her exactly where he had been.

Totally baffled as to what this was all about, she exclaimed, "Jock, what are you…?"

"You've had your turn to speak," he said. "So can you please just shut the hell up for one minute?" With Charlie now dumbfounded, he took a breath and went on, "As I was hatching this new career plan over these last twenty-four hours or so, I kept thinking about something. How I couldn't wait to share the news with you. I kept thinking that although it seemed to make my life everything I had waited for, my life would *not* be everything I'd wanted unless you were included in it. I thought about all the things I've learned, thanks to you; co-writing, you know, and the fact that my musical endeavors can go on, come what may." One more deep breath, and it was as if it was time for the counselor to now proceed with his closing remarks. "But I now have to say…"

She looked at him, full of dread, shaking a bit. But something happened she wasn't prepared for, something that she was to never forget. Jock Pritchard, the handsome, cocky, self-assured, hard-headed young attorney, right here in the back parking lot of a restaurant was going down on bended knee before her and taking her hand.

"Miss Charlene Cohen…I wish to ask if you would do me the honor…"

Chad came to Melinda's apartment a little after 8:30 p.m. in a taxi to take her to dinner. He'd asked Melinda about a really excellent place to dine with atmosphere and great food, and she'd suggested Antoine's in the Quarter. A famous restaurant with excellent food, she said. He'd then invited her to join him.

They took the cab into downtown from her apartment, which was in the Lakefront area and not far from Jobert's. At Antoine's they enjoyed soft-shelled crabs and warm conversation.

When seeing her home late that night, he wrote down her address, phone numbers, and email address and gave his to her as well. He then gave her a short goodnight kiss on the cheek, ending the evening.

It was, in a way, heartbreaking for Melinda to see the evening come to an end. She had no idea that that Chad shared the same feelings.

PART III

SPRING

Without music life would be a mistake.

- Friedrich Neitzsche

30

FOR ALL PRACTICAL PURPOSES, the new symphony hall was completed and ready for dedication. Even the landscaping about the exterior had pretty much been brought to a finishing point, with only time and nature left to effect its embellishment.

Inside the hall, plush seats faced the stage from multiple levels. Magnificent chandeliers hung from the ceiling of the auditorium. It was a place of total aesthetic beauty.

All around the Grand Tier, arguably the best seating location in the house, were Founder's Boxes, which had "sold" to wealthy individuals and a few corporations. There was a private entrance leading to the section of boxes as well as private restrooms and a lounge area.

Vision Artists Unlimited had come forward with a generous corporate contribution toward the symphony's capital campaign when it was learned that Chad Harmon was to be a featured act in the nationally televised concert. This had secured several tickets in the orchestra seat section for Vision Artists.

"Walkin' On" was a tune Chad had rather quickly co-written with Tommy one evening, the night before word came of Chad's booking for the concert. It was, ironically, the first time he and his friend had collaborated on a song. Both Chad and Tommy thought it one of the best that Chad would ever sing, making no apologies for their prejudice. The ballad had then been submitted to the symphony office on a work tape, which would be used for orchestration and by the pops conductor in his preparation.

Chad had still not signed with a label, though he had continued playing some bookings. In February had come the invitation from the Nashville Symphony. Orchestration backing his music had always thrilled him, and this was to be televised. People would know that he was still among the living and doing well.

It was the Saturday morning before the symphony dedication. Melinda Holstrom was in town for the weekend, having flown to Nashville for three visits already since Chad's surprise trip to New Orleans.

The two had eaten breakfast at the Pancake Pantry in Hillsboro Village. Even standing in line to wait for a table, let alone dining in public, was something that Chad was becoming more comfortable with, realizing he couldn't sequester himself forever.

They had now finished their breakfast and were driving back to his place.

"I have to admit something," he said.

"What?" Melinda said.

"I really counted on your being here for the concert."

"I know, Chad," she said, "but I've rearranged my schedule so many times to come to Nashville. And a Saturday is possibly the worst time a manager could take off from the restaurant. And yet I've done it once already for this weekend."

Chad thought a moment then said, "Given any more thought to our Plan A proposal?"

"I think that was *your* Plan A," she said, smiling. "It might be somewhere between B and C for me right now."

"What's to keep you from coming here to live? A restaurant job?"

"Chad, we've been through this before. And, you know, I do like my work. I take great pride in it."

"Sorry. I didn't mean it the way it sounded."

She drew a breath. "But, as I've said, it's a huge step to take, and I want us both to be sure. About everything."

"I don't know how I could be any surer."

She looked over at him as he drove, feeling something like joy and fear combined. "Chad, I feel the same way," she said, "but what assurances do we have that we'll feel the same way six months or a year or five years from now?"

"I guess we don't," he said. "People can't live their lives trying to bank on things like that."

"I've known a lot of people who've fallen in love, only to end up hurting each other after time had passed and they had to start paying the price. And I mean the price that commitment requires." After a moment's pause she went on to say, "And, to be honest with you, Chad, I'm not even sure about my own motivation."

"Motivation?"

"Despite anything I might have said to you that first night we met at Marlene's – because I was quite enamored of you, in case you don't know – I want to know that I'm in love with *you*, not the famous, gorgeous country music hunk that women dream of and fantasize about."

"I wouldn't exactly say I'm that hot a commodity anymore," he said flatly. "Maybe at one time."

Chad had by this time received only one token nomination with the Academy of Country Music awards held each spring in Las Vegas, and that had been for the single "Card Carryin' Country." He'd been passed over completely by the Grammy Awards.

"Oh, you'll make a return," Melinda assured. "Everybody who knows you is sure of that; Tommy, Sandy, Kris. Maybe it won't be quite like it would have been if what happened last fall had never happened. But you'll make it back up again."

"Glad you think so. But back to the primary subject. I want you in my life. And I mean all the time. Melinda, if everybody was afraid of taking chances there never would *be* such a thing as commitment."

"I think we both need time. I think we owe it to ourselves."

Neither of them said another word for a time as they kept driving south down Hillsboro Road.

Finally Chad broke the silence. "Call me selfish, repetitious, pushy, but it truly means the world to me, your being at that symphony concert next weekend." She was silent. "But if you don't, I guess I'll understand," he finally conceded, though with a bit of a pout.

She looked at him and reached over to stroke the back of his hair as they drove on.

"I think we should just go on and have it at St. John's Church," said Charlie.

"What's wrong with a simple outdoor sort of thing," Jock said, "somewhere out in the country, maybe just a civil ceremony?"

"You seem to be the only one against having it at your own church," she said and then paused. "Come on, what's this really all about, Jock?"

Charlie, now sporting a large, shiny diamond on her left hand, was at Jock's house, where she spent a great deal of her time these days. Currently she was seated on the couch in the office-den with pad and pencil in hand, as she'd determined it was time to at least make a start on some wedding plans. Jock, sprawled out on the same couch, rested his legs across her lap.

"If you must know, it's about dear old Snooks," he said with some repugnance.

"What's your mom got to do with it?"

"What's she got to *do* with it??" he exclaimed. "Jesus! You mean, what *won't* she have to do with it? She'll take charge of the whole show. She'll make up for you not having a mother by being worse than ten domineering mothers. She can't wait to show off to all her friends by putting on the wedding of the season and making this whole thing the talk of the Boulevard."

"Well, why not let her have her fun?" Charlie cajoled. "You know I don't care. Besides, we already declined to be at her table at the dedication ball. This could make up for it."

"We wanted to be at Tommy's table at the ball with the Vision Artists people, and that's our own business," he declared.

"Uh, correction: *you* wanted to be at Tommy's table," she said. "And don't get me wrong, I'm glad we're going to be. But it just seems like you've got, well, almost a vendetta going with your folks."

"Aw, whatever," he replied. Then, as he nudged her playfully with his foot, he quipped, "I know why *you* wanna be at that table. That's where that cute Chad Harmon'll be, ain't that right?"

He suddenly sat up, grabbed her and began tickling her, which had recently become one of his favorite pastimes.

"Jock!" she squealed as he continued. "Stop! I might just pee all over you!"

"Promise?" he laughed.

"And I know what *your* motive is about Tommy's table. To pitch one of your, excuse me, *our* songs to Harmon! Jock, *don't*!"

"Come on, baby," he said becoming more frisky and nibbling her neck, "let old Jocko have his way, and I'll concede to whatever wedding plans you want to make. Deal?"

"I don't make any deals with sex fiends!" she shouted while squirming and giggling. "And 'Old Jocko' has had his way three times already this weekend, and it's only Saturday."

"Ah well, you're all for collaboration; you know, making all that beautiful music together," he panted, now nibbling her ear.

She squealed, "*Jock!*" though truthfully liking the interplay.

Just then the phone on his desk rang.

"Jock, answer the phone," she said in between giggles when she noticed he was ignoring it.

"Aw hell, let it ring," he muttered, continuing to tickle, nuzzle, and do other things to her as the phone continued ringing. "The machine will get it."

"Jock, go on, answer it," she said, trying to get both her own laughter and Jock Pritchard under control. "What if it's something important?"

"Okay," he finally said grudgingly and ceasing his shenanigans on the couch, at least momentarily.

He reached over and pushed the speakerphone button.

"Hello."

"Hey Jock, it's Tommy," came Tommy's voice.

"Uh, hey, Tommy," he said but was soon silently grappling with Charlie again.

While Tommy and Jock talked, and while Jock continued to molest her, Charlie quietly mouthed the words "*Stop it*" now and again, though registering delight on her face and obviously not wanting him to stop it.

"Man, I'm sorry to have to bother you on a Saturday," Tommy said, "but we gotta put a rush on Chad's contract with the symphony. It was the symphony people that delayed in gettin' it to us, but, with the concert a week away, we need to go ahead and get it done."

"Is it at the office now?" Jock asked, reaching inside Charlie's blouse while constricting her from behind, which almost caused her to emit an audible screech.

"Yeah, wouldn't you know it, it finally came in the Saturday mail," answered Tommy. "I'm down here now at the office."

"Not a problem," Jock said, fondling Charlie's breasts, while she tried, though not too diligently, to free herself from his grip. "I'll come on by and get it a little later, so just leave it in my mail slot. After I've gone over it, I'll be happy to run by Chad's place and get it signed, if you'd like."

"That'll be just great," Tommy said. "It'd help to have it fully executed and turned in to the symphony office by Monday."

"I'll take care of it," Jock said, feeling proud of himself for the art of juggling business and pleasure so discreetly.

"Thanks, bud," Tommy said. Then before hanging up he added, "You and Charlie get back to business now." *Click.*

Both Jock and Charlie froze and looked at each other.

"Well, you know I'd be honored," said Father Kris over the phone to Jock that evening.

"We're looking toward a June or maybe July wedding at St. John's," Jock said. "Guess we'll have to make sure it works on the church calendar."

"Right. Just check with Nancy at the church office."

"Oh trust me, Madame Snooks will be there first thing Monday morning. I warn you that she's going to waltz right in and take charge."

"I wouldn't worry," Kris laughed. "Nancy can handle her. Uh, Jock, naturally I'm delighted you're having the wedding at St. John's. And I can't help admiring, if you don't mind my saying so, how Charlie is evidently so amenable to the church choice. I mean, I know she's of the Jewish faith."

"It was *she* who talked *me* into it," Jock answered.

"Is that so?"

"Ironic, huh?" said Jock, looking over at Charlie, who was lying beside him in the bed, basking in the afterglow. "You see, we sort of cut a deal this afternoon."

"Excuse me?" Kris said.

"Never mind," Jock said dismissingly.

"Well anyway," Kris continued, "I'll be honored to perform the ceremony, and I'll look forward it."

They said their goodbyes, and Kris put the phone down, glad to have heard from Jock and Charlie. They had recently become two more of his closest friends. They were a spirited couple and full of passion, but it was plain that they also were soul mates.

Kris's phone almost immediately rang again.

"Hello," he answered.

"It's Chad, Kris."

"Hey, pal. How's Melinda?"

"She's fine. She says 'hi.' Listen, Kris, Tommy, my manager, called me earlier today."

"Oh yeah, how is Tommy?"

"Fine. But I have news. I can get a couple of extra tickets to the symphony hall dedication concert. Vision Artists got a block of comps. I was wondering whether you'd like to go."

"Man, what a week this has been," Kris said happily. "I was just yesterday invited by Mrs. Greeling to be a part of her table at the ball. It was only after I'd said yes and hung up that it hit me I didn't have a ticket to the concert itself."

"Well, you do now," Chad said. "Whoa! Check it out! Sarah Greeling's table, the chairperson herself, along with all those big, important people."

"I'd say you're the important person," Kris said, "being one of the guest performers. And now, thanks to you, I'll get to see the whole thing in person. I guess you're getting excited, huh?"

"Yeah. As much as I *can* get." Chad had said this a bit dully while looking across the dinner table at Melinda. He'd just finished some of the New Orleans style bread pudding, which she had made and served following the dinner that he had cooked.

"What do you mean?" Kris asked.

"Aw, nothing. Forget it," said Chad. "Well anyway, I'll get the ticket to you somehow this week."

"That'll be great, man. Thanks for thinking of me."

"Anytime."

They said their goodbyes. Chad hung up the phone.

Melinda smiled her sweet and unassuming smile, which always made Chad melt like butter.

"Coffee?" she asked.

"Yeah, I'll put it on," he said, getting up.

As Chad went to the kitchen counter and began filling the pot with water she followed him. She caressed him from behind and laid her head against his back.

"Do you feel like I'm putting you off?" she asked.

He said nothing at first. Then, turning to face her and taking her in his arms, he added, "I just want you around all the time, that's all."

Suddenly it seemed very strange to Melinda that this man, now transformed by divine power, and one with whom women everywhere had been infatuated, was in love with her. And *she* was the one keeping *him* on hold.

Following the phone call from Chad and Melinda, Kris went into his kitchen to begin looking for something to have for dinner. Franklin followed close behind, always staying underfoot when his master had been gone all day, which was almost every day.

Kris thought about his life of solitude while most of his close friends these days were paired up. Only at infrequent times was he a bit lonely. Basically his life was good.

"Guess I'm not really alone at all, am I, Frankie?" he asked the devoted animal as he sat at the kitchen table and reached down to stroke him. "We've got a good life, huh?"

The thought of Hunter Jamison still nagged at Kris. There was to this day a lack of closure to the situation.

There was, in addition, a new issue – no, actually an old one – knocking at the door of his mind these days. It was something that he wasn't sure he was prepared to deal with. Perhaps he never would. Was it something that could cost him everything?

No, this wasn't denial. It simply wasn't the time yet, whether it ever would be at all, to deal with what he'd begun realizing about himself.

31

"IT'S ALMOST AS IF the term Music City USA is taking on a broader meaning," said news anchor Carolyn Rucker on WAB-TV. "When asked to name the most significant musical performance venues in Nashville, people think of such facilities as the Grand Ole Opry House, the Nashville Arena, the theaters of TPAC, and of course the historic Ryman Auditorium. But a stunning new performance hall, unlike any the city has yet seen, will finally be opened to the public this weekend..."

The worlds of the socially elite and the music industry seemed equally enthralled over this moment. The Nashville Symphony Hall dedicatory concert and ball were now just days away. The production crew from A&E rolled into Nashville a couple of days ahead to begin surveying the hall and setting up for the telecasting of the big event.

"Undoubtedly this symphony hall is something the caliber of which our state has never had until now." These were the proud words of Governor Bennington, one of the honorary co-chairs of the dedication ball, in an interview with Carolyn Rucker for WAB taped while the two stood outside the new facility. "And it's been built, I've been told, according to the standards of the best concert halls in the world."

One final rehearsal in the hall itself would be held during the day of the concert, much the same as the CMA Awards, Chad noted. Also like the CMAs, artists were assigned blocks of time to run their various numbers with the orchestra, while camera and lighting checks were simultaneously conducted.

Chad's rehearsal time had been slated for 11:00 a.m., and once again Tommy would be driving him to the rehearsal, as he could always be counted on to do. However, on Friday Chad called Kris about a ride to the concert.

"Tomorrow night Tommy and Sandy are having a couple of folks from a record label as guests at the concert, and they'll be at their ball table afterward," he'd explained to Kris. "Tommy still prefers for me to be driven to a major concert. I guess I agree."

"Say no more. It would be an honor," Kris had said.

Many Bel Terre socialites had committed to hosting tables for the lavish ball, tables of ten. By the same token, several record labels and publishing houses had been solicited and had agreed to sponsor tables. People all but fought to have an invitation to the ball, which, or so it had been rumored, the national media would be covering.

A few ladies of the Boulevard had commissioned their gowns for the event from major designers, much as they might have done for Nashville's annual Nightingale Ball. Other ladies had shopped theirs from consignment stores, cast-offs of the wealthiest who had worn the garments but once. The gentlemen who did not own their own set of white tie and tails either purchased them or rented them.

Charlie had been loaned a gown by her future mother-in-law Snooks, one worn in her earlier days but still quite fashionable, Snooks assured.

"Ah just feel it's a bit too, shall we say, youngish for mahself these days. Ah always say that a woman ovuh fawty ought to dress at least somewhat consuhvatively."

Jock withheld a guffaw at the "ovuh fawty" remark. Over forty and then some, he'd later commented to Charlie. And admitting to age was, in Snooks' case, less of a disgrace than admitting that it no longer quite fit her in the ass, he concluded.

Everything was in place for one of the most important events the city had seen in a while. As good fortune would have it, a clear day and night was predicted on the weather front, with temps in the 70s. The gowns wouldn't be rained on. It would be a night to remember.

A grim bit of news was breaking in the city, news that had at least temporarily eclipsed the symphony hall dedication. Gary Segal had finally been taken into police custody and charged with the murder of his wife Beth. To everyone's astonishment, Segal's own father had come forward with new evidence against his own son linking him to the killing. As it was now being reported, Beth Segal had threatened to leave her husband, and this had reportedly led to his beating her to death with a hammer and disposing of her body in the countryside north of town.

Jock, Charlie, Father Kris, and others, though appalled by the sordid details, felt relieved that Abe and Liz Feinstein could finally begin finding more and better closure to the situation with their daughter. There would be a long process of healing ahead for the Feinsteins, but the final chapter of the nightmare was at last being written.

Jock would for days to come be haunted by the fact that he'd once made a choice to form a professional acquaintance with Gary Segal, due to his own run-away ego. He'd heard Abe say that although recovering addicts might have their drinking and drugging problems under control, the program was still there and still needed to control their self-centeredness problems. But, as Abe went on to say, and as Jock now knew, those were one and the same problem.

Chad's excitement remained a bit hampered by Melinda's absence. One of the finest moments of his career, and hopefully the marking of a sort of comeback, should be shared with the woman he loved.

In truth and unbeknownst to Chad, Melinda had contacted Kris Hartley by phone on Thursday of that week. She'd had a change of heart, and she wished to surprise Chad with her appearance at the concert. She had in fact done something even more drastic. She'd tendered her notice to Jobert's with respectful apologies. It was to be effective in three weeks, at which time she would relocate to Music City.

She remained nervous about the whole thing, nonetheless, until she'd had a particular conversation with Marlene.

"I think it has to do with self-image," Marlene had said to her.

"I just don't want to hurt Chad or *be* hurt," Melinda insisted.

Melinda had dropped by Marlene's establishment to give her the news.

"He loves you, Melinda," Marlene said. "But, darling, I think perhaps you still have a picture of yourself as being the girl with whom he was placed under arrest, the girl who was practicing prostitution." Melinda just looked at her a moment, then looked away. Marlene continued. "Having begun a relationship that way makes you feel somewhere deep inside that it's not right, you don't deserve him, or maybe that you don't deserve each other."

Melinda thought about this a minute, then she gave Marlene a huge hug. She'd always cherished the motherly affection that she'd received from Marlene, and she was realizing that they'd soon be separated. She loved Marlene dearly and had long depended upon her for guidance, which even now she was receiving. From here on out she'd be forced to truly grow up, to depend on herself and on Chad.

As if sensing her thoughts, Marlene said, "I'll miss you, baby." Both of them fought tears as they embraced again. But after a moment Marlene said, "Well, we could stand here all day, but it seems to me we have to find something for you to wear Saturday night."

She quickly led Melinda to her huge walk-in closet where at one end was quite a selection of elegant gowns. She already knew that Melinda and she were about the same size.

"I think maybe this one would be darling on you," she said pulling a dress out. "But you should try on several."

The night of the concert Father Kris was to meet Chad at his place at 5:15 to deliver him to a makeup call at 5:30. Presumably, Kris would then be going on to the cocktail reception being held for ball attendees at 6:00 in an elegant new hospitality room, which had been included in the symphony hall's construction. In truth, Kris was to secretly drive to the Nashville airport where he was to meet Melinda, whose flight was due in at 5:40, her big surprise for Chad. Kris had successfully obtained an extra concert ticket for Melinda from Tommy, the last remaining one.

Trying to get comfortable in the newly rented white tie and tails, Kris arrived at Chad's house with a suggestion.

"Chad, how about we take your Saab instead of my car?" he asked. "I'll still be glad to do the driving, but mine's a little dirty. After all, this is a big night, and we ought to go in style."

"Fine," Chad agreed.

Kris's true reason was that his MR2, being a two-seater, would prove too small a car for when he, Chad, *and* Melinda would all be riding together at evening's end.

Chad grabbed his Gibson guitar and off they went in the Saab with Kris at the wheel. Chad was soon delivered to the stage door.

"Thanks, Kris," he said before getting out.

"Break a leg, man," Kris replied.

Kris looked lovingly and a bit wistfully toward his friend walking toward the stage door. Chad would never know that it was he, Kris, who'd engineered this special performance opportunity for him.

He now headed quickly to the airport. He concluded that if Melinda were forced to change into her ball clothes in the restroom of a service station along the way, that's how it would have to be. The concert was to begin at 7:00.

To his amazement, as he waited by the car in the lot outside the baggage claim area, suddenly Melinda came promenading out the door, suitcase in hand and dressed in a stunning black gown that would have been suitable for the highest occasion at the White House. She had changed in an airport restroom on her way to the baggage claim, having carried the dress aboard the flight.

"You go, girl!" he shouted as he ran to fetch her suitcase from her.

"Just a little something I dug up from my old high school prom days," she laughed as she accepted a kiss on the cheek from Kris.

"Ready to go to a concert?" he said after putting her one piece of luggage in the open trunk and closing it up.

"*Quite* ready," she answered.

She hopped in the passenger side and began touching up her makeup as Kris got in and took the wheel.

The concert program was perfectly conceived with the flow from the classical to the pop artists carefully planned. The commercial breaks were covered with short symphonic pieces, seeing to it that the orchestra was never left idle nor the audience left to boredom.

Tommy and Sandy were seated with Mr. Orson Chambers, an executive with Galaxy Records, and his wife. The Mathesons were bursting with pride that Chad was about to make his symphony debut, and appearing live on nationwide television for the first time in quite a while.

Also in the Matheson party, seated just past Orson Chambers and his wife, was Father Kris Hartley, who just had arrived with Melinda Holstrom, here to surprise her man Chad. They were growing to love Melinda as they did Chad, and she seemed good for him. As for Kris, he'd almost become a member of the Matheson "family" in his own right, due to his close friendship with Chad. On the other side of the Mathesons were Jock Pritchard and his fiancée, Charlie Cohen, whose occasional kisses and provocative pawing at one another seemed to indicate they needed desperately for this concert to end so they could get home and take care of business.

Conspicuously absent from the audience tonight was Rick Richmond, despite the fact that Pioneer had purchased a block of seats and was sponsoring a table at the ball. Word had gotten around the Row over the past week that not only had his wife Estelle filed for divorce, but he was also facing an alienation of affection suit from a disgruntled husband in town.

Finally the moment was here. Chad made his entrance and took his place in front of the orchestra to the sound of welcoming applause throughout the hall. His band members were already in place behind the small platform where Chad would perform. Spoken introductions were not being given of any guest artist all evening, formal concert etiquette being the format. However, the stars were identified as they first appeared by the broadcast host, whose voice was heard only by the television audience. The tuning of all guitars had been checked during the preceding commercial break. Chad took up his acoustic guitar, looked toward the pops conductor, and gave a downbeat.

"Walkin' On" was the most beautiful testament to survival Melinda had ever heard, and many would agree with her. The ballad touched her because of her love for the man singing it, but also because she herself was a survivor and daring to forge ahead in life.

The newest thrill to Chad and to those close to him was the rich, lush orchestration beautifully enhancing a ballad that he had co-written and was performing. It made the experience even more splendorous.

The song ended, and the audience applauded. As Tommy beamed with great pride, he hoped and prayed this could mark the end of the time in which Chad Harmon was known merely as the guy who'd "screwed up." He looked out of the corner of his eye for Orson Chambers's reaction. The record executive's apparent pleasure caused Tommy to feel at least a little encouraged.

At any rate, and whatever came after, this night was seeing the creation of an incredible memory.

"Oh my God! When did you get here?!"

Chad had been at first speechless, then unable to pull his lips away from Melinda's, and now was still holding on to her as if she might slip away from him. He, Melinda, Kris, Tommy, Sandy, Jock, and Charlie had all rallied backstage following the concert.

"I flew in just before the concert," Melinda said. "Kris picked me up."

Chad looked at Kris, reached over, and grabbed his shoulder. "You're a sneak," he said to him with a grin.

"Surprise! I didn't make it to the pre-concert party!" said Kris. "Had other matters to tend to."

"Ah well," Jock cut in, "you sure as hell didn't miss anything. Plenty of champagne, but nothing else to wash down the caviar."

"I noticed that too," said Sandy.

"You were dynamite, bud," said Tommy to Chad, putting an arm around his back.

"It was just wonderful, Chad," said Charlie, "and the new song is beautiful."

"My husband will take part credit for that," beamed Sandy, holding on to Tommy's arm.

"Well, anyway, grab your stuff and lets get to the ball!" shouted Tommy in a jovial spirit to Chad, and the gang shouted their agreements.

As everyone started moving on, Melinda whispered to Chad, "Can we talk a moment?"

"Sure, babe," he said. Then he said to Tommy, "We'll be along in a minute!"

"I have something to tell you," she said.

He looked at her, turned to face her straight on, and took her in his arms again. This seemed serious.

"I'm listening," he said.

"There's so much to talk about, Chad, the concert, how very wonderful you were, how beautiful the new song is, how it spoke to me, how much I care for you, how I miss you when we're separated by the miles…and…how nervous I still am."

He started to speak, but she cut him off.

"I know I'll get over it…with time." She looked down, took a breath. "But meanwhile I'm not really happy with the way things are."

"You're not?" he said.

"No," she said. "That's why I'll be here to stay in about three weeks."

There could not have been a more celebratory spirit anywhere at the ball more so than at the Vision Artists Unlimited table. Sandy whispered to Tommy that this was the soberest group she and her husband had ever hosted, though that fact certainly did not dampen the partying attitude.

The ball tables contained tall centerpieces, which were actually artificial trees decked in tiny white lights. The trees rose up over the tables to form a sort of arbor over each table.

A full orchestra provided the dance music. It was made up of the Nashville String Machine, a session group, plus other contracted musicians. They were situated on a stage designed and decorated to resemble the new concert hall stage. It was meant to seem as if a symphony actually furnished the dance music for the ball.

Couples danced the night away on the crowded dance floor in between their dinner courses, which consisted of corn chowder, salad, crab cakes and Chicken L'Orange with grilled vegetables for main course, pineapple sorbet, and Flaming Bananas Foster over ice cream for dessert.

Cameras flashed here and there, not just from the local media, but from the national scene as well. UPI had sent photographers, and videotape footage was documenting the ball. A photographer got a shot of the entourage at Tommy and Sandy's table as they all smiled in true merriment.

Mrs. Greeling's distinguished table, where all of the honorary chairpersons were seated, was photographed again and again. Kris was enjoying himself but felt that he would have had more fun had he been at the table where his close friends were seated. He was thinking of going over to ask Melinda for a dance, with Chad's permission, when suddenly he felt his cell phone vibrating in his coat pocket.

He turned himself away from the table a bit to take the call.

"Hello."

"Father Kris," said Bill Jamison, "you've said that I could call you anytime. I hope it's not a bad time for you."

"Of course not," Kris assured him.

"It's about Mary, Kris," Jamison said, "and Hunter."

"Bill, let me get where I can talk a little more easily," Chad said.

He stood, excused himself to the others at the table, and walked toward a connecting hallway.

"What is it, Bill?" he said when arriving outside the ballroom.

"I feel like I've caught you at an inopportune moment."

"Don't worry about it."

"But you see," Jamison began, "well, this is hard to explain. It's hard to even talk about at all."

"Just lay it out, Bill."

"I'm out in the garage using my cell phone. You see, Mary thinks…I mean she feels that…that Hunter's still here."

"You mean she's lost touch with reality?"

"Well, it's not quite the way you think." It was evident that Bill was trying to explain something that he himself was still struggling to get a handle on.

"I don't understand," said Kris.

"She says that…that Hunter's spirit is still here. She feels that he's still in the house and hasn't moved on, that he's been here all this time since his physical death."

Kris waited, his heart pounding, then said, "Go on, Bill."

"She's as serious as she can be about this. And, please believe me, Kris, she doesn't seem as if she's gone mad. It's like she's concerned about the welfare of her son as any mother could be."

There was a time when Kris would have been ready at the report of such a thing to suggest that a person like Mary was in need of psychiatric help. He no longer felt the same way.

"Father Kris," Jamison went on, "what's so sad is that Mary is certain that Hunter is afraid. She says he's alone and afraid to move on. And she, out of love for her son, is afraid *for* him." He stopped, got control of his own emotions and then continued. "And there's something I've never told you, Kris. She talks to Hunter and has for a long time now."

"I see," Kris said. "But that's not so extraordinary, Bill."

"There's something more, Father Kris. Something that changed this evening."

"Go ahead," Kris said.

"Mary's crying. It's like she's kept all these emotions trapped inside for months, and now it's pouring out. She's just…crying. And I…I do think…"

"Yes…?"

"I think she knows somewhere deep inside that she's got to let go, but she just can't."

Kris took a deep breath. A chill was running up and down him. "Everything's going to be fine, Bill."

"But what do you think I should do? I wanted to call you, not a doctor. I felt you'd understand."

"I do. More than you know." Kris hesitated for a second or two wondering about the next actions to be taken. There wasn't time to debate or ponder the issue. Bill Jamison was desperate. Mary was in pain. And then Hunter…"Bill," he finally said, "give me a little time. I'm coming over."

He could hear Bill heaving a sigh. "Thank you, Father Kris. Thank you so much. Of course I feel terrible pulling you away from…"

"Forget it. Believe me, nothing could keep me from coming."

After hanging up, Kris went immediately to his table, thanked Sarah for including him, but asked to be excused because something important had come up. Next he went to Chad who was sharing a moment of intimate conversation with Melinda.

"Hate to interrupt, guys, but we have a problem."

He explained, though not in detail, the situation with a couple that needed help, members of his parish who'd lost their son. He felt that time was important in this matter. The problem of course lay in the three of them being in Chad's car together.

"Chad," Melinda said, "we've finished our dessert. It's getting late. Why don't *we* go on and leave now? We can drive him."

Chad, as touched by Melinda's good will as Kris, said, "Sure."

"Thanks, guys," Kris said. "This is sweet of you."

They said their goodnights and exchanged hugs with the rest of the table.

"I've never been more proud of you in my life," said Tommy to Chad as they embraced.

Even Jock and Charlie tore themselves apart long enough for Jock to say, "It's a real honor to be working with you, Chad."

"Best wishes to you two," Charlie warmly said to both Chad and Melinda.

"The same to you and Jock," Melinda replied.

Kris asked if Chad and Melinda could please give him one minute, as there was something else he had to quickly see about.

As they waited he moved swiftly across the room to another ball table. He approached a vivacious lady seated there.

"Good evening, Nelda," he said.

"Well, hello there, Father Kris," Nelda Fairbank answered. "I haven't seen you all evening."

"Nelda, I'm sorry to disturb you," he said, "but could I please speak with you for a moment?"

"Why sure, honey," she replied, getting up as Kris helped her with her chair.

32

CHAD WAS NOW AT THE WHEEL of his Saab, Melinda at his side, Father Kris and Nelda in the backseat. They were traveling west on Interstate 40 toward Bel Terre. Kris pondered the present company; a disgraced though back-on-the-rise country star, his prostitute-turned-girlfriend, a society spiritualist, and himself, an African-American priest, all heading toward God knows what at the Jamison household.

At this point Kris hadn't explained anything further to Chad and Melinda regarding Mrs. Fairbank other than to say that she was a very special lady who could possibly be of some help to the family in need. Conversation had remained almost nonexistent in the car at first. It was Nelda who broke the silence.

"Well, young man," she said speaking toward the front seat, "I must say that you sang quite well in the concert tonight."

"Thank you, Mrs. Fairbank," Chad replied, making a quick eye contact through the rearview mirror.

"Call me Nelda, honey. I confess I'm very much a *classical* music lover, but I do have to say that there was something very, shall we say, *engaging* about your song."

"That's nice to hear," said Chad with a smile.

"Well, Father Kris," she continued, "Are these good people going to be joining us in our visit or are they going to drop us by the Jamisons?"

"Actually," Kris faltered, "we haven't discussed the details."

Kris gave a brief account to Chad and Melinda of the Hunter Jamison story, the young man's untimely death, and the ongoing situation with Mary Jamison's withdrawn despondency.

"That's heartbreaking," said Melinda.

As they took the White Bridge exit from the interstate, Kris went on to describe Mary's desperate feelings and her claims of Hunter's lingering presence in the house.

"The poor woman. I've been where she is."

This unsolicited remark had come from Melinda and had taken aback even Chad.

"Have you really, honey?" asked Nelda.

"Yes, in a way," said Melinda. "Except that in my case it was my father."

"No kidding?" said Chad with fascination. He'd never heard this story from Melinda.

"After he died," Melinda explained, "I really felt that…that his spirit was still in the house for a long while afterward. I had this feeling that he was worried about me and felt like *he* couldn't leave *me*. You see, he knew that my mother wasn't…well, let's just say that she wasn't the motherly type."

"Oh, honey, that is *so* often the situation," said Nelda. "Talking about your daddy, I mean. Departed ones do keep on caring about who and what they've cared about in life. How could we expect that they wouldn't? Matters of the heart do not, I repeat, *do not* leave us when *we* leave this world."

Feeling that one more thing needed to be explained, Kris described in the most delicate terms he could what Nelda's ministry was all about. Neither Chad nor Melinda seemed to flinch at this. In fact, Chad actually commented that he found it very interesting.

"Something else that you might find interesting, Chad," Kris said, "is that Hunter was a fan of yours. It took me a while to remember that, but he definitely was."

"Wow," was all Chad could say.

Kris was at this point merely assuming that the entire party in the vehicle would be welcome at the Jamison house. It was a lot to expect, but it seemed fitting somehow.

The car turned from Harding Road onto the Boulevard.

"She's in Hunter's room right now. She's calmed down a bit since I spoke to you, Father Kris."

Bill Jamison and all four of his newly arrived guests were seated in the grand living room of the home. Though Jamison had at first been taken aback to behold an entourage of formally dressed folk arriving at his doorstep, Kris had explained the reason for their traveling together.

"Do you think she's open to our help, Bill?" Kris asked.

"I guess I don't really understand what help you're proposing, Father Kris," he replied.

Kris looked to Nelda.

"Mr. Jamison," she said, "I'm aware that you and I have had until now only a passing acquaintance with one another, but I'm no stranger to your situation. I've faced it many a time." As Jamison was looking at her with total receptivity, she continued. "We all have our gifts and talents within God's family, and as a family we reach out to one another as need arises. I'm very willing to do whatever I can to help you and Mary come to a peaceful resolution to *your* great need."

Kris now knew as never before that Nelda, so strong in her devotion, was as sincere as could be in the work she did. Bill, who never had taken his eyes off Nelda as she spoke, somehow knew this too.

"Thank you, Mrs. Fairbank," he said.

"I introduced Mr. Harmon as we arrived," said Kris. "Do you know of his career at all?"

"I do," Bill answered. Then looking warmly at Chad he added, "and Hunter certainly did."

Chad smiled and said, "I take that as a special compliment, Mr. Jamison."

Kris continued, "It was a coincidence, my being with Chad at the time you called."

"Your presence is welcome, Mr. Harmon," Jamison assured. He then turned back to Nelda and, after a moment, said, "What do we do, Mrs. Fairbank?"

"Mr. Jamison, have you a Bible that I may borrow?" she asked.

Mary had greeted Father Kris and Nelda with a faint smile and a nod. She, her husband, Kris, and Nelda all were standing in the upstairs hallway of the house, Nelda with Bible in hand.

Kris had suggested that Chad and Melinda remain downstairs for the moment. Mary didn't seem to react negatively to her guests.

"You've known already of Father Kris's concern and his closeness with Hunter," Bill said. "They wish to help us, Mary."

Almost like a child Mary asked very simply, "How?"

"Mary, we understand what you're going through, although I know full well that we can't feel what you feel," said Kris. "But, you see, I lost a part of myself too when Hunter left us. And Mrs. Fairbank has dealt with painful situations you could not imagine. That's why she's here. She's here on an errand of love."

"I'm grateful," Mary said. "But I still don't understand."

"Would you mind if I spoke to Hunter, Mrs. Jamison?" Nelda boldly interjected to everyone else's surprise.

There was a moment of silence.

Mary looked at Nelda's kind and warm face, a face that could have spoken quantities of peace to anyone, Kris thought. After several seconds of looking directly into Nelda's eyes, Mary nodded her head.

Kris thought it almost an inappropriate moment to mention one last thing to Mary, but his heart told him to go ahead. "Do you know of the country artist Chad Harmon, Mary?" he asked.

She looked at him. For the first time she registered something other than a wide-eyed stare or deep grief.

"It's strange you should ask, Father Kris. I was just today playing the CD that Hunter loves so much."

The grandfather clock on the landing of the staircase now struck midnight.

All six people were in Hunter's bedroom, a small bedside lamp serving as the only dim light to the room. Nelda, with reading glasses now on her face, sat in a chair next to the lamp with open Bible in hand. Bill and Mary were seated on the bed, Bill's arm around his wife. Chad and Melinda occupied a small window seat. Kris sat in a chair near Nelda, though he was keeping a low profile in the proceedings for now.

"He will swallow up death in victory; and the Lord God will wipe away tears from off all faces; and the rebuke of his people shall he take away from off the earth: for the Lord hath spoken it."

Nelda had read the text from the book of Isaiah, the hope being that faith would be encouraged in everyone present. A moment passed, then she flipped over to a Psalm.

"The Lord is my light and my salvation; whom shall I fear? The Lord is the strength of my life; of whom shall I be afraid?"

She paused and looked at Mary.

"What is it you wish to say, Mrs. Jamison?" Nelda asked. "What do you need to say to Hunter just now?" Mary looked at Nelda, not quite sure as to what she should do at this point. Nelda reassured her. "Just whatever you feel like saying. You're among caring friends who understand. I can assure you of that."

Chad and Melinda were in awe of the moment. There was something about what was happening that they didn't quite comprehend, but they didn't disdain it.

Mary balked a few more seconds. Then she spoke quietly into the room. "You know how we love you, Hunter." It was as if she just didn't know what to say or do. "Oh Hunter darling…"

She was becoming emotional. It seemed Mary knew that there was more needing to be said, but she wasn't capable of it just now.

Nelda turned to another Psalm. "How excellent is thy loving-kindness, O God! Therefore the children of men put their trust under the shadow of thy wings. They shall be abundantly satisfied with the fatness of thy house; and thou shalt make them drink of the river of thy pleasures..." Nelda looked over her glasses at Mary before reading the final verse: "…For with thee is the fountain of life: in thy light shall we see light."

There was something with which Mary was struggling. She shook her head, her husband all the while trying to comfort her.

"You don't understand," she said. "He's afraid. He's afraid of the unknown. He's so young, and he's…afraid."

It was dawning on Kris what Nelda, through her experience, had already surmised. He felt he had to speak. "Mary, we all share your pain with you. But are you so sure of Hunter's fear?" A pause. "Could it be, perhaps, that it's *you* who's fearful *for* him? Could it be that that's what this is truly about, Mary?"

She couldn't answer. She could only hang her head, crying all the more.

Nelda looked up and spoke softly but directly. "Hunter…" she said. "Hunter, you know it's time to say goodbye, do you not?"

Mary continued weeping. Bill gently rocked her in his arms where they sat. Kris looked pityingly at Mary. After a minute or so she raised her head again.

"Oh, Hunter, my precious darling!" she wailed.

"He knows of your love and your husband's love," said Nelda emphatically. "There's no doubt he knows. I think the only thing that's difficult for him now is *your* fear and *your* concern. You see, his love for you is just as strong as yours for him." Mary continued weeping. "I believe, Mrs. Jamison, you know that it's time. And though Hunter knows it too, perhaps he won't…until you let him know it's all right."

Kris had to speak one more time. "Hunter, my friend Chad Harmon…" He looked over toward Chad, who was startled by the mention of his own name. "…Chad wrote a song and sang it tonight. It was a song all about going forward…" He looked over at Chad.

Chad, wide-eyed, looked back at Kris. He felt very reluctant, uncertain. After some hesitation, and without guitar, backup band, or symphony orchestra, he slowly began to sing. He was at a loss doing it this way, yet he proceeded.

"I…I'm walkin' on now, How good to see the light. It's been dark and it's been lonely, But I'm almost through the night." More crying was heard from Mary as Chad continued. "I've waited and I've wondered, And I've stayed here all the night. But I'm walkin' on now, How good to see the light."

Chad almost hadn't gotten the words out before choking up himself. He held tightly to Melinda's hand.

Kris silently begged God to give Mary the strength she needed.

She slowly lifted her head and said. "Hunter, sweet Hunter." And it now seemed as if she was trying desperately to find all the courage she knew she lacked. "Goodbye, my precious darling," she finally said with an eruption of emotion as her husband held her even more tightly. "I love you so dearly. I love you so very much."

"And I love you too, son," Bill said rather quietly, tears in his own eyes.

"Walk on toward the light, Hunter," said Nelda. "It's all right now. You can walk toward the light."

For a very long moment there was silence in the room.

Then it happened. It was indescribable, but everyone present experienced it. Something moved over the room, something that might have been likened to a strong wind. Yet it was nothing that could be heard or seen or physically felt. After a moment it passed. A deep sense of serenity was then present. All of them knew that they would never be able to explain it, but each also knew that it would be forever etched in his or her memory.

The Jamisons embraced one another. Mary was still weeping, though seemingly from release now more than from tragedy. Time passed as everyone merely sat in awe. After a few minutes Bill stood and slowly helped his wife up from where she sat. His arm around her, he led her toward the door.

They briefly stopped when arriving near Kris, and Bill smiled a faint smile of appreciation toward him. Without looking up, Mary simply said "Thank you, Father Kris." She caught her breath. "And Mrs. Fairbank." She still was in tears, but Kris knew that somehow Mary would be fine with time.

The Jamisons walked out the bedroom door. Soon after, Chad and Melinda quietly made their way out and down the stairs. Kris walked over to Nelda, who was still seated and with a look of satisfaction on her face. He placed a hand gently on her shoulder.

Still gazing across the room, she said, "Peace has come to this house, Father Kris."

"Yes," he replied. Though Kris fully believed that his young friend Hunter had found peace some time ago, never again having to deal with his mental or addiction problem, now the Jamisons themselves could begin to move on.

Feeling almost as if he were on hallowed ground now, he quietly walked out of the room. Nelda soon followed.

"What do *you* make of it?" asked Melinda as she and Chad walked out onto the front porch of the house.

"I never experienced anything like it," he answered. "I guess common sense would tell me that it was just, well, you know, a delayed bit of closure for Mrs. Jamison. Just an exercise in letting go of a memory."

"Yes," Melinda said.

"That's what my mind says," Chad mused. "But my heart tells me maybe it was something more than that."

"Spiritual things aren't experienced through the five senses," Melinda said. "They're not for human reason. Science can't prove or disprove them."

Chad just looked at her. He was an incredibly fortunate man and knew it. Nothing more needed to be said. She went into his arms.

Mr. Fairbank had been waiting for several minutes outside the Jamison's house in his Cadillac, Nelda having phoned him to come and pick her up. After she had bade her goodbyes to both Chad and Melinda, Kris saw her to the car.

"Goodnight, Nelda," he said.

"Goodnight, honey," she said. "You be sure and tell that young singer friend of yours that that is a lovely young lady he has with him."

"I feel pretty sure he knows," Kris said, "but I'll be glad to tell him that you highly approve."

He waved a greeting to Mr. Fairbank while closing Nelda's door for her.

The Fairbanks drove away. Kris walked back into the house to speak briefly to Bill who had now come downstairs for a moment.

"Thank you again, Father Kris,'" he said, taking Kris's hand. Then noticing Chad and Melinda visible through the doorway on the porch he added, "And thank you both for…for being a part of our lives tonight."

"We're grateful you allowed us to be," Melinda said.

"Yes," Chad agreed.

"I'll call Mrs. Fairbank with our special thanks tomorrow," Bill said.

After embracing Bill, Kris walked with Chad and Melinda down the walkway to Chad's car.

The three arrived back at Chad's condominium. After they'd gotten out of the car, Melinda exchanged a goodbye kiss with Father Kris.

"Thanks for everything. It really was sweet of you to pick me up at the airport," she said. "I'm sure I'll be seeing more of you soon, Father Kris."

"Just 'Kris' will do. And you're welcome. I guess we'll look forward to seeing more of *you*," he said. Looking toward Chad and with a smile, he added, "Some of us maybe more so than others."

After giving Chad a quick kiss she said, "I'm heading upstairs now."

"I'll be in soon," Chad said.

"Bye, Kris," she said.

"Goodbye, Melinda," said Kris.

As she went into the house, Chad looked at Kris, leaned onto the fender of his car, and then gazed up at the star-filled sky. It was one of those perfectly clear nights, too beautiful to describe. Kris soon walked over and joined Chad in gazing upward.

"It's a pretty awesome thing, huh?" Chad said.

As there had been a good many things awesome about the day, Kris asked, "What is?"

"The Higher Power's love toward us. The importance and the preciousness of each one of us."

Kris looked over at his beloved friend then up at the sky, the eternal abyss, and said, "Yes, it is awesome, Chad."

"Before realizing myself to be a drunk and coming into the program, I never had been one to delve into the metaphysical, Kris. I just had pretty much gone about doing my thing and trying to stay out of trouble…sometimes unsuccessfully of course. And my mother took me to church when I was a kid." He took a deep breath. "But I never did really try to *live* on a…a spiritual plane."

"It's going to be a great thing for a lot of people that you've now chosen to do so," Kris said.

"What do you mean?"

"You're going to make the world a better place. Each one of us does when we make that sort of change and live in it."

"That's a bit…" Chad smiled and searched for the word, "…*grand*, isn't it? That each of us, small and insignificant as we are…" And then he suddenly realized it. "We are, each one of us, precious. Important."

"Exactly," Kris confirmed. "That's how it works."

Chad simply nodded.

"Tell me," Kris said, "how did things go with the record label guy? Did you have a chance to get any feedback from Tommy?"

"No. And I don't have the slightest idea." Then he added, "But do you want to hear the latest news flash, something you might not believe?"

"Sure. Go ahead."

"It doesn't matter. Whatever comes, whatever doesn't, that'll be fine. Life's going to be what it's going to be, and it'll be good. I just sort of…well, I just sort of know that."

Kris noted that Chad had said this with true conviction. "I'm certain of it too," he confirmed.

After a second or two Chad said, "Goodnight, Kris."

"Goodnight, Chad," Kris said, looking lovingly at his friend.

They embraced. It was a beautiful and yet painful moment for Father Kris. Chad would never know the extent of Kris's love for him.

Chad was the first to pull away. He looked Kris in the eye and said, "And thank you for being the friend, as well as the sponsor, that you are."

As Chad headed toward the door of his condo, Kris slowly walked to his car. Stopping at the front door, Chad turned and waved goodbye to Kris, who waved back, still hurting a bit inside.

Kris got into his car and sat a moment, surer than ever before that he would never fully understand the ways of God. *We see though a glass darkly.* Of late, he'd begun realizing something undeniable in himself. But no, it wasn't really just lately. He'd suppressed this thing all his life because it had seemed to make more sense to do so. Perhaps there'd even been a connection between the stifled truth and his disease of alcoholism in earlier years, the drink having helped him medicate the denial. Who could say? Now he wondered, would he be able to hide it away forever?

He was still alone, while the rest of his friends, if not most of world, seemed to be traveling in twos. He would get over the "loss" of his buddy, the friend that he'd come to love in a way he couldn't fully understand. But how would he ultimately address this? How could he deal with it when it wasn't comprehensible to him? Could it cost him his ministry if he were to become open about it? His own denominational church was greatly divided over this very issue even now.

Time would tell. He knew that God would lead, lovingly and certainly. For now, life was actually quite good. *We are, each one of us, precious. Important.* A thankful smile crossed his face, though this was at once a moment of pain and peace.

He started up his engine and began the drive toward home where Franklin would be waiting anxiously for him. Kris was a blessed man, and one who, like Chad, had an adventure ahead of him.

Acknowledgements

It will no doubt occur to some, if bothering to read this at all, that there are scores of women, more women than men, on my list of people to whom I must express appreciation. But then I've lived in a household full of females for years, and that includes the dog. So I've learned all about relating to and listening to the "fair sex."

A lot of gratitude goes to my editor Jane Tanner, who was nothing short of ruthless in her criticism. (As a first time novelist, I wouldn't have it any other way). Jane, you're quite wonderful.

Special thanks to Dorothy Campbell not only for legal consultation but also for advice regarding "lawyer stuff" being written about in the story.

A huge thanks to Carolyn Eakin, my wonderful sister. She has been invaluable for her advice and help in the writing of this book.

Thanks to Danny and Sherri Morrison for help regarding music industry issues in the story, as well as for being excellent friends. Danny has written hit songs and managed some of the greatest country artists in the business, while Sherri has been a hair and makeup designer for stars on both coasts and in Music City. (Any guesses what two characters they inspired?)

My gratitude goes to Bill Myers for his fine design of the dust jacket (and you should see the incredible portrait he did of our daughters a decade ago).

I also have to mention Mildred Gulbenk, who was the perfect source for other story issues. Thanks, Mildred.

Finally, my wife and two daughters have always made my life something wonderful. My thanks to them for their love and their support. They make me know that I am among the most blessed men on the planet.

Printed in the United States
110128LV00005B/64-81/P

9 780615 189499